HONOR BOUND

Also by Rachel Caine and Ann Aguirre
Honor Among Thieves

HONOR
BOUND

RACHEL CAINE & ANN AGUIRRE

KATHERINE TEGEN BOOKS
An Imprint of HarperCollins Publishers

Katherine Tegen Books is an imprint of HarperCollins Publishers.

Honor Bound
Text copyright © 2019 by Rachel Caine LLC and Ann Aguirre
Frontispiece art copyright © 2019 by Patrick Arrasmith
HarperCollins Children's Books, a division of HarperCollins Publishers, 195
Broadway, New York, NY 10007.
www.epicreads.com

Library of Congress Control Number: 2018946242
ISBN 978-0-06-257102-1

Typography by Katie Klimowicz
19 20 21 22 23   PC/LSCH   10 9 8 7 6 5 4 3 2 1

First Edition

For everyone who ever dreamed of flying.
You belong among the stars.

Interlude: Nadim

Pain blooms like the darkness between stars, and it blurs until I cannot separate the wounds. Typhon struggles against damage both on his surface and inside; the Phage hurt him badly, and the agony is in his spirit as well as in his healing flesh. He holds Marko and Chao-Xing at bay and cannot allow them to offer comfort.

I am injured but fortunate. I have Zara Cole. I have Beatriz Teixeira. I have bonds that nourish and heal my spirit. I know that I am loved.

We have survived the Phage, an enemy I did not know until it struck. An enemy that has slaughtered my kind by the hundreds.

I am a soldier in a war that I did not know existed, and into this war I have taken my Honors. It would be easy to blame the Elders for this, but perhaps the Elders had no simple choices. I only regret that this new, dire enemy puts my Zara and Beatriz at greater risk.

We must find shelter.

We must find the means to fight and the will to survive.

The Phage must be stopped.

SLIVER, The

A renegade outpost on the fringes of the Segarian galaxy, established after the fall of the Segarian Communal Reign. When the Segarians fell, Fellkin raiders stripped industrial outposts for resources to power their mag ships.

Outpost 1473, built into the dense alloy of a naturally occurring planetoid, survived nearly intact. For generations, remnants of Segarians held the outpost. Upon their extinction [note: original sources conflict as to cause] the entity Bacia Annont [see separate citation] seized control of the outpost and began an extensive building project that welcomed trade from Fellkin raiders, Bruqvisz pirates, Elaszi traders, and other species dealing in unlawful or quasi-lawful salvage. Bacia Annont renamed Outpost 1473 as the Sliver.

Trade with the Sliver is strictly interdicted by 942 treaties.

This does not prevent its successful, and profitable, operation.

—Entry in the Journey database, logged by historian Sanvarell, ship Trellven, bond name Santrell. Santrell is recorded as lost to a Phage swarm.

CHAPTER ONE

Binding Wounds

"DOES THIS HURT, Honor Cole?"

Our autodoc, EMITU, poked my wounded arm with an extended probe. I only knew that because I opened my eyes and saw it happen. "No," I said. "I can't feel anything."

"Ah," EMITU said. "Well, that's probably unfortunate, since I haven't numbed you."

I tried to sit up, but I was too tired, and the medbed too comfortable. "Are you kidding? Because if you are, I'm going to scrap your drives."

"If you're paralyzed, that might be difficult," it shot back. "I haven't given you any nerve blocks because it

3

appears the alien blood—if all this fluid smeared on you *is* blood—has a quite adequate numbing effect."

"Is it *toxic*?"

"Oh yes," it said cheerfully. "*Highly* toxic. Please brace for chemical bath."

I was drawing breath to give him some choice words when a high-pressure liquid jetted down from the nozzles above, so strong it flattened me against the bed. It tasted like cherry-flavored vomit, and I tried not to notice the gross aftertaste. Once it was done, the bed rippled and stretched around me and calmly flipped me over like a half-done pancake. More spray pressure on my backside.

"Excellent," EMITU pronounced, while the bed flipped me to the upside again. "Ninety-nine percent clearance. Intensive treatment required on wound. Please try not to scream."

Thanks to Bea's hacks, EMITU was ghoulishly gleeful, and of course I did scream, a lot, when the high-pressure spray hit inside my wounds with pinpoint precision, like a diamond drill. I passed out for a second or two. When I opened my eyes, EMITU was leaning over me, and with all its metal surfaces and flexible extenders moving it looked like a nightmare . . . only this nightmare was skillfully knitting fresh skin back over the mess of my arm.

"Done," EMITU said in its typical cocky voice as it whipped away from the bed and plugged back into its charging port. "Regrets, Honor Cole, but you will live. Now get out. I have to mop up your copious loss of blood."

EMITU had been reprogrammed as a joke, but I wanted to keep it this way. The gallows humor suited me, especially when I was scared and off-balance.

Like now.

When Nadim—the intelligent ship I was living inside, the one who cared for me, who'd bonded with me in ways that neither of us fully understood yet—suffered, it was worse for me than my own injuries. If you'd told me a year ago that Zara Cole, survivor of the streets, would have been picked for the greatest adventure in the world—the Honors—and sent into space like this, I'd have called immediate bullshit. I wasn't Honors material. But here I was, wearing the grimy, torn remains of an Honors uniform.

Surprisingly enough, until the Phage showed up, I was . . . happy, being an Honor. Panicked half the time, but there was an edge of roller-coaster adventure to it too. This was the best and freest I'd ever felt, yet I'd also witnessed the destruction of the Gathering—where the Phage had slaughtered Nadim's fellow Leviathan—and I couldn't forget the shredded corpses, bleeding starlight.

That had reduced everything to survival.

Now I was afraid for Nadim. For all of us.

Elder Typhon, the only other known Leviathan survivor, was all jacked up too, bad enough that his Honors,

Marko Dunajski and Zhang Chao-Xing, were still with us a day after the fight. Typhon wasn't saying much beyond no, and we were all worried, especially his exiled crew.

The door to the medbay slid open while I was putting on a fresh uniform. I only had three left. I'd have to find something else to wear, and quick. You wouldn't think space would be so hard on the wardrobe, but I'd run through fewer outfits living on the streets in New Detroit's Lower Eight.

Chao-Xing surveyed me head to toe, which was discomfiting, since 40 percent of me wasn't yet covered up. She looked spit-perfect, from her glossy black hair tied in a bun behind her head to the spotless uniform she'd put on. Like mine, it was an Honors uniform, but hers was black with red stripes, the sign of an Honor who'd been matched to a Leviathan for the Journey and become a permanent partner.

"You seem better," she said.

I tried not to wince as I pulled my pants up the rest of the way and fastened them. Thank the stars the boots were self-sealing, so I jammed my feet into them and let them do the rest.

"Yeah. I'm great," I lied. In fact, I felt shaky as hell. "What's the situation?"

"We have a problem."

"Just like every other damn day," I said. "What is it now?"

"Yusuf," she said. "He's not well."

He was a human Honor we'd saved from the destruction of the Gathering, along with Starcurrent. "Lucky for us, EMITU's ready to go," I said. "Bring him in."

"I have already seen Honor Yusuf," EMITU piped up. "Unfortunately, although my technical abilities are unmatched, my diagnostic matrix does not identify the specific type of illness that he has contracted, and as such, my ability to treat him is classified as 'bullshit' by Honor Zhang."

"I assume that was a free translation," I said to C-X. She shrugged. "So . . . if EMITU can't fix him, what do we do?"

"We already need help for Typhon," she said. "He's got serious wounds. So does Nadim, for that matter."

"We need to find stars for them." Leviathan healed themselves using starlight—and the more specific the frequency of the light waves was to the Leviathan's specific physiology, the faster the healing. But so far, no one frequency had worked for both Typhon and Nadim, so that meant two potentially long trips and extended stays . . . and Yusuf wouldn't get any better, meanwhile. "How bad is Yusuf?"

"I estimate at his current rate of failure, he will be excess baggage in less than two ship weeks," EMITU said. "I might be able to maintain him that long with creative treatments for specific symptoms."

That sounded even worse than I'd thought. Two weeks? We were on the run from the Phage swarm. We needed refuge and a place where our Leviathan could heal and restore their full strength. Not to mention a place where we might be able to upgrade Nadim's skin to some kind of armor and get him some weapons.

"Hey," I said. "Were you aboard Typhon for any part of his upgrades?"

C-X gave me a quick look. "No, but if the question is where were they done, I have some ideas." Without waiting, she executed a perfect military turn and strode out of the medbay, leaving me to follow, or not. I did, matching my stride to hers. She managed to lengthen hers just a bit more. Not that we were competitive.

"I assume there are aliens out here who operate some kind of facilities, right?" I said. "That's where the Leviathan negotiate for upgrades?"

"There are several places it could be done," C-X said. "I'll link Nadim's database to Typhon's, and we can see what's nearest to us."

"Can one of these places also treat Yusuf?"

"Humans are still rare out here, and relatively few of us have ever needed more than an EMITU could provide. But it's possible."

"Okay," I said. "You look for someplace that fits what we need. I'll check on Yusuf."

She nodded, and we split at the corridor's end—her toward what Beatriz and I had dubbed Ops, and me toward the rooms we'd used for our new refugees: Starcurrent, who was a confusing mass of tentacles and good humor, and Yusuf. I didn't know which door was which, so I reached out to Nadim. *Hey, help me out?*

Nadim had been in the background through everything: through the agony with EMITU, and the conversation with Chao-Xing. So he knew what I was talking about. *I didn't want to intrude*, he said, and as ever, there was a warmth that filled me when we talked, something that felt steady and perfect, like two different notes making harmony . . . but beneath that, I could feel that he was blocking me from his own pain. I hadn't held back on mine.

How are you? I asked.

I am well enough at the moment, he responded. *My injuries are not as severe as Typhon's. You are going to speak with Yusuf?*

If you tell me which door he's behind.

On cue, one door glowed a soft, pearly white. I knocked, and it slid open.

I expected Yusuf to be lying down, but he stood at the far wall, gazing out on deep space. Nadim had made the wall transparent for him. He turned to look at me, and I was struck by how *old* he seemed—not in years, but his eyes looked ancient and exhausted. He was about thirty, with long braids, and rich, deep-brown skin. His eyes were bloodshot.

"Honor Cole," he greeted me. "Shall we sit?"

I nodded, and he perched on the edge of the bed. I took the chair set off from it, near the small table. "Are you, uh, comfortable?"

That got me a shadow of a smile. "As well I can be," he said. "Given the circumstances."

Yusuf had been deep bonded to the Leviathan Artemisia, as few people had been, and he'd lost her in the massacre back at the Gathering. In her last moment, his ship had launched him in a lifepod, trying desperately to save him.

And she had. But it looked to me like the battle wasn't over yet.

"So, what's wrong with you?" I asked.

"You're blunt."

"So they say. But rude is incurable, and you have an illness EMITU doesn't recognize."

"It's an alien viral strain I contracted a few months ago. My Leviathan obtained treatments for me, but they were lost with her." I could see him reliving it again: the terror, the agony, the utter desolation. It was like watching someone die and grieve and revive, all in a microsecond. "Lost with her," he repeated.

"Okay." I kept my tone brisk, though it was hard to watch him suffer. I didn't think he'd appreciate sympathy, even if I offered it. "Where do we find more of this treatment?"

"Most trading stations will have it," he said. "But it's expensive."

"You warning me that you might not be worth it?"

"I'm just saying. If you can't pay, I understand. EMITU could make me comfortable enough." *Until the end.* He didn't add that part, but I heard it nonetheless.

"You think that's who we are?"

"I don't know you," he said. "You don't know me."

"I won't get a chance to, if we don't save you. We're searching for stations that have what we need anyway. Your medical supplies will be one of our priorities." I got up, but then I hesitated. "Is there, uh, anything else you need?"

"Nothing you can offer," he said softly.

And the finality of his response broke my heart. I wasn't just talking when I said it was good to have Yusuf here. No matter how much I loved Nadim and Bea, there was a certain comfort in having another black person on board. In his eyes, I felt seen.

Still, stepping away from his sorrow was like escaping a gravity well. The grief was depthless in there. I took a few deep breaths and felt Nadim's gentle presence, warming me from the inside out. I knew what he was asking.

"Yeah," I said. "I'm okay. Hey, he's the one . . ."

I know, Nadim said into my mind. This time, I could see

his emotions, painted in my head . . . a pale lavender, for sadness. A raw edge of red, for pain and anger. *We will find a way to save Yusuf. But I—I find it difficult to be near him too.*

For Nadim, this must have felt like a personal failure, but I understood. Yusuf was, right now, the specter of what faced both of us if the Phage got us again. One of us living. One dead. Neither whole.

"Never gonna happen," I said out loud, for emphasis.

Nadim didn't answer.

Ops was crowded. Chao-Xing, of course. And Starcurrent, and my shipmate Beatriz . . . and Marko, Typhon's other Honor.

"Let's get this party started," I said, because everybody seemed way too quiet and morose. Starcurrent, I could understand; like Yusuf, he'd lost his Leviathan. But Starcurrent seemed to be rebounding faster.

"How are you?" Beatriz eased by Marko to get to me. Before I could answer, she took my arm in her hands and turned it carefully, examining the repairs. Then she looked up to meet my eyes. She had her bouncy, curly hair pulled back in a ponytail, and I missed the spill of it around her pretty face. She looked like she meant business. "Don't lie to me, Zara."

"I'm fine," I told her. "EMITU washed all the dead off me. I'm good to go." My tone made light of her concern, but she saw the gratitude in my eyes.

Bea squeezed my hand lightly before letting go and turning to the older woman. "Chao-Xing, any progress?"

"It's not good," she said. "The most therapeutic range of starlight for Typhon is less effective for Nadim, and both choices are too far away. Additionally, they both take us back into Phage territory. Or at least, where we know the swarm was concentrated last."

I sighed, my heart sinking. "Our options are bad and worse, then?"

"There's an alternative to certain death," Marko said, bringing up the data in holographic form. I didn't know what the hell I was looking at; this place was oscillating geometric angles and planes that didn't make sense. "That's the Sliver. They have programmable starlight baths for our Leviathan—not quite as effective, but our best shot right now. And they have advanced medical facilities for Yusuf."

"Not recommend," said a new voice, and we all turned to Starcurrent. Our tentacled alien refugee was still fiddling with a translation matrix. "The Sliver, primarily outlaw colony. Used to be industrial shipyard for . . ." The matrix cut out, denying us the name of whatever aliens once built starships there. Starcurrent fluttered face tentacles, which I was starting to understand meant ze was frustrated. Some emotions crossed evolutionary boundaries easily.

Starcurrent had said that the pronoun *ze* fit best. Starcurrent's species had nine gender identities, a complex spectrum of sexual preferences, and I could likely spend a lifetime learning about the Abyin Dommas without quite grasping all the details. For now, though, respecting zis preferences was the best I could do.

"I like the sound of an outlaw colony," I said, just as Bea blurted, "Is this a good idea?" Beatriz Teixeira was my partner aboard Nadim, but she was also a nice girl who'd never stolen or slept rough in her life. Core of steel, though. At first glance, we weren't much alike . . . but underneath? I could see Bea surviving some shit.

She already had, with me.

I winked at her.

Marko turned, and I noticed he was still favoring one leg. Finally, he spoke up. "I've analyzed the nav charts. At the speeds Typhon and Nadim can currently manage, the Sliver is the only option that doesn't lead us back to the Phage."

"No stars that could function as, I don't know, waypoints to someplace safer?" Beatriz asked. "If they could have a chance to fuel and heal a little to make the next leg of the journey . . ."

"It's a long way between stars out here," Marko said somberly. "They won't make it."

That was worrying. Nadim and Typhon were born sailors

of the stars; Leviathan navigated space the way whales swam the oceans on Earth, though they were vastly larger creatures. They ate starlight and bathed in it to accelerate healing. Though we were currently orbiting a small star, Nadim's energy levels were dangerously depleted. He was keeping me at a distance while he conserved his strength, but I still sensed his pain and his struggle to stay awake.

"They can't heal and travel at the same time," I said. "I don't know about Typhon, but Nadim doesn't have too many reserves left." C-X and Marko wore identical expressions that told me Typhon had even less.

"Anything else we can shut down?" I asked. Bea shook her head, ponytail swinging. "Shit. What about playing something for him?"

The Leviathan were singers. They sang to each other across the lonely, dark distances among the stars; they appreciated music of all kinds, and in some strange way it helped them build their strength. Maybe because it reminded them they weren't alone. Same reason they liked having crews on board, life-forms they could sense and sometimes touch in deeper ways, as Nadim and Bea and I had done.

"Sing?" Starcurrent perked up, tentacles undulating in what I assumed was excitement. "I sing!"

"Me too," Bea said, glancing past me. "Yusuf, what do you think?"

Sure enough, Yusuf was in the doorway. Propped up, looking ill and miserable and still radiating that terrible loss.

"No," he said. "Music helps, but the Leviathan can't recover on that alone."

"Should we make for the Sliver, then?" Marko asked.

That earned a shrug from Yusuf. "It's hard for me to care. For me, the worst has already come to pass."

Chao-Xing took exception to his attitude. "You still have your *life*. That's more than a lot of Honors can say right now."

I saw a brief burst of anger in his dulled eyes. "I expect you'd tell me I'm lucky. Don't. Not while your Typhon is still alive and drinking starlight."

Never thought I'd be the one to play peacemaker, but I wasn't about to let Chao-Xing step on Yusuf. I had his back, even if he felt completely alone in the universe.

Bea spoke before I could. "This isn't helping. Since Typhon and Nadim need aid desperately, shouldn't we ask what *they* want to do?"

Nadim answered at once. "The Sliver is our only hope," he said. "Though it is the most dangerous for all of you."

Chao-Xing's eyes went black, and Typhon spoke through her. "We must go to the Sliver. It is a matter of survival."

Once her expression cleared, I could tell she wasn't 100 percent on board with this plan, but since her Leviathan still had gaping holes bleeding starlight from the last fight, she probably got that it was a shit idea to contend with him. Not that Typhon usually allowed any arguments.

Beatriz went over to Marko, frowning over his bad leg. They bickered a little, but eventually he agreed to go back to the medbay. Funny, I'd never noticed Bea's tendency to mother people before, but come to think of it, she always took great care of *me*. You'd think I might have some of those feelings, since I was the one who'd dragged him off Typhon's smoking deck and saved his ass, but nope; my job was done. I had too much other shit to worry about.

"I guess we're doing this," I said to Nadim, but there was gentleness in my voice, and a question, and I mentally opened the doors wide to let him know he could get closer if he needed it. He responded carefully, holding back that constant grate of pain and giving me warmth and the sweetness of trust. We couldn't go deep, not here and now, but surface contact was good enough to make me feel weak with relief. To any outside observer, I was still Zara Cole: hard-ass, but inside? Inside I let myself be something kinder with him.

"Setting course, moderate speed," Nadim said from the speakers. *I have to slow down for Typhon*, he added silently. That allowance for the Elder's wounds was necessary. If we tried for too much boost right now, he'd bleed out trying to keep up. Chao-Xing was already edgy about not being with him, but Typhon was adamant that he couldn't offer safe conditions to his human crew just yet. That was more consideration than I would've expected out of him.

All Leviathan were massive, but Typhon was *frightening*. He was an armored war machine, scarred and cold from the moment I'd met him. Violence was his default. He kept his crew at a chilly distance and controlled them like puppets when needed; there was no partnership with him, not for humans. I'd gotten close once, slipped inside his defenses, and glimpsed the weary soldier on the battlements. That was Typhon. He'd left behind consideration, kindness, and love. For him, it was all about survival.

Hey, I understood that.

Now that we'd come to consensus, I retreated to my room. Nadim needed more from me than I felt comfortable providing in public. A deeper bond could assuage some of his pain, but I wanted a door between me and relative strangers before I let my guard down like that. I set my door to NO VISITORS and then sat down, flattening bare hands and feet against Nadim. His sweet green warmth flooded me, laced with red-and-orange pain.

The colors of discomfort glowed in my head, and I could feel his various injuries; I hummed—however badly—to help make them less. Nadim gentled like a sigh, settling into the speed that would carry us to the Sliver. Eventually. I sank into Nadim, and he sank into me, and we slowly became something new. Zadim, we privately called ourselves. We dwelled together in that quiet place, drifting together. Waves of peace and happiness, bright and nourishing as sunlight.

"Has Typhon told you any more about the Phage?" I asked Nadim later. I did it out loud, so he could choose to edit his response if needed.

No matter how close we'd become, we still required personal space. It was more than just being polite. There would be things he needed to keep to himself, and stuff I needed privacy for too. This intimacy was frightening in its intensity, dangerous too. Tricky, when it came down to sharing minds and emotions. I might screw it up, but I'd do my best to keep it to small mistakes. This meant too much to me.

I belonged here, with Nadim. And with Beatriz.

I got chills realizing that I could have lived my life on Earth only half-aware of who I was supposed to be. Before, I would have said I wasn't Honors material, but now I understood that if the Leviathan needed you, then you fit. Period. There was no "Honors type." Maybe there never had been.

Of course, we were well beyond the formal boundaries of the Honors program, where I wasn't supposed to know about the Phage, and humanity wasn't permitted to interact with other intelligent life beyond the Leviathan; we'd veered from the path plotted for us on the baby steps of the Tour. We'd started out playing explorer, and now . . . now we were at war.

"Typhon has promised to transfer full information once we're out of danger," Nadim said.

"Why not now?"

"The pain doesn't let him focus."

"Okay, but we need some intel before we reach the Sliver, then. What do you know about the place?"

A series of images cascaded through my mind, too fast for me to process. When they receded, I retained a glimmer of what he'd shown me. I had the impression of grungy, pitted metal and garish lights, as if someone had transplanted a run-down Las Vegas to deep space and flooded the place with crims from the Zone.

"You're even *more* excited now," Nadim said, and his tone clearly conveyed a sigh. "That was meant as a warning."

"Yeah, not sorry. But I *do* understand the dangers."

Danger is where I live. That sounded badass in my head, but it wasn't just a slogan. I'd survived lots of difficult years in the Zone.

"Good."

"How long until we get there?" I asked.

"Three days at our current speed."

Even if the Sliver had never seen a human, they'd

probably let us do business; Earth natives seemed to be the only ones who had an adjustment period for adapting. The ones I'd met so far found humans as dull as dirt.

Haggling was an art where I came from, and I had been surviving around fringe types in the Zone forever. People like Conde, the fence I worked with so often—that thought broke abruptly, leaving me with a smoking hole of a memory. *Shit*. Things were messed up out here, but there was nothing good waiting for me back on Earth either. Conde was dead. I'd left Derry McKinnon—a drug-addicted boyfriend who'd sold me out—and gotten on the wrong side of a major drug kingpin, Torian Deluca. I had to make this situation work for me, because running home wasn't an option.

Not to mention that leaving Nadim would probably feel worse than dying.

"Zara?"

Nadim couldn't read my thoughts, but he sensed my shifting mood. "Just thinking about some long odds. Nothing to worry about."

"I do worry about you," Nadim said. I knew he did. That spread through me like a ghost of an embrace. "You're very tired, you know."

"Thanks, I'm aware." With a weary groan, I took out the silk scarf that protected my curls—I was getting real fond of my grow-out—and wrapped my head. Then I flopped backward and hauled the blanket down from the bunk and spread it over me. The grav felt like it was twice as heavy as it ought to be. "Don't wake me unless things go sideways."

"I won't." His voice dropped to a whisper through the speakers. "Sweet dreams, Zara."

I brushed my fingers across the soft skin of the wall, and felt colors trailing after. Nadim's answering touch. It soothed something in me, something wild, and then I was gone.

I must have been dead tired because I was out for eighteen hours. At least that was what Nadim told me when I roused at last. Time for a shower. Since we had two whole days before our arrival at the Sliver, I did it up right, finger combing my hair after I wet it. Out in the Zone, I kept my hair short, almost skull cut, because I couldn't care for it in those rough conditions. Now, I had co-wash and luxe conditioners in stock from Earth, and it was nice to feel the springy weight of clean hair. I felt flash, and most of all, I felt *free*.

Suddenly, I had an unsettling realization that my Earth products wouldn't last. I'd stocked enough for the year of the Tour, but what about when that was gone? It wasn't likely we'd be swinging by home for a quick shopping trip. I didn't even know if other races out here *had* hair, much less product.

Guessed I'd be shopping for more than just weapons at the Sliver.

I was thinking about shopping because it was better than worrying about war, but we needed to gear up for that too: Weapons. Armor. Shields. We had to acquire all of that for Nadim, and fast. Hard not to be mad at the Elder Leviathan, who had tapped us for their war games without explaining the stakes. I mean, you wouldn't sit down at a poker game without knowing the buy-in.

I was sure that if I checked the old first-contact records, they'd show the Leviathan had never lied to us; that wasn't their style. No, they'd just told us half-truths, and dazzled us with vaccines to cure our rampaging diseases and biotech to stabilize our wildly imbalanced climate. They'd saved billions of human lives over the last hundred years, and maybe more importantly, they'd given humanity something it had lost in those desperate years . . .

Hope.

But it was all built on a cracked foundation.

Nadim probably felt my surge of bitterness because a surge of warmth trickled in, the equivalent of him asking if I was okay.

"I'm up," I said.

Not quite the answer he wanted. A deeper touch, and he knew why I was pissed. "I'm sorry. The Elders didn't tell us, either."

Younger Leviathan weren't informed about the Phage, or the dangers. It was the reason for the Tour, for the safe routes they were kept to during their training. Like us, they were learning.

Graduating from Tour to Journey meant putting on armor and taking up the battle. Unfair? Sure. The transition must have been tough for most of the young, innocent Leviathan who saw the universe as their playground . . . and found it was a jungle, and they were the prey.

That was the difference between me and Nadim. I'd always known there were monsters.

"That doesn't make me feel any better, but thanks for trying," I told him, and patted the skin of the wall. No starbursts of color this time.

After dressing quickly, I headed out to see how everyone else was coping. I found Marko playing cards with Beatriz and Yusuf at the kitchen table. I poured whatever was in the pot—luckily, it turned out to be coffee—and took a seat.

"What's the game?" I asked.

"Pai gow poker," Marko said. "Chao-Xing taught me. Deal you in?"

I knew pai gow from the Zone. Normally, they played it with Mahjong tiles, or dominos, but gamblers were flexible; they could play with pebbles if necessary. I wasn't surprised to learn there was a card version. "Hell no," I said. "I know a wolf when I see one."

Marko raised his brows without cracking a smile; he looked drawn and tired, just . . . not himself. We probably all seemed off our game. Even me.

"Speaking of Chao-Xing, where is she?"

"Combat sim," Yusuf said. He looked even worse than before, if that was possible; there was an unhealthy shine to his skin, and I doubted he could hold anything heavier than his cards. But he was here, being social, and that was better than grieving alone.

"Starcurrent?" I asked.

"No idea." Marko shrugged and played a card.

I'd find out from Nadim in a minute. But first . . . "Any Phage sightings?"

Bea nodded, looking grim. "There's something you need to see." She put her cards down and stood, and I followed her through to the control center, where she brought up a holo screen with images queued for playback. Yusuf and Marko, I noticed, had trailed along, though Yusuf quickly took a seat. Bea spun the playback and showed me what she was worried about.

I didn't see it at first. Looked like another Leviathan, very long range. I punched in on it with magnification, and that was when I started seeing the damage.

The rot.

This Leviathan was still clumsily swimming through

space, but its solar sails were folded, and the sleek, silvery body had blackened sores on the skin that pulsed and heaved. It made me break into a cold sweat to look at it: a living dead thing, colonized by a deadly parasite that was piloting it in search of more prey.

If it was still alive, it was dying in agony.

If it was dead, the Phage knew how to puppeteer the corpse.

Both possibilities were chilling.

"Did it see us?" I asked.

"Can't tell," Bea said. "But it couldn't possibly catch us even if it did. We're doing better time."

For now, I thought. "Can the Phage talk to each other across distances? Coordinate attacks?" I asked, and there was silence. I turned and looked at Marko and Yusuf. "Anybody?"

Yusuf finally said, "I don't know. Individually they don't seem very intelligent. But as a swarm . . ."

"Great. Just great." I raised my head. "Nadim, please tell Typhon that sooner would be better on that intel he's hoarding, okay?"

"Okay, Zara," he said. "But I don't think he will respond just now. He's sleeping."

That quickened my heartbeat. "What do you mean, sleeping?" Because my only experience with Leviathan sleep was the dark sleep that Nadim had entered—a coma state, where he'd drifted, powered down and helpless. It was a kind of chrysalis, and he'd come out of it stronger, but the idea of Typhon powering down just when we needed to be on our guard—

"Not dark sleep," Nadim immediately qualified. "He is . . . dozing, I suppose you would call it. It is helpful for his healing. In a few hours, he will wake, and I can ask him for the information."

"Yeah, well, don't just ask. Tell him we need it."

He didn't agree, but he didn't argue, either. I re-ran the playback and watched it again. My guts churned, and I regretted the coffee I'd downed, but I made myself view it again. Then again. I swore. "This is nuts. Do the Phage eat Leviathan? Do they prey on other kinds of ships too?"

Though I wasn't expecting much info at this stage, Yusuf said, "I've heard they can overtake a mechanical starship, but they don't feed on it. They crack it open and feed on the crew."

"So the Leviathan are shelter, transport, and a food source to them all at the same time." A cold shudder worked through me. "Preferred targets."

"They will hunt my kin to extinction," Nadim said softly.

If they hadn't already.

"Nadim, is there any immediate danger you can sense from this . . . thing?"

"No," he said softly. And then, a moment later, even more quietly, "I don't know who it is. There is no song inside anymore. Just . . . noise."

The noise of insects, burrowing, breeding, eating. I shuddered again. Maybe—hopefully—that Leviathan was dead.

We can't let it happen here. Not to Nadim. Not even to Typhon.

FROM THE SUNG HISTORY OF THE ABYIN DOMMAS

Comes now the day of pain and silence
Lost we have the greatest number of Dark Travelers
And their bound pilots and starsingers
Loss comes not from sickness
Or the dry burst of a dying star
But from a thing between the light
A thing of no reason
Only cruel hunger.

Beware now the shine of armor
The hiss of unmaking
The cut of edges
And ravaging mouths.

Many bodies, many teeth
One purpose
Eat, and eat again
Beware of the devouring dark
Between the safety of stars.

CHAPTER TWO

Binding Ties

I STAYED IN Ops long after the others were gone, searching obscure data files for anything, *anything* on the Phage . . . but didn't come up with much but a bad temper and a budding ache behind my eyes.

The pai gow game was back in action, though I could see something was off as I stepped into the room. Bea was too chipper and full of smiles; she'd gone into denial-cheerleader mode. Marko seemed impassive as ever.

And Yusuf looked ready to drop. I didn't like the way he looked. Not at all.

"Hey, Zara! Do you want me to deal you in?" Bea asked me. "Marko's a good teacher."

"Yes," Yusuf said. "You should take my place." He dropped his cards and stood up.

Tried to, anyway. Instead, he tipped out of his chair and began convulsing. Marko rolled Yusuf onto his side and said, "Get a hoverbed. We need to take him to EMITU."

I swallowed the taste of ashes and sprinted to medical, where EMITU was powered down in his cradle, but he shook awake as I grabbed one of the portable hoverbeds and started pushing it out. "Excuse me, those are not for hallway racing!"

"Yusuf's down," I yelled back over my shoulder. "We'll bring him to you!"

"Take precautions," EMITU said, and I wanted to turn back and ask why, but I was already moving too fast. *Precautions.* Did he mean Yusuf was contagious? I pushed the hoverbed faster, and as I shoved it into the canteen area, Bea jumped out of the way.

Yusuf was so still it scared me.

"He's unconscious," Marko said, reassuring me without realizing I needed it. "Help me roll him onto the bed."

I pushed the hoverbed down until it was flat against the floor, and together, we rolled Yusuf onto his back on the mattress. I stuck a hand under the grooves at the bottom and lifted, and the whole thing rose effortlessly up until I stopped pulling at about waist height. "Let's get him to the medbay."

Beatriz wasn't saying a word. She was just standing,

helpless, and I knew just how she felt. I took her arm and pulled her with us as Marko led the bed back to where EMITU waited.

Our medical unit surged at Yusuf as soon as we had the bed locked in place, and we all three stepped well back from the flailing appendages as EMITU drew blood, ran scans, and adjusted Yusuf's position all at the same time. He wasn't making jokes right now, which I found alarming. He was working fast and silently, and the three of us stayed quiet, until suddenly all the appendages stilled at once, and EMITU whirled around to face us.

"He is now stable," EMITU announced. "I do not appreciate you bringing me patients in this condition. It looks bad on my record."

"How is he?" Beatriz asked.

"By stable, I mean he is dying. Honor Yusuf is circling the drain. Approaching room temperature. Kicking the oxygen habit."

"Stop it!" Bea shouted.

"I cannot," EMITU said. "Unless you reprogram me. It does not mean I am not doing all I can to preserve his life. But the end is inevitable if you leave him within the boundaries of my care. I simply do not have the facilities or understanding to treat the underlying cause of his illness."

In that moment, EMITU sounded very . . . sober. I didn't like it. I liked jokey EMITU, rude EMITU, anything but serious EMITU. It made me jumpy. "How long?" I asked.

Bea sucked in a breath, bracing herself.

"A week," EMITU said. "At most. And the last few days I will have to sedate him, for his own protection."

Protection. That made me remember something. "You said earlier, take precautions. What did that mean?"

"The condition that Honor Yusuf suffers from is not airborne or touch-contagious, but it can be spread through contact with infected blood."

"Good thing he's not bleeding, then—"

Marko said, "He is. He hit his head when he fell. I got some on my . . . hand." There was a studied calm to the way he said it, and I looked over and saw he was studying his right palm.

The one with blood smeared in a thin red streak across the skin.

EMITU streaked across to jerk to a halt right in front of Marko, and one set of appendages grabbed the fingers and spread them. Chemical liquid foamed out over Marko's entire hand, bubbled, and vanished. EMITU turned his hand to examine it, then dropped it. "Done," it said. "Please strip and enjoy the full-body chemical shower you have now earned. Your uniform must be incinerated."

"Yeah, Marko, go on," I said, and forced a grin. "Strip."

He sent me a look that told me now was *not the time*, and he was right, because EMITU whirled toward me as well.

"Also you, Honor Cole," he said. "And you, Honor Teixeira. Chemical showers for everyone."

Zara? Nadim was listening, of course. And worried.

It's fine, I told him. *It's all going to be fine.*

I persuaded EMITU that my hair didn't need disinfecting, which saved it from a crunchy acid bath, but the rest of me got another nasty cleanse that left me tasting rotten cherries again. I wore the medbay robe back to my room, where I pulled on one of my last remaining uniforms. Man, I hoped the Sliver had something human-sized to wear that wasn't gag-ugly.

EMITU had taken blood from each of us. I tried not to think about the tests it was running.

I ran into Beatriz again in the kitchen, where she was pouring some of EMITU's chemical disinfectant over the floor where Yusuf had fallen. She'd put on her EV suit, which was smart; it was a thin, flexible, tough layer between her and whatever nasty was in Yusuf's blood. Not that there was a lot of blood—couple of drops, couple of smears—but it needed to be obliterated, fast. "Hey," I said. "Need help?"

"No, I've got it," she said. "EMITU kept Marko. He's running more tests."

That didn't sound promising. We looked at each other but didn't say it out loud. I switched gears. "Any idea where

Starcurrent is?" I asked. Bea shook her head.

Nadim answered. "Starcurrent is in the media room," he said.

"Thanks. I'll go check on zim, get our tentacled pal up to date."

The Abyin Dommas was sitting in the dark, watching real space footage, shots of Earth, the colonies we'd established on the moon and Mars. Starcurrent didn't respond when I came in or when I sat down, and I wondered if ze was sleeping. It occurred to me that Nadim might not have anything on board that Starcurrent could eat, as the live ships were provisioned according to the crew they carried.

"You all right?" I asked.

Dumb question, because ze's definitely not. Can't be. I remembered how Beatriz had said that zis people were born singing. In that context, zis silence took on a mournful air, a grief too deep for weeping. There were cultures on Earth that grieved by keening out loss in a poignant, ululating song. For the Abyin Dommas, maybe the opposite was true; they grieved in quiet, in stillness.

"I am all wrong," Starcurrent answered.

Either someone had fixed the translation matrix or that was the most accurate error ever. Because I understood exactly what ze meant. Just picturing how I'd feel without Nadim left a hollow sickness in the pit of my stomach. Starcurrent—and Yusuf—might have been deep bonded with their ships like Nadim and me, and their Leviathan were ripped apart by the Phage.

They'd watched someone they loved die, horribly. There was no consolation adequate for that grief.

But still, I tried. "Anything I can do?"

Tentacles quivered and flared, but now that I got that we were on the same team, the movement didn't strike me as threatening. It hit me more like a thoughtful gesture, equivalent to a human shrug. Or maybe I was just making stuff up to suit my own preconceptions.

"Talk," Starcurrent said finally.

"About what?"

"Anything. It will help . . ." More alien sounds that didn't translate.

"Sure," I said. I understood what ze meant: anything to provide a distraction. "You're watching stuff from Earth."

"We have never seen Earth," ze said, and two tentacles knotted up in complicated patterns. "A pleasant world. Your technology is . . ." Ze trailed off. I didn't think the translation matrix was the problem there. More like a desire not to offend me.

"Hey, I'm fine with you saying *terrible*," I said. "Because it was, back in the day. Wasteful, dependent on fossil fuels, polluting the atmosphere with toxins—"

"But powerful," ze said politely. "Many, many species never attain space. Few have the . . . curiosity. Courage."

36

"Yours did."

I was pretty sure that all-over ripple of tentacles indicated pleasure. Everybody liked flattery. "Ours heard the songs," Starcurrent said. All zis tentacles lifted and formed a shimmery, fluttering curtain. Disturbingly pretty. "Ours knew something waited beyond. Yours . . . did not. You had no assurance of welcome, only of danger. This is brave, venturing into the dark alone."

"Yeah, or stupid," I said, but I was a little pleased myself, on behalf of brave, stupid humanity. "You heard the song . . . which song? The Leviathan?"

"All songs," Starcurrent said. "We hear so many songs. Deep humming of Leviathan. Chorus of galaxies. Singing of suns. Whispers of races long gone, stars long drawn inward, singing backward. We hear all."

That was sobering. I wondered what that was like, being so in tune with—well, everything. "Must be loud," I said.

"Oh, no," ze said. The matrix was getting more comfortable, because this time, it moderated zis voice down to a lower volume, giving it a nuance that had been missing before. A faint wisp of sadness. "Never loud. All things balanced. The turning of stars, the laughter of children, the cry of pain . . . song is beauty. Song is life. Never too loud."

Something about that, and the wistful tone, made my vision mist a little. I'd never heard anything so hauntingly poetic before. Starcurrent's words made me feel small and heavy, but they made me feel part of something else too.

On the holoscreen, the International Space Station archive footage showed the awkward, cobbled-together structure that was the best humanity could do at the time . . . and then, the arrival of the Leviathan, coming to save dying crew members and open a new era for humans. Our efforts at creating a home in space looked ridiculous now, fragile and bound to fail, but there was a beauty in that too. A defiance.

A song in the dark.

"I'm sorry," I said to Starcurrent. "You must feel so alone."

Starcurrent stayed quiet for a long moment, and then ze said, "My ship's song lives in me. I sing it for the next cycle, so it will not be lost. Grieve for Yusuf, who has no song to hold, who cannot hear eternity. He sings too, but his song is lost and broken, disharmonious. Sing with him, as you sing with me now."

That reminded me what I needed to tell Starcurrent. But it didn't feel like the time. So I nodded and settled back, and we sat quietly in the darkened auditorium together, watching the ghosts of my ancestors flicker across the screen.

If I was singing, I did it silently. Like praying.

A day passed. Marko got kicked from the medbay with a clean bill of health and ended up having to wear an old

Honors uniform that Nadim still had stored away from his time on the Tour; it fit, but it wasn't the black and red that indicated Marko was bonded to Typhon. Maybe it was my imagination, but I felt like Marko's mood lightened considerably when he was back in those clothes.

But it didn't last.

When Typhon woke up, he was cranky, to no one's surprise. I knew the Elder was up when Marko suddenly dropped his pai gow cards in a flutter to the table, stood up, and walked away. I caught a glimpse of black eyes, the sign that Typhon had, without warning, taken control of him.

"Marko!" I yelled after him. I was going through food packets with Starcurrent, trying to see what ze'd find nutritious; so far, we hadn't come up with much besides vegetable broth, which ze'd tried reluctantly, but pronounced good enough to choke down. EMITU had provided us blunt but helpful comments on the relative lethality of ingredients, ranging from *agonizing but survivable* to *might as well space the patient now and save the trouble.* I wasn't sure the sarcasm translated to Abyin Dommas, but Starcurrent didn't seem too distressed. I turned to zim and said, "Hey, you okay here? I'll be right back."

"Good," Starcurrent said, with a flutter of tentacles I read as confirmation. Like a nod, but with more motion.

I ran after Marko, while Bea sighed and gathered up

the cards. "Tell him that was rude," she said. "Typhon, I mean."

"Are you kidding? You tell him!" I called back.

I caught up with Marko just as Chao-Xing stepped out of the sim chamber door; she was sweaty, dressed in a damp workout uniform, and her hair was down in loose clumps that stuck to her face.

Her eyes, like Marko's, were lightless black, pupils expanded to cover the iris completely. Without speaking or acknowledging either me or Marko, she fell into step with him, and they headed for the Hopper bay.

"Hey!" I was just a couple of steps behind, but they ignored me. "Earth to Typhon. Come in, jackass!"

Marko and Chao-Xing were moving in lockstep, and as one, they came to a halt so sudden I nearly plowed right into them. I backpedaled as they turned around. It wasn't just the eyes that had changed. Typhon had a *presence*.

Marko/Typhon said, "A jackass is a stubborn creature. Correct?"

"Stupid too," I said. "Annoying. Unbelievably frustrating. Shall I go on?"

"What do you want?" This time, it came out of Chao-Xing's mouth. I wondered if Typhon ever accidentally talked in stereo.

"Give us everything you have on the Phage, and no bullshit about protocol. Also, we need full med records for the Abyin Dommas, so we can make sure Starcurrent gets everything ze needs, and so we can treat zim in the event of emergency." I was working hard to sound calm and in control. Hoped I was selling it. C-X and Marko stared at me with demon eyes, and even though my nerves were usually steely, it was tough not to look away. "How are you doing, Typhon?"

That last made them both blink, in perfect harmony. "You're concerned about my condition for what reason?" He *did* speak in stereo. It was unnerving.

"Because you're commandeering Marko and Chao-Xing and piloting them back to you when you wouldn't let them come aboard before."

After a long, cool pause, Chao-Xing said, "It is now possible for humans to survive."

"When you say *survive*, do you mean that it's comfortable?"

Her mouth curled into a faint, alien smile. "No. But their assistance is required for necessary repairs. Is that enough explanation? Because it is all you will receive."

They pivoted, and off they went. I didn't follow. No point. Even if I suited up and got on board the Hopper with them, I doubted they'd let me come on board Typhon, and I knew myself well enough to grasp that I might be able to take Marko, with a whole lot of luck I might take Chao-Xing, but there was no way I'd come out on top fighting

41

them both. Certainly not with Typhon's strength behind them.

"Don't come running to me if it all goes south," I muttered, and reached out to touch the wall. Lights zipped in from all directions to coalesce beneath Nadim's skin in the shape of my fingers. He was feeling better. "Did he give you the info?"

"Yes," Nadim said. He sounded preoccupied. "There is a significant amount of data. It will take time for me to . . . understand all of it."

"How can I help?"

Wordlessly, he pulsed the light under my fingers, and it zipped away down the wall to lead me somewhere. I had a notion where he was directing me, but I didn't let myself assume anything until I was standing in the open doorway of my own quarters.

"Nadim—"

"Deep bond will make this faster," he said. "I only ask out of need. You have a gift for assimilation of information. You can parse the importance faster than I can."

"Flatterer," I said. He laughed. It was soft but woke deep blue ripples inside me that warmed to green, then orange. Intimate, those colors. I could feel *and* see them, even at this light bond level. "Okay. But tell Bea what we're doing. Have her hit the alarm if we're not out in . . . what, an hour?"

"An hour," he agreed. "Thank you, Zara."

He didn't need to thank me. The idea of going into a deep bond with him made my skin tingle, my breath come faster, and gave me a guilty rush of adrenaline. It wasn't strictly speaking *forbidden*, not anymore. But dangerous, a little. Nadim and I were both very new at this, and Nadim had a—I suppose it wouldn't be unfair to call it a condition—that made him prone to slip into dark sleep, which was dangerous at the best of times.

He was, I'd discovered, more likely to do it after a deep bond when all his inner defenses were down. But we'd installed a device to wake him in that event. Hence, Bea's finger on the button.

I made myself comfortable on my bed, pulled a blanket over my body—because it would chill quickly—and flattened one hand on the wall. My fingertips moved in a slow, gentle pattern, and his light followed.

"Ready," I whispered.

The universe exploded around me.

Deep bonding to Nadim meant becoming *one* . . . a single mind, a single creature, existing beyond the boundaries of flesh and bone and bodies. A sweet, perfect mingling of everything that made us individuals to create something *new*.

Zadim.

There was no *we*. Only *I*, a blending so complete that our barriers were almost all swept aside. It was like falling and flying and screaming and laughing and being so high that I'd never come down from the thrill of it, and the *stars*, the dizzying, blinding whirl of stars and the seductive whisper-song calling me on into the dark . . .

Focus, part of me chided. The Zara part, I thought. *Typhon's information.*

Zara remembered reading, but this was not that. It was experiencing data in a blinding rush, like memory and voices and pain blending together in a red wave. The Nadim part of me worked to slow the rush, and the melded *I* submerged in the flow, swam in it, absorbed and learned and grew and drank until full to bursting . . .

And the *I* spun apart into two, and Zara cried out and reached for the synthesis again, the warmth, the *perfection*, but it was gone, and I was back in flesh and bone that wanted to skim the stars and drink the songs. My skin was too tight, just as my body felt too small. I'd thought I understood isolation before, but this took it to a whole new level.

I drew in deep, whooping breaths, and felt the flush of warmth rush through me—an aftermath of the intensity made physical and real in all my senses. My body relaxed, though my mind was racing desperately to understand everything I'd just seen/known/experienced. I'd acted as a kind of filter for Nadim, helping him prioritize what Typhon had directed his way. It was weird and wonderful and fascinating, because I'd never thought of the human brain like that before.

"It's unique," Nadim's voice said from somewhere near my head. Soft, almost a whisper. "The human brain has the capacity to analyze information in a way that few other species can duplicate. It's one of the reasons we are so intrigued with you. You are complex creatures."

There was a warmth to his voice, and to the room around me, that felt like an embrace. Like he couldn't quite let go.

And I didn't want him to, either. "Not sure if anybody ever called me complex before."

"I neglected to note that humans are often unable to see the glory that's right in front of them," he said. "Pity."

Glory. The way he said it made my skin feel tight and luminous. It almost swept me away on a tide of bliss before I caught onto a solid, rocky thought. "In all that information, is there anything about how to kill these damn things?"

The bliss faded. The warmth around me chilled.

Nadim said quietly, "I do not think so."

The next day, we got our first look at the Sliver.

It looked like post-apocalyptic Las Vegas had crashed into a junkyard, and then rusted in the rain for a hundred years. I'd seen more inviting hideouts in the Zone, and that was as low as you got on Earth. Seemed like space crims should be a lot flashier than this. You'd think with all the tech, they could do something better than . . . well, than a ramshackle tangle of metal, garishly grafted. Bioluminescent strips, a maze of levels with no real organization, and ships hanging on to the thing at every possible angle as the station/planetoid spun in drunken spirals.

"How do we even land?" I asked nobody in particular, and got an appalled silence in response, because we were all staring at the Sliver the same way. Even Starcurrent had gone still, except for random twitches. "We have to match a Hopper to that spin?"

"It's part of the bar to entry," Marko's voice said over comms. He and Chao-Xing hadn't come back, likely because they still had a shitload of repairs left on Typhon. The list of stuff to replace was probably enormous. From the phrasing, he sounded like himself again. "Or so I heard. Honors don't come here. Leviathan come very rarely."

"Until now," I said. "Okay, so . . . Bea? Can you handle this?"

She tilted her head to one side and watched the rotation. "I think so." Better her than me, because I wanted to puke just staring at the trajectories involved. "It's not so bad once you get over the oscillation."

It burned me that I was supposedly the *pilot*, and I didn't have the natural feel for it that Beatriz did, but she—the singer—didn't have the ability to freely meld with Nadim the way I did, so it evened out. There was no way I was heading into a place called the Sliver without Nadim, however. We'd figured out how to jury-rig a remote connection before, and Nadim's input would be considerably more important here. I kept our bond open. Light, but present, so he could look directly through my eyes.

I still wanted a backup.

"Bea, do we still have the tech we used on Firstworld?" I asked.

She got where I was headed straightaway. "Should be with the other gear. I'll look." Soon, she came back with the unit and attached it to my skinsuit, adding, "Nadim, would you rather have this installed on a bot or a drone?"

"That is . . . an intriguing suggestion," Nadim said, but I could tell he had reservations. "I prefer to stay with Zara, for now."

I grinned. "My legs are your legs. So, what, we grab a Hopper and jump right in?"

"Not so fast," Yusuf said. "What will you use for currency?"

Great question. Honors were given a lot of good stuff, but bags of cash weren't included, and Earth money wouldn't do us any good out here. "What's considered valuable?"

Starcurrent scuttled forward, a little *too* eagerly. "If I may? All value the _____." That was a fantastic time for the translation matrix to blip on us. Ze waved tentacles as

47

if ze'd ended a galactic war or something.

"Try again." Starcurrent fiddled with the device. For the first time, I realized ze was no longer wearing a skinsuit, just the device, held in place by a tangle of smaller fringe tentacles. "Hey, are you okay? With the air in here?"

A dismissive wave of too many fronds to count. "I have grown a filter," ze said. "For the toxins. Given time, is easy. Ah, there. All species value stillsong."

"Stillsong? You mean, song," I repeated. "We're going to *sing* for what we need in a space-crim scrapyard?"

"Not livesong," Starcurrent said. "You have recordings. Those are stillsong. Rare, to have such from new species. Very valuable."

I blinked. We had a music library, sure; it held hundreds of thousands of musical pieces, everything from old-instrument classical to glasspipe, which had been raging when we'd left Earth. "Any particular way they want to have it?"

"Share by datastream," Starcurrent said. "Sample first. Full song on receipt of goods."

I shared a look with Bea, who covered her mouth with one hand to smother a sharp laugh. "Wait," she said. "Are you trying to tell us that we might be rich because we have a lot of music on board?"

All the tentacles splayed, and the tips went bright pink. "Yes!"

"Well, shit," I said, and picked up my H2 handheld. I tapped it against the console and called up the music library, then ported the whole thing into the handheld's storage. "I kind of love this dump now. Let's go make some trades."

All of us—except Yusuf, who remained in EMITU's care, heavily sedated now—decided to go down to the Sliver, which might not have been the safest choice, but we were running out of time, or rather Yusuf was.

"Right," Chao-Xing said as we got settled. She'd claimed the pilot's chair with Beatriz copiloting beside her, and me, Marko, and Starcurrent were all stuffed back into the crew seats. Starcurrent, I was interested to notice, could fold up *very* small. I assumed, from the ninety million tentacles holding on to everything in reach, including the back of Bea's seat, ze didn't like the idea of landing the Hopper on the spinning, gyrating, uneven surface of the Sliver. "I've sent each of you priorities. Stay in teams. Marko, Starcurrent, Beatriz, you stay together. Zara and I will work our own list."

"Which of us is looking for Yusuf's medicine?" Beatriz asked.

"On your list," C-X said. "Along with specific supplies and repair parts. Also, food that Starcurrent likes. Zara and I will arrange for the Leviathan's star baths and try to locate armor and weapons for them. Stick to your lists as much as possible. The faster we do this, the faster we're safely out."

Safe was not usually an incentive for me, but looking at the chaotic swirl of the Sliver, I was starting to understand the attraction.

"You got this?" I asked C-X as she did the final adjustments on her course.

Bea was running the numbers, and she nodded at Chao-Xing. "Approach looks good."

"Brace yourselves," C-X said. "Acceleration in three, two, one—"

I didn't even have a chance to ask her why exactly we would be *accelerating* before it felt like a fist punched me in the back, and the whole Hopper started to tumble and twist. Everything spun, and I heard the normally calm Chao-Xing let out a sharp, bitten-off cry as she wrestled the controls. Starcurrent made a yowling sound, and tentacles surrounded me. I cussed until the air should've turned blue.

We spun faster. I felt like my eyeballs would pop out. "Chao-Xing!"

"Almost there—"

"Hey!"

"Got it." Her words were calm, and rich with satisfaction, and the spin slowed down as jets fired, and then we

50

were down, the Hopper fastening to the metal skin of the Sliver with a harsh, jolting click. *Magnetic,* I realized. The whole damn landing pad was magnetic. Which was why the surface was littered with crouching ships.

Now, nothing was turning except the stars, and if I didn't look at them, the motion sickness wasn't so bad.

"Helmets," Marko prompted. "We'll need to keep them on in there. The air's borderline toxic at best."

We slid them on. Thin and filmy, the coverings felt like plastic, but there was really a breathable biotech that adhered close to our faces, locked down onto the skinsuits we wore, and immediately began feeding us a rich oxygen mix. Starcurrent's filtering system must have been feeding zim something else. "Okay. We ready to do this?"

"Weapons check," Chao-Xing said. She stood up and drew one of the sleek black laser guns that both Typhon and Nadim had aboard; I had a similar model at my side, as did Bea and Marko. We checked charges. All full.

"No weapon here," Starcurrent said. "None is needed, bless."

I had no idea what *that* meant, but I hoped it didn't mean ze thought the people who lived out here were good at heart. In my experience, fringe dwellers were loyal to their own, but everybody else needed to stay sharp.

"Got your tunes?" I asked. All four of us humans held up H2 units. Starcurrent's tentacles flared pink at the ends again. I wondered if that meant ze was excited. "Let's boldly go shopping."

That was when someone banged on the Hopper's armored side. Loudly. With what sounded like a hammer big enough to flatten a Leviathan.

"Open up!" The roar came across all our comms at a volume that made my ears ring.

FROM THE UNOFFICIAL PUBLICATION A GUIDE TO
THE SLIVER
Source: Bruqvisz Planetary Database, unlicensed copy

Welcome, brave traveler! To dare the Sliver is to declare your independence and show survival in all excellent forms. Your first challenge will be minor: landing and paying for the privilege of not being undocked.

Your second will be finding allies upon tiers, to assist in earning your way while on the Sliver. Bold thought and bold action are needed. The rule of the Sliver is lack of rules, but for two: never steal from Bacia Annont, and never steal from the Sliver bank. Killing in defense is allowable, but check alliances prior to such or could bring worse consequences. Theft from vendors is expected. Cheating, lying, deception: all are art.

If such is not your nature, brave traveler, move on. The Sliver is not for you.

If it is, many riches may be found.

The difficulty is leaving with riches intact.

CHAPTER THREE

Binding Agreements

"THEY ARE DEMANDING a docking fee," Starcurrent said. "Or they threaten harm."

"Yeah, got that part," I said. Chao-Xing and I took up positions, and Marko hit the control to power the Hopper doors open with the hiss of pressurized seals releasing. Scanning, my skinsuit helmet told me with a scrolling datafeed that I was in low-G and that oxygen was poor. Like Marko had warned, didn't look like I'd be taking off my helmet anytime soon.

Magnetized boots clanged against the metal docking floor, alerting me to company before I spotted the twin figures in power armor. Rounding our shuttle, they were slick as hell, impossible to tell what this species looked like, except that they had four arms, two legs, and what I suspected might be a tail. After hanging with Starcurrent, I was totally chill with all of this. Totally.

"We don't want trouble," I said, like that wasn't my damn middle name. I hoped their matrix could factor Earth talk.

Evidently it was highly adaptable. "State your business," Thing One snapped.

"We need to make some deals."

I was apparently speaking the right code because the hostility ramped down as the two conferred. Then the first one turned to me. "You have barter?"

I suspected that wasn't exactly the right word, but close enough. At least nobody had gotten shot yet.

"Tons of original music. You won't have heard anything like it!" To my own ears I sounded a little desperate, like the guy in the night market trying to unload the last of his shoddy bootleg chips.

If they asked about proof of intellectual property own-ership, we were so screwed. One of them made a call and talked to someone higher up the food chain. "Show us," Thing Two said. At least, I thought it was Thing Two. Hard to tell. The translation field was omnidirectional, to my ears.

Bea played some classical tune snippet on her H2; it wasn't my jam, but it made all Starcurrent's tentacles flitter around like ze was a sea anemone riding a strong tide.

At my cue, she cut the sound. "We can upload that to pay for docking, just say the word."

"Word," said the guard.

Bea must have been rolling her eyes, but she sent the data, and a light flashed on the handheld Thing Two was brandishing. Well, I called it that, but it looked nothing like Earth tech. This was pretty and crystal and to me, the way the colors and symbols flashed, they might've told me it was a magic gem, and I'd have halfway believed it.

"Accepted," Thing One said. "Scanning to decrypt format."

That took a bit, so we cooled our heels. It didn't make sense that they'd use the same type of files we did, but with their tech level, it would likely be a cake walk to reverse engineer our code. Finally, the green light flashed, and music pulsed from Thing One's hand—loud, industrial grindhouse stuff that nearly made him drop the unit.

"A trap?"

Uh-oh, Thing One sounds pissed. Bea edged closer to me. "I sent the wrong file," she whispered. "What do I do?"

I stepped up. "Hey, that first thing? That was nothing. *This*, this is the good stuff," I said. "Don't want it? Fine. But I guarantee you, nobody here has anything like it."

The guards conferred. Blared the grindhouse some more. Finally turned back to us. "Too much like _____ ," they said, and whatever the word was, the translation matrix gave up on it. "Other one."

Bea took a deep breath and tried again. This time, when the decryption finished, the classical melody washed over us, rendered weirdly wrong by the thinner air, but the guards seemed happier. Too happy, since they kept listening. Chao-Xing tapped her foot, and I felt the weight of her glare, even if I couldn't see her eyes.

This shit takes time, okay?

Thing One finally said grudgingly, "Open line of credit? Give access to ship database?"

"Don't give them access," Nadim whispered in my comms.

Having him perched on my shoulder was all kinds of handy, but did he think I was that fresh? "I wouldn't," I whispered back. Too far for telepathy. That would be more discreet. "'Cause I'm not nine kinds of fool." I raised my voice. "Not gonna happen. Separate line of credit, no ship database. How much does that song buy us? A week's docking?" I just made it up, but at least it was a starting point.

Thing Two let out a sound that was like metal grinding. I hoped it wasn't laughter. "Half day."

"Four standard Sliver days."

"One."

"Two."

The guards stepped back. More convo. Then: "Agreed."

One song, two days of docking privileges? Not bad. I was starting to like this place.

"What business you want?" Thing One asked. Didn't seem mad that I'd shut down his effort to outright rob us. Maybe that was just a polite opening gambit in the Sliver.

I opened my mouth, but Chao-Xing said, "Not your business. We need a vendor list."

That set off the bargaining again, but we got by for an additional pop song. Thing One handed us a shimmering white crystal. I had no idea what to do with it. "Where do we use this?"

"Kiosk," Thing One said. "Welcome to the Sliver. Have a nice day."

Behind them, part of the dock clicked, then tilted down to reveal a rusty metallic hallway.

The guards clumped away down the ramp.

"Follow?" Marko asked.

I shrugged and fell in behind the guards.

As soon as we stepped off the landing pad, we were in alien territory. The shape of the hallway reminded me of a honeycomb, made out of ancient, rusty metal, scarred with faded traces of what must have been graffiti. Too bad I couldn't read the faded yellow glyphs. Maybe they were ads.

My weighted boots kept me from floating away in low-G, but I wished I had magnets too. *That's going on the buy list.*

Behind us on the other side of the Hopper, a blue energy field shimmered, all that stood between us and a quick, cold death in vacuum. These fools could vent us back into space any time.

I looked over at Marko, who was hanging close to Bea. "You locked the ship down, right?"

"I don't know what kind of slicing tools they've got, so I can't guarantee security, but yeah, I did my best."

"Nadim?"

"No one will get inside," Nadim said. "And if by some miracle someone steals the Hopper, I won't allow the shuttle to dock. If any intruder tries Typhon, the Elder will crush them. We will be fine."

The guards must have been aware of that probability. Whether or not they would give it a try depended on how risk-averse these crims were. I suppose hijacking a Leviathan was right up there with stealing a planet. Probably beyond their pay grade, at least without serious authorization.

Our group followed a curving corridor that ended in an impressive-as-hell door. I wouldn't be surprised if this beast could stand up to a starving Phage legion. Thing One inputted a complicated code, and then lifted the visor to breathe on the panel. Interesting, that. DNA-based access? I glimpsed vaguely reptilian features and a set of sharp teeth before the faceplate came down again.

Probably not the time to ask if I could see more, huh? But I wanted to.

The bulwark groaned open, sounding like an airplane giving birth to a hovercraft. Thing One pointed through the opening. Plainly the guard didn't intend to show us around, so I reached for Bea's hand. She squeezed her gloved fingers around mine and we led the way into the Sliver, boldly going where no humans had before. Cheesy, I knew, but it felt right to think that. I'd seen the old vids.

Well, as far as we knew we four were the first humans here, anyway. Could be there were some delinquent, reported-dead Honors who had jumped ship as soon as they learned what the Journey was all about. If so, we might find them hiding here.

All of us clustered together, and I took my first look around.

The initial impact was . . . breathtaking.

From the silence of that entry conduit, now we were swallowed by controlled chaos. Everything about this place reminded me of the Zone—in a good way. This seemed to be the bottom of the structure, and I could see tiers above us, thronged with . . . people? Independently moving aliens, anyway. Pink lights flashed, advertising something. I couldn't read the words but the picture next to them made me think the ad was for a tavern, three levels up. Even this bottom tier was crowded, with aliens shoving past us while we gaped like tourists; I couldn't focus on any of them, and they were wearing bulky armored space gear—dented, scratched, patched together. The exceptions who didn't need it were a species that floated like jellyfish in the low grav, flashing with their own bioluminescence. Beautiful and frail-looking, but when an armored form brushed up against one, it got thrown back three steps, clearly dazed.

Right. Don't touch anything.

I straightened my shoulders and let go of Bea's hand. "Let's get to it. Bea? You see that kiosk they were talking about?"

"I don't know what I'm looking for . . . wait." Bea pointed. "That?"

I nudged her hand. "Just tilt your head and watch your gestures. We don't know what people find offensive around here."

She indicated a small crowd gathered around a translucent screen, displaying what had to be a map. We headed that way, and I checked to make sure no one was wandering off. They weren't. We worked our way up to the map.

It immediately powered down.

"I guess it needs this," Bea said, and took the crystal out.

She slid it into a small slot, and it fit perfectly, and the map lit up again. I didn't exactly know what I was looking at, though. Couldn't read the symbols. For an irritated second I thought we'd been ripped off already by the welcoming committee, but then a net of glowing white particles shot out and encircled Bea's head. As I reached out for her, a harsh tone came from the unit, then it said, "Analyzing cerebral matrix. Please stand by."

I lunged for her, but a dozen tentacles restrained me. Starcurrent. I considered biting. I *had* to teach this Abyin Dommas about personal space.

"Engram-mapping," Starcurrent said, like that could clear it all up. "Is fine."

"This is incredible," Nadim added in my ear. "She is not in distress, Zara."

"Well, I am! Let go!"

"Please to wait," Starcurrent said. "Is standard."

Ze must have been correct, because in another few seconds, the map deciphered Bea's brain. The kiosk lit up with information . . . in English. Names, mostly, which didn't help, but when I tapped one, a callout described a list of goods and services. Okay then.

Chao-Xing said, "Marko, start over there. I'll start here. Note any vendors that have items on your list, and I'll take care of ours."

It didn't take as long as I expected, but while they were

marking locations and figuring out logistics, I turned and took a visual survey. This place felt . . . understandable, which didn't make much sense, but there it was. The lower the level, the grimier it seemed. Scrap and crap, Tier One. Salvage, Tier Two. Possibly illicit services, Tier Three. By the time it ascended to ten tiers, it was obviously clean and well organized.

Like everywhere, the rich stayed above it all.

For my part, I wanted to roam around, get a feel for the place, but I imagined C-X wouldn't be down with such a strategy. She'd be all about making methodical progress.

"Bank," Marko said. "We should probably put something on deposit there. Not everybody's going to take trade, especially if there's an established currency system."

"Two kinds of banks," Chao-Xing added. "This one says it deals in datamynt."

"*Mynt* is Norwegian for 'coin,'" Nadim said. "Also in Swedish and—"

"Not the point," I cut in gently. "Marko? What about yours?"

"Something called fita. Isn't the same, I think."

Bea was still stuck on the first thing. "Wait, didn't there used to be virtual currency called Bitcoin? Maybe that's what the translator was going for."

"Sure," I said. "Probably. Whatever. So . . . which bank?"

The board suddenly said, "The Sliver uses two types of

currency, honored newcomer. The Sliver bank accumulates fita, which is required for premium station services such as fueling, major ship repair, armament, reinforcing armor, and drive repairs. Datamynt is lesser currency, to be used for nonstation services and products. The two are separate and noninterchangeable."

"So, selling our music would get us what, exactly?" I asked.

"Datamynt," the board replied. "Stillsong exchanges may be made at the Bruqvisz Bank on Tier Four for datamynt."

I was really, really hoping for a barter economy. Probably existed down here on the crap levels, but once we got above Level Three we probably needed legit currency.

Chao-Xing asked the obvious question. "And how do we get fita?"

"Several ways, honored guest. Fita may be granted for extraordinary services by Bacia Annont, owner of this station. May be earned through long service to Bacia Annont, likewise. May be accumulated through the Pit."

Bea busted out laughing, and I shot her an inquiring look. "What?"

"The station owner is named Bacia? That means 'bowl' in Portuguese."

"Let's hope that bowl is full of something good," Marko said.

In a place like this? I had my doubts. Time to get back on track—I addressed the screen, which had produced a list of definitions for Bacia's name in a hundred languages. I didn't like the look of "divine vessel," the meaning in Abyin Dommas.

"Enough. What route is fastest for earning fita?"

"The Pit," the board said. "Great risk for great return." It lit up a sublevel below our feet: an amphitheater. Giant gambling hall? I wasn't sure. "How may I further assist?"

"You can't," C-X said, and turned to Marko. "Got your vendors?"

"I've made a list."

"Then your team can go to this Bruqvisz Bank and make exchanges for datamynt, and go about your tasks," C-X said. She glanced at me. "Ours will be more difficult."

Because datamynt would buy almost everything on Marko's list.

But it would take fita to acquire what we needed for our Leviathan.

"Anyone gets in trouble, signal," Marko said. "Let's sync up and use our H2s for time- and position-keeping. Understood?"

"Rendezvous back here if something goes wrong with the comms," C-X said, because she was a worst-case-scenario kind of woman, and I liked that. "Watch your backs."

"Good," said Starcurrent, and as always, accompanied that with a flash of upraised tentacles. Ze had been watching the crowd while we interacted with the board. "Enjoy!"

That seemed unlikely, but okay.

Chao-Xing led our two-soldier military march along the bottom level. No proper storefronts down here; these junk merchants were selling merch off hover dollies and out of half-wrecked storage containers, and though I didn't understand the tech, I totally understood the concept of scrapping. I wondered how this place smelled. The filtering helmet blocked out all that, and I really, really wanted to know.

Against C-X's wishes, I did some browsing, and lots of cool stuff caught my eye. Eventually I bargained for a personal-force-field device. When I got done with the alien vendor, the gizmo was cheap enough, and I tested it with perfect glee.

Let's see. You push the button, drop it, and it surrounds you in . . . I counted ten seconds before the field appeared. I could picture this being useful in any number of situations. If I wasn't careful, I might also cut off some limbs.

"You don't need anything else," Chao-Xing snapped. "Let's move. If we have to do this Pit thing, let's find out what's involved."

I spotted the way down before she did, and the hair stood up on the back of my neck in pure exhilaration. Without a word, I kicked off the wall and sprinted for the platform; I didn't hesitate before leaping into the sparkling slip-stream. Hell if I knew what this was exactly—anti-gravity well, maybe—but I zipped down in what felt like free-fall, only it wasn't. There were mini-platforms to kick to indicate what tier you wanted, and I bounced off the next one down, landing on the dais with a glee so profound I couldn't stop laughing.

How's that *for public transportation?*

"I *love* this place," I half sang to Nadim.

"I can tell," he said, and I heard his shared pleasure. "It seems . . . exhilarating."

"Ow!" I said, because C-X had caught up to me and smacked me in the back of the head. She tried it again, but I dodged that whack. "What? That was efficiency in action!"

"You could have killed yourself!"

"And you followed," I pointed out. "Couldn't have been that bad."

There was another information board down the tunnel a bit, and we walked toward it. Traffic wasn't heavy in here, and what crowd there was clustered up by the board. It was displaying characters I didn't recognize, but as we came into range, they shifted into English. None of the others studying the board seemed to notice, so it must have only been that way for us.

Apparently, this was the signup system for the Pit. I read the instructions:

Only sponsored contestants may submit for matches. Teams preferred.

Artificial enhancements must be certified.

There are no rules in the Pit.

Death of an opponent wins, but at half pay.

Medical assistance provided for datamynt only.

Huh. This sounded like . . .

"It's a fighting pit," Chao-Xing said. "Betting on matches."

"Cage matches?"

"Doesn't sound like they have any rules, so . . . probably," she said. "Only sponsored contestants . . ."

I stepped up to the board. "Where do we find sponsors?"

"Sponsors may be obtained through direct request," the board replied.

"Where?"

In response, a bunch of blinking lights appeared on the board, at a variety of levels.

We both stared at them for a few seconds, then at each other. "You're good at the sims," Chao-Xing said. "You were good with the Phage. What do you think?"

"We don't have a choice, if we want to get our Leviathan the starlight they need. We can't spend years building up the social coin, can we?"

"No," Nadim said quietly. "I'm sorry. But we need your help. Typhon is improving a little, but it will fade the longer he's without the frequencies of light he needs. I will last longer, but to heal properly . . ."

I didn't know if C-X could hear him until she said, "Understood, Nadim. All right. Then we should start at the top, with the most prestigious sponsors."

"People at the top only bet on sure things," I said. "Try Tier Three. That's about our speed right now. We're unknowns. From the look of most of the beings around here, we're not very imposing. Getting someone to give us a shot could be . . . challenging."

"I like a challenge," C-X said.

"It didn't say anything about weapons," I said. "Would that be cheating?"

"Let's find a sponsor and ask."

I pointed to the place on Tier Three. "There," I said. "Looks like a dive bar. Just what we need."

This time, I let C-X go first, jumping into the upcurrent before I leapt in and followed. It felt like flying, like rocket fuel in my boots as we rose straight up past the entry level, past Levels One and Two. It would be a blast zooming around the Sliver like this; wild that none of the other travelers were turning flips or striking action poses as they zipped along. They seemed as bored as business commuters. Tensing my core, I managed one spin, dangling upside down long enough to catch a wicked smile brightening Chao-Xing's features.

At the last moment, I righted my body and landed on Tier Three with C-X close behind.

"That's . . . growing on me," she admitted.

"Damn right. Just like I am."

"Keep telling yourself that. I like your confidence."

Tier Three was a little more organized than the prior two levels, with small shops built out from the deck walls. Some had style, while others were bare bones, make-a-deal-or-get-out types. Conde would've vibed with those joints. A pang went through me, thinking of him, so it was just as well that Nadim couldn't catch my every emotional flicker; it wasn't that I'd *liked* Conde so much as I'd *known* him, in ways that I'd known few other people. He'd taught me early on how to navigate the Zone, what to steal, when to stop. Not a father figure, but . . . something.

"Hey, Nadim?" I asked. I felt the rush of warmth from him, but it seemed muted now. Distance, eating away at our connection. "Any updates on Yusuf?"

"EMITU reports that he is keeping him in an induced coma. His life signs are steady, but another crisis may occur soon. If it does, bringing him back may be more difficult."

More difficult than last time? That was terrifying. "Okay," I said. "Everything good with Bea?"

"She, Marko, and Starcurrent are at the bank on the next tier from your position," he said. "They are now arguing the merits of jazz music with a currency exchange specialist. I don't think they're in any danger."

Well, we probably would be, because the place the Pit board had directed us? Was a garish bar. I nicknamed it Pinky's, because of the hovering fuchsia spotlights swirling out front. When I shared that with Chao-Xing, she cracked a faint smile. A bot buzzed the open doorway, bleating a welcome message, I guessed. It looped in at least ten alien languages. Then I stepped into the translation matrix field, and it wasn't so much welcoming as warning us that the management took no responsibility for crimes committed on the premises.

"Wretched hive of scum and villainy, take one," I muttered.

From the quirk of her mouth, Chao-Xing got the reference, but she didn't smile. "Let me do the talking in here."

"Sure," I said. "I was gonna suggest that, seeing as you're such a people person."

"Zara." I recognized the tone of someone who was tired of my shit.

"I hear you," I said.

"This is making me anxious," Nadim said. "Perhaps you should try another option."

I paused as Chao-Xing pushed through the doorway.

"This is going to involve some risks, getting what we need. You understand that, right? You're going to have to trust me."

"I do," he said, without any hesitation at all. "Zara, I do. But being so . . . helpless is hard. I hate for you to put yourself in danger because of me."

"That's what a pilot does for her ship," I said. "And . . . you'd do the same for me, if it was necessary."

The whisper of our connection was still there, even at this distance. I looked up. The atmosphere above was topped by a shimmering blue force barrier that dimmed the stars beyond it. I couldn't see him up there.

But I could still feel him, and I knew he could touch me in return.

"It's going to be okay," I said, and plunged into the bar after Chao-Xing.

Inside, it didn't feel warmer or colder; my skinsuit was regulating the temp. Otherwise it would have been sweltering, because the bodies were packed tight in here. There was no central counter like you'd find in an Earth canteen, but servo-bots were hovering, basically flying drink trays, and the customers seemed to be placing orders on terminals scattered throughout, like smaller versions of the info boards. I didn't see any signs that said FIND SPONSORS HERE. Unfortunately.

Lights splashed the room with color, fading white to

yellow to green to blue and onward through the spectrum, so that it felt like the bar had a permanent filter, making wildly different patrons look vintage or melancholy by turns. Industrial-sounding noise blared from the walls; some local music, probably, but to my human ears, it sounded like a bunch of engines revving out of sync, with an army of toddlers banging pans in the background.

I processed the scene while looking for Chao-Xing. Lumpyhead alien, check. A few Abyin Dommas, which might make Starcurrent happy. I spotted a cluster that resembled what I'd glimpsed of Thing One: lizard face, pointy teeth, scaled, serpent eyes, and a ruff that flared on the back of their necks and curved up like a hood, and shifted hue, according to . . . I had no idea what.

I finally spotted Chao-Xing, who was also checking things out. "What do you think?" she asked, pointing at the lizard-faced aliens around a wide table. "They're the same species as one of the docking bay guards. Maybe a good place to start?"

"Sounds good," I agreed, and let her take the lead.

Given what I knew of her personality, I expected her to immediately start demanding to know their rates for sponsorship; instead she edged carefully up to their table, bowed politely, and said, "Hello. May I have a moment of your time?"

Then she waited. Eight snake eyes, varying shades of

brown and gold, locked onto us. *Shit, we might as well have "noobs" tattooed on our foreheads. She's probably using some bullshit Leviathan first-contact protocol guide.*

If she was, it seemed to be working. "Why?" the biggest one asked.

"You have the look of knowledgeable beings," Chao-Xing said. "And perhaps, interested in the contests conducted in the Pit?"

The four of them made a sound that reminded me of bones breaking. Took me a second to identify it as amusement. "Interesting approach," the biggest said, and took a drink from a bot that swept in bearing it. "You have until I finish this to make your case."

"Nadim," I whispered. "Is this a her?"

"No," he said. "Male. Use male pronouns."

"How can you tell?"

"Do you really need to know now?"

He was right. I cleared my throat and said, pitched to carry to both Chao-Xing and Mr. Lizard, "Sir, how about if I buy everyone a round while you and my friend talk?"

"*Sir?*" The reptilian eyes blinked. He had two sets of eyelids, and this one was weirdly transparent. "You dare make assumptions of gender?"

"I'm not assuming," I said as C-X threw me a half-desperate glance. "Sir."

That earned me another bone-grating cascade of

laughter, and Mr. Lizard drained the rest of his glass. He tossed it straight up in the air, and before it could fall (slowly, in this gravity), a bot whizzed in and caught it on its tray. "Better understanding than most newcomers. Your mynt to spend." His inner eyelids blinked again. "What gender are you?"

"What, you can't tell?" I shot back, and this time, all four of them hissed.

Taking that for approval, I headed over to the order terminal, and I was ready when the glow-dots encircled my head, just like they had for Beatriz at the first information board. Nadim had been right; it didn't feel like anything at all. I wasn't prepared for one of the hovertrays to zoom by and swipe a saliva sample from my mouth, though. Gaping after the thing, I turned as the interface listed the things it could synthesize that wouldn't poison me. Sweet. After minimal reflection, I ordered two Fizzy Riffles, whatever the hell that was, and when I thought about the lizards, a new bar selection popped up. Incomprehensible name, but the word REORDER was next to it, so I hit it four times.

The terminal asked for payment. Right. I hoped that Team Leviathan had come to an agreement at the bank. I pulled out my H2, and sure enough, there was a message from Marko. *We have plenty of datamynt,* he said, and provided an account link. I quickly held the link up to the terminal, and it must have worked, because nobody came to evict my ass.

A message came up on the board. *Order in preparation.*

I headed back to C-X, who was making small talk with the lizard aliens. *Not* a sentence I ever imagined myself putting together. I nearly got my head taken off by a hovertray bearing two neon-yellow drinks with white smoke roiling from them.

The lizards were laughing again. C-X was holding her own, and somehow, she'd acquired a drink already. It was a vivid pink, like the lights outside the place, and a faint fog drifted off the surface and over her hand. She hadn't touched it. Free drinks? Suspicious. We'd be lucky if they didn't drug us and haul our bodies off for science.

"Nadim?" I asked. "Still with me?"

"Always," he said. "The being you are speaking with is from a race called the Bruqvisz. They are known to be aggressive. I have never met one myself, but be careful."

I grinned. "Why don't I promise to be clever instead?"

*A FRAGMENT OF A RECORDING SMUGGLED FROM
THE SLIVER, REPUTED TO CONTAIN THE VOICE OF
BACIA ANNONT*

NOTE: The validity of the recording is in dispute. However, no member of the rare Biiyan race has been seen beyond the Sliver for a thousand recorded galactic grand rotations.

Biiyan Elder: . . . honored by the light of your regard, O Majesty, please allow gifts of rarest value.

[Indecipherable sounds]

Biiyan Elder: I freely gift all this to you, O Majesty, for the favor of your approval. How may I serve you?

[Indecipherable sounds]

Biiyan Elder: More I may not give without indenturing my people to Your Majesty's service.

BACIA ANNONT: Then it will be so. You serve me now.

[Indecipherable sounds and screams]

Biiyan Elder: Then let it be so.

CHAPTER FOUR

Binding Promises

THE ROUND OF drinks arrived with a hiss of approval from the lizards. Two of them raised hoods at the back of their necks, which flared sunbursts of gold. I guessed/hoped they liked the gesture. C-X quietly replaced the pink drink on the hovertray and took one of the Fizzy Riffles. She passed the other to me. I wondered how we were supposed to drink through our masks, but my helmet feed said I could remove it briefly, though I'd soon suffer from the imbalance of oxygen and carbon dioxide. I lifted it just enough to bare my mouth and tasted the concoction. It was both bitter and peppery, nothing I'd choose to have again, but low toxicity was an excellent quality in a place like this. Following suit, Chao-Xing downed hers like medicine, and even the lizard dudes seemed impressed.

"Cheers," I said. They echoed it, though beyond the translation matrix, they might be bidding me to drink the blood of my enemies. At that point, introductions seemed natural. "This is Zhang Chao-Xing. And my name is Zara Cole."

"Zeerakull," he repeated. "And JongShowJing."

I guessed our names had no literal translations. *Close enough.* Zeerakull sounded badass.

Then Big Lizard gave me their names in return: Followshome, Ghostwalk, Fairweather, and Suncross. He spoke them all so fast that I couldn't match them with faces, but I felt 90 percent sure that the large guy speaking was Suncross.

"Now to business," Suncross said. "Your offer of beverage has earned time. Go. Tell me why we risk fita to sponsor such . . . small creatures. The Pit is no place for weakness."

"Small doesn't mean weak," C-X said.

That got a grunt in agreement. "True, true, I know fierce opponents smaller than you. But they have poison and more legs than two. We have a large fund of fita. Sponsorship splits your winnings with us, fifty percent. Need proof of your skill, of course."

"Of course," she said, and didn't even lose the little smile she was holding. "But we keep seventy-five percent."

I'd have started at ninety, but she was new at this. I kept quiet as they went back and forth . . . and then, I realized what Suncross was doing.

Misdirecting us.

When the one next to him—Fairweather, I thought— came out with a knife and lunged, I was ready, though I wasn't looking. Didn't need to be. I grabbed the arm, felt the scary-thick muscles tensing underneath, and let momentum carry the weight across the table, with me guiding the creature face-first down onto the floor. I grabbed the knife as he fell, and buried it point-first next to the Bruqvisz's head. Good knife. It didn't even break.

I'd like to say the bar went quiet, but in truth, we were totally ignored . . . except for C-X, who'd paused to look down at us, and Suncross, who'd jumped to his feet. The other two followed his lead.

I was leaning my entire weight on the point of my elbow at the nape of Fairweather's neck, and the Bruqvisz was squirming. But not getting up. "Sorry," I said. "Please go on."

Chao-Xing looked at Suncross. Suncross looked at her.

And then he let out a low rumble of a growl, and I thought, *Well, shit, had to go this way, didn't it?*

Then Suncross picked up his drink and raised it. "To a marriage," he said. "Us to you."

"Uh, what?" I blurted.

Suncross thought that over. "Partnership," he said. "Is better? Sixty percent to you. Forty to us of any winnings. You will make first round, maybe second before you are taken seriously. Then . . . ?" He shrugged. "Then we see." He glanced down at Fairweather and said, "Let my friend rise. He will buy drinks to seal this celebration."

"I'm keeping the knife," I said, and pulled it out of the floor as Fairweather rolled up.

"Fair," Suncross agreed. "Will take it off your percentage, though."

"Come on."

"Is family treasure."

I handed it back. "So, how fast can we start in the Pit?"

"You are in a hurry?" Suncross sounded surprised this time, if the translator got it right. "Most not so eager for pain."

"We're not masochists," Chao-Xing said. "We have injured Leviathan to care for. They are the only survivors of a Phage attack."

Silence dropped on the table like a tarp. Suncross and Fairweather sat down, and as one, the four Bruqvisz's hoods slid up and turned dark. "Was not aware," Suncross said. "We mourn. The Singers are important to all of us. You are Honors?"

That startled me, and Chao-Xing too. "Yes," she said. "We are."

"Bonded?"

"Yes."

"Then we will advance you the cost of healing stars," he said. "A loan of fita, from the Bruqvisz. The Singers should not suffer." There was some murmur from the other three, but Suncross rapped two of his four fists on the table, and it died down. "Is a great gesture for us. You understand? But you must repay in the Pit."

I felt short of breath. The urge to blurt out yes nearly strangled me, but I stayed quiet. I could feel Nadim hovering on the fringes of my consciousness. Maybe he was listening. I didn't know. But Chao-Xing was cool and formal as she bowed toward the Bruqvisz and said, "We take this as a matter of honor. How may we arrange this treatment for our ships?"

For answer, Suncross tapped Fairweather on the shoulder, and the other Bruqvisz left the bar. "Will return once order is placed," Suncross said. "Do not let us down, little beings. Loss of fita is a serious business on the Sliver." He took a drink of his new concoction and fixed his eyes on me. "Why the Pit? Why not safer way, like Sliver service?"

I shrugged. "This way's faster." I didn't want to tell him the other reasons, like *I like to fight* and *I'm not that good at taking orders,* both of which were true. "You made a good decision," I added.

Suncross grunted. More drinks arrived. The other

Bruqvisz started to talk, finally, and I was surprised to find that they were discussing what sounded like . . . music. The merits of the terrible bar band we were enduring. Apparently there was a great deal of pride involved. It didn't quite come to blows.

Fairweather came back in a few minutes and took his seat with a nod.

"Done," Suncross said. "Your ships have healing stars as long as you win in the Pit."

No pressure, right?

As soon as we stepped out of Pinky's, I felt the vague connection to Nadim strengthen. "Hey, Nadim," I said. "Did you catch all that?"

"The Bruqvisz have loaned you the fita to purchase the use of star baths for the two of us," he summarized nicely. "I don't like this idea of fighting for money, Zara."

"You'd rather I do it for fun?"

"Zara."

"Okay, point taken, but . . . look, we *will* run into the Phage again, right? You saw the effort it took for us to survive them. Sharpening my skills isn't a bad move. Plus, if it earns you healing, armor, weaponry . . . I'm willing."

I could tell that he wasn't, not entirely, but he let it go. "Marko has located a possible source of medication for Yusuf."

"Where?"

"Tier One," he replied, and when I glanced at my H2, it showed the location. Amazing that their tech could integrate so swiftly with ours; theirs must have been incredibly advanced. I tapped Chao-Xing and showed her; she nodded and surged ahead.

I was a couple of steps behind as she dove into the grav well, and I admired the graceful arch of her body as she fell. It was amazing there were no midair collisions; traffic was pretty heavy. I picked my spot. Then I hit the tier selection and plummeted, wishing I could feel the freefall on my face, in my curls; the suit muted all that. I bounced twice on landing at Tier One, and then we headed for the glowing dot where Marko, Bea, and Starcurrent were clustered.

It was a junk shop, unsurprisingly. As we rolled up, Chao-Xing dropped a hand to her weapon and I was about to draw mine, because the last time I got this vibe from body language, Deluca's man Enzo died in an alley. I couldn't see Bea's face, but the rest of her body language telegraphed terror. Marko looked tense as a suspension bridge. And Starcurrent was strobing colors down zis fronds like ze'd been plugged in as a glitter ball, tentacles waving all over.

The Abyin Dommas was saying frantically, "No, the human girl is not for sale. I repeat, *not for selling*."

"Well, shit," Chao-Xing said.

For once, she spoke for both of us.

The booth owner—a big, protean thing that I instantly nicknamed Blobby—oozed toward Beatriz, and she tried to head for the safety of the exit. It extruded a limb to block her path. In the flashing, glowing lights of the Sliver, the limb shone silvery on the surface, with flecks of gold and black tumbling inside like a living snow globe. Could have been pretty, if it wasn't boxing in my friend.

"Hey!" I charged. "Appendages to yourself, and nobody's for sale, get it? Nobody!"

Blobby retracted, rolled around for a second, then expanded again into an alarming explosion of sharply pointed spikes, a snow globe with anger issues. A growl rattled the metal around us, and I could feel the vibrations through my boots.

In my comm Nadim said, "Zara? Are you in danger?"

I registered his tension, struggling to keep myself calm. "Nope," I told him, and was proud that my voice sounded so even. "We're okay. We're fine. Right, Bea?"

The last thing I needed was for two wounded Leviathan to decide they needed to charge to our rescue. The Sliver *looked* like a ramshackle wreck, but I doubted it was. And it certainly would have defenses suitable to protect the criminal activities conducted inside it.

Bea nodded. "Stand down, Nadim. We can deal with this."

The translation matrix field cut in, and Blobby said, "I didn't say I'd *buy* the thing. I said I'd *rent* it, squid."

I was pretty sure *squid* wasn't what Blobby had called Starcurrent, but it was probably an insult that had to do with tentacles. Close enough. Starcurrent's tentacles flared out in a threat display, and instead of the strobe effect of anxiety, they went a thick, dark blue.

And sprouted *stingers*. Every single one of them produced what looked like a thin, curved spike. As I watched, liquid formed at the tip of one, and dripped off to the floor. I half-expected it to hiss and bubble like acid.

"Hey!" Chao-Xing shouted. "Put it away. We're *talking*! That's an order!"

I didn't know that C-X had any kind of rank to pull, but it seemed to work; Starcurrent's stingers retracted, and zis colors faded from a violent navy to a more serene, but still disturbed, blue. "Apologies," ze said. "I will not see friends hurt again."

It hadn't occurred to me that Starcurrent, like Yusuf, was going through PTSD, but that was what it looked like: outsized reactions to stress and stimuli. I'd seen it in the Zone. I was willing to bet that Starcurrent hadn't pulled those stingers out for years, if ever, but ze was shaken and prone to overreactions right now. Which nobody had counted on, least of all me. I'd thought of zim as the steadiest among us.

Blobby must have understood the value of de-escalation, because the spikes sank down, and the central mass expanded and formed something roughly bipedal. Roughly. It looked like dirty cooking oil inside a transparent human skin, which was severely not right, but I managed to keep my hand away from my weapon, though my fingertips ached to skim it just for reassurance.

"Tourists," it scoffed. "Amateurs. Barter offer rescinded. I sell you nothing. Out!"

"Wait a second," Beatriz said, carefully pushing past Starcurrent to put herself front and center. "What are you talking about?"

"Livesong," Blobby said. "Lost my last livesinger to another booth. Nobody has heard your kind. Will draw business. Will trade information on healer for this."

Marko glanced at Bea. "What do you think?"

She answered, a touch uncertain. "As long as it gets us the meds Yusuf needs . . ."

"This job come with fita?" I asked.

"Can," Blobby said, very smoothly. So smoothly I didn't trust a word of it. "I know those in high places."

I didn't doubt it. "How much?"

Blobby did *not* like that question, or maybe it just didn't like me, because its form expanded again, and now the spikes were on hands *and* shoulders, and bristling like a beard from the vague shape of a jaw. "I offer legal employment," it said loftily. "Fita is Tier Two."

I muttered to Chao-Xing, "How many tiers are there?" She shook her head. "Nadim? Can you find out?"

It took him just a few seconds to reply. "Seventeen," he said. "Tier Two is low."

Chao-Xing smiled and said, "We're strangers here, friend, but isn't a fresh livesinger worth more than merely two fita? Many singers start at ten."

"How the hell do you know that?" I whispered.

She kept it equally low when she said, "I don't."

She kept smiling and waiting while Starcurrent's blue digits slowly faded to a color like Earth sky, and finally, Blobby plopped its aggressive spikes back in and said, "Eight fita is fair. But no more. Full work cycle of livesong, two breaks for nourishment. Contract renewable daily, either party can cancel. Piracy-proof field."

I gave Beatriz a look. "Your call," I said. "What do you think?"

"Three breaks," she said. "And I decide what to sing. In addition to the fita, you introduce us to the healer who has the medicine we need."

"Agreed," Blobby said.

We were already earning fita, we had treatments for our Leviathan, and were on track to finding Yusuf's meds. Sweet. This outlaw station wasn't *that* different.

"Employment begins," Blobby said. It sprouted about a

hundred little appendages and began putting things out on the rough, uneven surface of the booth's table—parts, pieces of shiny objects, tubes of liquid, nothing I could identify at a glance. "Sing."

"Now?" Bea drew herself up—even though she feared performing in public, pure determination shone in her eyes.

"Healer details first," Chao-Xing said.

Blobby flipped an appendage, which I first thought was an impatient gesture, but something emerged from the fluid and extruded a crystal that fit into the info boards. We all looked at each other.

Marko plucked the jutting shard out of Blobby's essence. "Great," he said, and wiped his fingers on his pants. "Thank you."

Blobby's spikes rippled out again, then back in, as it activated a glowing red field around its booth. "Sing. Now."

Bea started with a quiet scale, working up to it. Blobby went still, listening, and its skin vibrated in ripples as she grew louder. It didn't have eyes, or expressions, but I had the feeling it was impressed . . . and she hadn't even really started yet.

I was curious, so I stepped back until I was outside of the carmine field.

Bea's voice cut off completely, though I could see her lips moving. The red suppression field not only prevented recording but made sure crowds weren't getting the show for free. Interesting.

The red bubble was clearly the signal that something exciting was going on, because all around us, shapes started heading our way. Lizards, Lumpyheads, a few Blobbies, a couple of those delicate, beautiful Jellies. More I didn't recognize, wearing armor that was so blocky, anything could have been in there.

I pushed back through the field—there was mild resistance—and Bea's beautiful, clear voice launched into one of her favorite Elza Soares songs, *"Mas Que Nada."* Starcurrent's tentacles swayed in samba rhythm and pulsed with bioluminescence like Bea had brought zim as her own light show. *Nice.*

"I think eight was low," Chao-Xing said.

I was thinking the same thing, but it was a start.

We headed over to the info terminal, and Marko slid the crystal into the slot.

It didn't work. "Try cleaning it off first," Chao-Xing said.

"I wish you hadn't reminded me where it came from," he said, but he scrubbed the crystal against his uniform until it shone, then tried it again.

This time, it lit up a sublevel—the Pit level—and a small tunnel off to the side of the main area. That didn't look like a promising place to find a healer, unless the doctor specialized in gladiatorial injuries. But it was the only lead we had. At worst, we could check if we were registered for the next bout in the Pit.

Marko said, "Interesting. We found about a third of what we needed and had it delivered back to the shuttle. We only went up the first two levels, though. Things get more expensive the higher up you go. How'd you two do?"

"We made some new friends," Chao-Xing answered. "A consortium of Bruqvisz."

"Like the bank?"

I nodded. "They loaned us the fita to get treatments for the Leviathan. Now we have to earn it back."

Marko narrowed his eyes, radiating dubious curiosity. I didn't blame him. "How?"

"We'll show you," I said. "Let's go."

As we turned to go, the information booth spoke. "Would you like to load a VA to help you navigate the Sliver?" the terminal asked. It had a strange voice, just one tone away from being terrifying. Maybe some species found it soothing, but it raised my pulse level like a crim with a knife.

"Uh, I don't know? Do we want one of those?" I asked the other two.

Nadim said, "I believe that stands for virtual assistant. Partition your H2 before you accept any data transfers. We can't risk a security breach."

"I'll pass," Chao-Xing said. "But one of us should take the chance."

Risk-taking was my thing, I immediately got that, so I set up my handheld and got the shiny gold flash of a completed task. Now I was ready. To the terminal, I said, "Please install virtual assistant."

My H2 started vibrating, which was both cool and alarming, and when the transfer completed, I had a swirl of light dancing over my handheld. "Ready to assist."

A talking sunbeam—why not? I could probably ask it what I wanted to know, so I tried various phrases, until I hit on "help adapting to habitat." That one triggered a data stream so detailed that I had to pull back the info and pause to get the gist.

I turned to Chao-Xing. "Looks like we can pay for an injection that will let us go suit-free, nanobots that regulate our physical needs from the inside out. Expensive, and doesn't last forever, though, so we'll need regular boosters. Thoughts?"

I was already on board. Fighting in the skinsuit didn't seem too practical. If the enemy damaged our helmets, we wouldn't be able to see, hear, or *breathe*. Not the way to earn fita and victory in the Pit.

C-X tapped the side of her helmet and I figured she was probably tired of the weird insect vision the helmet created. It didn't make me dizzy or disoriented, but it was still strange to have images beamed to my brain at 360 degrees;

safer, sure, but over time, I suspected it would give me a migraine. I was in no way eager to return to those days.

"How expensive?"

I read off the price, within our reach with the songs we'd already sold. "I think it's worthwhile. The suits will limit what kind of moves we can do."

Nadim didn't seem sanguine, though, with an endearing blend of concern and caution. "Are you sure about this, Zara? This is an invasive procedure with unknown alien protocol. I don't have any records of the Sliver or this nanotech if anything goes wrong."

"It'll be fine," I said.

Probably.

If they could map our brains and figure out our language, it made sense they could do the same for our physiology. Theoretically, anyway.

"Zara . . ."

"Before we get injected, I'll analyze it with the H2. You see anything wrong, you sound the alarm. Okay?"

"I don't understand why you risk yourself so easily."

"That's okay. I don't understand Leviathan stuff too well sometimes, either." Except in those perfect moments where we were Zadim, and I could hear the starsong, drink their light. I understood more than I wanted to admit, and . . . so did he, most likely.

Chao-Xing glanced between me and my shoulder unit,

and she smirked a bit. "You two done? If so, let's get Yusuf's meds."

Marko had the hang of the grav well already, so there was no need for training; we all jumped into the downdraft and went to the Pit level. Bottom floor, lowest social standing for anyone living or working down here. Up ahead, the info board glowed, and when we checked it, sure enough, the Bruqvisz had entered a sponsorship with a new team.

They'd called it JongShowJing and Zeerakull, of course. I asked my new VA about our schedule. "You have twenty hours to report. Failure to appear results in team forfeit."

"Noted," I said. "Set the clock for me, all right?"

"Done. Anything else?"

"Take us to the doctor."

The VA led us down a maze of rusty, chancy corridors, to a door that looked like it could withstand sustained weapons fire. I didn't see any doorbell, or even a viewscreen. Chao-Xing stepped up and delivered an authoritative knock that echoed on the metal.

The door made a horrible screeching sound, like she'd hurt it. "Hey!" I covered my ears, and so did Marko; Chao-Xing clenched her teeth and knocked again.

The horrible screeching shut off, and after a delay, the door swung open on a dim room with a reclining medical chair that looked the opposite of reassuring, and a gaunt, cadaverous, human form shuffled out of the shadows.

It took me a second to even realize that much, because he had hair grown down to his shoulders in a ratty mess, a beard to match, and he was wearing a shapeless mass of gray fabric that I supposed might have doubled as a medical smock. Under the hair, the skin that showed had a sickly tinge, but he looked pretty white by nature too.

He seemed as shocked to see us as we were to see him . . . and then his milky gray eyes filled with tears.

"Oh my God," he said in English, and reached out a trembling hand toward us, but didn't touch. "*Oh my God. You're . . . from . . .*" He staggered backward, hit a gritty wall, and slid down to a limp collapse. He covered his face with shaking hands. They, at least, were clean. "No. No, can't be true. Can't be."

"Hey." Marko stepped forward and crouched next to him, put a hand on his shoulder. "Hey, we're real. I'm Marko. And you are?"

The old man gulped and coughed and swiped at his eyes and stared at us like we were angels fallen from heaven. "Henri," he said. "Henri Justineau." His gaze roved from one of us to the next, and I could see he was about to lose it again.

His name rang a distant bell, and I used that to keep him on track. "You're from Earth. You were an Honor," I said. "Right?"

He looked at me, and I saw more tears well up. "Once. Once, I was. Not anymore."

"Where's your Leviathan?" Chao-Xing asked.

"Dead," he whispered. "Torn apart. I survived. The Bruqvisz saved me. Took me out of a lifepod long ago and brought me here. I never thought . . . never expected . . ."

"To see humans again?" Marko finished, and patted him awkwardly. "Well, here we are. Honors from Earth. We're happy to meet you, Honor Justineau."

I admit it, I had a little tight spot at the back of my throat, and I cleared it with a cough. "How long you been here?"

"Here?" Justineau looked around as if he didn't quite remember where he was. Shock, probably. "I—time is different here. Many, many years."

Chao-Xing had been checking her H2. In a low voice, she said, "Henri Justineau went on the Journey almost forty years ago. He was twenty-two when he left Earth."

Forty years, scraping out a living among strangers, so far from anything he'd ever known. Alone. I understood his shock now. And his shaking. The fact he'd survived the death of his Leviathan was amazing, but somehow making it this far? Even more impressive. I thought I was a survivor, but I didn't know if I'd have those guts. Or that luck.

Justineau did some deep breathing, and then accepted Marko's offer of a hand to help him back to his feet. He attempted to push his hair back, but it sprang back out in a wild rebellion until he rummaged around and found something to tie it back. "Well. This is quite a day. I'm . . . I'm thrilled to meet you, and I'm sure you understand what an understatement that is. But from the looks on your faces, you didn't come here expecting to find me, either. So why *are* you here? To rescue me?"

We all glanced at each other, and since neither of the other two opened their mouths, I said, "Sure . . . ?" I drew it out and made it a bit of a question. "If you want to leave, that is."

Justineau let out a shaky laugh. "Oh, no, how could I resist all this luxury?"

Chao-Xing didn't let that go on long. "We came because we heard you had an effective treatment for this disease." She pulled the notation up on her H2 and handed it over. He took it and gazed at the thing like it was a wonder—I guessed it was, seeing human tech again—and then focused on what was being displayed.

"Oh," he said. "Yes. One of you?"

"No. A survivor we rescued earlier. He's sick."

"Very sick, if he didn't have his meds," Justineau said.

"Yes. I do have what you need, but I warn you, it's costly. Sliver regulations require me to charge datamynt and fita for extraordinary treatments, and this qualifies."

Of course. I saw C-X square her shoulders. "How much, exactly?"

"That depends on the stage of his disease. I'd need more

information to calculate dosages and strength. But in the vicinity of one million datamynt, and ten thousand in fita for enough medication to see your colleague through the worst of the disease. If it's kept at bay for five years, the parasitic fungus that's colonized him will die and be flushed away from his system. Do you know how long he's been ill?"

Nadim said in my ear, "EMITU is sending the data to your H2." I looked down and checked, and then handed it off to Dr. Justineau.

He reviewed it quickly, and nodded. "Yes. He's in the middle stages. You'll need enough to see him through another two years. I can do that."

"For a million datamynt and ten thousand fita," Chao-Xing said.

He gave me my H2 back. "Regretfully, that is the price."

"Even if we're willing to give you passage off this rock."

"I don't set prices," Justineau said. "Bacia Annont sets prices. And Bacia Annont can kill me if I don't comply. You can't protect me."

Probably not.

"Huddle," I said, and the three of us stepped away and put our heads together. "So . . . do we actually *have* a million datamynt?"

"We do," Marko said. "But not a lot more."

"Enough to take care of the rest of our supplies?"

"No," Chao-Xing said. "Not to mention that we don't have ten thousand fita. What we were loaned went straight to the purchase of the starlight treatments for the ships."

"So . . . ?"

Chao-Xing sighed and stepped out of the huddle. She turned to Henri Justineau. "Datamynt now," she said. "We'll pay you the fita after we win our first bout. Agreed?"

"Agreed," he said. "Upon transfer of the datamynt, I can release the medication to you. I'll need to record the agreement to station data. If anything goes wrong and you don't fulfill on the fita within one standard week . . . there are penalties. Harsh ones. And you'll have to turn over the remaining medication."

Chao-Xing didn't poll us for opinions. She just nodded.

As Justineau slid back a thin curtain to show what must have been a station records access terminal, I looked at Marko. "You okay with this?" I asked him.

"Saving Yusuf's life? Obviously."

"That's a given. I mean, with Chao-Xing being in charge."

He sent me a strangely amused look. "Ask yourself that question, Zara."

After reading the terms, which were just as the doctor had stated, Chao-Xing signed the screen in agreement and Justineau dispatched a drone to deliver the treatment to

Yusuf and EMITU. I wished I could deliver the meds personally and spend some time with Nadim, but if I didn't report to the Pit with Chao-Xing, we'd have some pissed off lizards demanding fita forfeits from our hides.

That fast, we were in debt to the station for ten thousand fita, more to the Bruqvizs, and I had a feeling we might soon drop from the frying pan into the fire.

Justineau, it turned out, couldn't—or wouldn't—give us the shots to acclimate us to station atmosphere. Instead, he sent us to another doctor. We rode the slipstream again, all the way up to Tier Fifteen, posh as hell, white and chrome, nothing you'd guess existed from the shabby station exterior. I'd visited a few apartments like that in the Zone, all broken cement block and graffiti outside, but when you stepped inside, it was fresh paint and shiny floors, beautiful antique family pics in silver frames. Usually, those were historic families who'd had the chance to move to Paradise but had such deep roots in Old Detroit that they couldn't be dislodged with a backhoe.

I called up my virtual assistant. "Which way to the clinic?" Or whatever you called a place where they gave injections that would let your body survive on the wrong ratio of breathable gases.

The light swirl gave excellent directions, chipper as you please, and I led the way to a neat shop that was run by one of the species I referred to as Jellies. They seemed to communicate entirely by bioluminescence, which was weird but cool. My new VA was all over it, providing vocal translation services.

"The doctor welcomes you and asks what procedure you require."

"Nanobots that let us breathe and walk around without suits," I said.

My H2 flashed a sequence of lights, so quick and complex that I thought I might have a seizure. Some small part of me couldn't believe I'd maintained my calm for this long; I was surrounded by entirely new sights, sounds, stars, and I really wanted to retreat to Nadim and just curl up on the floor and *feel* him. This separation wasn't great for either of us. Adrenaline would only take me so far. The higher I got in the tiers, the closer I thought I'd be to him, but instead our bond felt frayed and fragile.

More back and forth between the VA and the Jelly-doc. God, when I thought about trying to describe this scene for my old crew in the Zone . . . I nearly snorted a laugh. I couldn't have described half of what had happened to me since I left rehab.

Finally, they settled the price, and I authorized the data-mynt transfer from our thinning supply of cash. Not like I could haggle in this situation.

Chao-Xing flourished a hand. "This was your idea; you go first."

"Gonna wait five minutes, make sure I don't die in a puddle of blood?"

She arched an eyebrow and didn't answer that, which I assumed meant she was doing exactly that. Marko made a *be my guest* motion.

"This is not amusing, Zara." Nadim sounded anxious.

"I'm kidding." *Mostly.*

I took my helmet off and held my breath when the VA told me to and felt a hiss and pressure at the back of my neck—and when I turned to look, I saw a translucent cable disappearing back into the ceiling. The Jelly-doc hadn't moved, except to wave tendrils with slightly more speed. It flashed lights again. The VA said, "Injection complete. You may experience some light discomfort. Please report any significant pain, failure to breathe, contraction of limbs, dissolution of organs, or more serious side effects."

Oh, damn, it was like our EMITU on board Nadim, only without the fun side, because I was pretty sure the Jelly-doc meant all that literally.

I said, "That's really not funny—"

That was all I got out before the convulsions hit me.

FROM THE UNOFFICIAL PUBLICATION A GUIDE TO
THE SLIVER
Source: Bruqvisz Planetary Database, unlicensed copy

The goal of every resident of the Sliver is the same: pursuit of data-mynt, amassing of fita. Mynt is traded for goods and services. Fita, much more valuable, can win patronage and items controlled only by Bacia Annont.

Beware, traveler: the Sliver is designed to rob you of datamynt as quickly as it is earned, ensuring you never win free of the station. Many are the bandits who arrive thinking to take what they wish. Few are those who leave with even a fraction of what they had on arrival.

Beware also of those who would trap the unwary to serve in crimes too dangerous to survive. Open no boxes. There are no free gifts.

CHAPTER FIVE

Binding Vows

I DIDN'T DIE, but the next twelve hours were hellish.

Chao-Xing responded better to the treatment, and she was on her feet in eight; Marko helped us both by getting food and water when we could keep it down. On our way out, the Jelly-doc gave us a scrolling list of What Not to Do, based on my reaction. One proscription was *overexertion*.

Fuck that. We'd already taken a loan from the lizards, and Yusuf would die if his meds were confiscated. We had to get the fita payment for Justineau ASAP. I wasn't sure what the consequences of failure would be, but probably worse than I'd like. Never had so much hung on me winning a fight, and I felt like shit.

Maybe we should've fought in our skinsuits?

Too late for second-guessing.

Nadim was twitchy over our separation, and it wasn't comfortable on my end, like a glass shard embedded beneath my skin. "Come back," he told me when I was well enough to pay attention. "Take the Hopper and rest with me instead."

"We can't," Marko said, which clued me that Nadim was addressing all of us. "Leaving would mean paying the docking fee again, and Yusuf's meds drained our datamynt reserves. We can't afford to go back to Nadim until we earn more. To be honest, right now, we can't even afford the next docking payment to keep the Hopper where it is."

I called up our virtual assistant and asked the light swirl, "What happens if we don't pay our docking fee on time?"

"Your docked vessel is confiscated," the swirl chirped, and somehow made that sound cheerful. "You will need to pay significant fines and penalties in addition to regular docking payments to retrieve. In one standard station month, ownership of the vessel is forfeited, and an auction is conducted to satisfy fines and penalties."

Great. We were screwed, stranded, *and* in danger of losing our way back. But at least Yusuf was getting treatment. *We saved him.* That did make me feel better, but separation from Nadim *hurt*, and I damn well knew I'd see him again soon. Even so, I was ready to take it out on someone, so when I imagined how Starcurrent and Yusuf must feel, a sympathy and sorrow welled up in me. I'd treat both of them better from now on.

When we went looking for Bea at Blobby's, she wasn't there. The booth was shuttered, all the junk locked away behind glittering mesh that probably could withstand lasers and whatever high-energy weapons this place could bring to bear. Our H2s showed her on Tier Two. *If something's happened to her . . .* I didn't finish the thought, racing through the dirty, dimly lit hallway to where the H2 said she was.

I banged a fist on the door hard enough to raise an ache in my arm. "Bea? Starcurrent?" I yelled. "You in there?"

The door slid open, and there Bea was, Starcurrent behind her. Her smile was a little wobbly, but she stepped back into the room and spread her hands. "What do you think?"

Starcurrent flared tentacles, trying to be positive, I guessed, but the color flares of distress were a dead giveaway.

This looked like a Zone flop. There was no furniture apart from the metal ledges that could be used for sitting or sleeping, if you were small and slept on your side. As I explored, I found a table that pulled down from the wall and a bar hung perpendicular to the ceiling, like for species with interesting sleep habits. Well, I'd crashed in worse places.

"Not bad," I lied.

Bea tried to smile, didn't quite manage it. "This is all we could get for what we had to spend. Maybe we can buy some pillows? Brighten it up a bit?"

"It's fine," Chao-Xing said. "We can sleep on the floor."

Starcurrent waved zis fronds. "Do not need much sleep. Will work instead and earn datamynt and fita. We need this."

"Damn right we do," I said. "In fact, I think the less time we spend here, the better. We're awake, we're earning. Right?"

Every one of us nodded. We all understood the urgency.

If we lost the Hopper, we lost home.

Before the others were even awake, Chao-Xing and I headed to the Pit. Time was ticking on us, and I stretched as we moved, conscious of how much expectation was riding on us. The need to cut and run—fuck all this responsibility—and go to Nadim chewed at me, a low-key impulse that I could control. For now.

"I wish there was another way," Nadim whispered from my shoulder.

"Me too," I admitted. "I miss you."

The feeling was growing, minute by minute, and I wasn't sure how I'd cope when my emotions hit critical mass. Somehow, I locked the yearning down and focused while wondering if it was hard on Chao-Xing in the same way. She had her game face on, not inviting me to ask personal questions.

Okay then, down to business.

Fight notices had been posted, and when we checked the info board, there we were. But it wasn't quite what I expected. "We're fighting separately?" I pulled up my VA. "Hey, swirl, why are we fighting alone?"

"Must prove qualifications first," the virtual assistant said. "It is customary."

"Do we earn for these individual fights?"

"Yes. If you win, payment counts toward your team and sponsors."

"And if we lose?"

"You are charged appearance fees." The VA obligingly showed us how much. My stomach clenched, and Chao-Xing gasped. "It's advisable to win."

"Yeah, no shit," I muttered.

Our third match would be tag-team. Provided we got that far. We *had* to get that far. If not, we'd end up worse off than before.

From here, I couldn't tell the audience from the gladiators, but once we stepped out of the main hall, lights directed us down the corridor to the actual . . . pit. There was no other word for it, a depression in the floor, where I waited to be called to fight. Beside me, Chao-Xing was calm and quiet, scanning the aliens around us for signs of weakness. Or so I suspected.

Nadim suddenly said, "Zara, I don't like this. Come home now. Come back to me. Let's find another way."

"I know," I told him. "But we don't have a lot of choices right now. I *have* to do this. Not just for you. For all of us."

A grim silence, then he said, "Understood. If you can bear it, I must as well."

Six bouts later, they finally called me for my first match. The announcer rolled with the Suncross-style mangling of my name, but no worries: "Zeerakull" sounded pretty badass for a professional fighter. I strode into the center square, more of a polygon really, with metal mesh and force fields between us and our screaming audience, to face off against a giant Lumpyhead alien. He had to be over two meters tall, and I didn't know enough about his physiology to estimate weight. Good reach. Speed? Likely below average.

I had to use that. Somehow.

"You are the challenger, Zeerakull. Weapon or barehand?"

Shit. Seemed unlikely they'd let me shoot him, and I didn't have much experience with what else they had to offer in here. "Barehand," I said.

The starting tone sounded. Lumpy let out a terrifying wail and flushed bright orange, head to toe. He charged me, and I slid aside. Basic gymnastics and fleeing-the-scene parkour let me rebound off the wall, whirling a kick that landed strong. Lumpy barely grunted while I felt the impact all the way up to my kneecap.

Damn. Maybe I bit off more than I could chew.

A massive arm drew back, and I arched and twirled, gliding right under the strike. From behind, I could see a gap in the plating or scales or head bulbs, whatever you called them. The flesh was soft and pink, a small-ass target, but as I'd guessed, Lumpy was strong, not fast. While he was turning, lumbering like a confused buffalo, I knifed my second and third fingers and jabbed them into his soft spot. Sank into that squishy flesh up to knuckles, and Lumpy let out a screech that gave me chills. Goo oozed over my hand as he collapsed.

The crowd booed me. *Dirty trick? Did I kill him?*

"Zeerakull wins! A punch in the junk is not against the rules. There are no rules!"

Grimacing, I wiped my hand on my pants as I strode out of the polygon. Chao-Xing high-fived me as I checked the H2. *Yep, datamynt and fita received, our first payout.*

Maybe somewhere deep inside I was hoping to hear "nice job." Instead C-X said, "Your technique is sloppy. If you hadn't gotten lucky, he would've pulled your head off."

"Untrue," said a nearby Abyin Dommas. "These aren't death matches. Beaten half to death, probably."

"Thanks for the support." I got a cheerful flash of tentacles in response.

A few matches later, C-X threw down. Her style was cleaner, and she took longer to drop her opponent, so she was sweaty as they cheered her out of the ring. I took some pride as our avatars skimmed up the rankings. Not a huge leap. But this . . . it was fun.

I just wished Nadim could be here, share the rush and the pride with me. The tag-team matches wouldn't be starting for a while, so I got something to eat from a nearby vendor. Tasteless, texture like tofu, but the machine assured me it was "nutritionally adequate." Fantastic slogan; I could see that catching on.

Reluctantly, Chao-Xing ate some too. Keeping our strength up mattered. We had to blaze this datamynt and fita bullshit and get back to our Leviathan. I paced; waiting to be called up was more exhausting than the moments in the cage. I caught C-X leaning against the wall, eyes closed. If it had been Bea, I'd have hugged her or patted her shoulder, but I wasn't in that place with C-X.

Then they called us up.

"Zeerakull and JongShowJing, challenging!"

We were fighting three blue aliens. Should be fine. I

went in with a touch of swagger. We chose weapons. And then something went upside my head; I hit the ground so hard that I could hardly hear or see.

"Zara! Zara, *get up!*"

Chao-Xing's voice rang in my ears, weirdly flat, and I opened my eyes. Overhead, a black sky glittered with stars that glided past, time-lapse fast.

"Zara!"

The command in her voice made me forget the stars and roll over on my side. I felt something under my hands and picked it up. *A stick. Why was I holding a stick?* No, not a stick. A shock stick, long as my arm, balanced like a sword.

Right, I was tag-teaming with Chao-Xing. In the time I'd been out, she'd managed to drop one of the blue dudes. Two left. These enemies seemed to be both elastic and electrified, which sucked for me. I wished I could ask C-X how she'd done it while I was out, but the battle tips would have to wait until we won.

We *had* to win. Our way home hung on this fight, not to mention our only hope of repaying the lizards.

One shock treatment was enough to make me cautious. Since C-X had done well, dropping one and keeping the other at bay, I watched her and positioned my weapon as she did, defending successfully against two lightning-fast strikes. When she struck, so did I.

It wasn't like I was up to strategy, but reactions? I was

good. The blur came for me, hit the ground again in a roll, came up with the shock stick (sword?) held out in a firm grip. I lunged forward and sliced the weapon sideways, and caught my lanky blue opponent as he overextended those two-meter-long arms. He didn't need a shock stick.

His touch had knocked me down and nearly, nearly out.

My hit was on target. I tapped my shock stick on his right side, just above his hip; he had short, stubby, insect-thin legs, and the upper half of his body towered over me by three meters, but I got him just about in the balance point. I felt the muted buzz as the stick fed current, and then Blue was down, folding up and slamming facedown onto the mat.

A glance over told me Chao-Xing was still standing too.

A roar went up from the stands—sound *and* light, because the bioluminescent species started flashing like mad. I raised both arms in triumph and turned in a circle. A score holo counted down, and our opponents didn't even try to get up until the holo proclaimed that we'd won.

Sweet, sweet *fita*. Top level, a full seventeen units credited to our account. Aliens loved a good fight, especially my lizard homies. They'd won both fita and datamynt today from betting on C-X and me. From where they stood guzzling victory drinks, Suncross gave me four arms up, and I heard the roar he let out over the rest.

"Challengers win! Up-rank, team of JongShowJing and

Zeerakull," shouted the announcer. "Next game, four station hours. Bet early, bet often!"

Nanobots or not, I was gasping for breath; the atmo here on the Sliver was thin, and not at all friendly to humans. Jelly-doc's admonishment sprang to mind, but screw that. C-X and I had gone to near mid-level in the alien fight club.

"If you're finished basking in the applause, it's time to go," Chao-Xing said. She took my shock stick away—probably because I liked it too much—and returned it to the weapon rack. "I checked. Our *fita* is pushing us up the scale quickly. If we keep winning, we might get an invitation to the Peak."

The Peak, we'd learned over the last couple of days, was where Bacia Annont had offices, a spectacular jutting spire made of sleek, hard metal that had an opaline shine to it in starlight. Biotech? Even Nadim wasn't sure.

"Do I have time to shower?" I asked.

She shook her head.

I'd just stink, then. It wasn't like there were a lot of humans to be offended by my sweat, which glittered in beads on my skin; let C-X wrinkle her nose if she didn't like it. She didn't smell any better.

"Where are we headed, anyway?" I asked.

We slipped out the private exit reserved for fighters, new to me, but any VIP privilege was cool as hell. "I found a day job—enforcement at Pinky's."

It tickled me to hear Chao-Xing using the nickname for the bar that I'd mentioned in passing. "Perfect. Good fita?"

"Would I waste my time otherwise? Mynt's not bad either." C-X was already talking like a Sliver space crim regular.

Her job made sense too. There were no rules in the Sliver, but that didn't mean bar owners let patrons get away with starting shit; here, as everywhere, bouncers were critical. Bouncers who could eject people politely, even more. From what I knew of her, C-X would have the touch. She was strong enough to handle most of these crims, and I'd seen that she could also be icily polite when she needed to be to soothe ruffled feathers.

"Any other perks?"

"Two free drinks a shift. You can have one."

When we popped out onto Tier One from the arena, Nadim came through my shoulder unit. Just hearing his voice relaxed me. "Zara? Are you and Chao-Xing all right?"

Damn. I wished I could hug him. *This sucks.*

I didn't mention my fresh injuries. He wasn't complaining about the pain left from the battle with the Phage, either. "We won our fights, earned some fita and datamynt. Hope we'll be good to repay the lizards soon, keep up on docking fees and Yusuf's treatment." I paused. "How's he doing?"

"He doesn't talk much," Nadim said. I heard that

sadness again, that streak of real and painful loneliness. "He seems better today. I've made sure that he is comfortable and tried to interest him in entertainments. I haven't been very successful."

"Try putting him to work, if he's well enough. Sometimes we need to busy our hands to quiet our minds."

"A thing I can't imagine," Nadim acknowledged. "Thank you, Zara. I will try that. When are you coming back?"

"Yeah, I don't know yet. Soon, I hope. I'm getting on the express to Pinky's. Will talk to you later." That was a cowardly way out of the question, but I didn't have a conclusive answer yet.

Another ride on the slipstream, and I lost Nadim again. Reception was spotty in certain parts of the Sliver, maybe on purpose. My stomach tightened. Maybe I wouldn't linger; I didn't *have* to stay here while she was working. Not like C-X asked me to, but it seemed safer for us to travel in pairs. I wrestled between opposing urges—watching Chao-Xing's back against my desire for Nadim.

One drink, that's fair. If C-X gives me the all clear, I'm out of here.

I sat down and whistled up a hovertray to place my order—another Fizzy Riffle, since I knew they were safe. The taste was still gross, and Chao-Xing seemed to have the bouncer thing down pat, so I was just about to get up when someone slipped into the seat next to me.

Not Suncross, or one of his crew. I said *slipped* into the seat, but this alien oozed; the creature was either Blobby or Blobby's kin. I was guessing kin. Blobby's booth had exploded in popularity since Bea started singing there.

"You often come here?" Blobby Two asked me.

I groaned. "Don't even," I said. "What do you want?"

"I have a job for you," it said. "Only you. No others."

"Fita?"

In response, the blob—this one, I realized, had more golden outer skin than Blobby, but I couldn't see any other identifying features—extruded a limb, and something pushed *out* of the limb and plopped damply down on the table. *Ugh.* It was, I realized, some kind of case. As I watched, the slime sucked together into a thick, golden droplet, and then slid back into Blobby Two's appendage.

"Open," it said.

I nudged it with a fingertip. Nothing exploded. "What is it?"

"You see when you open."

"I'm not the marrying kind," I told it. "In case that's what you were thinking."

"Is *job*," Blobby Two said, and the exasperation sounded just like every other person who'd met me. "Open!"

I poked the thing again and looked around for Chao-Xing. She was showing somebody to the door and taking no notice of me. I opened the box.

Lights flashed, and I winced and closed my eyes. When I opened them again, the box was open, and nothing was inside it. Not a damn thing. I turned on Blobby Two. "What the hell was *that*?"

"Code," he said. "You carry now. Take to this spot." Liquid dripped from its appendage and raced to form an alien curlicue of an address, I guessed. I was starting to get the rudiments of some of the written forms, but not this one. I tapped my VA swirl on my H2, and it obligingly read it off as *Tier Nine, booth seven.*

"What do you mean, I carry it now?"

"Nanites," Blobby Two said. "I codejacked. They will retain in memory for one hour. You should hurry. My associate will give you fita on delivery."

I had no idea what was going on here, but it sounded like I was both hostage and smuggler, like an old-time drug mule. Didn't like it. "What if I tell you to screw off?"

Blobby's appendages drew back in. So did the liquid and the address. "Then you must try reprogramming nanites before you die," it said. "Or get paid. You choose, Zeerakull."

I wished Chao-Xing hadn't taken my shock stick away, because I really wanted to try it out on this creature. "How about if I choose to cut you open like a fish?"

Blobby Two formed itself into a bipedal replica of a human, and a parody of . . . of *me*. That weird thing on its head was meant to be my curls. And it managed two blind eyes and a nose and a mouth that were so wrong it made me roll my chair back. "How if I kill your friend?" it asked. I looked at Chao-Xing. She was in no danger, but she was seven kinds of busy. "Not that one," it said. "This one."

It shifted form again, this time into a profusion of tentacles that I recognized. *Starcurrent.* But Starcurrent was with Beatriz, at Blobby's booth.

Unless there was no Blobby and Blobby Two. "Are you from the booth?"

"Of course," it said smugly. "When required, I split a part of myself for errands. Still me talking. I can tear your friend apart at the booth and you cannot hurt me. No one can. Why bring violence? Just go to address. Get paid. The end."

Like all smooth gangsters, he knew just where to push, how hard, and when to hold out the cookie. *Son of a bitch.* Crims really were the same everywhere. I knew he had me. Maybe he was bluffing about Starcurrent; maybe he was bluffing about the nanite recoding too. But I couldn't take the chance that Starcurrent could die, and I could end up gasping my last on the floor in an hour anyway.

"I'll get paid," I said. "Seems like the only smart play. But you'd better not screw me over. I'll find a way to hurt you. Count on that."

He oozed off, and when I looked down, I couldn't see any trace of the protean bastard. He was *gone.*

I've got an hour. I'm carrying code in my actual body. This shit is so messed up.

Thoughts swarmed my head like angry bees. I could've gone straight to the drop site, but I'd never been the obedient type, plus this asshole had uploaded his whatever into me without asking. I looked around for Chao-Xing, but there was no sign of her. I was wasting vital seconds searching.

Bea. She's a hell of a data slicer. Maybe she couldn't do a damn thing, but I'd be a fool not to check in with her. I sprinted out of Pinky's and zoomed off to find Bea.

Nadim spoke as I was falling. "Zara, please. I know you're doing this for me. For Typhon and me. But I want to leave. I've drunk enough artificial starlight. We can wait for repairs and upgrades."

"We can't." My voice sounded curt, and I hated hiding this from him, but if my fear disturbed him this much, I could only imagine how bad it would be if he knew what a mess I'd stumbled into.

"I don't care!" He sounded almost frantic. "Please, Zara. Let's leave. I'm afraid, and I think you are too."

I kicked off and landed on the tier where Blobby's booth was housed. "There's nothing to be afraid of," I lied.

"I'm afraid you won't come back," he said, and it was the most broken tone I'd ever heard from him. "You and Beatriz. I'm afraid that we'll be left here alone. We've never been more alone, Zara."

That stopped me for a second. He was right. The Leviathan had always heard each other at great distances—how far, I didn't know—which meant that they were never *really* alone. But if there was silence out there . . . our two Leviathan must feel crushed by it.

"I'm sorry," I told him. I was saying that a lot, and I hated it. "Soon, okay? I'm on my way to something important."

"On your way to what?"

As I dropped onto the platform, I wished I could share all these problems with him. But right now, he was wounded and grieving, and it would only make it worse for him to know just how screwed I might be when he couldn't help. I got out of the way for all the other aliens kicking up and falling down, and tried to calm my pulse. I wedged myself back in a little alcove to get out of the jostling traffic flow of armored suits, flowing limbs, and floating tendrils.

"A job," I said, which wasn't a lie. "I'll tell you all about it when things are squared away. It's not that I'm trying to be secretive. It's just that time isn't on my side right now."

Blobby meant for me to head straight for the drop point . . . but I knew crims, and if I obeyed Blobby like a pawn, I'd likely end up dead. Mules didn't live long down in the Zone, and I needed a plan to counter the "Zara's expendable" one Blobby had laid out.

I imagined I could feel Nadim's hurt, but the remote didn't allow for that. He didn't insist, and his reluctant capitulation made me ache. "Very well, Zara. Is there any way I can be of help?"

"Do you know anything about nanobot recoding?"

"I'm searching all databases now."

"Thanks. I might need that soon."

Running flat out, I reached Bea's booth in record time. She was just stepping out of the bubble, thankfully. I grabbed her, surprised to find that my hands were shaky. "Bea."

"What's wrong, Zara?"

Nadim was probably listening, so I had to risk him flipping out when I filled her in. Deep breath. "Where's Starcurrent?"

"Mandy asked him to stay to sort some stock for extra fita," Bea said. "Why?"

"Mandy?"

"That's his name. The blob."

I didn't have time to deal with that cognitive shock. "I need your slicer skills. I'm on a clock, Bea. It recoded my nanites, and I don't know what the hell's inside of me, or what will happen when I make the transfer." All the words came out in a rush, revealing more clearly than I'd intended how damn terrified I was.

Reckless was my way of life, but there were risks worth taking and risks so dangerous that only a suicidal daredevil would step up. I was nowhere near that league, and outrage and violation warred inside of me. This wasn't a job I'd chosen, and I couldn't have been more pissed at Mandy for making me its tool.

Bea took my hands in hers, locked her eyes on mine, and I steadied. "Slow down. Your nanites have been recoded? Tell me the whole story."

Excruciatingly aware of the ticking clock, I forced myself to tell a coherent version of events. No doubt that Nadim heard it all, but he didn't freak out, as I'd feared. Instead he started reading off all the data he'd uncovered on the subject. Sadly, it wasn't a lot.

"So, you want me to . . ."

"Switch the code back? Hack my nanites?" Even I thought that was too much to ask.

"What if I get it wrong? Zara, I could *kill you!*"

I took another deep breath, aware that my time to do that was probably running thin. "Mandy threatened Starcurrent if I didn't deliver this . . . whatever. Hell of a stick to beat me with if this was just some no-big-deal data transfer, don't you think?"

"He *what*?" Her face—rounded and pleasant and nearly always smiling—hardened, muscles tensing underneath, and her mouth took on a stiff line. "That evil son of a— that's it, we are *quitting!*"

I loved that Bea's idea of punishment was quitting. Mine was more along the lines of seeing what kind of chemicals would melt the rancid creature into sludge.

She started to dart back inside the bubble, but I grabbed her and held her back. "You can't," I said. "You try to get Starcurrent out of there, and Mandy might carry through. Ze's an unknowing hostage. Let's keep it that way."

She looked at me with real fear in those dark eyes. "So, what do we do?"

Probably I should have just resigned myself to being used, but that didn't sit right. I was nobody's mule. Plus, this stain of a task smelled wrong, bad wrong. "Nadim, can you hypothesize as to why Mandy's doing this?"

His answer made me spit every colorful Zone curse I'd ever learned.

Interlude: Nadim

Zara is silent.

I miss the stars.

The songs are still calling, but I am trapped in this orbit, bathing in artificial light. Some beauty cannot be replicated, only approximated. Nearby, Typhon broods. He is a dark shadow, no longer the Elder I once respected and feared. In saving him, he feels I also lessened him, because he judged me weak and impulsive, unfit for the Journey. Yet I have done what no Leviathan has before me, chosen my own partners for the Journey. It feels like a freedom all others ought to be afforded. How can any Elder know my private heart or understand what I need?

Now I need Zara and Beatriz. I need to spread my wings and circle the sweetness of a white dwarf, bask in the starlight, and call to my cousins, desperately hoping for an answer in the silence.

I cannot have those things.

If I lose patience, Typhon will crack. I must be strong enough for both of us.

FROM THE UNOFFICIAL PUBLICATION A GUIDE TO
THE SLIVER
Source: Bruqvisz Planetary Database, unlicensed copy

In the event you are given a gift and unwarily accept such, be advised that you must only admit such humiliation to your closest of allies on the Sliver. Bargains may be struck to relieve you of responsibilities associated with such gifts.

Worst cases require extreme measures to win freedom from such indenture, which almost certainly would require offenses against the ruling orders of Bacia Annont. No amount of mynt or fita will protect you, should such occur.

Recommend you make appropriate funerary rites and gift possessions prior to attempting, and leave recording exempting your planet, kin, and family from all involvement.

Good luck, brave traveler. You will require such.

CHAPTER SIX

Binding Blood

GETTING IN TO see the official Jelly-doc took time, and I didn't have any, so I took Bea with me back to Pinky's, and this time I was in luck: Suncross and his boys were at the table. They all roared and held up four arms each to celebrate my arrival. That was a lot of arms. "Zeerakull, Zeerakull, Zeerakull . . ." They made it into a chant as they hammered on the table in a complicated rhythm that almost bent the metal.

"Thanks, friends," I said, and took a seat. "This is my friend Beatriz Teixeira."

They all locked attention on her, instantly, and I was

reminded of a holo recreation I'd seen of a group of ancient raptor dinosaurs stalking prey.

Bea smiled bravely anyway. "Hi," she said.

"Another human," Suncross said. "Beetreshra."

They all repeated it, and Bea gave me a look. I hoped mine conveyed *Don't bother trying to correct them.*

Suncross suddenly banged two fists on the table, hard enough to make the whole thing quiver. "You are the singer! Mandy's singer!"

"I don't belong to Mandy," she said. "But I sing there. Yes."

The hiss that followed was full of approval. "We like singers." I hoped that wasn't something lost in translation, like *We like them cooked medium well.* "Zeerakull, you and JongShowJing made us much mynt today. Well fought."

"*Fought?*" Bea said, and looked at me with open-mouthed shock. "Seriously?"

"Well, a little."

"Zeerakull punched a Fellkin in the—"

"Okay, great, so, let's get on topic," I interrupted. "Any of you know a good doc who can reset programming on nanites?"

Suncross's lizard eyes blinked, both eyelids, and he growled low in his throat. "Nanobot repair only on top levels," he said. "Officially."

"Unofficially? And I'm kind of in a hurry."

The lizards all exchanged looks. Suncross sat back as the lizard next to him ordered rounds of drinks. A hovering bot swooped in near Bea's face, probably to gather a saliva sample, and she waved it off impatiently. No drinks for Bea. That was probably good. I was going to need her dead sober.

"You hacked, Zeerakull?" Suncross asked. He slid a small, oblong box across the table. The one I'd left behind, the one Mandy had used to sucker me into this. "Code box."

I debated hedging about it, but then I nodded once. Sharply. Suncross hissed softly. This time, it didn't carry any hint of approval. "How long?"

"Under an hour," I said. I assumed the matrix would shift that into the proper time scale for him. "I'm screwed, right?"

"Depends," Suncross said. "First, what does codejack do?"

"Not sure, but . . ." I bit my lip. Wasn't wild about sharing Nadim's speculation, but he'd found references to it in communications going in and out of the Sliver. "It could be that it'd hack the mynt database. A big score for somebody."

Suncross grabbed a drink off a flying tray—probably not his own—and guzzled it in a single, long swallow. He slammed the glass down on the table, where it sat radiating a smoky cold. "Bad for business," he said. "Bad for every-body. No rule-keepers here, but many who would kill for such. Don't touch mynt or fita. Only real precept."

"Uh-huh," I said. "Figured that. Nobody likes having the bank looted. So . . . what do I do? If I go where he told me, I'm dead as soon as word gets out that the bank's been robbed. If I don't, I'm still dead. Right?"

"Second problem," Suncross said. "How much pain can you take?"

"Sorry?"

"Did not translate? Pain." He flicked out alarmingly long claws and dragged them across his bare palm. The scratches filled with pale pinkish blood. He didn't flinch.

"I'm pretty tough," I said, but inside, I was already start-ing to shake. "Why?"

"Down-low doc not the best with anesthetics," he said. "But fast. Can wipe programming. But cannot reprogram without original dataset. Must hack doc ops to get. Down-low doc will not do. Hacker must be fast too."

Ah, he's talking about Doc Justineau. I'd met him already, so I didn't need the lizards to guide me further. I did have other questions, though.

"Back up. Is there a reason I can't put on my skinsuit to buy some time while we figure this shit out?"

Suncross made outward slashes with his claws, a ges-ture of negation, I thought. "Skinsuit doesn't help with hacks. Is like . . . software. Skinsuit is hardware. Can't connect with nanobots blocking."

Dammit. Desperate measures it is. Since there was a doom clock running in my head, I circled my fingers at Bea, signaling for us to move out. Chao-Xing stopped us on the way, and she wasn't happy. "We've got a fight in a few hours," she said. "You should be resting. You look like hell. Are you all right?"

I looked down at my hands. They weren't the rich, healthy color they usually were; they'd gone a little ashen, and under my fingernails, there was a faint tinge of blue. I was breathing deeply, but getting less oxygen. There was a headache building like a thunderhead behind my eyes.

"Fine," I lied. "I'll rest. What about you?"

"I don't need rest," she said. "I could fight all day."

I believed that. I wanted to explain to her about the codejacking, but I was afraid that she'd try to take control of the plan or trash it altogether, and I didn't have time for a debate. Not anymore.

She had to turn away to deal with a scuffle near the stage, and we moved off fast.

Henri Justineau seemed happy to see us again—until I explained our problem. "Codejack?" He took a deep breath. "Guess you ran into Mandy. Codejacking's his specialty. Got me when I was just getting started here." He swallowed and managed to get to his feet on his own. Steadier. "I can reset, but you'll need to upload original specs. You want me to just dump the code?"

"Can you capture it on media?" Bea asked.

"Sure," he said. "There can't be a lot of time between when the last of the code is burned and the new code gets flashed, or we'll lose her. Understand?"

"Yes," Bea said.

I cleared my throat. "Heard there's likely to be some pain."

"Agony," Henri said. "And it's going to take a while for all the nanites to wipe. Ten minutes or so to get them all. Can't give you anything while that's underway or it'll interfere."

"You had it done."

"No," he said. "I didn't. I couldn't take the pain. My codejacking was a ransom demand. I complied. I lost my fita and nearly died. That's why I'm down here in the dregs, patching up arena losers and addicts, because I couldn't hold out for the whole procedure. You sure you can take it?"

"Only one way to find out," I said, with absolute bravado. "Nadim? Are you there?" As I said it, Henri flinched.

"I'm here," Nadim said. He sounded distant. Quiet. I'd kept this from him as long as I could, but he must have heard me talking to Bea. "You're going to hurt yourself."

"Don't think I have much of a choice. You can't feel it, can you?"

"No," he said. I didn't know why, but I thought that *might* be a lie. "I can't lose you, Zara. I can't."

"You can," I said. "But trust me. You won't." I pulled in a breath that felt stale and empty. My headache was building into torture. "Let's do it. Now."

I'd like to say that I was a badass about it, but I wasn't. From the moment Henri hit the controls and began the process of wiping the programming of my life-sustaining nanobots, my whole body went into overdrive. Every nerve screamed. Every muscle contracted. He'd strapped me down on the chair, but even so I nearly fought free while I writhed and screamed and begged it to stop. I couldn't remember why I was doing it, only that it was killing me.

It didn't stop, and it didn't get easier as the minutes ticked by; I was trying to breathe, trying to *live*, and it felt like the worst agony a human being could endure, and *it didn't stop . . .*

. . . until suddenly, with a snap, it did.

The vastness of all my muscles relaxing, all my nerves falling silent, was like euphoria buzzing in my veins. The headache was still there, but distant as a storm blown halfway across a globe. I panted and sucked in breaths that did nothing, *nothing* to nourish my cells, and I started to cough.

"Flash code now!" I heard a voice shout, and Bea let me go, stepped back, and her fingers flew across her H2.

Not fast enough. Not *nearly* fast enough. The headache came roaring back, consuming my brain in a black storm, and my body took on weight, as if an invisible force was slowly crushing it. I felt unfocused and frantic and terrified as everything spun and spiraled around me, and my last, desperate effort was to reach out to Nadim through the vast distance between us . . .

And he caught me as I fell.

I relaxed into him. I was a mindless, screaming thing, but his embrace quieted me, and his love flooded every cell of my body like cool water.

I'm here, he told me. I don't know what it cost him to do it, but he held me. He stayed. *I won't leave you. If you go into the dark, I go too.*

And for a long, long moment, I thought I would die, and kill him with me. The emptiness screamed around us, pulling us apart cell by cell . . .

. . . and then the code kicked in on my nanobots.

It didn't stabilize all at once; the ramp-up took long moments of feeling terminally ill, but at least I wasn't dying anymore. I was healing. And Nadim held on until he felt the headache's black shadow contracting. I felt the exact moment, with exquisite detail, when he withdrew. I felt small, but not alone. Never alone.

"Nadim?" I whispered it and closed my aching eyes. "Nadim?"

"Here," he said. "Still here."

"Makes two of us." I felt a smile play at my lips, and I let it stay. "Thank you."

"Don't do it again," he said. "Please, Zara."

The sound of my name, in those quiet, longing tones, made me go still inside. Breathless, but not in the way that I had been. I felt lifted on the force of it.

"Z?" Beatriz's hand was on my cheek, and I opened my eyes and looked at her. "Are you okay? I'm sorry, I tried to get it uploaded as fast as I could . . ." She sounded half-frantic. I aimed the smile at her this time.

"I'm okay," I told her, and tried to sit up.

Bea and Henri unlocked the restraints, and by the time I sat up, the worst I had were a few bruises from the strug-gle, and the last remnants of a headache melting away as the nanites industriously scrubbed me clean of toxins.

"Wow," I said. "Let's never do that again."

Henri shook his head. "I don't know how you survived it. The codejacking had deep defenses. It nearly killed you."

I knew why it hadn't managed it. Nadim. "New Detroit girls are tough," I told him. "Where you from, Henri?"

"Carolina," he said. "United Raleigh."

"You got the code saved off?"

"I did," he said, and held up a small vial swimming with

red. "I drew blood. Don't worry, I disabled the comms functions, so it can't beam itself out anywhere. It's a dead virus."

"Nice." I took the vial, stared into it for a second, and slipped it in a pocket of my one-piece station suit. "What time is it?"

"Time?" Bea asked, and frowned. "Why?"

"Because I've got a job," I said. "And I'd like you to tell Mandy that if he doesn't pay up with max fita for your next performances, this goes straight up to Bacia. I'm pretty sure Mandy doesn't want that."

"Careful," Justineau said. "Crossing Mandy is dangerous."

"I didn't cross Mandy, Mandy crossed us," I said. "And we're getting paid for staying silent about it. Fair?"

"Fair," he said. "But watch out. Mandy never sleeps."

"I got it." Wincing, I flexed my arms as Bea unstrapped me.

My entire body felt like someone had gone over every inch of it with a hammer, and my knees wobbled when I tried to stand.

She shook her head at me. "You can't fight today. It's impossible."

Shit. When I tried to bring my arms up in a fighting stance, pain lanced through me. Even my knuckles hurt, like I'd spent hours with my fingers cramped into a fist.

"Not impossible," I argued, though it was semantics. "Winning, though? Yeah."

"Well, you shouldn't today," Justineau said. "Not unless you want to end up back here with ruptured organs."

I shot the wretched-looking refugee a look. "Thanks for the warning. Listen . . . are you . . . really okay down here?" He'd joked about my offer of help before.

Something like a smile broke the withered solemnity of his face, though his eyes were so sad that I had to look away. "Not so much. But at least I'm alive. And now you're here. I can't tell you what seeing another human's done for me. Made me feel . . . almost normal again."

"Right, well . . ." Awkward as hell, but I settled the bill, paying in both mynt and fita. "Thank you for the help."

Even leaning on Bea, it took me a lot longer to limp out of the sublevel than it had to come in. As we hit Tier One, Chao-Xing's face popped up on my H2.

"Where are you?" she demanded.

"There was a situation . . ."

She set her jaw, eyes sparking with impatience. "Are you coming or not?"

Suncross leaned into the screen from behind C-X's shoulder. "You survived down-low doc? Good. Will call in favor, postpone fight."

"Thank you." I was surprised how much I meant that. Shit. I didn't trust people who did good deeds. "Wait, what's this costing me?"

"You forfeit, I lose mynt. Doing this for me, not you."

Spoken like a true gambler. I felt better knowing he had an ulterior motive, but it seemed like I'd forgotten some important detail. But what . . . ?

"Fill me in later." Chao-Xing cut the connection and I shuffled onward to the slipstream platform. I didn't leap into the flow so much as fall, and I swallowed a shriek as I landed. If Bea hadn't caught me, I would've dropped.

"I've got you." Her arm went around me, both supporting and protective.

That . . . I didn't know how I felt about it, except I had a sudden warmth in my chest. People had been finding me too hard to handle all my life, but here Bea was, helping me, having my back, no matter what shit I got myself in. The Honors had done me a real favor when they paired me up with this girl. Smart, sweet, and tough all together.

My H2 flashed, a brief vid message from Suncross. "Delayed to tomorrow. Will notify you of new match time." His broad grin bared knives. "You will make us mynt."

FROM THE UNOFFICIAL PUBLICATION A GUIDE TO
THE SLIVER
Source: Bruqvisz Planetary Database, unlicensed copy

Should you be brave in battle, and lacking in mynt and fita, best way to survive the Sliver is enrollment in the Pit. This is only for those who do not mind giving damage and can sustain such. Is not recommended for soft species lacking formidable defenses. Aggression is advised.

Survival of battle rounds earns mynt and fita at a faster rate than other duties available to new travelers. However, rise in rank is unlikely, and mynt and fita may be quickly lost if bets are placed by combatants.

Wisdom says to allow allies' bets only.

No rules in the Pit. Be warned that only best survive to be hired by Bacia Annont.

Good work comes if you achieve.

CHAPTER SEVEN

Binding Resolution

"STARCURRENT!" EYES WIDE, I clutched Bea's arm and gave it a shake. "He's still with Mandy. We need to—"

"I got this," she said.

Rarely had I trusted anyone else to get the job done, but I locked eyes with Bea and figuratively passed her the torch. "Thanks. I'll get myself to our squat."

She hurried off, trusting me to do as I'd promised. As I trudged that way, Nadim spoke in an anxious tone. "How are you?"

"Better," I answered. "You? How're your battle wounds coming along?" During those moments when we'd been deep bonded because of the procedure, my own pain had been bad enough that I couldn't remember anything about his.

"Not perfect, but well enough to travel. Typhon too. We should leave now, Zara. You've been there too long." What I heard in his tone was too complex for simple anxiety.

I stopped. "What're you afraid of? That I'll get settled on the Sliver and I won't—"

"Want to come back?" he finished. "Perhaps you shouldn't. It is a huge risk, traveling with me. There is so much we don't know about the Phage, and so many of my cousins have gone silent. Part of me thinks that I should stay with Typhon, and away from you. Safer for you and Beatriz." The pause was painful. "You have found another human there. Marko and Yusuf could also stay. We could go on alone."

Damn, Nadim was having a crisis, undercutting my resolve. I couldn't afford to break dock, as our Earth music had been a fad, interesting only because of its newness, so to earn mynt and fita, we had to work.

But it didn't sit right with me, ignoring Nadim's pain.

If I was honest, I wanted to go home—and home meant Nadim. It didn't mean curling up in that metal cube and feeling sorry for myself. This was a reckless idea, and really, if I had the energy to try this stunt, I should probably go help Bea and Starcurrent, but after what I'd just gone through, I deserved to be selfish.

It took me a while, asking around, and with my VA's help, but I eventually found a stall that sold me an extra oxygen pack that I jury-rigged to my skinsuit. Next, I needed the magnetic boot attachment I'd coveted when we first arrived on the Sliver—easier to find and worth haggling over—and finally, a limited-use jet pack. Already, I was exhausted, but I'd committed to this course. I headed up to the top public tier and groaned coming off the gravity well. Falling hard, I stayed down for a few minutes—no surprise that the aliens kept moving around me. People in the Zone would act about the same.

I'd scoped out the station well, so I knew where our ships were in relation to the rest of the Sliver. Resting near the top, beneath four arched metal beams that emitted the energy currently allowing them to heal, and those beams were huge by human standards, more than big enough to walk across. If the guards caught me doing this, there would probably be a fine.

What the hell? I'll risk it.

Keeping a sharp eye for witnesses, I tailed a bot on its rounds and followed it right into the restricted area. As I'd suspected, the unit eventually went outside for routine maintenance, and I got outside the Sliver, keeping close. From there, I climbed, slow and exhausting, especially with my burning muscles and residual headache, until I got to the first beam.

Just walk, I told myself.

Like being in zero gravity was no big deal with the station oscillating behind me. Nadim couldn't come on board the Sliver, but I could go to him. And I would.

Sheer determination got me to the center of the beams, where they curved above my Leviathan like a steel ribcage, steadily beaming a star bath. Emptying my mind, I fired the jet pack and jumped. Solid landing.

"Zara? You're here? How?"

Thankfully, Nadim had been quiet until right then, maybe trying not to guilt me, and that focus had allowed me to ignore my pain and get here. "I found a back door. Give me time to get inside, and then—" The inside of my head went white and crimson with the discomfort I'd shut away, but determination could only keep it at bay for so long.

"Zara? I'm sending Yusuf!"

That was the last I knew for a while. When I woke, Yusuf was pulling my skinsuit helmet off, his brow furrowed in concern. I pushed his hands away. "Thanks for the save, but if you're recovered enough, we could *really* use you on station."

To me, he already looked a lot better, alert and no longer shiny with pain sweat. In breathless bursts, I explained about the codejacking, and how Bea and Starcurrent were facing off against an unkillable blob.

When I finished, he was shaking his head. "You couldn't call in an SOS?"

"I wanted to see Nadim. And I needed to find out if you

could get inside the station this way—without paying the docking fee again."

"There's cheap, Zara, and then there's crazy. You know which you are, right?"

"Never mind that. Just go. Help Bea and Starcurrent. Please. We *need* you, and I . . ." Shit, it hurt to admit this. "I've got nothing left, okay?"

Yusuf squared his shoulders, and for the first time, I got a glimpse of what he must've been like when he was first recruited as an Honor: sharp-eyed and commanding. "Yes. I'll take your gear and tell Marko how to follow. Are you fine from here?"

Not so much, but . . .

"Sure."

Somehow I crawled out of the airlock, and Nadim lit the way to my quarters with concerned pulses of light. *This was such a self-indulgent idea.* Maybe I should've stuck it out on station, but when I hauled myself into bed, I regretted nothing, especially when Nadim tapped lightly and I let him in. We spilled into a light bond that eased both pain and exhaustion. His care trickled through me like a warm summer rain, soaking into the places parched by our separation.

I hate being away from you, he whispered.

Me too.

When I drifted off, it was just like he held me while I slept.

Twenty-four hours later, I was a lot better off—and we had a secret back door in and out of the Sliver. Marko and Yusuf had extracted Starcurrent from Mandy's murderous clutches, and the Abyin Dommas was getting medical treatment, while the rest of our crew tried to talk Chao-Xing and me out of more gladiator combat.

Just outside the arena, I waved the others ahead of me. "Be right there." To Nadim, I added, "Try not to worry. We'll lose touch while I'm fighting, but it'll be fine."

"I believe you will prevail, Zara. But I don't like that you risk yourself this way. Not for me." Nadim sounded borderline despondent, and my heart ached at the way he was trying to feign bravery. That was a human trait, not a Leviathan one, and I wished I hadn't taught him that.

"Trust me. Talk to you soon."

The arena was packed. I'd have liked to say it was because of Chao-Xing and me, but there was a massive alien named Mangler in the next bout who was apparently all that. Bodies jostled around me in the pit. If not for the holos, I wouldn't have been able to see the match at all. The view was better for spectators than fighters, so I stretched, trying to work out the kinks.

Chao-Xing was warming up next to me. She didn't miss my winces, even though I tried not to let them show. "You sure you're up to this?"

The only possible answer had to be yes. Briefly I wished I had some flavor of chem to mask the traces of pain still buzzing in my nerves, but I didn't want to chance stumbling on a buzz I couldn't quit. Plus, fighting drugged was a likely way to get injured.

"I'll manage," I said finally.

She looked none too sure, but I glimpsed Bea, Marko, and Yusuf in the cheap seats, ready to cheer us on. When Bea caught my eye, she raised both arms. *She believes in me.* Problem was, I couldn't miss how fragile she looked in this crowd. Like one of the Jellyfish, but without the apparently deadly stings. I needed to get her out of here, and the sooner we up-ranked, the faster I got back to Nadim for good. Resolve firmed my spine, and when I raised my fists, I hardly noticed the soreness in my shoulders.

"That's the look I was waiting for," Chao-Xing said. "I thought maybe the Blob had sapped your spirit."

"You try having your nanites hacked," I muttered.

"I'm not dumb enough to look in every random box a stranger hands me."

"Hey!" Before I could say more, the announcer called, "Zeerakull, challenging!"

Taking a deep, bracing breath, I strode off with the confidence the audience wanted. I paused at the weapon rack, now used to the customary "weapon or barehand?" choice. It would have been nice if they'd showed me my opponent beforehand, but since I'd learned a little about the shock stick in the tag-team fight with C-X, and my foes would only get more dangerous as I climbed, I grabbed the long, elegant weapon.

"Zeerakull chooses shock stick. The champion declines a weapon. Let the battle begin!"

Thankfully, it wasn't the Mangler. But the alien that skittered into the ring might have been worse: eight legs, a coiled tail with a barb, and a face like a nightmare. Really, this was a blend of a scorpion and a spider. On some level, it reminded me of the Phage, only it was much larger, and it seemed capable of independent thought.

And trash talk, apparently, because it hissed, "Will suck out your guts."

Dammit. The shock stick might not help much. From what I could see, this enemy was covered in chitin. As it charged, I used the haft of my weapon to vault over it, and I landed if not gracefully, then soundly. The tail strike smashed into the metal floor so hard that it *pierced through*. A shudder rolled over me.

Imagine what it'll do to me. These aren't supposed to be death matches. But there aren't any rules.

No time to waste; the alien was already wheeling, and it was *fast*. I'd never fought anything like it before. I only had one idea, and I'd lose in a spectacular fashion if this went bad. Pretending to lose my footing, I toppled backward and then acted like I was losing my grip on my shock stick in the panic. I was dimly aware of the crowd, reacting, cursing, shouting encouragement to me or my foe.

Nightmare Face came on without caution, seeing me as small and weak, already defeated. I was on my back, right? No need to fear me. But cats are most dangerous when on their backs, and I'd clawed my way up in the rankings. No way I'd stop now. My opponent committed, full lunge, mouth open.

In a flash, I whisked the shock stick in front of me and braced. Perfect angle: the electrified tip went into its gaping beak, past the ridged chitin and into the soft, wet tissue of its throat.

I jammed it in at an angle and made sure the charge kept running.

Flesh sizzling, my enemy thrashed as it choked on my shock stick. I rolled away, barely dodging the slamming strike of legs that could've impaled me, and then the flailing barbed tail. As the champion jerked and eventually stilled, the timer counted down to zero.

For a few seconds, the roar from the crowd was deafening as medical personnel came to check on my opponent and give treatment. I didn't think I'd killed the thing, but its throat would probably be sore as hell for a few days. As the adrenaline surge trickled away, I absorbed how shaky I was. Somehow, I managed to keep my feet and pose for the crowd. My face shot up-rank, to a mixture of cheers and boos.

When I got back to Chao-Xing, she wore an expression I couldn't read. "This is where you say, 'good job' or something," I prompted.

Her look didn't waver. The longer I scrutinized her, the more I thought she had something important to say. Then she put a hand on my shoulder. "You may not have the best training, but . . . I think you have a gift that cannot be taught."

"I . . . what?" Of all things, I wasn't expecting that.

"When you fight, you spot your opponent's weakness. You instinctively see how to defeat them."

"Well, yeah. Isn't that normal, looking for a way to win?"

"Looking, yes. But most people don't find it as fast as you. And I've watched you now, several matches, and your ability to pinpoint weakness? Uncanny."

"It's not that weird," I said. "Where I come from, that's just . . . it's street fighting. You do whatever you need to, put your enemy down. You survive."

Chao-Xing shook her head. She didn't have time to argue with me, though, because she got called up next. Watching her fight, it dawned on me that she was *right*. Her strikes were fierce, but she didn't seem to see what I saw. If *I* was up against this opponent, barehand, I'd go after its knees. They were knobby, spindly, and I could *see* how the match would proceed if I took that course. But C-X didn't seem to pick up on it, so it took her much longer to win. I would've ended that bout in less than two minutes.

She was sweaty when she joined me, trembling with exhaustion. This time I didn't care how she reacted. I gave her my shoulder. To my surprise, she leaned for a minute as the next fight was called. C-X mopped her face with her sleeve.

"Do you believe me now?"

"I think I might." I told her what I'd noticed about the alien's leg joints.

Seeming unsurprised, she said quietly, "I couldn't pinpoint that, Zara. This is an advantage you must exploit in our next match."

"Last time when we tag-teamed—"

"You were blindsided, and then you were watching *me*. This time, I need your full focus on the enemy."

Otherwise, we'll get owned.

She didn't need to add the last part. The more we up-ranked, the tougher our opponents got. We were hanging near the top-middle now. If we passed this tag-team match, we'd be in the top ten, enough fita to access the upper tiers. *Hello, starship supplies.*

I bounced on the heels of my feet, shaking out the tension that came from waiting. We both needed to hydrate, so I got us some water from the vending machine.

"Here." I handed C-X the tube, and she drained it without protest. "You think Nadim and Typhon are okay?"

"Is that what you should be concerned about now?" It was a reprimand, so I did my best to get my head in the game.

Five matches, five winners called. The ranking board changed according to those decisions, and then the avatars blurred and scrambled, their way of upping the tension and excitement. No joke, it worked too, because I tensed, waiting to see who Chao-Xing and I would face in the next challenge.

"Zeerakull and JongShowJing challenging!"

Since C-X had led the way last time, I followed her lead when she chose a long stick with a padded metal ball at the end, kind of like a bo staff, with a weight at the end for bludgeoning. "Challengers choose the xersis. Interesting selection. Champions decline weapons. Let the battle begin!"

Four aliens swaggered into the ring—not great odds for us—and they were a race I hadn't seen before. I should have been awed by all the diverse types of life there were in the universe, but mostly I needed to focus on how to incapacitate them, which kind of took the wonder out of the equation. Gray skin, thin bodies, two arms and legs, but these weren't the big-eyed grays from human lore; they were more like if someone mixed shark DNA with a primate to see how that would play out.

Claws, check. Teeth? More like fangs; jaw might have a second joint like a croc.

"Zara," Chao-Xing called. "What're you seeing?"

"Nothing yet."

Their legs looked strong; same with their joints. The champions didn't give me time to complete the assessment. Charging, two on one, they tried to overwhelm us with a flurry of powerful strikes. Those claws would do major damage, even in a nonlethal fight. Possible that we'd bleed out before medical personnel arrived.

I barely blocked all the hits, and the impact resonated into my elbows and set rockets of pain off in my shoulders. These bastards were *strong*. They attacked in perfect concert too.

I unfocused my gaze, trying to watch all four at once. And that was when I saw it: the perfection of the timing.

"They're linked!" I shouted.

"So? Plan?"

"Working on it."

"Work faster!" She fell back under the flurry of blows.

Murky eyes, holes in the side of their heads, but I couldn't strike fast enough to get to anything that might slow them down. It was taking almost all my ability to block; I had no idea how to mount an offensive. These assholes were fast, fierce, and completely coordinated. Block, block, smash. I got lucky and whacked the end of my xersis into the alien's earholes. Immediately they all stumbled and for a few seconds, they couldn't seem to *find* me.

"I don't think they see well! They hear! Earholes, now!"

In unison, C-X and I wheeled, slamming the sides of our enemies' heads in a one-two strike. They staggered, and I smashed my xersis harder, digging into the soft flesh on the side of the skull. A shriek went up from all four, and they lashed out, no longer a perfect dance of death, but chaotic and agonized. I didn't even have to hit them hard, but the repeated percussion put each of them on the ground, writhing in pain.

Unbelievably, Chao-Xing strode over to me and took my hand, raising both our arms in the air as the timer wound down. For a few seconds, I basked in the victory glow. She was feeling it too, all sass and swagger. I would not have believed C-X could showboat if I hadn't seen it with my own two eyes.

"JongShowJing and Zeerakull, champions!" That was new. I guessed it meant we'd joined the Sliver's elite warriors.

Damn right.

I strutted a little as we claimed our stuff from the lockers that held our personal gear. When we got out of the arena, fans practically mobbed us. C-X iced them out with a look that sent all but the most determined scuttling away. Bea, Marko, and Yusuf threaded their way toward us. In the short time since I'd seen him, Marko was thinner, with new lines by his mouth, and a layer of brown scruff that highlighted his pallor. Finally, he looked like a scraggly deep-space astronaut instead of a PR pretty boy.

While Marko radiated exhaustion, Yusuf had perked up some. It was good to see the man smiling. He had dimples too. Maybe the best cure for grief was being needed.

"Hell of a fight," he said, bumping his fist against mine.

Before I could answer, I smelled something rotten. And familiar.

Mandy oozed up from the cracks in the metal flooring in a gooey rush. I could see why the bastard had claimed nobody could hurt him. *Heh. We'll see.* Yusuf already had a weapon in his hand, and Marko was drawing, not that human tech could defeat this thing. While Bea looked like she'd wanted to run, her feet stayed firmly planted.

The crowd around us dispersed so fast it was like they'd teleported. In the viewing stands I heard shouts, cries, and hisses echoing as people started calling attention to what was happening down below.

Free show.

Mandy growled out, "Came for the debt you owe me, Zeerakull. You are dead."

As he lashed a pseudopod at me, I dived and rolled.

Mandy chuckled this time. Sounded like a bad toilet draining. "You cannot escape me, softskin. I can find you anywhere. You and your friends. All know this. All know I am invincible!"

"Oh yeah? Let's find out." As I came up behind the blob, I took out the personal-force-field device that I'd bought on the junk level, tapped the button, and chucked it. The small box sank into Mandy with a plop. Mentally, I was counting the seconds.

"You fool. This is not a weapon," the blob taunted.

Not in most people's hands.

As the unit settled into the blob's core, the timed force field flared on ten seconds later, turning Mandy inside out. Controlled expansion was one thing, but this push happened so fast that the alien splattered, exposing a glittering cluster of nerves that must have served as its brain—something like it, anyway. Before it reformed, I stomped the nerve cluster, grinding my foot against the floor plating until those delicate tissues were paste on the bottom of my boot.

"Can't hurt you, huh?" Scrape and spread. I pulled the matter apart, breaking connections one by one. "*Nobody* screws with me or my crew. Don't you *ever* threaten us." I added that last bit for witnesses who might want to try me.

There was a hush on all the upper levels, and when I looked up, there were a thousand alien faces turned toward us. A whole bloom of Jellies, dozens of them, clustered above, floating in midair as they—presumably—watched.

Beneath my feet, a pseudopod trembled, tried to form. *Nope.* One last twist of my heel, and the sentient goo stopped receiving signal. The spatter was just residue to be scrubbed away by cleaning bots.

I turned again to look up at the crowd. "Don't start none," I said, "won't be none. Got me?" Casually, I bent to pick up my slimy force-field gadget, wiped it on my pants, and shoved it in my pocket. *Hope it still works. I don't care what C-X says. This will come in handy.*

It might have been one of Suncross's crew who started the chant, but it picked up and thundered, seasoned with dozens of accents and translation matrixes. "Zeerakull! Zeerakull! Zeerakull!"

Bea was staring at me too. "You—you killed it."

"Damn right I did. It nearly butchered Starcurrent. And it was gunning for every one of us." I didn't understand why she looked so shaken. "Had to be done, Bea."

"But—"

"Beatriz. *It had to be done.* Best it be done out here where everybody sees it."

"I agree," Marko said, putting away his weapon.

Sure enough, he wasn't the same bright-eyed boy who'd pulled me out of Camp Kuna.

Yusuf sighed softly and shook his head. "Sometimes we

must do bad things to prevent worse, but that does not make them right."

Necessary, not right. I could live with that.

"I have no idea how you thought of that," Bea said. "Using the shield that way."

"Hey, you have your area of expertise. I got mine. Mine mostly involves ruining somebody else's good day."

"Attention."

I'd never heard a station announcement before, but this commanding tone overrode every sound, every conversation, and rang like a bell through the entire Sliver. A cool voice. Calm. Assured.

"Zara Cole, Zhang Chao-Xing, champions of the Pit, you are summoned. Bacia Annont will see you now."

We'd earned a visit with the Sliver's big boss.

FROM THE UNOFFICIAL PUBLICATION A GUIDE TO
THE SLIVER
Source: Bruqvisz Planetary Database, unlicensed copy

If you are summoned to the dread presence of Bacia Annont, the unquestioned ruler of the Sliver, we have only one piece of advice to deliver:

Do not go.

CHAPTER EIGHT

Binding Command

BACIA MIGHT BE a big deal on the Sliver, but I understood crim bosses down to the bone. They waited until they had you at disadvantage, and then they summoned you, so you'd be conscious of the great gap between their grandeur and your squalor. I wasn't about to answer a summons straight from the arena.

Maybe I couldn't get a shower, but there were ways around it, even here. Spending some mynt got me hygiene kits and clean clothes. I handed one to C-X, saying, "If we start by jumping the exact second Bacia says jump, we'll already be at a disadvantage in this sit-down. We aren't hounds that heel on cue, okay?"

C-X nodded. "You make a fair point."

"Plus, I'm dying to see if this helps," Bea added, as she took her kit.

Our room was big enough that three of us could wash and change at the same time. I'd lived in enough group homes and rehab centers that I had no modesty. Mostly I was curious if these glorified wet wipes could help, and they did remove the salt and sweat from certain key areas. Once I'd tidied up as best I could, I put on the new outfit and then went to work on my hair. I needed to wash and condition it, but for now, I settled for doing the front in a crossed twist, leaving the back in a cute puff; I'd never been able to braid the back of my hair, but this, I could pull off.

"How is it?" I asked Bea, striking a pose.

"I love it. Can you do mine?"

In my whole life, I'd only done braids for my sister, Kiz, when my mom was too busy or too stressed. Bea had a lot of hair, probably type 3B, but I didn't hesitate. "Sure. What'd you have in mind?"

"Fishtail?"

That wasn't too complicated or beyond my ability with the limited product we had. I damped her curls as I had mine and got to work. C-X alternated between pacing and tapping her foot against the floor. "I can't believe you're actually doing each other's hair."

"What, you jealous I'm not fixing yours too?" I grinned at her.

"Just get dressed already," Chao-Xing said to Bea.

Unintentionally, I'd gotten us matching outfits: yellow for me, blue for Beatriz, and red for Chao-Xing, who was grumbling as she pulled on her jumpsuit. "You think we're a superhero team?"

"I got what was cheapest and looked like it would fit us." The fabric was strange and milky, seeming like it should be transparent, and somehow it wasn't. I could get used to the gossamer softness and how breathable the material was.

"These are probably pajamas," Chao-Xing muttered.

"At this moment, I can't stress how much I don't care. Look, do you know how hard it is find clothes that fit us in a criminal squat that doesn't even *have* humans? I think these are meant for those weird little gray guys. We need to move. A minor delay can be excused as us wanting to be courteous by looking our best. But if we screw around too long, it'll seem like this is a power play."

"Isn't it?" Bea asked.

Shushing her, I found Marko and Yusuf pacing the corridor. "It's probably not good to keep Bacia waiting," Yusuf said.

"It'll be fine."

I hope.

Since Bacia had only summoned the pit champions—Chao-Xing and me—we probably couldn't bring our whole entourage. I pulled Marko aside once we got to the main tier. "Take Bea and Yusuf; watch over Starcurrent. Ze's in medical right now and we can't leave zim unprotected."

"Understood. Be careful, Zara."

"That was some good tactical thinking," Chao-Xing said as we moved off.

We leapt from the transit platform together and kicked off for the top tier. Other commuters dropped off at each tier, but we kept soaring, up and up, until it was just the two of us, and when I looked down I could see the entire rusty, chaotic beauty of the Sliver spread below us.

What could I say? It had grown on me.

As we entered the last zone, a recording began to blare. It was a translation-matrix field: *Warning, you are approaching a restricted area! Do not attempt to depart at this level without prior authorization. Death or severe maiming will occur.*

Bacia did not play.

My heart thumped harder as I landed. Crimson lights flared all around as Chao-Xing settled beside me. I couldn't see any threats. Didn't mean there wasn't a big-ass gun pointed at us, ready to shred our asses into space confetti.

"Maybe red means go," Chao-Xing said. "Bacia may not see in the same spectrums, or have the same cultural—"

The lights suddenly flared gold, and a high, pleasant tone sounded. The words that followed were just a blur of sound until the translation matrix kicked in. "You may proceed to authentication."

Turning, I glanced back at the dizzying view below, absorbing how small the tiers looked. At this remove, I couldn't hear any of the gambling dens, none of the drinkers in the dives, none of the merchants' patter. It was a different world in the Peak, one that gave me vertigo. Quickly I wheeled to follow C-X.

Security was *tight*. We walked up to a blank wall, where a featureless black plate emerged like it was rising out of a sea of milk, ripples and all. Was this thing liquid? I didn't dare touch it to find out. "What now?" I asked.

"Breathe on it," Chao-Xing suggested. "It's probably for DNA collection."

"Yeah, or they like a sobriety check." I shrugged and leaned forward, and gave it a good sample of my breath.

The black screen flashed blue and cycled back to darkness again. I stepped aside, and C-X went next. Same result, and then the whole wall just . . . melted. Splashed in a curtain into the floor and disappeared, and we kept walking forward. When I looked back, the wall was back up behind us. No way out now.

Don't suppose this is how Bacia gets rid of enemies, I thought, and wished I hadn't.

The corridor curved, and the sides were the same featureless white. Grav was lower here, and I could feel the slow bounce of my curls as I walked. Felt like I might float if I wasn't careful, but the soles of my boots stayed firm on the surface, so I guessed there was some mysterious adhesion on it.

We were moving up, I realized, in a long spiral, and when we reached the next level, there was a shimmering golden curtain of light that blocked our path.

A Jelly bobbed and floated in the space right in front of it. It was a big-ass thing, with elongated tentacles—deadly, I guessed. It bioluminesced in lazy waves of muted colors, and the translation matrix said, "Welcome, honored guests, to the office of Bacia Annont. All weapons please surrender, except for those biologically grafted or inherited."

I was carrying a pack with a knife and the personal defense field in it; I put the bag down, and Chao-Xing started unloading her arsenal into it. I wasn't shocked to find it impressive. I *was* surprised that she'd found most of it on the station. That was some crunchy good tech.

"Hey, how are we supposed to pronoun Bacia anyway?"

Chao-Xing flashed me a superior look. "You're only now asking? Word is Bacia uses they/them."

I filed that away. *Good to know.* Nothing like getting your host's gender wrong to sour an impression.

The Jelly must have judged us honest in disarmament, because the curtain of light fell, and Jelly-butler floated ahead of us into a room the entire width of the tower, which was big enough to make me feel disoriented after the noise and clutter below on the Sliver. The floor beneath us was firm and polished, and what I guessed was artwork floated in carefully chosen spots around the room. Some of it was two-dimensional, some 3D. For all I could tell, some of it might have had some multidimensional aspects too. Some pieces were so beautiful I wouldn't have minded a long look, and others made my head hurt.

Suddenly, a song started playing in the background. Classical rap, all beats and drops and burns, and ahead, I saw a wide, curving desk in what looked like real wood, only purple. Behind that was a chair big enough to be a throne, and the back of it spread out in shimmering fronds that resembled feathers, but were probably something else: organic tech, maybe. No idea what purpose they served, but they were colorful.

Bacia Annont said, without the translation matrix, *in English*, "I hope that I have chosen appropriately from your musical collection. I rather like the music of your people. It's uncomplicated, but full of . . . energy."

The Sliver boss was—well, the word for it would be *giant*. Shockingly huge, sleek, mind-numbingly beautiful, smooth gold and luminous curves, and my mouth dried up looking because all I could think was that they were the kind of creature that back in the day would have made humans on any continent, in any culture, drop to their knees and call them a god. I couldn't tell if Bacia wore armor, or they *were* the armor; those eyes held eternity, and I couldn't look for more than a couple of seconds without nearly melting into a puddle of pure attraction.

"Hello, pilots and starsingers," Bacia said, and their voice was bells and harps and the most profound kind of music I'd ever heard. "Hello, Nadim of the Dark Travelers, here by proxy. I am Bacia. The Sliver is mine. I am its protector." They paused and listened to the music. "Yes. I like the music of humans. This is worthwhile. I shall collect."

I had the sense that meant something, but I couldn't think what. I couldn't *think*, period, because the presence of this creature was . . . vast. Bigger even than Nadim's, or Typhon's. I didn't know if they meant to be that overwhelming. They just were.

No wonder they didn't walk out on the tiers.

"Take it," Chao-Xing said in a dreamy tone. "You can have our whole collection."

I considered arguing; I mean, she was giving up currency, and I had just enough sense left to know that ran directly to our best interests. But I didn't say anything. I couldn't summon up that much will.

Bacia inclined their head just a tiny bit, and it felt like the greatest gift I'd ever gotten. *Get hold of yourself. They're just another alien; you've seen dozens now.* But they didn't *feel* alien, even though Bacia wasn't like anyone I'd ever seen. They felt like home, and home meant love, kindness, and safety, even though I'd rarely had those things in my life. Bacia was the sweet, perfect moments in my mother's arms, the safety and power of bonding with Nadim, the laughter and light of everything clean.

It took everything I had to pull in a deep breath and say, "Stop playing us, Bacia. Why did you call Nadim a 'dark traveler'?"

I got their attention, and with it a flicker of annoyance that felt like an open flame on my skin. It died as soon as I flinched. "His people live to wander, surviving the silence between stars. Isn't it natural?"

Their explanation was simple, and it made sense, but the words felt ominous in a way their description didn't. "Bullshit." I fought to force that word out.

They laughed. Even their laughter was warm, and it swirled around me like a current, trying to sweep me away. "I do genuinely like your music, human of Earth. It is heartfelt, if not complex. You are a passionate people."

The pressure on me increased. A headache burst from seed to storm in about a heartbeat. I had to fight this. Sweat broke out cold on my skin, and I concentrated on that, on the smell of my half-washed skin, on the flutter of my clothes and the pulse drumming in my head. "We're here to talk, not bow down. You called us. So, let's trade."

Bacia's smile—if it was a smile, maybe I was imagining that—faded, and so did the warmth, leaving the cold shimmer of power. Their kind had to be rare in the universe, because if they weren't, they'd have taken *everything*.

"I did," they agreed. "You brought Travelers to our station. Travelers draw the parasites—"

"Wait, parasites? You know about the Phage."

Bacia's amusement hit me like a wave; I wanted to smile for no apparent reason. "The names we give to what we fear can tell others much about us. I want you and your Dark Travelers gone, as quickly as possible."

"Well, we're flying the same course, because we want the hell out of here too."

"But you have been earning mynt and fita as if you mean to stay. I have been watching your exploits."

I was ready for that, though it hinted that Bacia had a use for us, echoed in the subtle swelling of power again to try to gain advantage. I had the feeling our time on the Sliver had been one long audition for a job nobody else wanted. Even if that was true, Bacia was *not* going to get one over on me.

"What can I say? We have bills to pay. I might be interested in better-paying work, if the offer includes armor for our Leviathan," I said. "Both of them. Full work crews to install and repair what's already there. Oh, and whatever weapons you've got that the Leviathan can use, we want."

"That is a significant request."

"Yeah, well, we're good for the mynt. And the fita."

"Not for this," they said. "This transaction requires more than mynt, more than fita. This requires a more personal service."

I didn't like the sound of that one bit. "Nope."

Bacia laughed again, and I thought of silver and stars. "Let us make a bargain, Zara Cole. Let us be allies. The Sliver has many things that could strengthen your Dark Travelers and preserve them against the parasites you call the Phage. Some might even ensure the survival of their kind. I ask one small thing in return for this great gift you ask of me."

"Wait, I never said anything about a gift," I said. "This is a trade. Value for value. No favors, and we don't owe you shit when it's done."

The pressure closed around me again. Felt like I couldn't breathe, though I knew my lungs were working fine. My brain tried to tell me I was about to die, and I should get the fuck out of this place, but I made it shut up. I needed calm. I needed strength, but alone, I wouldn't be able to resist forever. Closing my eyes, I reached for Nadim, and since we'd set new parameters of possibility when he saved me during the codejacking, he leapt in response to my silent call, no longer an unconnected observer.

Nadim filled me, diminishing the alien's hold, and then

the bond locked in. Zadim. Our eyes opened. Bacia didn't seem to notice the difference, but they didn't even look as large as they had before, nowhere near as looming.

"Little human," Bacia said. "I deal fairly with all. I built the Sliver from nothing. I face all species without fear or favor. You would be wise to think before offending me."

Our eyes opened. Zadim spoke. "No favors, no debts. Straight deal. You don't want it, we take our ships and go."

"Go where?" They flicked dismissive fingers—were those fingers? They looked shockingly human, but I suspected that was an illusion. "Your Travelers are sick and wounded, blackened by grief within. The Phage have been rare in this sector, but where the Travelers go, the Phage follow. They will catch yours and core them hollow without the proper plate and weapons. These, I can supply."

"Then let's get to price. We're here to haggle." The Zara part of Nadim was forming words, but the strength, the intention, that was the meld of Zadim.

Bacia's ancient eyes studied us, and we had the sudden, eerie feeling that appearance was a beautiful shell they wore for our benefit, an outfit they'd put on because it might speed things along. "Why are you not like the others?"

"You don't know? Truly?" Perhaps they had never witnessed a perfect deep bond.

"You don't treat me with the reverence others do."

Irritation pricked at the superficial calm of those words. Bacia stared harder, trying to work out the puzzle of how a mere human could resist such power. "You're a true pilot."

"We are Zadim."

"I have never known a Dark Traveler who could bond at such distance."

"We're not here to discuss that. You want something. Something all your other Sliver rats can't give you, or you'd have already made deals with them. So?"

Bacia didn't like us. The charm turned off, as if a switch got thrown, and what was left was not gold but ice-cold iron. "Very well, if you wish to dispense with the pleasant conversation, I will. I require payment in service. I require you to bring me something rare and dangerous. Will you do it?"

Whoa, whoa, whoa. "Depends. What the hell is it?"

"An artifact," they said. "It is located on a long-deserted planet located a distance away, but with a ship like yours, you should be there and back in a few station days."

"Anybody watching over this *artifact* of yours?" We considered the possible dangers. "Guards? Alarm systems?"

Bacia blinked those dark, eternal eyes and said, "No. It lies alone and forgotten. There is no danger."

A lie; it rang hollow to us, and we could read small cues that had been invisible to Zara alone. Bacia . . . was nervous.

"Then why haven't you claimed it already?"

"I do not leave this place," they said. "And there are reasons I do not wish to send those I employ."

"Somebody else owns it."

Bacia's smile came slow, and it gave us a bad feeling. Worse than we had already. "Not anymore." There wasn't just a story behind that; there was probably an epic, several intergalactic wars, and maybe a few planets left in rubble. "Do you agree?"

"What exactly are we getting in return for this?"

"What you requested. Defenses against the Phage. Weapons to repel and destroy them. Time grows thin, little human. It is time to decide. Agree, or leave the Sliver."

"What happens to our mynt and fita if we decline?" We weren't sure where we stood financially, in all honesty. Borrowing from the lizards and taking meds on credit from Dr. Justineau had left us scrambling to run some numbers.

"If you leave to complete this request, then it will be held in trust," they said, smooth as melting butter. "If you leave without agreeing, it reverts to the Sliver for redistribution. This is fair."

The hell it was. We started to argue about it, but right about then, Chao-Xing took a step forward. It looked like the movement took all her strength and grit, but she did it, and came shoulder to shoulder with us. She didn't speak, but I understood: she was fighting Bacia's influence and standing strong.

"What do we think?" Zadim asked. "Take the job, or not? Your call."

Chao-Xing was staring at Bacia. I couldn't read the look on her face. "What are you?" she asked.

Bacia's large, perfect head tilted to one side. "What do you see?"

"You ought to be ruling a galaxy, yet you're hiding in a tower. Maybe the proper question is, what are you afraid of, Bacia Annont?" Chao-Xing stood straighter, lifting her gaze in unmistakable challenge.

The air chilled, icy as the vacuum of space, and that bottom-of-the-ocean pressure built again. Something hid behind the gilded mask that I *really* didn't want to meet.

"I fear nothing," they said, and I knew that for a lie the second I heard it. "But you, little humans . . . you should fear *me*. Last time. Yes or no?"

Chao-Xing shrugged. "Yes," she said. "But I warn you, you should know something about us humans."

Bacia sat back. Bored now. "And what is that?"

"We've worshipped lots of gods in our history," she said. "We've killed most of them. You might want to be wary."

Zadim heartily agreed with that sentiment. "Send the coordinates. And Bacia? No charge for breaking dock. Call it a good-faith payment."

Bacia said nothing, but Jelly-butler drifted forward, delicate membranes flashing an agitated light show, and led us out. The minute we stepped past the milky white wall, Zadim splintered. I stumbled, feeling cold and alone; Chao-Xing caught me. I didn't know if they'd even noticed my eyes in the middle of that intense negotiation. A faint squeeze on my shoulder implied that C-X had.

I leaned over and braced myself with hands on my thighs, breathing deeply. "What did we just do? What *was* that?"

"Next best thing to a god out here in the black," Chao-Xing said. "But vulnerable, or they wouldn't be hiding. If anyone can give us what we need, they can."

I was feeling a little giddy, rather than shaken; we had just—holy shit—faced down a being that would have scared most creatures into a fetal position, if they had one.

Chao-Xing and I headed for medical to brief the others, and C-X—slick as hell—had been recording the whole encounter. Starcurrent's tentacles went blue at the tips as ze stared at Bacia's image on the H2.

"Not good," ze said. "Such beings . . ." Here, Starcurrent hesitated, as if there was a story ze didn't want to tell. "They acted as gods," ze finally said. "Once, such ruled far-spanning galaxies. Many wars between them. Many worlds gone in fighting. My people suffered much. Thought they were only dust now, dust and forgotten songs."

"Yeah, well, we're not dying, and we're singing on," I told zim. "Cheer up. We're getting the hell out of here."

And back to Nadim, I thought. I craved him like oxygen.

OFFERED SALE: A FRAGMENT OF A RECORD OF THE
BIIYAN
Source: Unknown, no provenance exists. Unverified.
Value of collected material may either be nothing, or
incalculable. Buyer beware.

Long we wait
Weightless
Longing
Freedom taken
Crushed by their regard
Descendants lost
Must win free
Or die

CHAPTER NINE

Binding Destiny

WE DIDN'T BREAK dock right away. Bacia hadn't asked us to punch a clock, and we had interests on the Sliver to protect. That meant looking for Suncross, our primary ally here on Stab-You-in-the-Back Station. He'd sponsored us and earned fita on our fights, so that should mean we were still on good terms.

Chao-Xing went to collect her wages from Pinky's, and Starcurrent took Marko and Yusuf shopping, gearing them up for the mission to come. That left Beatriz and me to head for the arena, where we might find our favorite lizards.

Since C-X and I were still listed as champions—which would only stand for another few hours, and we'd get downgraded when we didn't register for the next match—I got free admission and took Bea in as my guest.

There was a low-level bout on below, and I was a little shocked to see that it was an Abyin Dommas fighting. Somehow, I'd been thinking they were heavily pacifist . . . until I saw how this one took down zis opponents. Those tentacles were *damn* fast, and strong, and ze wasn't even using the barbs. Fastest win I'd seen yet. Also, the first where the winner solicitously stuck around and helped revive the loser.

We were looking for Suncross, but the big reptile was absent. Ghostwalk was there, though, betting heavy, and he greeted us with a hearty shout and double sets of fists pounding his chest. "Zeerakull! Fighting today?"

"Not today, buddy," I said, and taught him the fine art of the fist bump. "Listen, where's Suncross? I need to talk to him."

Ghostwalk was already shaking his head. "Not now," he said. "Not today. Today is day of pleasure."

"Uh, you mean, like a day off?" Beatriz asked. "Because—"

"No, no, *pleasure*. Tier Twelve. He will not want talking. Come tomorrow."

"But—" Beatriz said, and evidently she thought the translation matrix was off.

"Let it go," I told her. "Tier Twelve is brothels."

"*Oh.*"

"Let's see if Justineau has any useful intel," I suggested.

Beatriz went with me when I headed down to the warren of rusted hallways where Justineau had his medical closet. We had to wait while he attended to one of the Lumpyhead aliens, this one a sickly shade of orange. Once his patient left, he ushered us in with a bewildered smile. "You didn't open another code box, did you?"

I snorted. "Not hardly."

"We were wondering if you knew anything about this." Bea showed him the coordinates and summarized the job Bacia had ordered us to complete.

If anyone had asked me, I'd have said it would be impossible for ol' boy to get whiter, but as he listened, he went from regular milk to spoiled and developed a tremor in his hands.

I tilted my head. "Looks like you do. Know something. And here I was about to offer you a ride out of here."

"No thank you," he said quickly. "I mean, you have a mission first. If . . . when you return, we can talk about your kind suggestion then."

"I need info." When I leaned on the door, I didn't mean to be threatening. I was just making it clear I wouldn't be leaving until he opened up.

Now Justineau wasn't just pale; he was sweaty too.

"This is only low-tier gossip. Not from a verifiable source."

"Do I look like I'll judge you for getting me gutter intel? Lay it out."

Bea added, "Please," because apparently, we were doing good cop/bad cop all of a sudden. I smothered a smile.

"Well, what I've heard . . . it's not a lot. But it seems like you're not the first."

"To be sent on this job?" I asked.

Justineau nodded. "Every so often, somebody makes a splash on the Sliver. Makes a name for themselves."

"Like we did," Bea said.

Justineau clearly didn't want to have this conversation, twisting his bony fingers together. "Sometimes in the arena, sometimes cons or slicing. Whatever way, a new crew winds up with the mynt and fita to get a meeting with Bacia."

An icy hand crawled down my back. "You're telling us that nobody ever comes back from this, like it's a suicide run where they send people who could potentially threaten their power base on station?"

"I never said that." Justineau's gaze darted toward the walls, wild as a cat in a box. "Bacia is all-powerful. It's just an arduous task, that's all."

Shit. I wasn't thinking about surveillance.

Living like this would make anybody paranoid, though, and it was likely poor Justineau had mental problems as a result of losing his Leviathan and then having his nanobots codejacked. The human brain could only bear so much. We needed to take his info with a big-ass grain of salt.

"Do you know anything more about the actual job?" Bea's tone was gentle, and Justineau responded to that.

He took a breath, calming visibly, and then he ran an unsteady hand through his shock of gray hair. "Not much. I heard that a distress call came in from the last crew that attempted it."

"I don't suppose you have a copy?" I asked.

Quick head shake. "The only other thing I can tell you is, they said something about a vault down on the planet. The message was scrambled, and the translation matrix couldn't decide whether to call it a vault, a bunker, a sepulchre, or a repository."

Wary, I locked eyes with Bea. "None of those are remotely the same."

"We might literally be robbing a tomb? I did not sign up for this," she mumbled.

"I'm sorry I can't be of more help." Justineau stepped past me and put a hand on the door. I stepped away and let him signal our departure.

"Thanks anyway."

As we left the grimy, makeshift medbay, I said quietly to Bea, "Did you get the feeling he was holding out on us?"

She lifted a shoulder in a half-shrug. "Maybe? He was definitely scared."

Halfway to the exit to Tier One, it hit me. "We should've

asked who might have a copy of that distress call. He only said *he* didn't, not that nobody did."

"It's worth checking out," she agreed.

Down in the bowels, there was no exhilarating slipstream, so we had to trudge back down to Justineau's squat, probably no more than seven minutes, round trip. I rapped on the metal door, casual at first, and then harder when I got silence in response.

I cocked a brow. "You think he ran off to warn someone?"

"About what? I don't think he's in Bacia's circle."

"When you're right, you're right." I got out my H2 and activated my VA. "Can you tell me if Doc Justineau's at home?"

"Yes and no," the swirl of light said. "Would you like me to override his door?"

"You can do that?" Bea was surprised.

"Under most circumstances, no. This is an exception."

"Go for it," I said.

The door swished open to reveal the old man on the floor. Even at this distance, it was obvious he wasn't breathing. I raced in and flipped him over, thinking maybe it wasn't too late for CPR. But his throat was *crushed*, not just strangled but crumpled inward, with a ruby-violet burn on the skin, tiny blisters still forming. His eyes already had a white film, staring up at the grungy metal ceiling with an expression of such anguish and terror that I recoiled.

"Any idea what made those wounds?" I asked the VA.

"Scanning. Similar to attack of . . ." Bleep of the translation. "You call them Jellies."

I thought of the huge Jelly-butler up in Bacia's aerie. Too big to do scut work down here, but a lesser minion? Hell, yeah.

"This just happened," Bea whispered. "Like, right after we left."

No question, she was correct. I considered how easily I'd dismissed his fear and almost banged my head on the wall. Guilt wouldn't help, though. Only action could.

"Somebody shut him up," I said grimly. "And I think we both know who."

"Zara! Beatriz!" Nadim sounded urgent. "Get out. Get out *now*."

To say we got off station at lightning speed would be an understatement. There were no authorities to contact per se, so I used my VA to file a death notice on the station server. The swirl of light also provided Bea and me with an alibi, which was both creepy and convenient. Apparently, this thing had a geo-locator tracking feature, which could pinpoint us as nearby during time of death, but not responsible.

I couldn't wait for Suncross to finish his pleasure tour. If the lizard thought we were reneging on the sponsorship deal because we'd taken a job from Bacia, so be it. I sent a vid message explaining the situation; that was the best I could do. Next I called Chao-Xing as we headed for the docking bay. My H2 connected to hers after some static and interference.

"Don't worry about a day's mynt. We're going now."

"Why?" I should've known she'd ask, but I didn't want this story in the electronic wind—and it would be if we talked now.

Bea leaned in. "Trust me, it's bad. We should move. Stay alert and watch out for the Jellies."

That was enough corroboration. C-X cut the connection, and I blew past the sentries who were posted outside our honeycomb of a landing space. The Hopper felt blessedly familiar when I climbed in. Bea got in the pilot's chair, so I slid on back.

"Can you raise Starcurrent yet?" I didn't want to go back inside the Sliver.

She shook her head.

Every move I could make felt ominous and wrong. If I hurried off to the mission, maybe that was exactly what Bacia wanted. Or maybe the big boss would prefer for me to linger, so there would be an excuse to—

Fuck it. No matter what, I needed Nadim—and soon—to get my head right.

Finally, the H2 crackled to life, and Starcurrent was

on-screen. "Chao-Xing said we leave? Coming soon, with her."

I let out a sound that was all relief. "Hurry."

"Am rushing with all filaments."

Remembering Justineau's dead, staring eyes and his mangled throat, it was getting harder for me to stay calm. Nadim could probably sense it, because he said, "That death, it feels like both a precaution and a warning."

"Murder," Bea corrected, her voice faint but firm. "They murdered him."

And that was a hard weight to take. Poor man had survived a Phage attack, lost everything to Mandy's code-jacking, only to eke out an existence thinking he'd never see his own kind again. And when he did? We got his ass killed. Hard not to see a lesson in that, some kind of way—humans were dangerous as hell, even when we weren't trying to be.

"Think we can do this?" I asked, low.

Bea reached out, wrapping her fingers around mine, warm brown on brown. And it felt nice; I'd never been this close to another human who didn't have a history of hurting me. Beatriz, she was just . . . *good*, like getting an icy gulp of water on the hottest day.

"We've done everything else," she said.

And damned if that didn't bolster me. When I contemplated all the improbable shit she and I had survived, together, this might be another one for the record books.

Seemed like forever before Chao-Xing and Starcurrent rolled up, Marko and Yusuf moments behind. As they climbed in the Hopper, Bea powered it up. Her assurance had grown in leaps and bounds since the time she took us down to Firstworld. That felt like a lifetime ago, that carefree joy, that . . . innocence. I'd rarely applied that word to myself, but the universe kept teaching me how little I knew, even if I thought I'd seen some shit.

"You good?" I asked her.

Starcurrent slid in back with me as Bea nodded. She was analyzing trajectories, and soon, we swung out, away from the dizzying oscillations and toward the beautiful gleam of our healing Leviathan. Even Typhon looked fantastic to me now, and Nadim? A burst of love cascaded through me like fireworks.

"I don't like these circumstances," Nadim said. "But I'm glad to have you both home."

"Are you planning to tell us what made you scramble like scared sheep?" Chao-Xing demanded.

Since Bea was busy swooping the Hopper into Nadim's docking bay, I answered the question in a monotone. It wasn't like it was a long story, just a pitiful and tragic one. I also shared what snippets we'd gleaned from Doc Justineau before the Jellies iced him. Once I finished, Chao-Xing slammed the console with an angry fist, and Starcurrent was tinged in a violent blue that I was coming to recognize as rage.

Zis tentacles unfurled, trembled. "Cowardly. That human threatened no one."

I had no energy to grieve. Maybe it was terrible, but I'd burned through all my reserves, and I just wanted to retreat to my room and be with Nadim.

I didn't linger in the docking bay. The others could debrief.

Not me.

Trailing my fingertips against the walls, I quietly delighted in the colors that rayed from that small point of contact. As soon as the door closed behind me, I set it to NO VISITORS and I switched my H2 to DO NOT DISTURB. Then I stripped off my boots, flattened my hands and feet against the floor, falling *into* Nadim.

"I ate nutritionally adequate food on the Sliver," I said. "So why am I so . . . hungry?"

"I'm the same. The artificial light bath can mend me, but I wasn't whole without you, Zara. There were so many places in the warren where I could not follow. That silence . . ."

"I know." Because for him, silence was like death. And I'd been so results focused that I'd forgotten he was mourning so many of his cousins. "What can I do to make you feel better?"

"You're doing it, you and Beatriz. You are shining for me, and she is singing."

Once, I would've scoffed at the idea that I *could* shine, but there was no doubt in me anymore. To Nadim, I was a damn candelabra.

Likewise, once it would've made me faintly jealous to hear that Bea could comfort him, just as I could, but with a different method. Now I wondered how it would feel if we both bonded with him at once, if it would be warm and tender and sweet, an echo of her hand in mine. I suspected she didn't want a bond name with him, and hell, I wasn't even sure that was possible—for a Leviathan to form a complete bond with two beings.

There were still nuances I didn't understand, but for now, I would lie here and drink Nadim's peace through my fingers and toes. I needed him now, like vitamin D or sunlight. His voice soothed me. The touch of his mind quieted my fear.

And I would need that strength soon. For Bacia's suicide mission, because no matter what Justineau had said, I was sure that no crew had come back from it before.

We will. I intended to be first to complete the job and come back alive. But that meant going in eyes open, heads turning, every sense on high alert. "Nadim, did you get any answer from Typhon about these coordinates? Did he know anything?"

I felt his faint blush of chagrin; he'd forgotten to tell me, in the pleasure of our reunion. "Yes, he did. He has not been to this area, but others have. Most . . . did not return."

"Hang on a second. Leviathan were killed?"

"I don't know if they were killed. They only haven't returned."

"Not reassuring in the least, though."

"No," he admitted. "Typhon says that two of us went to investigate and found a deserted planet, far from its sun. Dark and cold, and no life that they could detect."

"Any buildings down there? Installations?"

"One," he said. "It was very large. Three sides, pointed at the top. One side was black, one silver, one white."

A pyramid, each side a distinct color. I didn't know what that meant. "Okay. Any kind of readings coming from it? Energy? Communications?"

"No. It was silent and appeared to be inert."

I was guessing it wasn't. I wondered why two Leviathan got away, and others were lost. Maybe it had to power up after it destroyed its enemies. They caught it at low charge.

"Working theory," I said. "Whatever that is, it's a weapon, and we need a way to find out how it works from a great big safe distance. Thoughts?"

"A few." Nadim sounded smug. I wondered why, but he didn't share anything, at least not yet. "It will take us three ship days to reach this system. We can discuss with everyone. For now, Zara . . . rest. And . . ." He hesitated, and I felt the pulse of his amusement. "Perhaps a shower."

I groaned. I didn't want to get up. Ever. But he was right.

I really, really stank. My hair felt stiff and crunchy at the ends. My skin felt dry and abused. I didn't need a shower; I needed a spa day.

But I settled for carefully removing my front braids and taking two hours to scrub up and properly co-wash and deep condition my curls, apply finishing oil to my hair and lotion on my skin. When I finally padded out of the bathroom wearing loose silky pajamas, I felt as relaxed and pampered as I ever had in my life.

"Better?" I asked, as I dropped the station garb in the disposal. Hell if I was going to put any effort into cleaning it. I crawled into bed, under covers, and the mattress molded softly to my body and made me feel embraced. I put a hand flat against the wall. A pulse of slow light flowed from the contact.

"Better," Nadim said. There was a purr to his voice. He shared my relaxation, just as he had my tension. "Sleep, Zara. You are safe."

PHAGE, The

Since I can't find any record that makes sense in the official database, I'm recording this for future Honors. Look, if you're like me, you're already overwhelmed by the revelations about other inhabited worlds, other species crewing the Leviathan . . . and you're starting to realize that you've been lied to, at least by omission, your whole life. I can't help you with that, because what's coming is so much worse.

I have little scientific analysis to offer right now. We barely survived an encounter with these vile things, and I'm trying to help my ship heal as best I can from the encounter. They come on like a swarm—like ants, bees, hornets, something insectile and unstoppable. Not vulnerable to much. I'm asking my ship for more intel, but she's too hurt to reply, and I'll admit it: I'm scared. I want to protect her. I don't know how.

God help us if we didn't get away from them, and they track us, because we won't survive a second encounter. We're trying to make for a place called the Sliver to acquire armor and weapons against this species. The Elders are too far away to help us.

God help us all if these things ever attack Earth.

–Entry in the Journey database, logged by Honor Simon Chu, ship Cherys, bond-name Starblade. Starblade is recorded as lost to a Phage swarm.

Interlude: Nadim

I do not like this mission. I understand the necessity of it, but it was torture to have Zara and Beatriz separated from me for so long in that terrible metal cage, fighting for their existence.

Now we are together, and this is good; she and Beatriz are safe with me. But what we have agreed to do . . . I fear it is a wrong choice. I fear we may do something that ends us. Other Leviathan might have perished on this same course. I am alert for Phage as we glide to the destination, alert for any hostile forces that may emerge. I am stronger. Almost healed.

Typhon is not healed, but he will fight regardless of his wounds and damage. I do not want it to come to such things.

I wish we could run. Bathe ourselves in far, rich star-song and be away from the battles and blood and death. But my kin are a silence now, fewer than they should be. Weaker than they know.

We must defend.

We must avenge.

And most of all, we must survive.

Zara's Guide to Aliens on the Sliver

Bruqvisz, aka Lizards. Four arms, two legs, varying skin tones, with a ruff that stands up when they're riled. They like to gamble and fight, care a lot about their honor.

Oborub, aka Jellies. Bacia's elite. Their tendrils are poisonous, and they're stronger than they look. Never heard them talk; they communicate with bioluminescence.

Elaszi, aka Blobs. I hate these bastards. They're evil Jell-O and hard to perish. Do not trust them or open any gifts they offer.

Fellkin, aka Lumpyheads. Orange, insectoid with chitin. They're strong but not fast, and their genitals are in the weirdest place.

Abyin Dommas, aka Tentacle Squid-faces. They change colors by mood but don't communicate that way. They're born singing, peaceful, but extremely effective in combat when forced to it.

The Phage, aka My Worst Nightmare. [No entry]

—sourced from Honor Zara Cole's personal logs

CHAPTER TEN

Binding Allies

I SHOULD HAVE known there'd be trouble when I woke up.

I didn't sleep nearly long enough, and after so much time being on my guard at the Sliver, I didn't wake up calmly, either—maybe because it wasn't Nadim who woke me, but a human hand, shaking my shoulder.

I went for a knife, still mostly asleep, didn't find one, and flipped off the bunk in an instinctive attack. I had my hands around Beatriz's neck before I realized what I was doing, and quickly threw them up in the air and backed off a step. *Deep breaths*, I told myself. My skin was burning from the adrenaline, and the instinct to punch still hadn't gone away, but I had it on a leash now.

"What the hell?" My voice was too sharp. I needed to dial down the hypervigilance. The Sliver was out *there*, not in here.

"Sorry," she said. Her eyes had gone huge, and I could tell I'd scared her. "Should—should I not wake you like that?"

"Damn, Bea, sorry." I sank down on my bunk again, suddenly losing strength, and stared down at the pink surface of my palms. I turned them over to inspect the scars and calluses on my knuckles. I'd been fighting a long time. "Bad dreams."

That was a lie, but it sounded like the truth; if I'd been dreaming, I didn't remember. But Bea seemed relieved to have the excuse. "I had them too," she confessed, and I thought she wasn't lying about it. "That place."

"What's so urgent?"

"Oh. Yes. Sorry. It's Typhon."

I realized that Nadim wasn't saying anything. I knew he was *there*, his awareness hovering at a distance, observing but not interfering. I'd know if he was asleep, and he wasn't. Just staying out of it.

"What about that old bastard?"

That normally would have drawn a smile out of Bea, but not this time. She crossed her arms across her chest, looked down, and said, "He wants to leave."

"What the hell does that mean?"

"He . . . he feels he's strong enough to go his own way. He says it's urgent to try to contact more Leviathan, and he can best do that on the move, with song. He needs to sing to them about the massacre and tell them of the danger."

"And he can't do that here?"

"No," she said. "He says that this area of space has . . . I didn't quite get it, but something like soundproofing, I suppose. Signals are muted, or blocked altogether. It's probably why the Phage avoid this place."

"Huh. Probably Bacia's doing." I remembered how tough it was to communicate with Nadim back on the Sliver; the farther we got from our Leviathan, the tougher it was. Bacia was probably surprised we could do it at all. "Did you tell him it was a stupid damn idea?"

Bea's eyebrows arched up. "I thought I'd save that for you. I know how much you like that sort of thing."

"Being sensible?"

"Confrontational."

"Okay, yeah, I earned that." I stood up, stretched the tension out of my body, and sighed.

I wolfed down breakfast—*real food* instead of nutritionally adequate protein cubes—and reveled in the feel of my clean Honors uniform against my skin for about a hot second before I realized something was missing. Starcurrent was doing something in the media room; I was aware of that even though I didn't specifically go looking . . . Marko was on Typhon, but Chao-Xing hadn't gone back yet and was still knocked out in a deep sleep on the sofa. Beatriz was in the control room. Nadim was quiet, but present.

We were missing someone.

Yusuf.

"Nadim." I stood up, forgetting about everything else. "Where's Yusuf?"

"He is with Typhon," Nadim said. "Marko asked him to make the transfer."

"He . . . *what*? Wait a second, you let Marko order Yusuf around like that?"

I felt the cool purple pulse of Nadim's mild offense. "Of course I didn't," he said. "Marko offered Yusuf a place on Typhon. Yusuf sensed there is little space for him here. We are too . . ."

He didn't finish that, but I knew what he meant. Me, Bea, and Nadim, we were a *team*. A solid, tight-bound unit. Yusuf didn't need to be staring at that all the time, feeling outside. That must have been hell. I hadn't even really thought about it, but I could imagine when you lost everything you loved, seeing other people happy would be torture, at least until time scabbed over the raw places in your soul.

"So . . . he's going to be there with Marko and Chao-Xing?"

"Yes," Nadim said. "The medication you secured for

him has made him much better. We will keep Starcurrent with us. They will take Yusuf. It seems equitable."

I'd rather have Yusuf here where our EMITU could look after him, but nobody had asked me, and I guessed if Yusuf had wanted to stick around, he would've protested his new assignment. Typhon had a medbot too, with the same equipment as ours, and as long as Yusuf had his meds, it should be fine. Right?

"How's Typhon feeling?" I asked Nadim as I picked up my tray and cup and cleaned everything up. "Any better?"

"Yes," Nadim said. "Beatriz told you he wants to seek out others of our kind?"

"She passed that along. He's in no shape to do that solo, is he?"

"No."

"Didn't think so. And he's dragging Marko, Chao-Xing, and Yusuf off into danger along with him? Hell, no."

"You are not the boss of him," Nadim said.

"Who taught you stupid ancient slang?"

"Is it not correct?"

"For my *great-grandmother*."

"But the point is valid. We can't tell Typhon what to do. He is an Elder."

"He's a pain in my ass is what he is." I hadn't forgotten Typhon's brutal "teaching methods," which mostly involved slapping his pupils around. I hadn't forgotten the callous way he treated Marko and Chao-Xing, at least in the beginning. He was no saint, and I was not about to let him run his Leviathan ass off and get my friends killed. "Talk to him. Tell him that we're maybe a week out from having everything you two will need to defend yourselves against the Phage. If he wants to play at being a general in this war, maybe he ought to spend a little time thinking about strategy."

"I see," Nadim said. "Strategy is not something my people have mastered. We are not, by nature, warlike. It's a measure of Typhon's desperation that he has become so violent."

"Well," I said, and patted the closest wall. I let my fingers rest there once the motion was done. "That's why you picked us, isn't it? Humans? Because we do have that instinct. It's built into our DNA, to fight to survive against all comers."

"Yes," Nadim said. He didn't sound happy about it. "You are an aggressive species."

"Hardly the only ones. I mean, even Starcurrent can whup ass when ze needs to. Ze has *poison barbs*."

"It's a last defense," Nadim said. "Zis people are not warlike. They are peaceful by preference. Your friend Suncross's race are naturally prone to aggression, and there are a few others. But for the most part, dominant species lose the need to dominate."

So, the galaxy at large viewed humanity as bad seeds. I wasn't totally unhappy with that. "No wonder I liked

Suncross so much," I said. "Anyway. Tell Typhon what I said. It's dumb of him to go running off without full armor and weapons, and if he can't see that, Chao-Xing will give him a lesson." I figured C-X would like that.

But Nadim, after a moment, just said, "Typhon isn't happy, but he says he will agree to a short delay."

"Generous of him, since we're saving his big, scary ass." I only paused for a second before I said, "You don't have to tell him that."

"I didn't," Nadim said. A little pulse of emotion ran beneath my fingertips, golden and warm. Amusement. "I know when to pass your words on and when to use discretion."

"Better you than me," I said. "My filters aren't so good."

"Your filters are fine," he said. "You are as you should be."

That was a startling thing to hear. It woke warmth in places I'd always felt cold. Empty spaces I didn't know I had. *You are as you should be.* It was the kindest thing anyone had ever said to me, and it felt . . . pure.

I pulled in a breath, held it, breathed it out.

Nadim said, "Did I do something wrong, Zara?" I could hear the touch of anxiety in his voice.

"No," I said. I wanted to fold myself into him, to create our shared, perfect union, but I didn't. Just for this moment, I wanted to be Zara Cole.

Because Zara Cole was as she should be.

"No," I repeated, and put all the love I felt into my voice, and into my fingertips that rested against his skin. "No, sweetheart. You did something exactly right."

I could feel his startlement and his satisfaction. Pure, again. He hadn't said it to game me, or get something out of me. He'd said it because he felt it.

It came to me with clarity right then that I loved Nadim. Alien ship that he was in the flesh, I loved the bright, perfect core of *him*. Mind loving mind. I remembered thinking I'd loved my last boyfriend, Derry, but that had been a hollow, shallow kind of feeling, something built like a bridge over a vast, black chasm of yearning. It was just . . . bodies. I'd never trusted him. I never really could.

Nadim, though. Nadim was a kind of brilliant flame that only warmed, never burned.

If I trust him, and he betrays me, this will hurt worse than anything ever has. That alone made me quiver, made me almost draw back from the truth of what Nadim was, and how we fit. My instinct was always *hurt first*.

But that had left me alone. Left me cold.

And I knew in my heart that this was right. Finally and completely . . . right.

But I didn't say that. I just said, "Is Typhon coming with us to get this thing Bacia wants?"

"He will come," Nadim said readily. "He does not want to be alone."

I didn't know if that was because he was afraid—unlikely—or because Typhon's temper might snap and he'd smash the Sliver into rusty little pieces. Probably the latter. Typhon, like me, wasn't afraid of much.

"Fine. But let him know that he's not calling the shots here. We're the ones who brokered this deal, and the ones Bacia's dealing with directly. Okay?"

"Yes," Nadim said. "He understands. I don't think he likes it, but he understands."

"Good enough. We ready to go?"

"We are," Nadim said. "I'm waiting for your word."

"Word," I said, because he enjoyed that dumb joke, and I liked that he did.

I felt the leap of motion through my body, moving through my soul like a ripple of wonder, and I closed my eyes and bonded with Nadim . . . not deep, it wasn't needed, but like a surfer catching a wave. The feeling of gliding through space, then the leap forward . . . it was such a perfect, joyous physical thing that it felt like dancing. Like fighting.

Like other things. But I wasn't going there. Not now.

Beatriz came from the control room. "Did you know we're—"

"Yep," I said. "We're heading to the coordinates. I need you to be on top of what we're going to face when we get there. That okay?"

"Absolutely," our singer said, and hummed a little tune. I don't know if she even knew she was doing it. I felt the resonance within Nadim, a perfect harmony of songs I couldn't even perceive with human senses, but Beatriz could. Stars and Leviathan and universes, all vibrating at their own specific frequencies. I wondered if I'd ever be able to feel that too. "Anything special I should be looking for?"

"Death traps," I said. "Because Bacia's sending us right into one."

When I first joined up as an Honor, I'd never thought of the Leviathan as having predators. I mean, live ships with tech so advanced they could save Earth? How could they *not* be the top of the food chain, right?

But as we traveled, I kept a sharp eye out for the Phage. It was clear at first, closest to the Sliver, a sort of resonant dead zone, but the farther we traveled, the louder the Leviathan sang; sometimes it was joyous, and sometimes it was a mourning call. Either way, silence was anathema to them in large doses. While Nadim could dark run for a brief time, Typhon had no stealth mode, so that meant we rolled with full visibility.

That kept all of us on edge, though I tried to hide my nerves by digging into the files Typhon had shared with Nadim. The Leviathan didn't process information as humans did, so these were more like contact logs—who, what, when, where, just the facts. Humans would have tried to capture an alien creature, dissect it, experiment on it to find a weakness. Which was both awful and informative about us as a species. Our Leviathan brethren didn't have that same inclination or the ability to conduct that kind of invasive research. Not without human help, anyway, and that was where I came in.

Images from the contact log didn't teach me much, but I studied them anyway, logging how the Phage moved in space and the way they latched on, like space insects, with pincers to puncture and teeth that I couldn't get a read on. From some angles they looked more mammalian, but really, I needed a specimen to be sure. And *that* was not something I ever thought I'd say.

Mumbling a curse, I stood and stretched, flipping off the console screen. Hours had passed. I could hear Bea singing in the media room, and if I had to guess, Starcurrent was probably with her. I didn't feel great about Yusuf going off to Typhon without me making sure the man was good with it.

"You're troubled," Nadim said.

Before, that knowledge would've raised my hackles, but now I could see the benefit in not having to explain my every mood. "About a couple of things."

"The Phage." That was an easy guess, and he hesitated over the next one. "Yusuf?"

"Got it."

I activated the comm. It was a novelty to have Typhon

close enough for Marko to pick up straightaway, and there was no lag in response time, either. His face was a little grainy due to our travel speed, but it was still cool as hell to *see* him like this.

"How you feeling?" I asked.

Things had been too hectic on the Sliver for us to talk much, but hopefully, he wouldn't take it personally. Shit must have been rough for Marko, because he'd believed in all the shiny Honors propaganda, and for him, these unwelcome revelations had to be like learning that fairy tales didn't always have happy endings.

"My leg's better. Still sore, but I can get around. Or . . . were you asking about my mood?" His lopsided smile said that wasn't like me.

"Well, I could listen to some feelings, if you need an ear." Grudging offer.

Marko laughed, though he looked strained, twin lines pleating his thick brows together. "It's tough. Typhon is as grim as I've seen, Chao-Xing has never opened up to me, and I . . ." He trailed off, probably thinking I didn't give a shit.

Fair. I normally didn't.

"Anything I can do?"

"For *me*?" His brows shot up.

Admittedly, I wasn't known for being generous with my time or my emotions, but Nadim and Bea had softened me a little. "Sure."

"No. But thanks for asking."

"No problem. Can I talk to Yusuf?"

He might not want to chat, but he couldn't fault me for checking in. After all, I owed him one. If he hadn't hauled me inside when I collapsed, something terrible would've happened when I ran out of air . . . and Nadim would've gone mad. I shivered slightly.

"Just a minute," Marko said.

It took a bit longer than that, but Yusuf eventually showed up on-screen. His face didn't tell me much about how he was doing, but his eyes did look brighter, and his cheekbones weren't quite as sharp. *Hope that means he's been eating.*

"Are you okay with the transfer?" I asked.

"It's fine. There's more work here to keep me busy since Typhon is damaged."

You both are, I thought.

"Let me know if you need anything."

Yusuf didn't smile, but he did incline his head. "The meds are taking care of my illness, and I'm past the worst, Zara. I'll keep eating and sleeping and going through the motions. One day, maybe it won't hurt so much."

There was so much I wanted to say, but the words stuck in my throat. I could only get out, "I'm sorry. It must be so hard."

His dark gaze held mine, sharp as grief even through

the comm screen. "It's a fatal wound that somehow doesn't kill you."

"I'm here, all right?" That was about all I could offer.

"Thank you," Yusuf said somberly. "You have a truly beautiful soul. No wonder Nadim loves you so much."

I didn't fully process those words until Yusuf cut the connection, left me looking at a blank screen.

Beautiful soul. Lord.

"I do, though," Nadim said then.

"Huh?"

"Love you. As I do starlight."

That was what kept him alive, literally, no big deal. The blush came on hard, and I put my face against the wall. Even through my closed eyes, I could sense the pulse of light in reaction to my proximity. I was still curled up there when Bea came, somewhat later.

"Zara, you okay?"

"Yusuf and Nadim were messing with me," I mumbled.

"We were not!" he protested. "He only said—"

Nadim would absolutely tell her a bunch of details she didn't need to know, so I distracted them both, quick. "Marko said his leg's better," I said. "And I had an actual convo with Yusuf, so that's progress. Oh, and I've got some prelim data on this rock that we're supposed to be visiting. You want to—"

Nadim interrupted me this time. "Zara." His tone had

shifted, gone flat and urgent. "Something is approaching."

I tapped the wall and said, "Viewport please," but I wasn't expecting what we got. Even from so far away, I caught a shimmer of movement, distant light on shiny black plates. It undulated like a snake. And in the distance, the drifting, dark bulk of a Leviathan—dead; I knew it in my guts. We'd seen that ship before, piloted by the parasites, clumsily chasing after us.

They were abandoning it because they'd identified new, fresh prey. The Phage had found us.

"Shit. Nadim, analyze trajectory!"

"They're trying to intersect," he confirmed.

His horror shivered through me, rooted in my spinal column. Bea rushed over to the console, but before she could call, Chao-Xing was already popping up on the monitor from Typhon. "You spotted them?"

"Evasive maneuvers," I suggested.

She gave me a stern look. "Elaborate."

Did Chao-Xing not have a solution, or did she want to test me? Whatever, I was ready. I wasn't a trainee anymore and I *did* have a plan. "We separate, take alternate routes to the coordinates. The Phage will respond one of two ways. One: they pick a target and chase. Two: they split up and do likewise. Scenario one is good for us because one Leviathan is safe, and the other just needs to be fast. Scenario two is good for us, because we've already seen that they're slower and stupider in smaller groups."

"Agreed," Chao-Xing said. "On my mark, break formation and don't look back, no matter what. We'll rendezvous on day three at mission coordinates."

Talk about a snap judgment.

"Got it." I turned to Bea, and by extension, Nadim, since he was always present. "Are you ready?"

She nodded, and he answered by making light contact, mind to mind. Dropping into a nearby chair, I reached for him, and in the next instant, we were Zadim. On some level, we could feel/hear the weird scratching of the Phage at the edges of space, and their noise ate away the melody of starsong, leaving only discord. We corkscrewed away from Typhon in a smooth motion, and the devourers hesitated only a microsecond before choosing us.

Smaller Leviathan, easier prey.

Quicksilver amusement raced through us, but there was no time for laughter. Bea was talking, but we couldn't focus on her words when we had to run. Leaping, full speed, away, on a burst of energy that rippled in a silver shock wave. From star to star we leapt, passing through the colors, swimming them.

The Phage had played this game before, but there was little they could do but try to surround us, and the farther they spread apart, the slower and stupider they became. They were deadly in the swarm, but we were faster than them, smarter than them. Zadim swam close to the gravity well of a black hole, and some portion of the individual swarm—a quarter, I thought—lost the battle with the monstrous pull, disappearing into atoms as they fought the strongest force in the universe. It was dangerous; Zadim felt the pull too, an almost irresistible wind that tried to blow us off course, but the Leviathan had sailed these stars for eternities, and we knew what to do, how to flip and turn and break the dark tide.

The other stars sang. The black hole had no music but an eerie whistle like a hole punched in reality, and a great, vast silence behind.

The Phage were nothing against it.

We led the enemy away from Typhon, with his bleak soul and festering wounds. We danced through irrational suns that lashed out with whips of fire, vaporizing dozens of the Phage; we ran just fast enough to keep them on our track, singing exultantly all the way. When the tattered remains of the Phage had followed us too far to change course, we glided into dark run: silent, shadowed, and their chaotic rage followed until it echoed to silence.

We'd lost them.

I had no clear sense that it was safe, except suddenly I was sitting in a chair instead of out among the stars. It always took me a few beats to reconcile myself to being human again, all this skin, these fingers and toes, and what were elbows for again? Bea knelt beside me, holding my hands, which had gone very cold.

"You were together for a long time," she said in a neutral tone.

It would've been completely fair if she'd asked me if that was prudent, after what had happened with Nadim and dark sleep, but we had the alarm now, and Nadim was more mature. He could handle a deep bond now. We both could.

"How . . ." I tried to get out, but my throat was bone dry. Bea put a glass of water in my hands; I guzzled it. "Sorry. How long?"

"Eight hours. I was getting ready to pull out the opera and sing you both back home. We need to establish some rules, you two, about how long you can do that without damaging yourselves." Bea looked so fiercely beautiful that she kind of took my breath away.

Damn. When I joined with Nadim, it felt like *seconds* to me. I had no ability to track time at all. No wonder I was stiff and cramped as hell. Getting up took a couple of tries. Bea was right. We needed guidelines. I couldn't imagine how frightening it was for her, waiting and watching. Hoping not to die. Hoping we didn't drift off together into the dark and leave her trapped.

"We've lost the Phage." Nadim sounded tired too. "We're lucky. If we had run into another swarm, they would have surrounded us and closed."

I hadn't thought of that, and the cold possibility of it

tensed up my muscles. "How many swarms are there?" Somehow, I'd thought it was just one. But the idea that there were *lots* out here, hiding in the dark, waiting to attack . . . that was terrifying. Running wasn't always an option. And we didn't have the weapons to really fight back effectively.

Nadim would be a rich source for them, gutted and filled with their swarming bodies, piloted like a zombie back to Typhon. I couldn't let that happen. Ever.

I sighed. "I'd hoped we lured them so far out they died." Was that even possible? How long could they drift out there, waiting to hear a victim? Maybe years. Maybe forever. "Bea? Help me find a good star for Nadim to refuel."

We spent what felt like too long orbiting a smallish star, but it fit Nadim's needs perfectly, and when we struck out on the return, he set a good course and speed that let him catch regular infusions of light from his sails. We wouldn't arrive tired, at least.

Another day or so, and we reached the coordinates without further issues. During the journey, I caught up on delicious food, used the combat sim, and generally hung out with Bea, Starcurrent, and Nadim. I was feeling good about our Phage victory, though I guessed it counted more as an escape. Typhon should be here soon, and then we could . . . what?

"I have no idea what's down there," I said. "We should take some readings."

Bea would probably always be the careful one in our partnership. "What if that activates the weapon that destroyed Bacia's other pigeons?"

"We dodge?" I was half kidding. "Seriously, we're good at that."

"Zara!" Since she was laughing, I figured that meant forgiveness.

"Our sensors shouldn't trigger anything," Nadim said. "I'm not receiving any signs of sentient life from the surface."

"Plants and animals, though?" Bea asked. "It looks like it has an atmosphere."

Nadim said, "Yes. Like Firstworld. In fact, I detect some similarities in structural style in the ruins present on planet."

Huh. Bacia had provided detailed criteria on what we were looking for, and no matter what they said, this artifact must come with antediluvian, automated defenses. Otherwise, what killed the other crews they'd sent?

Typhon arrived as I was wondering that. *Seems we're about to find out.*

FROM THE SUNG HISTORY OF THE ABYIN DOMMAS

*We swim safe in the knowledge of the death of gods,
free in our world, free in our minds. We sing of them
in darkness. We sing of them in silence. We sing in
warning of what is gone, and never to return. As we
are born singing, we must always sing of this, but only
to ourselves, to remember and watch for the rise of new
gods, false gods.*

Such must never come again upon us.

CHAPTER ELEVEN

Binding Hope

IT WOULD BE beyond risky to jump in the Hopper without scoping out the planet, so I got Nadim to try something . . . unusual. We found a relatively small chunk of rock—plenty of them floating around, moving according to the dictates of distant gravity. The one we chose was small, about the size of an old-school round football.

That was good, because we were about to score a goal with it.

"Okay," I told Nadim. "Push it when I tell you to. Don't smack it too hard, just enough to send it into the planet's atmosphere and let it do the rest."

"Ah," Nadim said, and I felt the blush of his satisfaction. "We are creating a decoy."

"Exactly. Let's see what happens when something enters the atmosphere."

Bea and I watched tensely as Nadim expertly maneuvered the asteroid into position, then with a gentle flick of his tail, sent it spinning down into the gravity well of the planet. It arced, but he'd perfectly judged the angles and force, and it made straight for the coordinates that Bacia had given us. It wasn't big enough to cause much damage, with the lower grav on this planet, so we weren't worried we'd destroy anything vital; if it made it to the surface, it would be a pebble after burning so much off.

There was a sudden red flash that seemed to emanate from both poles. It formed a solid red curve that spread in a heart-stopping second all the way around the planet. It lasted for two seconds, maybe, pulsing with power.

Then it was gone.

So was the asteroid.

I mouthed a word I didn't say, but man, did I feel it. That was some heavy planetary defense shield. Maybe it had been designed to destroy asteroids, exactly as it had just vaporized the one we'd thrown down there . . . or maybe it was designed to keep people like us out.

Either way: not good news.

"Try again," Bea said. "Let's see how long it can keep it up."

"What if it detects us and targets us?"

"Nadim has a stealth mode."

"I do," he said. "Perhaps this is an excellent time to use it."

"What about Typhon?"

"Tell him to stay high and be ready to dodge."

Typhon also had armor. Stealth would have to be our shield.

"Go for it," I said, and felt the shift. I probably wouldn't have, if we weren't so attuned now; it was like a whisper moved through me, and a chill. "Let's try another asteroid."

We kept up the slow bombardment, making sure to vary our location so that there was nothing for any targeting system to extrapolate and lock onto. We were ten tosses in when the line suddenly flickered out.

Nadim flicked asteroid eleven on its way. Intuition made me urge him to move, and we went to another spot to watch as A11 made a clean, burning arc all the way down. We tracked it to a tiny negligible impact on the surface.

"Well," I said. "That's looking pretty—"

A beam of pure red light suddenly burst out of both poles, but this time, it didn't form a protective shield around the planet. The two spears of power crossed at a specific point in space, then winked out.

"Uh, that was exactly where we launched Asteroid Eleven," Beatriz said. "It would have sliced Nadim in half if we hadn't been moving." She sounded blank, which I guess meant she was terrified. I would have been, if I wasn't so damn angry. I wanted to rip someone's eyeballs out.

"Nadim, keep evading. These batteries run down, they have to, because other Leviathan said they didn't have a problem. Maybe if we keep making them waste their shots, we can get down there while they're offline."

"I don't like that plan," Nadim said. "I will be fine, but you—"

"We've got to go down there. There's no other way."

It was surprising that Typhon and crew had stood by while we played asteroid ball, less so that Chao-Xing lost patience and buzzed our comm. "How do you see this game ending? We can't just wait and hope the defenses run down. They might be linked to a self-sustaining reactor, or—"

"You got a better idea?" I cut in.

"Maybe. I'm thinking that if Nadim and Typhon join forces with an asteroid barrage, it might be impossible for the weapon to evaporate that many projectiles."

"It's a start," I said, still chewing on the problem. "But I don't like putting Typhon at risk."

"I still don't like your odds of survival, even supposing you're right about defensive downtime." Nadim could probably produce stats relevant to our potential demise, but that wouldn't help me think.

Suddenly it hit me, and as it did, Bea brightened too.

We traded looks, then I asked, "Is it possible that we could modify the Hopper to add shielding like we did before?"

Chao-Xing conferred on her end, while I did the same with Bea and Starcurrent. In the end, our separate teams reunited with the consensus that while we could get shields operational, the Hopper didn't have the power to maintain them. We could take one hit coming in, no more, and if the planet shot at us as we were making our getaway, it would have to be evasive maneuvers all the way.

"It *might* work," said Marko, from somewhere behind Chao-Xing.

"This is ridiculous. Get over here for a proper meeting." I could tell C-X was about to complain, so I added, "You've still got gaps and repair work ongoing, right? Nadim is more hospitable."

Nobody could argue with the facts, so Chao-Xing, Marko, and Yusuf arrived a bit later. Their Hopper lined up beside ours in the docking bay, and we were waiting for them in Ops, so we could strategize. I didn't love the one-hit-and-out limitation of the shield, but we argued for a while about how we could get more power to the shuttle.

Midway through the meeting, Bea ran off to check our supplies, but we didn't have much in reserve. Her return prompted another round of bickering. I took the chance to connect with Yusuf.

"We could really use some genius innovation right

now," I said, nudging him. "You've been on the Journey longer than all of us. Help us figure out how to survive the round trip."

Something sparked in his dark eyes, maybe my use of the word *survive*. "What is the point?" he asked softly. "There is no defeating the Phage."

"Bullshit. You don't believe that. So, come on, help us out. Pull your weight." I gave him a little shove.

Unexpected, probably, since I'd tried to comfort him the last time we spoke, but this situation didn't allow me to be patient or gentle. And let's face it; that was never my strong point anyway. My natural angle was up in somebody's face.

He stumbled, but I had his full attention. "Don't test me, little girl."

"Or what? You'll kick my ass? Go ahead, try." I made a face guaranteed to enrage anyone who didn't love me, and sometimes it worked on them too. "Nah, there's no point, right? Life is pain. No ass-kicking from you, my man."

There was that spark again, a little brighter this time. A little hotter. "Let's see some respect. I saved your ass once already."

I shoved him again. Harder. "What about it? I'm sick of tiptoeing around you. We need you for more than grunt work. I saw your file, man. You're fucking brilliant, so *be brilliant* now."

It took a little more verbal pushing, two more shoves, until he finally swung at me. Anger was better than apathy, a lesson I'd learned hard down in the Zone. The punch was half-hearted and slow, and I dodged the hit easily and smacked him on the shoulder. "Been a while, huh?"

"What the hell are you doing?" Chao-Xing demanded.

"Getting Yusuf to engage. According to his Honors vids, he's an expert in robotics." While I was distracted, he nailed me a glancing blow on the chin, interrupting me good. I didn't quite bite my tongue, but it was close, and Nadim rumbled. Yusuf followed up with a roundhouse that was backed by real power, and I weaved around that one.

I held up my hands, but Yusuf kept swinging until Marko grabbed him, and then he started to fight in earnest. The altercation ended in a bunch of us holding him, more of a group hug than real restraint. After a few minutes of wild struggle, he kind of collapsed and screamed, then broke into such heartbreaking sobs that I could hardly bear to hear them.

"Meeting adjourned," Bea said. She was shaking her head. "Zara. Really?"

I stayed in the huddle until Yusuf calmed down. Starcurrent didn't have a single tentacle in the pile; ze was probably trying to figure out what kind of human custom this was. Good luck with that. Yusuf took several deep breaths and then he nodded to say he was good. Marko let go, and I followed suit. Chao-Xing's expression said she was deeply fed up, but we needed Yusuf's head in the game.

He got up and brushed back his locs, wearing a new expression of determination. "Let me see some schematics."

The ideas flew fast and furious, with Chao-Xing and Yusuf doing most of the talking. I could install the tech like a champ, but I'd never done my own designs down in the Zone. Closest I'd come was combining parts from different tech into something else. Maybe I *could* innovate, but this shit was what teams were all about. We were all valuable; everybody had a part to play. Hours later, after some tweaking and rerouting of systems, overclocking some shit, and adding juice, it looked like we could get the shield up to two-hit sustainability.

I took Yusuf's and C-X's ideas and brought them to life, making the upgrades piece by piece with a 3D printer and some honest sweat. Between this shield and the asteroid barrage, which we'd need coming and going, we had a chance now. *Time to pick teams.*

"We need the best pilot in the Hopper on this run," I said then. *Sorry, Bea.* "That's Chao-Xing. I'm on tech support and combat specialty. I've also got the best physical scores on board, I think. Anyone object to me going dirtside?"

Marko shook his head. "I'd be a liability if you need to move fast. I'll return to Typhon and coordinate with Bea-triz on the bombardment." Put that way, shit sounded so damn serious.

"Understood." To my relief, Bea didn't seem disappointed to be passed over for the ground team.

Or maybe I was the weird one for being excited about this? The adrenaline was already starting to kick in as I glanced between Yusuf and Starcurrent. "We could probably use a third. I'm willing to let you two decide. C-X?"

"That's fine, as long as we get moving soon."

"I'm . . . feeling a little better," Yusuf said. "But still perhaps not the best person to take along on a suicide mission."

He had a point. Plus, he wasn't at a hundred percent physically, either. Whoever we took with us needed to be fully committed to the mission. "Starcurrent?"

"Will assist with all tentacles."

"You heard the Abyin Dommas. Let's roll out."

Once Marko told Typhon that we wanted real bombardment, the Elder Leviathan got seriously into it, like we invented Leviathan football. He and Nadim rounded up a giant circling swarm of small asteroids, and one after another, started flicking them down toward the surface.

Chao-Xing piloted the Hopper out of Nadim, and we hovered out from the two Leviathan and watched the light show. It was horrifying, and at the same time, fascinating. Nadim and Typhon danced, constantly on the move, and the casual flicks of their tails or bumps of their bodies to send the asteroids tumbling were as precise as a ballet dancer's spins.

The defense shields below ruthlessly devoured every one of those rocks, a relentless sustained assault, and when it finally flickered and failed to make a full revolution around the planet, I slapped the back of C-X's seat. "Go, go, go!"

She pushed the Hopper to full speed. "We're going to hit the atmo hard," she warned. "Hang on!"

The Hopper shuddered when we encountered the first layers of the exosphere, and the shaking got worse as we hit the thermosphere. The shielding was burning off heat nicely, and creating an unnerving orange blaze at the nose of the craft; I couldn't see a thing through the forward screen, so I relied on instruments to tell us what was happening downstairs. There were energy bursts from both poles, but they were weak and erratic. The defenses were trying to come up, but after guarding against *eighty-seven* asteroids, the goalie was sitting down.

We needed to be on the ground before the time out was over. Chao-Xing pushed it, beelining for the site where Bacia had told us we'd find their precious trinket, but like me, C-X also had eyes on the readouts.

When I saw the spike, I yelled, "Evasive!" as she yanked the controls, starting a sudden, corkscrewing twist that threw us off course. We dodged a thick, red beam slicing at us from the north pole. The forward view had started to clear, so I got a heart-stopping look at the brute force of the thing as it sliced the air only about forty meters from our craft.

Chao-Xing promptly swung *back* toward the beam, which was so counterintuitive that I had to bite my lip to keep from swearing at her about it, but she was right; the beam only held for a second, then blinked out. She kept pushing the Hopper to its shaking limits, and we dove. Fast, faster, and when we dropped below the level where the last asteroid had been incinerated, I finally remembered to breathe.

We were coming in hot, and only a pilot like Chao-Xing could have pulled us up in time to settle on that gray ground in a flurry of dust and made it gentle as a soap bubble touching down. Chao-Xing hit the button to release restraints, but she kept the door shut as we both scanned the sensors.

"Atmo is good for us," I said. "Air's thin but breathable. Starcurrent?"

"I can adapt my filter quickly."

Nodding, I added, "Keep your helmets on. Even if the air isn't toxic, there might be poisonous pollen or invasive alien spores. Better not to risk it."

Chao-Xing was studying the scan results. "I'm not finding any significant life signs."

"Nothing big out there," I said. "Plants, some small animals."

She nodded. "Then let's get in and out, fast as we can."

"I hear you, but this is my area of expertise. Understand?"

Part of me expected her to argue, but she said, "You take point, then. Starcurrent, if anything about this place looks familiar, sing out."

I already knew that was the wrong phrase to use for a race of galactic musicians before ze said, "Sing what song?"

"Tell us what you recognize," I said. "Preferably not in song."

That got me a ruffle of tentacles. "I am quite proficient in—"

"We're moving."

The second I stepped foot on this nameless, alien world, all my defenses came right up. The air was thin, and the sounds rang flat and tinny; the lower grav was nice, but I'd have to watch myself.

Reminding myself to be careful of sudden movements, I checked the coordinates. We were just over 400 meters from Bacia's target, and the early scans had been right: there was a temple there, similar to what we'd found on Firstworld . . . only this one stood tall and straight, translucent shards of crystal reflecting the light of the dim sun. There was an eerie elegance to it, and as a wind blew past me, it cut itself on the crystal edges, and the whisper of its passage vibrated, pulsed, rang.

Frightening and beautiful, all at once.

"Slow down," I said. "Follow my lead. That means step where I step, and don't touch anything. Got it?"

Starcurrent flared tentacles in a *yes*. C-X nodded.

I led the way, one careful step after another. I was acutely aware that we had no way of knowing how long we had before the defense batteries recharged, but rushing would get our asses killed fast. I was looking for traps, signs, *anything* that looked wrong.

"Starcurrent," I said. "What can you tell me about this place? What was it built for?"

"Beauty," ze said. "Song. Life. Protection."

"Hang on. Tell me about that last one."

"Protection?"

"Yeah, because mostly in my world that means *against attacks*."

"No," ze said. "Protection *for*. Not *against*."

I wasn't sure what that meant, but I had the feeling ze was at a loss how to explain it more clearly, and this wasn't let's-guess-the-meaning time. This was go time, and I had to decide how to proceed.

"Is the temple going to protect against *us*?"

I got a bunch of lifted tentacles. I didn't need a translation matrix to know they meant *Your guess is as good as mine*. Great.

I nearly took a last step forward, onto a shimmering crystal walkway, and changed my mind at the last second.

"Can you sing to it?" I asked zim. I got a confused wiggle. "That's not a metaphor. I mean, really sing a song to calm this place down if it gets angry?"

"I can sing. Cannot guarantee effectiveness."

"Well, if something goes wrong, go full opera. I'm counting on you." I glanced back at Chao-Xing. "You watch our backs."

"I've got your six," she said softly.

Unexpectedly comforting.

With a deep breath, I set my boots on the pathway. Charcoal sand gritted under my feet. Silvery plants swayed nearby, standing three times my height, and they made a pleasant, muted chiming sound when the wind stirred them. They also let loose a continuous stream of faint pollen, but the breeze blew it away from us. This was exactly the kind of shit I'd worried about before. No telling what it would do to our lungs.

I didn't see anything animal-wise. Here, the ground was mostly barren, though I could see lusher forests of the big bell fronds farther off in the distance, and beyond that, a massive thrust of mountains. The sky was a peculiar color of purple, like permanent twilight, even though the sun was at its peak just now. This place would be *very* dark when the planet rotated. I wondered how fast that spin was, and how long we had before darkness fell. No matter how irrational the feeling, I didn't want to be here when the curtain of night came down.

I was five steps up the path when the bells from the fronds chimed louder. The wind hadn't increased; it still blew a faint, loose pressure across the temple's crystal. So, what was up with the bells?

"Starcurrent?" I asked, pointing at the bell fronds. "Familiar?"

"No," ze said. "I have never seen such. Very pretty."

"I wasn't asking for gardening tips—never mind." I was asking a pacifist creature to be paranoid. "Keep your eyes on them, okay?"

"Of course."

Six more steps, the bells clanging with intense volume, and I set my boot on the first step of the temple.

The *bong* that rang through the landscape was so loud that I nearly fell from the shock of it, and it took me a disordered second to realize that it was coming from the bell fronds. Starcurrent said, sharply, "Alarm!"

"No shit," I said, but that was drowned out by *another* sound that came all the way from the distant bell frond forest, and it was deafening even in this thin air. C-X clapped hands over her ears, and so did I; I was breathing too fast, suddenly, and the thin, dry air had a bitter smell now, discernable even through my helmet's filtration system. I didn't realize why until I saw a shimmer of silver in the air around us . . . and a silver cloud rolling across the empty space, coming from the bell frond forest.

"Defenses," Starcurrent said. "Interesting."

"*Interesting?* Try singing something!"

Ze did, a caterwauling grate of sound that made me wish I'd never asked. It didn't last long. "Unfortunately, there is no effect on the bell plants."

"What does this silver stuff do?"

Chao-Xing had her H2 out, and she was already scanning. "It isn't microbial," she said. "Or bacterial. It appears . . . inert."

Yeah, I didn't believe that for a second. The silver cloud billowed toward us, driven by a gust of wind that *had* to have been generated out of the forest, and even through the skinsuit I felt the sting. This wasn't pollen. It was needle-sharp *glass.*

I whipped out the triangular device that I'd killed the blob with, programmed it for the widest possible circumference. "Huddle up!" Beckoning the other two, I dropped the device between the three of us, and activated it with a quick tap of my foot.

Ten seconds later, a bubble of lacy gold burst out around us. Protection field. The silvery stuff that was already inside hung weightless in the air for a few seconds, then began drifting down to the bottom, like glitter in a snow globe. *Just in time.* Outside, the storm crashed over us, a constant, brutal hissing stream of cutting edges. We'd have been flayed in seconds, skinsuits and all, if we hadn't come prepped with defenses.

It felt like standing in the middle of a tornado, and none of us made a move, like we were instinctively trying to avoid the notice of an apex predator hungry for raw meat. Chao-Xing was breathing fast. So was I, and I felt the hot prickle of sweat breaking under my arms and breasts, on the back of my neck. It didn't run, because the skinsuit quickly wicked it away and tidily stored it for later recycled use, but *damn*. I'd been through some intense moments, but at least during those I could run, fight, *do something.*

This, I had to stand still for, and hope the shield held up. My nerves burned with the need to move, but I held on. Outside the bubble, the bonging of the bell fronds kept going, sending wave after wave of silver dust at us.

Nadim said, via the remote, "Zara! What's happening?" He sounded frantic. I could feel it, and he could probably feel my rising, frustrated panic too. "Are you all right?"

"We're waiting out a storm," I told him. I kept it calm outwardly, and tried to force that inside too. Like the defense system, the plants couldn't keep this up constantly, either.

"It's fainter," Starcurrent said. "The sound."

Ze was right. The bells were softer now, and I could see a faint hint of sky, temple, ground through the attacking silver haze. Definitely lessening.

It ended with a soft, almost mournful *bong*, and then the silver dust settled into a cloud and floated to the ground. I realized we'd been walking through this gray dust on the way here, the eroded remains of this sharp pollen, cracked and broken by time.

Our shield popped with a sudden, audible *snap*, and I flinched as a rain of silver filtered down. Nasty, but not capable of killing us now.

"Come on," I said. "Before it reloads."

FROM THE OFFICIAL PUBLICATION LOST LEGENDS
OF PAST STARS
*Source: Bruqvisz Planetary Database, licensed copy,
DNA coded*

Imagine, if you can: a past so distant even old stars were not yet born, galaxies still close together in their Great Migration, and at the center of all, gods. Beings unknown, of vast power and great cruelty, who did not create life but instead took from it to enhance their own empty souls, for souls they had not. Creatures of power and hunger.

This seems a distant fantasy, yet two species remain who record this as a real time. Perhaps these records are lies to entertain. Perhaps they are true but slander a race long dead without even ruins to record them. Yet the Abyin Dommas quietly sing of this, and the Biiyan, whose resonant temples lie in broken crystals everywhere. The Biiyan are a dying race. The Abyin Dommas speak not of the past to those beyond their oceans.

Who is to say if these gods existed?

Or if they may yet wander?

CHAPTER TWELVE

Binding Actions

CRUNCHING UP THE path to the pyramid or the temple, whatever the hell it was, gave me the chills. Felt like we were walking on layers of dust that came from centuries of death, and that . . . was probably true. If other crews had landed here, that powdered glass storm would've flayed them alive, left them to decompose into the dust beneath our feet.

This entire *world* was a graveyard.

No danger, my ass.

As we landed, I'd noticed that this site wasn't ruined like the temple on Firstworld, leaving us the damn fine question of how we were getting inside. We mounted a black stone ramp that could've been jet or obsidian or some alien mineral I didn't know about. Time had stripped the shine and pocked it with holes. Some spots seemed like natural erosion.

Others could be blast damage.

Moving slowly upward, I didn't see anything as obvious as tripwires or pressure plates . . . not that I'd be able to second-guess how an alien species would rig traps, anyway. I wished I could stop and feel a little of the majesty of this thing: a real space pyramid.

A walkway went all the way around at the base, and I led the parade; the pyramid had a silver side, a black side, and a white side, which baffled me. There was a puzzle to solve in those choices, and one of those options would offer us a way in. Three brains were better than one, so I started speculating aloud.

"There won't be human associations with these colors or material choices. Starcurrent, does your lore cover any of this?"

From Starcurrent's posture, ze was checking out the seemingly impenetrable structure as well. A flare of tentacles. "Black is the abyss from whence all life springs. White is the nothing to which we return when our songs fall silent. Silver is the walk-between, for those who see both worlds, beyond life and death."

"Huh, okay. Anyone have thoughts as to where the door would be, the one that *doesn't* kill us?"

We were standing in the open, close to the temple, but not near enough to activate murderbots, if there were any. I didn't like the delay, but survival meant taking our time, even when all my nerves were urging me to smash and grab. The cool heist-planning part of my brain knew fast action would be fatal. There was a reason people didn't return from here, so we had to be smart and careful, more than anyone who had come before.

Chao-Xing scanned the structure and bounced the data to Nadim to be analyzed with Bea's help. We got back a stream of numbers, but nothing that helped with the symbolism or pinpointed the safe pathway. Per those readings, there were corridors that led inward from all three sides.

"I don't like theoretical bullshit," C-X said finally. "How do we know having different colors on the sides isn't just . . . alien design choices? Colors mean so many things to different cultures, even back on Earth."

"Well, it's safe to say human influences haven't made it this far," I pointed out. "Let's go with Starcurrent's analysis. From that point of view, it would be too straightforward for safe passage to come through the life door—"

"Silver," Chao-Xing cut in. "Which stands for gray, the in-between. The safest path would be between the two extremes. Logically speaking, it should be at most half-danger, which gives us reasonable odds."

All things considered, that theory made as much sense as anything, and we couldn't hesitate until the sun vanished. The temp was already dropping, frosting my skinsuit. I glanced at Starcurrent. "All in favor?"

"Have always wanted to be a walker-between, as in our stories."

That settled it. Still stepping carefully, I headed for the silver side. My heart hammered in my ears as I listened for the next alarm, but we got all the way to the faint outline of a door without waking up the bell fronds again—or anything else that I could tell. Problem was, there wasn't a control panel here, no handle, no sensors that I could spot. This wasn't the same interface as on the Sliver. The door looked like normal glass, but according to our readings, it was denser, comparable to titanium in strength, and utilized an interwoven smart crystal matrix that wasn't in production anywhere anymore. All Nadim could say about it was that it was a variation of Leviathan tech, but far enough off that he didn't have any idea how to hack it.

Dead-world tech, beyond anything I'd seen or imagined.

I shivered. "Nadim, are you *sure* there's nobody inside this thing?"

"There are no life-form readings of any kind inside," he said. "And there are no life-forms above the rudimentary at all on this world. The plants are the dominant species."

I could see why.

From a safe distance, I tried breathing on the door, since that had worked back on the Sliver. Nothing. Working up my nerve, I touched it, but that only left a smear of fine dirt gritting the smooth surface. Chao-Xing went next, same outcome. Of course, we were both in skinsuits . . . I didn't want to take off my gloves, but I did it anyway.

No result.

We both stepped aside as Starcurrent's skinsuit—which I'd never figured out how ze put it on in the first place, with all those tendrils—suddenly was absorbed *into* zis body. Ze flattened several tentacles and filaments against the glass, and then ze *resonated* it. That was about the only word I had for what ze was doing. I felt the subharmonic rumble ze emitted, and it seemed to me that zis appendages quivered at the same frequency. An answering tone came from deep within the temple, eerie as hell. What followed didn't sound like language—just bass rumbles and high-pitched hisses—but Starcurrent was flushed with triumph and zis head ruff was standing up when ze turned to us.

"It says, 'Welcome, singer in the deep, you are known.'"

I stared. "You mean, it knows *you*? Personally?"

"No. Only my people. I believe it is being polite." Since Starcurrent had said zis people had stories about the ruins, it tracked that ze could interface with this tech and we couldn't. Maybe these ancient aliens had kept tabs on the

Abyin Dommas for some reason.

"Okay," Chao-Xing said. "Carry on."

I wasn't sure I was totally down with that, but I nodded.

Starcurrent sang to the door a little more. A lot of it I couldn't hear at all, just a distant sense of vibration; ze was singing in ranges that human ears couldn't hear, I supposed. The occasional bass rumbles startled me. When the song moved into frequencies I *could* hear, it sounded heartbreakingly beautiful, and lonely, and incredibly alien.

Starcurrent went quiet, and the door slid up, showering silvery dust.

"Great work," I said to Starcurrent, who gave me four tentacles up as zis skinsuit formed again. Having a built-in seemed like a hell of a time-saver.

A hiss of stale air wafted over us, and C-X was all over it, scanning like a pro.

"Same mix as before?" Even if it was, my helmet was staying on. In vids, there was always some dumbass who was like, "The air is breathable!" and stripped off his gear without running necessary tests. Hell, even if the lung cocktail was breathable, it didn't mean there weren't spores that could grow into chest-bursting monsters inside your torso.

Vid monsters aside, we could be allergic to a thousand things here, and I wasn't about to succumb to anaphylactic shock.

"No new toxins or pollutants. Zara, take the lead."

I flashed Chao-Xing a cocky grin and a high sign. "Well, I've kept us alive this long. Go, Team Z."

"Mind on the mission." She was terse, as well she might be. We'd gotten this far. Lots of others might have too, and still ended up as dust under our feet. I needed to stay focused.

The gray corridor ahead was featureless, dull crystal lined with shards like the ones that made music on First-world. They didn't react to our passing, and I damn sure wasn't going to ask the Abyin Dommas to sing again; no telling what that would do inside here. Prelim scans showed a maze of sharp turns that led to an open space deeper in.

I kept my eyes on my H2 and let it do the analysis, and it immediately lit up with an alert when it detected a difference in the crystalline structure running beneath us. Crouching, I checked the floor and said, "These might be pressure plates."

I didn't dare step on one, but I lightly touched a fingertip down. Nothing. Still, better not to risk it, so we skirted them as we pushed deeper. Maybe because the place had recognized Starcurrent, we were logged as permissible visitors? I wished I had asked Bacia if any of the other teams had included an Abyin Dommas; that info could have helped me make some educated guesses.

I should have asked for full records on *all* the other teams, but I figured they would have said no regardless. Fine. I was used to doing without, and that included info too.

We got through the maze without casualties, and I let out a heavy sigh of relief that probably wasn't warranted. My whole damn spine was tight. This feeling hung heavy, dark and dreary. Pervasive dread. Probably came from breathing in filtered dead-people dust.

Not helping, brain.

Turning in a slow circle, I took in the heart of this ancient, alien temple, an open space filled with more of the shining crystal. It also ringed us on all sides. The shards marched up the walls, vanishing into a vast, shadowed expanse. Given how rough I'd come up, this was beautiful, but I couldn't shake the thought that the shards also looked like weapons poised for launch. Dropped with enough velocity from the upper reaches? Instant impalement.

I thought of Bea, and the way she'd so gloriously sung to make the crystals light up . . . but maybe that wasn't a *good* thing here. Human voices might trigger something worse than "Welcome, you are known."

But hey, we had an honored guest. "Starcurrent, stay ready to sing if shit goes sideways."

"Always ready," ze said. "Is interesting."

Starcurrent had an ice-cold view of *interesting*, because

I was freaked the hell out. My skin was crawling under my suit, and I wanted to wash all this silver shit off me. Who knew what the long-term effects of the stuff were? I checked the coordinates Bacia had given us. According to that data, we were right on top of whatever they wanted so bad. It was cold enough that I could see my breath.

I looked down. Under us, beneath the crystal, curled a shape. I couldn't tell what it was at first . . . it was too small to be a ship, and too big to be an artifact.

It took me a long few seconds to let the shape seep into my brain, and just as it did, Chao-Xing said, in a voice as tight as a bowstring, "Bacia wants us to rob a grave."

"Fuck," said Starcurrent.

Or, at least, that was how the translation matrix interpreted the strangled sound ze made.

Both Chao-Xing and I were frozen, staring at the cloudy mass beneath our feet. Now that I was looking down, I could see sigils etched in the floor, but I couldn't read them.

"Nadim? Anything in your database like this?" Worth a shot.

"It's like the glyphs from Firstworld," he said after a brief delay. "But there are some minute differences that may affect nuance."

"Give us the big picture," Chao-Xing said.

"'Here rests the fallen god-king, life-eater, song-swallower. Tread not upon him; never speak his name. Let him return to dust and may the silence never be broken. Death comes for any who forsake the way.'"

"This sounds like a damn Egyptian tomb curse," I said, as the chills got worse. Normally I wasn't one to say stop in the face of adventure, but . . . "Are we sure we should be messing with this? You know, certain doom. Death hexes."

"Do not wish to raise the dead," Starcurrent said. Sounded sensible.

"You *had* to put it that way," Chao-Xing muttered. "There's no other way for us to gear up against the Phage. And we know they're a real threat."

I saw it too. Letting visceral fear keep us from helping our Leviathan? I wasn't about to walk away from that fight.

With a sigh, I said, "It has to be you, Starcurrent. We need you to open the tomb. We don't know what will happen, so when it opens, you grab whatever's in there and run for the exit. You're the fastest. Don't wait for us, just *move*; get the goods out of here."

"Do not approve of this strategy," ze said.

Chao-Xing met my gaze, and I read a certain understanding in her dark eyes. "She's right. As long as you get out, Nadim and Typhon will be safe. This is . . . an acceptable risk."

What she meant was, we were tolerable collateral damage, when you weighed us against the fate of the Leviathan.

I didn't have a smile in me for this moment, but I did offer a firm nod, silently agreeing with her judgment.

"Zara, no!" The sharp cry came from Nadim on my remote.

There was no time to argue. With real regret, I whispered, "Sorry," and switched off the link unit. If this shit went bad—and it might—Nadim didn't need to see it live. He'd feel it, and *that* was bad enough. This . . . this was the best way for me to protect him. Bea would have to help him get through this.

Bracing myself, I said to Starcurrent, "Sing that thing open. It's go time."

It wasn't quite that simple, of course. Starcurrent began singing, and the shards glowed a soft amber, then rippled with a rainbow of colors. Like being trapped inside a prism . . . only the flickering light took on an ominous rhythm. A warning strobe, I figured. Starcurrent must have known that too, because zis tendrils shook, flared, and turned bright red at the ends.

Ze sang zis heart out, and I heard the crystals singing back. It was like a duet, an operatic argument, and then . . .

Then the floor melted in a square, like honey on a hot plate. The shards flared brighter than my eyes could stand, and I looked away, squeezing my eyes shut. Heavy vibration shook through me, and that deep buzz crawled up from the soles of my feet through every bone in my body.

"Going!" Starcurrent shouted, and I blinked away after-images. Ze was a blur of movement now, and when I finally had unobstructed vision again, ze was already out of the pit, hauling the curled-up body wrapped in a profusion of tentacles. Ze moved like lightning when ze needed to, and when I blinked again ze was *gone*, even as the walls and ceiling began to rumble without benefit of zis singing.

Didn't sound happy.

And then the lights went out completely.

Chao-Xing instantly triggered the emergency glow strips embedded in her skinsuit, meant for just this kind of problem, but everything looked the same now, three paths to the exit and no visible clue which one was the *right* one. Which way had Starcurrent headed? I thought I knew, but a mistake might be deadly. My head hurt from the flashing lights and the rumbling. Was I getting enough oxygen? *I hope my suit's not compromised.* My feet felt heavy.

"Zara!" Chao-Xing shouted at me, and I snapped back into the moment. "This way!"

We raced through the maze that led out the silver between-life-and-death door, and as we did, something knife-edged and as long as my arm slipped out of the darkness above us without even a whisper. A crystal shard, a monster of one with edges sharp enough to slice titanium. I dodged, gasping, and it hit the floor behind us and stuck point-first, vibrating there.

A second later, a whole *forest* of them dropped, and if we'd still been standing there we'd have been cut to ribbons.

We made it into the tunnel. The shards on the walls were dark, and more than big enough to do real damage if they were fired at us. I stared at them, forgot to watch my feet.

"Down!" Chao-Xing shouted, and tackled me to be sure I did it. We hit the gritty floor hard, and I barely avoided getting a crystal in my skull as it fired into the opposite wall.

We had to *stay* down, because the crystals kept breaking loose and shooting across our heads. I inched forward and hit *another* pressure plate.

The deluge paused. Something clicked in my head. "Get off me! I think we can control the flow," I shouted, and rolled to my feet, keeping my weight on the plate. "This is an off switch! Hit the next one while I'm on it!"

In answer, Chao-Xing leapt for the next plate and landed like a cat, crouched, staring at the shards and ready to drop if she had to. I could hear both our breaths in the silence. *No shit, we're both scared to death.* "Okay," I said. "So, in theory, if you stay on *that* one, I can jump ahead of you to the next one. We can leapfrog through."

"Don't miss," she said.

"Obviously."

I balanced. It was a long jump, and no way to build up momentum; this would all be down to precision and strength. Coiling all the power in my legs, I released it in an explosive move that sent me arcing past Chao-Xing. *Too much, too much, damn it . . .* But I landed at the far edge of the plate, nearly overbalanced, and settled back on my heels just in time. I crouched and took a minute.

"Ready?" Chao-Xing asked.

"Go."

She leapt, landed with perfect balance. My thighs burned. I'd never trained for the long jump, but I'd been rebounding off objects in the Zone for years. Maybe that was what I needed—a new angle of approach. I took two steps back on my plate and used the wall to kick off as I went sideways and back out again. This time, I landed square on the tile, and I grinned at Chao-Xing like this was a game we were playing.

"Nice," she said.

But I noticed she didn't try to copy my trick. Back and forth, we made the jumps, regular as a pendulum. Our timing had to be spot-on as we angled and arced past each other; the slightest misstep would bring down a cutting crystal rain. My skin stung from a hundred tiny slices; the silver dust was constantly abrading our skinsuits, and I could feel it working its way through. Chao-Xing couldn't feel any better, but her progress stayed steady.

In the maze, it was hard to see how far we'd come. I had a feeling these plates were designed for a much larger creature that could hit each one in a long stride. Bacia's people were huge, I remembered. It seemed like for human-sized visitors, two was the minimum number required for survival, preferably with an Abyin Dommas to sing for entry and make a quick getaway.

"I'm so tired," I wheezed, rubbing a cramp from my calf.

At least we could rest between jumps. I squatted, head between my knees, and tried not to imagine how freaked Nadim must be. Chao-Xing gave me about sixty seconds before signaling with a snap of her fingers. "If we wait too long, we'll freeze up."

"Muscles or emotions?" The joke fell flat since she didn't smile.

"Both. You're up, Zara."

This next leap would push us around the corner. Mustering my strength, I hit the wall hard and almost overshot the plate. My heels hit the edge, and I scrambled backward and caught myself on my hands. Enough weight, good, but now I was even shakier. Chao-Xing soared past me, but her grace was fraying, and her breathing had ragged edges when she stumbled to one knee. There was no way in hell Marko could've run this gauntlet with his bum leg.

From here, though, I could see the distant doorway, a rectangle of twilight against all the crystal that wanted to be our tomb. Five more jumps, max. *You can do this. Nadim and Bea are waiting.* This time, I didn't need Chao-Xing to prod me. Despite my aching joints, I stood on my own, straightened my shoulders, and launched.

Solid landing. Back and forth we went, gathering momentum like aerial dancers who performed on silken scarves. I swore Chao-Xing even added some twirl as we got closer to the exit, so close to safety I could taste it. On my last leap, my ankle bent sideways, and I screamed. The crystal came at me so fast, but Chao-Xing moved like a mother lion, more of a dive than the swan-like ballet leaps she'd been doing, and she hit me with her full weight. We went rolling together, as one, toward the doorway with shards raining down around us.

The frantic motion saved us from impalement. We were both bleeding, but together, we managed to pull each other upright. A few steps, and then Starcurrent was there, supporting both of us with all zis tentacles. I'd first registered the strength of the Abyin Dommas when one came aboard to help Nadim out of dark sleep, but now I appreciated how helpful that power could be.

"You stowed our cargo?" Chao-Xing managed to ask.

"Secured. Returned to aid companions."

"Thanks," I said.

We waited out the silver rain of pollen, and once it was a drifting mist, we limped toward the Hopper, and I activated my remote link with Nadim. He was immediately talking. "Zara! Do you hear me? Starcurrent said—"

"We're fine," I cut in. "Both Chao-Xing and I have minor injuries, no more. We'll be home soon."

"Don't ever do that again." He sounded furious.

"Nadim—"

"I mean it. Once, you said I'm not a child, so I shouldn't trust everything the Elders say, but if I'm *not* a child, then you must trust me. You think you're protecting me, but not knowing is worse, and that is not a choice you should make *for* me."

Chagrin cut through the network of pain. I had a lot of small aches, some burning slices, but he was right. "I hear you, and I'm sorry. Let's talk about it more when I get back."

"Fine," he snapped.

Oh, he is not *fine.*

Neither was I, totally, but we were all alive, having survived that death trap of an alien temple, so there was no quelling the satisfaction as I climbed into the Hopper. Starcurrent got in back, solicitous due to our numerous flesh wounds, I assumed. As Chao-Xing got in, I said, "Thanks."

"You would've done the same for me."

[unreadable due to damage]

. . . history shall not repeat. I have given sanctuary and safety to many hunted beings here; some races are extinct beyond these tiers. I have built an empire, and I am safe. Should my lineage be revealed, many of those beyond our shields would seek to eradicate me. What I do here I do for protection. For preservation. I defend what I am, and I defend those who take refuge here.

No gods shall walk my space. Yet I must find a god to learn how to destroy one.

CHAPTER THIRTEEN

Binding Pain

I LEANED FORWARD in my seat and groaned. My skinsuit was shredded here and there, but thankfully, the Hopper had its own oxygen supply. Warm blood trickled down my lower back and my upper thigh. No gushers, so it wasn't life-threatening, but I could use a minute with EMITU when we got back. I wasn't about to jinx us with the word *if*. After what we'd been through on this dead world, I had full confidence in Chao-Xing and Starcurrent.

Something was bothering me, though. The shimmer of discomfort made it hard for me to focus as Chao-Xing took us up. This low, the space lasers shouldn't be an issue, but . . .

If there was no life on this planet, what was directing the weaponry?

That question popped into my head as something exploded directly below us, rocking the Hopper. Chao-Xing was already taking evasive action, and Starcurrent had three tentacles wrapped around the seats for additional support.

As copilot, I had to figure out what the hell was after us. I scrambled to adjust the screens, checking, checking. Still no life signs. "Drone gunners, a damn legion of them, coming fast and hot."

There was the answer to my question. If there was no life, there had to be an AI of some kind with the infinite directive to protect this place. It was also probably in charge of maintaining the power source that ran the lasers, and there must have been a fully automated facility producing bots, some for repairs and upkeep, and these ships—

They were like nothing I'd ever seen. Small and maneuverable, but enough firepower to rock the Hopper even when they missed. Chao-Xing swore as she swung us left and right, evading fire while trying to gain altitude. The ride was choppy as hell, and we had no weapons. I scrambled for the comm.

"Nadim, we've got bogeys. Can you take some out by playing some asteroid ball?" My voice sounded shaky, and I hated that it did.

"On it, Zara." He seemed calm, thankfully.

Chao-Xing nodded in my direction. "Good thinking. Typhon's cannons are too massive for such small targets."

Yeah, chances were he'd blow us up too if he fired. Plus, we had no idea what else would swarm after us if he bombed the surface. Our mission was to escape this charnel house, not nuke it to cinders from space. A sudden flash of orange, and the Hopper shuddered, like the vehicle had been tased.

"Direct hit." Starcurrent didn't seem alarmed, though our shield would only hold for one more strike.

Per the screen, we still had hundreds of gunner drones after us, and some might have ballistic weapons. Our shield couldn't stop actual projectiles. My stomach heaved as C-X swooped us up and down, into cloud cover and out of it, but these damn things had expert tracking protocols.

"I can't shake them," she said.

"Keep climbing. And trust Nadim."

As I said that, the asteroid storm fell, balls of fire plummeting from on high, and they impacted behind us, taking out a vast swath of gunner drones. I could hear the booms as they collided, and others wheeled out of control, smashing into more units and creating a fireball that blazed all over our screens. Our temp gauge went insane, and I activated the cooling burst meant to settle the engines in case of a fire.

"Good," said Starcurrent.

We kept climbing, gaining altitude, and a few drone ships tried to pursue, but they crumpled and fell like Icarus and his wings of wax as they soared too high. *Designed for close combat,* I thought. The red lasers activated as we raced away from the planet, and I could almost feel the burn slicing through the Hopper as the beam swung toward us.

Chao-Xing did everything a human could, but the Hopper had no more to give, and it was already smoking. Red death zapped us, but the shield thrummed with its own energy, popped and gave just as we slid away from full impact. The shot sparked the tail end, shearing off the Hopper's dorsal plating, and now we had smoke in the cabin as well.

Shit. If the planet had fried our cargo in a last-ditch vindictive play, we were so boned with Bacia. Starcurrent scrambled for the extinguisher as the automated system warned us, "Exterior compromised. Life support failing."

We had half an hour of breathable air with the Hopper all jacked up.

It wouldn't take us that long to get to safety—and Nadim. I hoped.

With sheer willpower and a lot of cussing, Chao-Xing got us relatively close before the engines gave completely. Now we were adrift, floating like space flotsam, but thankfully, we were above the planet's atmosphere, within Nadim's reach. I almost cried when I spotted him on-screen, his graceful lines, the curve of his tail. Nadim took us in carefully, knowing we had no propulsion or steering. The Hopper hit the docking bay hard, even so. We bounced and slid with a scrape of metal.

Hopefully that didn't hurt him.

"Zara?"

"We're here. We're good." Okay, not so much, but we were all alive, which meant we'd beaten the damn odds.

I stumbled out of the wrecked shuttle to find it still steaming, missing part of the back end, and singed all to hell, despite the makeshift shielding. Those installations were worse than blown: black as onyx and half-melted too. This Hopper looked like it had flown to hell and back, which wasn't entirely inaccurate.

I tried to walk, and the ankle I'd wrenched in the temple of doom gave completely. I didn't fall, but only because a big form swept in before I could hit the deck.

Yusuf caught me and swung me up in his arms, bridal style. Intellectually, I knew he was fine, but my heart didn't flutter; I didn't hit him, either. He was just transporting me to the medbay, nothing more; I could read a man well enough to be sure of that. Since he was older, I might come to see him as a big brother, given time.

"What're you doing here?" I asked him. "I thought you were on Typhon!"

"I was," he said. "Marko sent me in case trouble followed you home. You have a certain affinity for complications, and I'm not bad in a fight."

I could believe that. Man was *solid*.

As we left, I heard Chao-Xing giving orders to Starcurrent about securing the cargo. First time I ever knew an Abyin Dommas to lose zis patience. "Worry about yourself, Zhang Chao-Xing. Injuries first, goods second."

Bea was waiting in medical with EMITU. Yusuf settled me in the treatment chair and said, "I'm glad you all made it back in one piece."

My laugh meant I wasn't sure if my condition qualified, but when he smiled back, I was *so* glad we'd pulled him and Starcurrent out of their lifepods. To know these two were alive because of us? That was an awesome feeling. Even if I was currently a mess, I could see that being over with Typhon had—weirdly enough—given Yusuf something that not even Nadim had been able to provide: purpose. Like me, Yusuf had a warrior's heart.

Bea shooed the man out then. And cast an appalled glance over me. "Look at you. It will take days for your skinsuit to repair! And these cuts . . ."

"Sorry." Rote response, as she helped peel me out of my gear, because I was trying to understand where this sudden flare of pain was coming from. Maybe adrenaline had iced it out until now?

The smell of copper nearly overwhelmed me, and I went lightheaded when I saw the scope of damage to my skin. So many red slices on the brown, smeared and trickling, and that didn't even encompass the wounds I could feel but not see.

"How are you still conscious?" EMITU asked. "This is significant blood loss, Zara Cole. Did you fight a brood of vampires?"

"How do you know about vampires? Is that critical medical info?"

"Even a medical unit has hobbies."

"Well, sure, could have been vampires," I mumbled. "Feels like it." No wonder I'd been so dizzy; it was a damn miracle I hadn't dropped back in the temple.

First, I got some quality pain meds, so that I tingled and then went numb. I also cared a lot less what was happening to my naked body—had to be naked, as that sharp silvery dust had gotten *everywhere* and needed to be removed before it cut me even more. Some of my slashes had to be laser-sealed; others EMITU treated with the flesh-caulk sealant he'd put on my hands before, but I was too muzzy and dreaming to really be sure what the autodoc was doing.

The meds wore off before he finished, though. My head got right again, and I looked down at my ankle, now tightly wrapped in a flex-cast. "Is it broken?"

"Snapped like a chicken's neck," EMITU said cheerfully. "Congratulations on a sincerely painful injury."

"Well, damn."

"I got your robe," Bea said. "And EMITU and I gave you a thorough bed-bathing while you were out. It'll be hard for you to shower for a day or two."

"Thanks." I smiled up at her.

To my surprise, she hugged me tight, gentle and careful, but with more affection than it felt like I'd gotten my entire life. Hesitantly I put my hands on her back. "Bea?"

"I was scared too," she whispered, nuzzling her soft cheek against mine. "When you cut Nadim off, you shut me out too. We don't want to lose you, Zara. Neither of us does."

Damn if she didn't make me tear up, and I tried to blink them back, but a few trickled out anyway. "I'm sorry. I really am."

Maybe I would've said something more, something sweet, but EMITU sure knew how to ruin the moment. "Get a room!"

I let out a snuffled laugh and so did Bea. We took the hint; she helped me to my quarters, and I hobbled to the bed. "Where's Chao-Xing? Is she okay?"

"Yusuf took her back in their Hopper. There was no waiting in their medbay, so . . ."

Yeah, that made sense. "You know I appreciate you,

right?" I wanted to say that she was downright precious, but I couldn't quite get the words out yet, and I was *so* tired.

"Same here," she said. "You're always willing to risk yourself, but I've got to say, I've had just about enough of seeing you hurt."

Once she left, I rolled off the bed onto the floor in movements so slow, I was sure I looked elderly. But I wanted my palms and soles on Nadim because I had some serious amends to make. He hadn't said much since we got back, and I'd promised we would talk later. I owed him that conversation before passing out.

"Nadim?" I made contact, but the lights stayed off.

In fact, it took a few minutes for him to answer. "Yes, Zara."

"Guess you're pretty mad." That was a statement, not a question.

"Angry? Yes. And hurt, as well. Did you think . . . *what* exactly did you think I would do if something happened to you down there?"

"I don't know," I said miserably. "I just didn't want you to be hurt."

"If something happens to you, Zara, I will be *eviscerated*. It will be as if my sun has gone out, do you understand? I would not plummet to my death because I must care for Beatriz. She is my singer, and I would live on for her. But without you, there would be an eternal darkness in me, like you've seen in Typhon. And for you to deny me your last moments, even a final glimpse of you to carry into the dark? That is heartless."

I imagined it then: Nadim, like Typhon, trapped in mourning throughout the centuries, missing me, wanting me, denied even the last touch with me, and I lost it. The tears I couldn't give completely to Bea in the medbay scalded my cheeks. The pain was too big; I couldn't swallow it down. It hammered the breath out of me.

My words came out choppy, staccato with sobs I was trying to hold in. "I'm sorry, all right? I messed up big. I won't ever do it again. I promise. Not for any reason." I cried into the curve of my arm, and I was sure Nadim could feel those tears, dripping slowly onto the floor, part of him now as they dried. My salt on his skin. "Forgive me, please? It's been a shitty day for me too."

"I know," he said softly. "I didn't mean for you to suffer."

The lights came on then, all around me, so my body was haloed in that brightness, and I could feel the surface warming where we touched. I played Nadim with my fingertips, painting in light, sweet colors that vibrated with life.

Yeah, we're both here. We're together.

That had to be enough. When we got back to the Sliver, we'd be gearing up for war. Against the Phage. Nobody knew how the hell *that* would turn out. I put my cheek against Nadim and held on, because this one perfect moment might need to last a lifetime.

I felt him humming, deep inside, in frequencies that soothed something in me. A lullaby, giving me permission to sleep safe and dream of drinking sunlight.

I got up to find an argument in progress. Not Bea and Starcurrent, but Starcurrent and—via the comms—Marko. I limped in—the ankle was going to be a pain in my ass—and draped myself on the couch as I spectated. I had coffee and a doughnut with sprinkles—not the same as a delicious deep-fried one, but close enough for my sweet tooth.

As ze quarreled with Marko, Starcurrent's tentacles went rainbow. I didn't know what rainbow meant, but it couldn't be good, because ze was saying, "—not recommended to move it! Have secured it in an armored safehold. Nadim grew new materials specifically for this purpose, to ensure no danger exists!"

"Nadim?" I kept it to a low whisper. "What are we upset about?"

"Typhon wishes us to surrender the body to him."

"And . . . we don't want that?"

"Typhon is still healing," Nadim said. "I am stronger. Therefore, it's a more logical choice for me to monitor the cargo."

"Yeah, but he's got a point. He's equipped with a shitload of interior defenses you don't have. If this body turns out to be not-so-dead . . ."

"All scans show it to be an inert corpse, long deceased."

I'd never really gotten a good look at the thing. I supposed I should, but right now I was basking in the sweet glow of not giving a damn. If it was dead, fine, be dead all day.

"You want me to step in and tell Typhon to—"

"No." Nadim's warmth curled around me like a blanket, encouraging me to stay where I was. "Starcurrent is more than capable of handling this zimself."

"Poor Marko," I said. "I've never seen Starcurrent go full rainbow."

It took longer than I expected, but Starcurrent finally got Marko to stand down. Ze settled down to normal bioluminescent flashes, like firefly sparks going off under zis skin. It was a good look. "Your friend is very stubborn," ze said to me, and undulated into a chair, tentacles dangling. "Confess not to understand why humans take such risks when it is unnecessary to do so."

"We jump off high bridges with rubber bands attached," I mumbled around a mouthful of chocolate icing and bread. "For fun. We're weird. But I think this was more about Typhon wanting to protect Nadim."

"Ah. Yes," Starcurrent said, and waved some tendrils.

"This I understand. Same among my people, instinct to protect the smaller and more fragile. Is why I like you."

I nearly snorted hot coffee. I hadn't been called small or fragile in a long time. I'd been a strong, wiry kid, and the Zone had put muscles on my thin frame. "Well, thanks," I said, because I didn't go around offending people *every* day. "I like you too, Starcurrent. That was some quality snatch-and-grab work you did down there. Without you, we'd never have made it."

Zis tendrils gently waved the compliment away. "Would like to take the opportunity to take samples from the body," ze said. "Is acceptable to you?"

Hell no, I wanted to say, but ze seemed so eager that I found myself saying, "If you think it's safe. But only if you're sure."

"Is inert," ze said. "Will be careful. I have seen the vids in your library, Zara."

"Even the scary ones?"

"For a species with so little experience of the galaxy, your vision of it is one of fear." Ze studied me for a few seconds, all zis tentacles gone quiet. "You should hope more, Zara."

"Yeah, well, I'll hope when I have reason to. And maybe our paranoia prepped us for space better than you think. The Phage aren't misunderstood. They're a plague."

"Acknowledged, am ill-equipped to understand," Starcurrent said. "Perhaps the Leviathan Elders were wiser than even they knew, to bring such a race as yours to us now."

I finished my treat. Every bite brought back bittersweet memories . . . doughnuts were something that could be made cheap in the Zone, fried up in old pots over busted camp stoves, slathered with sugary chocolate made from melted-down fancies from New Detroit. Sprinkles? Those were a luxury. The taste took me back to the streets, and I realized how far I'd run from them this time.

All the way to the stars.

"Shall be about my work," Starcurrent said, and slid out of the seat in a writhing rush. "Zara? Should rest."

"I'm fine," I said, and licked my fingers. Never let good icing go to waste. "A little blood loss? Nothing much. But hey, while we're on it—thank you."

Starcurrent's fringes flared a delighted pink, but ze just waved a few of them and slithered off, quickly.

I drank the rest of my coffee and said to Nadim, "I'll be with Starcurrent."

Nadim's reply came tinged with concern. "Why?"

"Because I want to see a dead god-king. Not very often you get *that* chance."

That wasn't the reason, and he knew it, but we both pretended it was. I stopped by the armory and picked out a discreet, high-powered weapon to carry on my hip. I wasn't sure what would stop a god-king . . . probably nothing, but I felt better for having it.

I clipped my trusty personal defense shield to my belt too. Damn thing worked just fine. We'd have been dead in five minutes down on that rotten world without it.

Beatriz found me as I trailed Starcurrent to the newly created secure storage. She fell into step with my limp. "What are we doing?"

"*I'm* going to keep an eye on Starcurrent and zis badass science project."

"Because you're all the backup anyone needs, even when you're hurt." Beatriz sighed at me and plucked the rifle from my hands. "Nadim, you'll alert us if anything weird happens, right?"

"Yes," he said. "Since I can't keep either of you from doing this, any more than I can Starcurrent."

I tried to reassure him. "We'll be okay. You said it yourself: the king is dead."

"What worries me," Bea said, "is what usually follows when people say that."

"Yeah." I tested the weight of the personal shield on my belt. "Long live the king."

Like the rest of Nadim's human-occupied interior, the special, secure cargo hold was a comfortable temperature. Honestly, it gave me the creeps to be hauling this carcass; I didn't want this sort of twisted power anywhere near those I cared about. Starcurrent opened the doors with a code that I didn't bother to memorize. After I satisfied my curiosity, I would *not* be coming back.

With a peculiar reverence, Starcurrent unwrapped the corpse. Then I got my first good look at what we'd dragged out of that temple, and my brain couldn't handle it. *Look away!* it must have ordered, because before I could even resolve what I was seeing, I was staring at a safe, blank, metallic wall. Beside me, Bea had turned away, hands over her face.

Come on, I told myself. *You've seen some shit.*

I made myself turn my head, slowly, trying to bring just a little into focus at a time. That wasn't so bad. Grayish flesh that looked thick as rubber. I was looking at . . . what? An appendage? Hand, foot, tongue? No idea. The god-king they'd sunk beneath a floor and protected with traps . . . it looked like a dozen of the universe's worst nightmares had been melted together, and formed something even worse . . . but when I finally brought the whole creature into view, that wasn't what I saw *at all*.

I hadn't averted my eyes because it was so horrible. I'd done it because it was too . . . too *beautiful*. That was what my brain kept telling me, anyway, but my eyes reported something entirely different. *Nightmare*, they insisted. *Miracle*, my brain interpreted. The dissonance made me feel sick, but I held on, staring at the thing. I remembered

269

how Bacia had overwhelmed us with their presence. This creature, even dead, had the same lingering, slick charm that convinced you something was wonderful when it was foul.

Dead, though, it couldn't quite pull it off. Makeup on a nightmare only made it more of a nightmare.

Starcurrent seemed unaffected, but then again, I guess ze would be; after all, ze'd had to wrap tentacles around this massive thing and haul it out of a lethal temple. If ze'd been overwhelmed like us, ze wouldn't have gotten far. Ze was coiled next to the misshapen, fungus-like bloom of what I guessed was a head, using a sharp knife to scrape a sample into a tube. Ze was wearing gloves on zis tentacles. Condoms, really. At least ze was being safe.

"Magnificent, yes?" Starcurrent said. "An unbelievable opportunity to view one of the _____." There went the translation again, fritzing out on what was surely a very strange word that didn't get used much. "Have always believed none remained, even as dust and bones. The honor of being here is beyond my experience."

"So, what is it?" I asked. I finally let my gaze drift away, because I could feel bile rising in my throat as my body tried to argue more strongly with my brain.

"Few records, more legends. Great voyagers. Conquerors. A hunger in them like that of humans, to explore and dominate." Starcurrent was using a medical drill. I didn't watch. I wanted to tell zim off for including us and this monster in the same sentence, but I couldn't. "Few still existed in the early days of the Abyin Dommas. We were singers to them."

"Great. They liked art."

"Singing soothes," ze corrected. "A troubled race. Hungry always for more, more devotion, more worship, more acquisition. Our songs calmed for the kill."

That got my attention. I forced myself to focus on zim, not what ze was working on. Tentacle condoms and all. "What do you mean, *the kill*?"

"Early days of my race, we were slaves," ze said. "Pets, perhaps. Of little consequence. We sang them to sleep." Ze calmly sliced off a thin strip of skin from what I might loosely call a shoulder. "In sleep, they were killed."

"By you?"

"Was not yet alive, Zara Cole."

"By your people, I mean?" This had taken on a whole new dimension for me. Ze wouldn't know it, but we had things in common. Half my heritage came out of slavery, out of being considered worth less than someone with whiter skin. The other half had been the ones doing the owning. Many generations had passed for us, but that didn't make it sting less. I had never expected to find slavery out here, for some reason. Or its toxic aftermath.

"Yes," Starcurrent said. Ze sounded a little sad. "We did

not wish to. We are not a violent people. But the _____
threatened more than we could allow. Is not something we
are proud of. Necessity."

"I don't understand."

"They destroyed many, many planets. Many races," ze
said. "That was why they were called Lifekillers."

The translation matrix had finally settled on words.
God-king of death. Lifekiller.

FROM THE ANNALS OF THE BIIYAN, BEAMED FROM STAR CLUSTER X3458
—audio* extracted from drifting detritus by Leviathan Moira, just before her disappearance

*translation from Old Biiyan by Bruqvisz scholar Mindshine Farlander

A sea of inky blackness surrounds me in this barren wasteland. No light.

The stars have been drained to ash. Strange and terrifying, there is immense pressure. Dread. He comes.

I am going to die.

This is a warning. We thought they could be appeased. If someone recovers this fragment, they will know what happened to me and be aware of the threat.

He draws near; I can feel myself growing weaker. Take my words; sow them far and wide. He has grown too powerful. He must be stopped. Tell my family I love them. Tell them—

[audio ends in static]

CHAPTER FOURTEEN

Binding Tyrants

I SHUDDERED, WANTING the answer to this question almost as much as I feared asking it. "How did you . . . defeat them?"

The Abyin Dommas paused as ze sealed up a large clear box full of samples. "We made them dream of their own ending," ze said. "We made them believe they were dead, until they ceased to function."

That was the most sinister thing I'd heard in a while, and I shivered, but this time, it wasn't because of the thing on the floor. No, this was about my *friend*. I didn't say anything. Neither did Bea, who hadn't turned around at all, but I could feel her listening to every word. The Brazilians had a complicated relationship with slavery too. They came out of conquerors and conquered, death and slavery and despair.

Seemed like everyone in this room had something to do with it. I'd never expected to find the Abyin Dommas at the center of it though.

"No need to fear me," Starcurrent said. Zis voice sounded mournful now, and I realized zis tentacles had drained of all color. Ze looked gray now. "Kill only when we must, to preserve life. Not warlike. Not conquerors."

I nodded, but I was thinking that ze had betrayed something earlier. Ze'd put humanity into the same category with these creatures he called *Lifekillers*.

If the people of Earth couldn't keep it together, maybe they'd end up sleeping too, convinced of their death until death took hold. A whole planet, slowly going silent under the weight of the song of the Abyin Dommas.

We're not like that, I thought. But we had been. The Leviathan had seen our violence and anger; they'd quarantined humanity, evaluated us, brought us out in carefully curated groups. They couldn't risk us becoming that kind of conquering, ravaging plague on the universe. They already had the Phage to contend with.

Obviously reeling from exposure to the corpse, Bea bolted for the exit, and I heard her gagging out in the hall.

She hadn't even really gotten a good look at the Lifekiller, but it had been enough. My head ached, my skin felt painfully tight, and my mouth had gone very dry. My broken ankle hurt like glass splinters had been driven into it. I just wanted to get the hell out and forget—if that was possible—what I'd seen and heard in here.

Starcurrent slid by me, heading for the door. Out of the corner of my eye, I caught something. Couldn't even say it was movement. Couldn't say it wasn't anything but tight-cranked nerves.

I turned around in time to witness the Lifekiller's awakening.

It was like a switch going on, a star going supernova. One second, the nightmarish shape of the Lifekiller was sprawled on the floor . . . and the next, it was sitting up, and it was *beautiful*.

I froze. My lips parted on a gasp. Exaltation flowed in me like sap in a tree, and I felt myself falling, but I didn't know why. Didn't feel the impact when my knees hit the deck. Pain was forgotten. Bacia's presence had been overpowering, mind-numbing, but now, in the presence of *this*, I realized that they were feeble, weak, *nothing*.

The creature that rose before me glowed, shimmered, gleamed with light. Its open eyes held dark universes.

And it was looking at me.

"Zara!"

Someone was screaming. Not me, or at least I didn't feel it if it was. A distant voice, echoing inside me like a gong being struck over, and over, and over. I could feel it, but not reach it, because I was caught in the thick, sticky glamour of a god.

Then someone grabbed me by an arm and dragged me, limp as a rag, out of the hold. I came out of my trance and started to struggle halfway out, not to get to my feet and run out, but to retreat to the god I'd just abandoned. I couldn't leave. Why would anyone want to? I tried to twist free, but the hand grabbing me dug in hard enough to make me wince, and I felt healing skin break and cuts open. Smelled blood.

Then I was out, and a door slammed shut, and I heard Nadim's voice *shouting* both in my ears and inside my head, and I groaned and rolled over as the hand finally let go, trying to block out the noise. I felt emptied out inside. Grief-stricken for what I'd just lost.

I knew what this was. I'd felt it before, seen it on others. Chems did this kind of thing, left you with this horrible craving for what killed you. Left you feeling incomplete without it. I'd had seconds of exposure to that—that *thing*—and it had left me hollow. Tears flooded my eyes. I was shaking with withdrawal. Ashes in my mouth, bile in my throat.

So much *longing*.

"Nadim," I whispered. I felt broken, and I needed to feel right. "Nadim?"

"I'm here," he said, and when he felt me reaching out to him, he reached back, flooding into those empty spaces I now realized were wounds gouged in my soul by that creature. That god-king. That *Lifekiller*. But Nadim . . . Nadim reminded me what I was. What *we* were.

When I stood up, favoring my aching ankle, my stance was firm and my eyes were clear, and I hugged Beatriz's distress away. Starcurrent was near, but ze wasn't at all affected by our emotional storm. Ze watched. I realized there was a very different dimension to it now, a color in zis limbs I hadn't seen before. I interpreted it as *on guard*.

"Lifekiller is not dead," ze said. "This is bad."

"No shit," I said, and let Bea go. Nadim was still with me, but we weren't deep bonded, not quite. It was more like a full-body embrace, holding me up and guarding me from harm, just as I'd done with Bea. I silently reassured Nadim that I'd be all right now. His presence kept the influence of the thing in that room down to a dull ache. "Nadim? Does that . . . that thing affect you at all?"

"It is uncomfortable," he said. "I can feel it trying to access my consciousness. I will not allow it."

Nadim had more control than I did, then, and that scared me; if Lifekiller could take hold of me, could he puppet Nadim through our bond? I didn't think so. Nadim had just pushed him right out of me.

Together, we could do this.

"What are we going to do?" Bea looked lost now but still strong, as I knew she would be. "I mean, against something like that . . ."

I waited for Starcurrent to speak. To suggest something. But ze stayed unnaturally quiet. *It's a test*, I thought. In zis eyes, we were already dangerous. I wondered what future humans would have in this hostile universe if we failed against the Lifekiller. I pictured the Abyin Dommas singing us all to sleep, all of humanity. The gentlest of murders.

"Easy. We kill a god," I said, and flashed her a cocky, confident grin I didn't feel.

"You're kidding, right?" Bea flicked a nervous glance at Starcurrent.

Before I could answer, a massive force slammed the door that separated us from sheer destruction, and the metal buckled. "That won't hold it long," I said.

"*Why* did it wake up?" Bea was asking in a thin, high voice. I hadn't heard that tone in a while; it was the nervous girl who'd nearly thrown up on the trip to meet Nadim. "It was supposed to be dead, right?"

"Obviously not. But maybe . . . dormant? The way frogs go to sleep and kind of freeze for the winter and then when they thaw—shit."

"You've thought of something." Bea hadn't been down in the temple of doom or she would've noticed this straightaway.

Maybe I'd have picked up on it faster if I hadn't been hurt. No way to be sure now, and it didn't matter anyway. Done was done.

Another gargantuan slam against the door, and I saw gaps, between wall, floor, and ceiling. We didn't have long.

Starcurrent started singing this eerie-as-hell tune, and it put pictures in my head, scenes I didn't entirely understand. Kind of reminiscent of the way I saw things when the crystals lit up on Firstworld. Dammit, I couldn't afford to be distracted now. The Lifekiller paused, though, and his next attack didn't have the force to break the door.

I AM COMING YOU WILL KNEEL

There was no sound that anyone else seemed to hear, but the words broke across my brain, as if they were eggs, and the yellow oozed into the seams and cracks, until I couldn't think. I'd just . . . my knees started to bend.

"What's on your mind, Zara?" Nadim's steady voice got me back on track.

Clutching the wall for support, I managed to say, "The temple, the tomb. It was cold there. Frosty. M-maybe that was on purpose."

"Like cryo," Bea said. I didn't think Lifekiller had reached out for her yet. Maybe I was the weak link, somehow. Not a thing I liked to be.

"Exactly. Nadim, can you lower the temp in the secure hold?"

"On it, Zara."

Starcurrent's song didn't seem to be enough on its own, and we needed this thing back in stasis ASAP. Could be it required a choir of Abyin Dommas to do this job, but we didn't have one of those . . . or did we? "Bea! Can you record Starcurrent's song and multiply? Make it a whole backup band?"

Her face flooded with understanding. "Yes! Yes, hang on!" She grabbed her H2 and hit controls, and as Starcurrent sang, zis voice doubled, tripled into a chorus that filled the ship. I felt Nadim's response to the song—he thought it was beautiful, and peaceful—but all I wanted to do was clap hands over my ears. Not for human consumption.

Another strike on the door, this one more like a toddler kicking his feet. Just in case, I threw down the portable force field, and it covered most of the gap.

Bea readied the rifle as Starcurrent kept singing. If Bacia was expecting a dormant god-king and we delivered a truly dead one, I figured we weren't getting paid. I didn't like the thought of giving this to them, but we couldn't fight the Phage without this devil's bargain. I swore beneath my breath as the thing kept chewing at my brain, working the edges, until my mind felt like a lace handkerchief.

I am coming you will kneel

This time it was an insidious whisper, ants crawling in my ears where I couldn't dig them out, and it stung.

Before I realized it, I was scraping my nails against the side of my head, and Bea had to physically stop me, grabbing my wrists with her full strength. The shakes came on hard, like Derry on some bad chem, and Starcurrent's song was making me want to peel my face off. I wasn't used to threats like this, where I couldn't punch it until it fell down.

"Leave Zara alone!" Bea cried, and then she took a deep breath, and her powerful soprano glided over the song of the Abyin Dommas, interweaving, counterpointing in alien beats and measures.

I was going to hurt her if she didn't let go of me, because I had to dig the worm out of my head, dig it right out of my brain tissue . . .

Then Nadim touched me lightly, mind to mind, and it was instant cool water. I stopped fighting Bea's hold and let out a breath. The music flowed over me, and filtered through Nadim's perceptions, it was soothing too. Bea's voice, Starcurrent's amplified, invisible chorus . . . all spreading peace like a thick, warm blanket.

I couldn't hear anything from inside the cargo hold. Best to ask, though, because I damn sure wasn't going back in. Bacia's people could come aboard and take possession when we got to the Sliver.

"Nadim, what's going on in there?" I had to swallow hard to keep my morning coffee down. All my aches and pains were back, and I smelled blood on my body again. EMITU was going to get another visit. If we lived that long.

"It appears to have gone dormant, Zara. Likely a combination of the lower temperature and the soothing song. Thinking to amplify and replicate zis voice was very smart. Beatriz's additions were beautiful."

"Music appreciation later. Keep it icy," I said. "I don't care if it takes a year to thaw out again. We can't risk it waking up again while it's on board."

Starcurrent's song faded into silence, and the eerie echoing digital avatars went silent too. We all listened for a long moment. I imagined the god-king slumped just on the other side of the damaged door. If he'd gotten out of there, what would we have done? He'd have taken me over, no problem. Bea too, most likely. And together, we could have created a pipeline for the Lifekiller to make Nadim a slave too. If this god-bastard had any memory of how his people had gone down, he'd have killed Starcurrent first thing.

It would be hard for me to sleep until we got rid of this Lifekiller. If I wanted to stay sane, I couldn't ponder long what Bacia planned to do with it. Some days you just had to choose between bad and worse. There were lots of Abyin Dommas on the Sliver. We could pass the word for them to work up a nice lullaby.

"Typhon reported some anomalies." Suddenly Marko was on my H2. "Everything all right over there?"

"More or less. I'll get back to you."

No reason to give details right then. First, we had to repair this door.

After I collected the personal force field, it took all three of us—Bea, me, and Starcurrent—using all our collective strength, to unbuckle the damage. After that, I used welding torches to make damn sure it wouldn't open again. Might be overkill, but right now, overkill sounded pretty good.

Still, as I'd predicted, I didn't sleep for shit, and I was cranky as hell by day two. The sick helplessness, the feeling of being in thrall? I wouldn't forget that anytime soon. Oh, I knew Nadim could've pulled me back—if we'd gone Zadim, I'd have been fine, just like I was in Bacia's sanctuary.

But there was a small, haunted part of me that felt ill over knowing that that sort of power existed. And we were handing it off to Bacia. I tried to imagine what the two of them would do together, and it was impossible not to let fear simmer on low, especially when I remembered Starcurrent's stories. Whatever might come of this down the line, it probably wouldn't be good for the universe at large.

There was some faint comfort in knowing I wasn't alone in my dread, however. Bea came knocking about halfway through the sleep cycle. She had shadows starting beneath her eyes, and it struck me that neither one of us should have to be making choices that were so damn big. We hadn't been trained for any of this; at least Chao-Xing and Marko had experience. Yusuf had more. I thought of my sister Kiz on Mars, taking trips outside the dome, doing science experiments and deciding which book from her reading list to tackle next. I needed her to keep that innocence. That trust that the universe meant her no harm.

Yeah, that's why we're out here, making these tough decisions. So they don't have to.

I stepped back to let Beatriz in without asking what she wanted. It was easy to guess that she was freaked too. We both desperately needed some peace, and maybe we could find it together. Pulling my pillow and blanket off the bed, I spread the covers out like a thin pallet, and we curled up close enough to share.

The light was faint, and I could see mainly the curves of her cheeks, the dark spill of her hair. Her lashes flicked slow and steady, a silent testament to the fact that she was tired but she couldn't get her mind to shut off. I knew the feeling.

I couldn't believe I was about to make the offer, but I'd wondered if it was possible, before. "You want to try something cool?"

"Maybe," she whispered.

It wasn't permission, exactly, but it wasn't denial, either. *Good enough.* I wasn't about to say something like *if you don't like it, we'll stop,* because I'd heard that in other contexts too often to count. I took her right hand in my left and flattened my right palm on Nadim.

"Are you touching him?"

Quiet rustling. "Now I am."

"Nadim? Can you feel us?"

Instant warmth pulsed against my palm, washed over me like a warm bath. "Yes, Zara. You and Beatriz are together."

"Can we, all three of us . . . ?"

"I would like that. As long as you're both willing."

"Bea?"

"Let's try," she said.

I closed my eyes. Nadim took me first and it was gentle, being carried on a wave. Bea slid into the water that was Nadim next, and I could *feel* her, like I never had before. Her sweetness, I'd known it, but never experienced it; she was warm and open, and it was all goodness, especially when I stretched farther and could soak in everything of Nadim. Our edges blurred, and I felt the worry and tension drifting. We weren't deep bonded, but it was a beautiful between, with an intimacy that stole my breath. He was, and she was, I—oh, we were, together.

It was impossible to say when that exquisite peace and

soft connection shifted into actual sleep, but I woke up snuggled on the floor with Bea, her head on my shoulder. I'd been with people before, but never like this. I stared down at her sleeping face. This was . . . different, and deliciously complicated, and some part of me wondered what it would be like, kissing Bea and letting Nadim feel it, and—

Maybe no Honor ever entertained such thoughts until now. Whatever, it wasn't like I planned to act on them. Well, not yet, anyway.

Quietly I put on a uniform and crept out—well, limped, because even with EMITU's fast-heal treatments, the ankle would make me wince for a while. I left Bea sleeping. She needed the rest.

First stop, check on the secure storage hold. I found Starcurrent there, watching the door like it might explode. Couldn't really blame zim; ze must have been twice as twitchy at the idea of turning this thing over to Bacia.

"Everything okay?" I asked.

"Quiet," ze said. "Not good. Should kill this while we can."

It wasn't that I disagreed with zim, but . . . "Our mission is to deliver it. Otherwise, we don't get the upgrades. And we can't fight the Phage without them."

"Death is death," Starcurrent pointed out. "Phage or the return of the god-kings. Either way, death."

"You're so much fun before breakfast."

I ate, and then checked on how long till we reached the Sliver. Eight more hours. I wanted to ask Nadim how last night was for him, but that seemed strange, along the lines of *was it good for you?*

A couple of hours later, I gave in to my curiosity. "Nadim?"

"You've been quiet today," he observed. "But . . . thank you for last night."

Hell. From the heat in my cheeks, I was *definitely* blushing. "Uhm, what?"

"It was clearly your idea, Zara. Beatriz is shy. But that was . . . good. I wasn't alone, and it was perfect. It put us all to rest."

If I could, I'd bury my whole self, because here he was calmly leading a conversation I hadn't worked up the nerve to start. "Clearly. All the best ideas are mine."

"And the most dangerous ones," he teased.

Bea joined us in the media room a little while later and damn if she didn't mess with me too. "Do you always run out on people after you sleep with them, Z?"

"I wouldn't say *always*," I muttered.

She flashed me a wickedly beautiful grin, and shoulder-checked me before she got serious. Clearly not freaked about the events of the night. "Everything's okay with . . ." She gestured, and I knew she was talking about our cargo.

"Okay's a stretch, but it's still asleep," I said. "Starcurrent wants to kill it."

Bea took that in without the horror I'd have expected. "Is that possible?"

"Don't think so. What do you think, Nadim?"

"I am not in favor of killing a thing because I do not understand it."

"Well, the Abyin Dommas understood it well enough to kill off the whole race, or give it a damn good try. They don't seem like the type to overreact. The only reason I'm voting to keep it alive is to get our shit from Bacia."

"Bacia is not full parentage, like the Lifekiller in our hold," Nadim said. "Their song is in different frequencies. A distant component of Lifekiller, mixed with that of another species. The Lifekiller's song is unique."

"Let's talk about something else," I said. "Either of you ever heard of zydeco music? Chris Ardoin?" I spun up an album before they could keep going about killing a god. Thankfully, my choice of music distracted the two of them and kept them talking until the Sliver popped up on our visuals.

With no other options, I opened a comm channel to docking control and recognized one of Suncross's kind, despite the helmet. "We need you to pass along a message to Bacia."

The guard made a skeptical sound. "Sure, everyone says that."

"Check in or you'll be sorry. This is Zara Cole."

Lizard made me wait five minutes, but when he came

back on-screen, he was apologetic. "Sorry, what's the message?"

"Tell them we've retrieved the cargo, but they need to collect it, as we've sustained some damage. We need a special refrigeration container or a slew of Abyin Dommas or both. Preferably both."

I could tell the guard thought I was scrambled, but Bacia *did* send a crew of singers in the deep to board Nadim in a shuttle, and with them, they brought a huge freaking cryo unit on a hover dolly. My entire body went tight when they cracked open the door to our special secure storage. I looked away for the entire transfer, unable to bear the idea of seeing it, or worse, hearing it in my head, scraping like the long, yellow nails of someone who had long ago lost any claim to reason.

Bea held my hand so tight it hurt. "Are we sure this is a good idea?"

"Hell no."

"Breathe please to acknowledge transfer of cargo," said one of the Abyin Dommas.

Automatically, I breathed on the tablet ze held up. The screen came alive. Startled, I took a step back, because there was Bacia. The image didn't carry the same impact as their presence, but it was still impressive.

"Congratulations. You have exceeded my expectations. I will arrange for a full work crew to commence repairs and upgrades for your Dark Travelers. There will also be a substantial bonus added to your accounts, if you wish to partake in certain expensive celebratory revels while the work is being completed."

We had their blessing for some R&R, but I had no idea what costly pleasures they might be talking about, unless it was some freaky shit up on Tier Twelve. Bea still hadn't let go of my hand, and I didn't breathe easy until I saw the cryo unit loaded on Bacia's shuttle and the Abyin Dommas flew off with the Lifekiller.

Our singer in the deep was silent, a detail I couldn't help but notice. Starcurrent likely thought we'd screwed up big here. My mama used to call this kind of move borrowing from Peter to pay Paul: you better be good at hustling when the final bill came due.

"Well," I said to Bea. "Hail the returning heroes, roll out the red carpet, we've got mynt to burn. Should we hit up the Sliver one last time and make some noise?"

I didn't say so, but this might be our last chance to cut loose.

Interlude: Nadim

What we have done terrifies me. Bacia Annont is a creature I do not understand much about, but I know that they will defend this station with all strength. But is Bacia more? Are they of a kind with the evil being we have brought back?

Having the being awake within me felt like a dire sickness, and if not for the brave actions of my Honors, I might now be a mindless slave to the Lifekiller, doing . . . what? Terrible things. I do not like handing this god-creature to Bacia. I do not like many things. But my cousins are perishing, hollowed out and eaten alive, and I must do what I can to preserve them.

I hope we have not done something even more dreadful, out of our fears.

CHAPTER FIFTEEN

Binding Compact

BEATRIZ NODDED, PUSHING the curls back from her pretty face. "Damn right. Let's show them how it's done."

"Meet me at the docking bay in an hour. I need to glam up."

I took my time in the bathroom, using my precious stash of Earth products to take care of my curls. If Yusuf knew how to start locs, I might ask him to hook me up. His hair still looked fucking great, despite everything he'd been through. I finished up with premium lotion that left my brown skin looking and smelling beautiful.

Too bad Nadim can't really appreciate how fine I am.

Bea whistled when I strolled into the docking bay. Girl acted like she was playing when she gave me that once over, but I didn't think it was *entirely* in fun—and I was good with it. Plus, I did look fantastic in a funky combo of a sleeveless zip-front shirt and calf-length pants with plenty of pockets, storage for the concealed weapons I was carrying. No point in formality here.

"That's a good color on you," I told her.

Bea had on a vibrant, silky scarf that floated like it had anti-grav; it changed colors depending on her moods. Right now, it was warm, sunny yellow that complemented her rich brown skin and eyes. "Thanks! You ready?"

"Just waiting on Yusuf."

The older Honor had agreed to supervise Nadim's upgrades since he'd overseen the process with his own Leviathan, and he didn't seem interested in shore leave. The man would work himself to death if we weren't careful. I'd keep an eye on him, make sure he didn't push himself too hard. I was still worried about the parasitic fungal colony that was living in him too. We had to keep him healthy for two more years before he'd be clear of it.

Yusuf jumped off the Hopper as I got in and Bea settled into the pilot's seat. "You have everything you need?" I asked him.

He hefted the bag slung across his shoulder. "I'm fine, thanks."

"Then take care of Nadim for me."

Zara, Nadim protested. *There's no need. You'll be back soon.*

It's for him, not you.

That settled Nadim a little, but it was nice that he didn't see Beatriz and me as replaceable.

Having one Hopper to serve two Leviathan was a bit inconvenient, but ours would be fixed soon. As Bea started the engine, Starcurrent joined us. Ze had been quiet since the whole waking-the-god-king issue, and true to form, ze climbed in back with Marko without saying a word.

Landing was much different this time. Bea had learned from watching Chao-Xing, and she maneuvered us in with admirable aplomb. Likewise, the guards in the docking area treated us like real VIPs, and we rolled through to the Sliver without a moment's delay. Starcurrent broke away from the group immediately and hurried off, maybe to warn other Abyin Dommas about what we'd done.

Yeah, I don't feel great about it, either.

Bea drifted ahead, toward the map at the center of the promenade. It had the latest info on what merchants were running hourly sales, where you could get grub for cheap, and what brothels on Tier Twelve were offering discount alien fun times. Beside me, Marko wore this complicated expression. Before, we were too pressed for time to debrief on the reality of the Sliver, and I wondered what he made of the place.

"What's on your mind?" I asked.

"It's unbelievable. All these *races*. All this—and we didn't know about any of it. The Leviathan meant it for our own good, but . . . I spent a *year* on the Tour, and Nadim never even hinted that all this existed."

I swallowed the urge to defend Nadim. Not helpful.

"You know why they did that, right?" I asked. "They were testing us. Trying to see if we were what they needed for the Journey . . . and the Journey is going to war with the Phage. Oh, sure, some badass space adventuring too, but mostly? It was about using us, and our human instincts, to help them fight the Phage."

"And do you think that was wrong?" Marko asked quietly.

"Damn right it was. You don't recruit people to a fight without telling them the odds, that's a given. But they basically promised us a sea cruise with open buffet, and once we got on board, we ended up on battleships. Ever heard of a bait and switch?"

"No," he said. "But I understand your point. Still. They're fighting for their lives. And if we can help, then we should."

"Not sure all those folks back home who keep your picture on their wall feel the same way about it," I said. "Not sure they'd send their kids off with tears and pride if they knew what was on the other end."

"That's not our problem anymore," Marko pointed out. "Our goal is survival."

"Survival's something I'm good at." I nudged him. "So are you." But he was right, and I couldn't help but look for Beatriz. I watched her as she dodged and skipped around the bobbing flow of aliens on this tier. Grace and beauty, our Bea.

"She's gorgeous," I added quietly. "She may never be a fighter the way we are."

"She doesn't have to be, as long as she fights in her own way," Marko said, but he was watching me, not her, and reading between the lines. "Have you told her?"

"What?"

"Zara."

I glared at him. *"What?"*

"Nothing," he said, but he was smiling as he said it. "None of my business."

Bea joined us, and our eyes met just for a second. A flash of recognition, and something else. On some level, I understood her in ways I hadn't before last night. But like he said, that was none of his damn business. I wasn't ready to make a move, and he shouldn't tease me about it, either.

"I'll be at Pinky's," I told her. "I need to talk to Suncross. If you're planning to shop, take Marko with you. He needs some gear."

"Sure. We'll find you there, then?"

"You bet."

Her smile was like starlight on Nadim's sails. Maybe Nadim and Bea and I *could* have something more . . . delicious and complicated.

Hell, what out here conformed to human conventions, anyway? There were more possibilities than I could count. And we were just starting to see the outlines of it, after living so long in the dark.

I left Marko in Bea's excellent company and moved on with confident purpose. I was secure here now, and when I jumped into the transport and kicked off at the right tier for Pinky's, I felt like a local.

Pinky's was, as usual, packed. No bouncers I knew this time; Chao-Xing had been replaced by an Abyin Dommas, and I had the impression, though it was tough to differentiate them even after so much time with Starcurrent, that this one was the victor I'd seen in the arena. The one I never wanted to fight. I'd guess that an Abyin Dommas with a victory down there would swing a very big stick around here, and sure enough, the crowd seemed boisterous, but they gave zim a wide, respectful berth.

Suncross and his boys were at their usual table, but they were different this time. Suncross raised a hand in greeting and kicked a chair toward me, and Ghostwalk nodded, but all in all it was a pretty morose welcome. No table-thumping. No chants for Zeerakull. Just grunts all around.

"Somber around here," I said. Guilt nipped at me when I remembered that we'd bailed without waiting for a response to the hasty vid-message I sent. "I have a hell of a story for you."

"We lost," Suncross said, tossing his empty cup in the air. A hovertray grabbed it and zoomed in to offer another. He hardly seemed to know it was there, but I noticed he wasn't slow on grabbing the glass, either. He batted the tray away irritably and lapped up the liquor, more like he was trying to deaden pain than just enjoy a drink. "Bet on stupid Abyin Dommas in finals. You would have won, Zeerakull, you and JongShowJing. Very disappointing. We lost much mynt." He brightened up a little, and I saw he'd been drinking a while, and with dedication; his reflexes were slow. "But now you're back! We will make good our losses, yes?"

"I'm sorry," I said. "You sponsored us in good faith, but we're not here to fight in the arena. We're getting our upgrades and heading out again. What happened? I thought the Abyin Dommas dominated in the semifinals."

"Did," Suncross confirmed. "Very stupid race, very stupid. Could have won easily, chose not to in last fight. *Felt sorry* for his opponent." Suncross snorted salt out of his nostrils. The tabletop was already crusted with it. "Sobbing story of brood back on homeworld, opponent needed fita to buy passage out. Abyin Dommas conceded. *Conceded!* Who concedes without a death blow, I ask you? Or loss of limbs?"

I acknowledged that truth with a nod. "Well, at least

I can pay you back the fita you loaned us when we first arrived."

"Good news," Suncross grunted. "Not good enough. We lost much on that accursed Abyin Dommas. Even with your reimbursement, there's not enough left to pay docking expenses, settle our accounts on Tier Twelve, fuel up, and go."

Somehow I didn't laugh. "Maybe if you didn't blow so much money on booze and cheap thrills—"

"Legitimate overhead! Do not sap our will to live, Zeerakull." Suncross glared at me.

As my lizard friend listed all their totally legit costs, I crunched some numbers on my H2. We had sufficient mynt and fita to pay for our needs. When I factored in the generous survivor's bonus Bacia had paid out, I was flush as hell, and there was nothing I wanted here. I'd already bought some alien tech, such as the personal force field. I wouldn't mind having a spare in case it broke, but since I was good at fixing stuff, even that wasn't *necessary*, strictly speaking.

When we'd first arrived on the Sliver, Suncross and his crew had sponsored us and provided good intel. In the Zone, such generosity was rare enough that it deserved a reward, and the same standard held out here on outlaw station. I started when Suncross slammed four clawed hands on the table, forcing me to look up.

"The least you could do is pay attention when I'm complaining, Zeerakull!"

"I heard you," I snapped. "Keep your scales on, or you'll be sorry."

"Are you threatening me?" Suncross hissed in my general direction.

These damn lizards had no chill. Still, I owed them a good turn, so I'd pay up. "It looks like I can front the mynt you need . . . and I just checked. If I sign off, I can gift some of my fita to you. It's enough for you to fuel up and get going."

Suncross's jaws dropped open, revealing *so* many teeth, but he was just surprised, not thinking about eating me. His crew quieted, the entire table just staring at me. Ghostwalk put all four of his hands on the table and turned them palms up. His scales were gray-green, palms a soft ivory, and I had the feeling this gesture had deep cultural meaning.

"What are your terms?" Suncross finally asked.

"Huh?"

"Interest. What percent?"

Sighing, I said, "I'm not a loan shark."

Ghostwalk still hadn't moved his hands. "What is a borrow fish?"

That translation quirk made me laugh. "Look, this is a farewell gift. It's highly unlikely that we'll be back here, and you were good to us. I want to help you, no strings."

"Why would there be strings?" Suncross demanded. "Slave ship?"

Why is it so hard to give gifts to lizards?

"No. If you don't want my help, just say so."

"Free help?" Ghostwalk clarified.

"Yes, completely free." Finally, it seemed like my message was getting through. Crims in the Zone weren't this wary.

"We cannot accept," Suncross said. "Unless you offer an employment contract. It is dishonorable to take charity. Worthy to work off debt."

This was getting so complicated. I had no use for another ship and crew . . . or *did* I? Their mechanical ship might come in handy against the Phage. Tapping the table thoughtfully, I wished the others were here to weigh in.

Is this a great idea or a terrible one? Only one way to find out.

"Okay," I said. "Let's explore our options. Does your ship have weapons?"

Suncross and Ghostwalk traded looks, like I'd asked something deeply stupid. "Of course."

"Since I don't know how much it normally costs to hire you, I'll have to trust your word. How long will you work for me in return for buying your crew out of Sliver hock?"

The lizards turned off their translation matrix and talked among themselves, snarls and growls that meant nothing to me. After a few minutes, Suncross restored the tech and answered, "Half a rotation, we follow your orders. Loyal to the bone."

Since I was willing to give them the fita before anyway, I took the deal without hesitation. I had no way of knowing if that was a fair trade for what I was paying, but they seemed pretty concerned about worth and honor. Didn't really think they'd cheat me. We wrote up the contract right there in Pinky's and signed off with our biometrics, then I made the necessary mynt transfer and fita grant.

One by one, the lizards—including Suncross—turned their palms up on the table. Sixteen palms, open.

I added my own human hands, and Suncross nodded.

"Our strength is yours, Zeerakull. Your honor is ours. Death before betrayal."

I didn't know the proper response to that, so I nodded back, and then sixteen hands clenched into fists and pounded the table in a thunder. I followed suit, drumming until my still-healing skin winced from the abuse. At the end of it, Suncross and his boys threw back their heads and roared, a sound like a T. rex shaking the world, and I joined in with a war cry that felt like it tore my throat open. Seemed like the thing to do.

Just wait until the rest of the team learns that I've hired mercs.

Partying with Suncross was a loser's game, so I tapped out after two drinks, fist-bumped the crew, and headed outside. Marko and Bea must still be shopping. Stretching, I reached for Nadim, and the mental threads wove together between us, and I took in a deep breath of recycled air, heavily spiced with alien body odor, food that smelled no better, and the sweat of thousands of desperate people, all rubbing crankily against each other in close quarters.

Felt like home.

"Nadim," I said. "Everything okay?"

"Yes," he said. "Yusuf has made an extensive list of upgrades. I will be fitted with armor, several rail guns, internal defenses, an upgrade to the force shield you installed before." He sounded like a kid getting the best birthday present ever. But then he chilled. "I wish I did not need them. But they will keep you and Beatriz safe."

"And you."

"Well, yes." He said that as if it didn't matter that much. I shook my head. I was going to have to work hard to train the martyr out of him.

"Has the station crew sent a schedule yet?"

"Yes, upgrades will begin as soon as the items are printed in the shop. Expected time is two station hours from now. Typhon's work is mostly repairs, and the crew is already on the way to him now. They are reinforcing his armor considerably."

"That's great," I said. "That gives me time to take care of something."

Nadim must have caught the tone in my voice, or the surge in my emotions, because he said, in a newly cautious voice, "Zara? What are you going to do?"

"Nothing dangerous," I assured him. "I promise, I'm not looking for a fight."

"No arena battles?"

"No."

That seemed to satisfy Nadim, at least a little, though I could tell he was on his guard now. Good. I wanted him to be. I'd be on the Hopper in an hour to be on site when the upgrades commenced; I wasn't about to trust Nadim to Bacia's people without being there to observe and shoot anybody who tried to hurt him. Yusuf was there, but it was unfair to ask him to do the job alone.

I found Bea and Marko sitting at dinner in a pretty, shiny restaurant up on Tier Fourteen. Unlike Pinky's, it wasn't crowded; there was a respectful space between tables, and everything looked freshly sanitized. The air smelled fresh and clean in here, and periodically, a mister above the tables drifted down a scent that was pleasing for the race of whoever was occupying it. In Marko and Bea's case, it seemed to be lavender. Relaxing.

I stared. "Shut up—is that *ice cream*?"

"Kind of," Bea said. "I don't think we want to ask where the milk came from. But it's delicious. Sit down!"

305

"This place is great," Marko added. "Expensive."

"Yeah, well, I was drinking with Suncross. I kind of, uh, hired them."

"To do what?" Bea asked.

"Well, not public relations," I said. "They're mercenaries. They'll fight with us for half a rotation, measured in Sliver time. We might need them if we come up against the Phage again. Or other problems."

I expected them to object, but maybe the meal had chilled everybody out; Marko just nodded and took a bite of the ice cream. I decided I'd better try the stuff before it was gone, because at the rate they were going, it would vanish before I had the chance.

I snagged a spoonful and put it in my mouth.

The taste exploded in layers: sweet first, then a dark, vibrant, mysterious richness that lingered beneath. It finished on a sting that was almost spice, which felt like the most perfect thing ever. I put my spoon in the bowl with Marko's and Bea's, and the entire thing melted into the pristine table. Not a drop to show it had ever been there. No servers here, I gathered. Not even servo-bots. Just peace, quiet, and damn amazing food.

"Would you mind coming with me somewhere?" I asked.

Bea's scarf turned a light blue. "What are you going to do, Zara?"

"Nothing dangerous," I said. "I need to buy something."

"What?"

"You'll see."

They paid the bill, and we left the restaurant. I back-flipped into the transport and took the route down, plummeting in a dive all the way to Tier One. The other two kicked out without trouble, and stood with me on the central plaza, where we'd first been welcomed in.

"Okay," Marko said. "What are we doing here? Aren't the shops on other tiers?"

"Yes," I said. "But that's not what we're buying." I turned and walked toward a giant holographic display filled with names. "We're putting someone on the memorial board."

Suncross had pointed the board out to me; it held the names mostly of arena combatants who hadn't survived matches, which was a daunting list considering it wasn't *supposed* to be mortal combat. But not all the names came from the arena. It cost to add one—a considerable sum of mynt and fita—and only those who had lots of friends and fans could afford to even be listed.

I tapped the interface and added a name. *Henri Demetrius Justineau. Citizen of Earth.*

"Oh," Bea said quietly. "I understand."

I added a staggering amount of mynt and fita, the rest of our remaining balance, and Justineau's name soared to the top of the memorial list and illuminated in gold. It would stay there until someone paid more for their monument. Unlikely.

I wasn't good at funerals, so I said, "Sorry, Justineau. You deserved better. We would have taken you out of here if we could have. Whatever faith you followed, I hope it welcomes you home."

Bea didn't say anything, but when she stepped forward, she began to sing. It was opera, an aria that I recognized; it was the emotional, heart-shattering, beautiful song she'd first performed when we'd come aboard Nadim. I felt Nadim enfolding both of us as the music soared up through the Sliver, amplified by space and passion. Tier by tier, all business stopped. Everyone listened. A shimmering cloud of Jellies floated out over the space, like a curtain of colors that pulsed with the emotions of her song. Her scarf had turned ice white, framing her face in light like an angel's, and her eyes were closed, tears tracking down her cheeks.

It was the sweetest, loveliest thing I had ever seen, and for it to be *here*, in the grime and rust and stench of the Sliver . . . I knew everyone, on every tier, was for a moment somewhere else. Somewhere beautiful.

She finished, and the silence that followed might have been unique to this place. Respect. Honor. No one seemed to breathe.

I said, into that silence, "Good-bye, Henri Justineau."

Someone echoed it. Then someone else. Then everyone standing on the tiers was saying it.

I didn't know, but I thought he would have liked it, because for one precious moment, everyone on the Sliver knew who he was.

Bea took a deep breath, wiped her face with her scarf, and said, "That was a good thing to do. Thank you, Zara."

"Yeah, well, don't expect me to make it a habit, because nobody else I like is dying," I said. "Marko? That includes you. Hell, it even includes Typhon. Clear?"

"Very," he said. "Although if I do fall, having Beatriz sing me to rest would be the best passing I can imagine."

She caught her breath and looked away.

"Enough serious shit," I said. "Come on. Let's get our upgrades and blow this wreck."

Observing while aliens did things that hurt my Leviathan was not my jam. At all.

I stood about two hot seconds of it before I stuffed my aching ass into my skinsuit, which had regrown itself good as new, rolled on the helmet, and spaced myself to go see what *exactly* these assholes were doing to Nadim.

"Hey!" I addressed a creature hanging motionless in space, fixed to Nadim by a cord that looked too thin to do any good. The alien I was talking to was a big, hulking thing, made anonymous by the metallic suit. It had to be the boss of this gang, because it wasn't doing anything useful. "What the *hell* are you doing that's hurting him so much?" I could feel every sharp, stabbing pain, though

Nadim was bearing it without complaint.

The helmet slowly rotated—the body didn't—in my direction. I couldn't see a damn thing through the dark faceplate. "Installing Level Twelve armor isn't a painless procedure on the Dark Travelers," whatever was inside said. The voice came from my translator as a high-pitched, almost childlike tone. Horror vid scary. "If you wanted pain relief, that should have been ordered."

"Well, I'm ordering it now!"

"Sure," the boss said. "But it delays us by another two days while it takes effect."

Nadim said, "No, Zara. Let them work."

"You're *bleeding*."

"I will heal. We should do this and go."

"Nadim—"

"No," he said, firmly. I knew that tone. I knew that feeling, unyielding as a steel wall. "You hurt yourself for our sake. I can do no less than bear my own pain. If you wish to help install the plating, then that is more useful."

Shit. He was right, of course; I had to treat Nadim like his own being. If he wanted to endure surgery without anesthetic, I might hate the hell out of it, but I didn't get to say he couldn't do it.

I pulled in a breath, blew it out along with my anger, and said to the construction boss, "Okay, no pain relief. How can I help?"

"Fasten yourself, take a crate, follow instructions," the suit said. "Ask if you don't understand. We're short-staffed, working two ships at once."

Well, I liked a no-nonsense approach, at least. I tethered my suit back to the airlock, kicked off, and tumbled through the gravity-free space to land on the side of a floating platform full of stuff. A helpful spinning icon hung over one box, and I checked the instructions attached to it. They were all visual, not words, which was helpful. All I needed to do was drive the crate, which had its own jets, over to Nadim, position it until the crate told me it was in the right position, open it, and position the plating. The bolts were self-drilling. It was slick, all things considered.

I was fine right up until the drills fired, bolting the plating deep into Nadim's body; I knew it was necessary, but I felt every centimeter of the drill, and the sharp, red agony it caused, even when Nadim tamped it down.

This is how he feels, watching me get hurt. It blows.

The drills finished, and the crate flashed that it was finished. I drove it back to the pallet and picked up another. There were at least a hundred workers involved, but a Leviathan was, well, vast, even at Nadim's size. This would take time.

It took hours of exhausting work—not physically tough, but emotionally—before I went inside and took a food-and-water break. Bea was monitoring, and she made sure I sat down for a bit before I went back at it, but I couldn't really rest. Not with the constant spike of drills entering Nadim's flesh.

The plating finally finished with the last drills cutting in and anchoring, the last silvery burst of blood from beneath leaking away into space. Nadim hung in the low light, and as I backed off and really looked, it was awe-inspiring what had been done in a Sliver day. Sleek, scaled armor overlapping like that of Earth fishes, in a black so deep that it would conceal him from most visual sensors even when he wasn't running dark. The only way to see Nadim now would be as a shadow against stars. The two big bumps that had been added at his tail and head contained shield generators, and there were backups midway on his ventral and dorsal surfaces. Two rail guns sat in sleek pods, ready to emerge and fire at any moment.

All he lacked now was the interior defenses, like Typhon had.

"How does it look?" Nadim asked me, and I blended with him to show him what I saw.

"Badass," I told him. "You look badass."

"Then we match," he said, and I laughed.

It was shift change, and the workers had all untethered and were hanging on the huge pallet vessel for the ride back down. The construction boss stopped next to me to say, "You ever need a job, I'll hire you, softskin."

I didn't think that was a particularly cute nickname, but I thanked him anyway.

I was watching the vessel and workers glide back into docking orbit with the Sliver when something caught my attention. I didn't know what it was and kept looking. Typhon's repair crew was finishing up too, and catching a ride home, was it that? No, the movement had come out of a different quadrant. The Sliver did draw in ships all the time, so I thought I'd glimpsed one of those coming or going . . .

. . . but it wasn't a ship. I caught the undulating motion first, the lucid gleam of starlight on shiny carapaces as the swarm twisted and changed shape.

"Phage!" I screamed, and kicked off for the airlock. "Bea, send word to the Sliver, *right now*! All defenses up as soon as I hit the door!"

FROM THE WORLD COURT INVESTIGATIVE FILES,
CASE 98305743

SUBJECT: DELUCA, TORIAN

Transmission intercept [date redacted], Recording Agent [identity redacted]

DELUCA: Don't tell me to let it go, Ashe. That damn crim destroyed billions in clear profit.

ASHE: You sure this isn't more about your kid? Look, her purse got jacked. She flashed money in the Zone. Anybody would have lifted her purse. Just bad luck it was this Zara girl.

DELUCA: She's no idiot. Second she clocked I was on her trail, she grabbed the prototype chem and tossed the box. You think it's an accident some no-hope Zone cooker ended up with the exact same formula that was in the box? That I have to buy supply from the Zone now instead of selling to it? She stole from me, burned me, and got away. I don't get her, my business won't ever recover.

ASHE: Sir. She's a damn Honor. She's in space. How do you think you're going to get her now? News says she's gone on the Journey. She's not coming back here.

DELUCA: Then we go get her. Bring me the boy, Derry McKinnon.

CHAPTER SIXTEEN

Binding Resources

THE CONSTRUCTION PALLETS weren't speedy. They'd take time to dock, offload their crews to the Sliver. While they were between us and the station, they were vulnerable, and the Sliver couldn't raise their defensive shields without abandoning the crews.

I wasn't shocked when the Sliver's shields flared silver around it. Bacia did strike me as ruthless. The construction pallets hadn't reached safety yet, and they immediately came to a halt, hovering in place. We had to defend ourselves, *and* them.

Heart roaring in my ears, I raced for the airlock. Bea

was there waiting to pull me in. Every second we spent spooling up my umbilical, the Phage were getting closer, to us, to the helpless workers Bacia had sentenced to die.

With Bea's help, I slammed the airlock shut and said, "Nadim, can we take these workers in? Like you did with our disabled Hopper?"

"Our docking bay can't hold the entire work crew," he answered. "But I'll save those I can and ask Typhon to gather the rest." I sensed him moving at speed to intercept the first, smaller work transport. It was *just* going to fit inside his hold, I thought.

Typhon was bigger, so maybe we could protect everyone—or, at least, keep them out of the direct line of fire. I pulled my helmet off because insect vision was distracting, and my curls sprang free. I was drenched with sweat under the skinsuit, which was trying to earnestly wick it away and stabilize my temp, but the sweat came from adrenaline and fear. When Nadim came about, I braced against the wall and *felt* him. He was scared, but not like our first, bewildering battle against the Phage. This time golden anticipation threaded through his fear, alongside the deep red of determination. He understood what we were facing now. I had no doubt that he'd spent time studying the recordings of everything we knew about them . . . how they moved, and what killed them most effectively.

If he's good, I'm good.

My nerves settled a little from that brief contact, and I rushed through the passageway to Ops. "Let's lock down the docking bay. I'm sorry to the contractors, but it'll be chaos if we let them run all over the place."

Bea nodded. "On it. Sealing the doors."

"Taking on extra weight in three . . . two . . . one."

I felt the jolt of Nadim rescuing the workers, which was good, but the maneuver brought us closer to the Phage. My stomach heaved when I remembered fighting them on Typhon's ravaged decks. Nadim didn't have any internal defenses installed yet, so if they boarded . . .

Trying not to think about the worst-case scenario, I said, "Shields up. Get Starcurrent on the comms to talk to the contractors; explain they need to hold on tight."

"Hear and responding, Zara," Starcurrent said over comms. "Am of little use to you here, will join them to explain in person. Less frightening to see the familiar. Workers may find ways to help. Will inquire."

The armor that had caused Nadim so much pain was now making me feel intensely better; it was a very fancy grade of impenetrable. The longer we kept them out, the more of them we could kill with weapons and maneuvers.

The weapons we'd just installed were supposed to be better than the ones that Beatriz and I had jury-rigged, and I'd asked for them to be specifically calibrated to repel the Phage; they'd fire not one large projectile, but a spray of small, high-energy pellets, like a giant space shotgun. No autocannons yet, and I wished for something like space napalm, though that was a physical impossibility since there was no oxygen in vacuum.

"Pulling away from the station," Nadim said. "Coordinating with Typhon. All workers now in our holds."

Moving away was a good precaution. When we went weapons hot, our fire might tear through the Sliver's defenses, and we couldn't afford to find out how Bacia would retaliate. Fighting on two fronts was an effective way to get dead.

I took a breath, two. *Calm down*, I told myself. I touched Nadim and found steadiness in him. We wove together—a light bond, the opening steps to plunge deeper when we needed it.

"Full-scene visual," I said then. A dreadful thought occurred to me. "Uh, you can still do that? Even through armor?"

"I can control the opacity of the armor," Nadim said. "It does not affect the durability. I can still give you full visuals."

Bea took a step back, because she didn't love it when part of Nadim seemed to vanish. As I watched through the transparent side of the ship, the Phage hesitated, torn between the Leviathan moving away from the Sliver and a tempting stationary target. I wasn't sure how smart they

were, but there was no doubting their predatory preference when they swirled after Nadim.

In the arena, Chao-Xing had said that I had an ability
to see weakness where others couldn't. Right now, all I
could glimpse was the fact that the Phage were slower and
weaker in smaller numbers. *Split them up, slow them down.*
I locked onto that thought as Nadim powered up his guns.
Typhon was already firing into the cloud, but the enemy
was small and fast, hard to hit. Even when a blast hit some,
more scattered; it was like shooting into a school of fish.
Even with a shotgun, only so many took damage.

The Phage split up into two twisting columns, and I was
weirdly reminded of spiral ladders of DNA as they whipped
toward Typhon and Nadim, gaining speed.

It'll be fine. We've got plating.

Still, sickness was rising in my stomach. We'd barely
survived that first battle, and we weren't ready for this.
Not really. But that was how life worked, chucking you
into situations you weren't prepared for. The real test came
in how you reacted.

Sink or swim.

Typhon was firing, lighting up the darkness around the
Sliver, and his barrage of projectiles tore the hell out of the
Phage column, scattering them like birds. But as soon as
it paused, they reformed and came on ahead. The silence
on our comm said that the Elder Leviathan and crew had

enough on their hands without worrying about us. I steadied myself. If I panicked, Bea might too. Nadim needed both of us ice cold and focused.

He can't do this on his own.

Just like that, I was good again. The jitters subsided, and I didn't fret about how shit could break bad. For Nadim and Bea, I'd shut down everything that scared me and get this done. *Phage. Weakness.* Something was stirring in the back of my head, but I couldn't pinpoint it just yet. *Fine, let's kick some ass while it simmers.*

"There's a disturbance in the docking bay," Bea said.

I hit the comms. "Starcurrent! Lock that shit down!"

"Am trying!" ze shouted back. "Is not going well!"

While the workers were probably scared, they should be at least glad we hadn't left them stranded. But if they knew we were moving away from the Sliver . . . "Tell them if they distract us now, we all die, will you? We've got this. They need to sit their asses down and wait!"

"Yes, Zara. Am communicating so."

Nadim dodged, turning and darting, drawing one long tail of the swarm away. Out here, though, it was darker. I didn't like that. Nadim was still healing. "Any good suns near us?" I asked him.

"Yes," he said. "I am going toward it."

The distance between Nadim and Typhon was increasing, as both Leviathan tried to actively split the Phage force. Bursts of brightness in the black, as Typhon fired again and again. This was old news to him, whereas we were green as hell, but Typhon was also moving slower than Nadim. More gravely injured before, and still healing.

"Marko! What do you need?" I asked, hitting comms.

"Focus on yourself!" he shouted back. I saw a blur of his face on the screen, stark and pale as he concentrated on the boards. "Try to take out as many on your side as you can. If we let them reform . . ."

The first of the Phage had almost reached Nadim. Bad for them, because he quickly dumped speed and let them overtake, and I fired a brutal barrage of projectiles into the swarm before they could dodge. Phage carcasses spun, trailing freezing blood in lacy patterns. Bursts from Nadim's railgun shook the whole ship, but Nadim leapt with the recoil like a teenager learning to dance. "What else we got?" I asked Nadim.

"Fire the particle laser on the widest beam," he said. *Shit.* I'd already forgotten about that one, and I quickly spun to those controls, but Bea was already on it. I didn't know when she'd made it to Ops, but there she was, and steady enough to flash me a quick smile as her fingers danced over the board.

"Setting up targeting parameters," she said. Before she finished talking it was already done, and she slapped the controls to let the computer execute, because that was faster and more accurate. "It'll fire when the maximum number of Phage come into alignment."

It took about two seconds for that to happen. I got my balance and watched the particle laser burn through a swath of the Phage. *Good.*

"How many more shots do you have?" I asked.

"Twenty, if we cycle down the shields," she answered.

"If not?" I didn't want those things on his skin, oh hell no, not even with plating.

"Fifteen?"

"Then let's make them count."

Bea said, "I'll see if I can free up some power, lower life support to minimal outside Ops and the docking bay." She was already on it before I nodded.

I studied the swarm as the Phage came at us again. Railguns were down by 20 percent already; once those were gone, we wouldn't be able to keep them off for long. I didn't want to test the plate, not yet. I held fire as the front runners of the swarm spiraled toward us, and I dropped deeper into the bond. *Hit them hard,* I told Nadim, and felt his muscles flex as he slowed to put them alongside, then rolled and slammed hard into more than a hundred of them. The impact of the defense shield into the column vaporized most, and sent the next wave scrambling apart, shattering their formation. Nadim didn't hesitate. He leapt forward again, toward the light of a distant star. I felt the far-off song of it, the waves of energy reaching into him. *Food.* I hadn't realized how desperately hungry he was for it until the radiation began to energize him. It steadied him, cleared his mind, and mine too.

I replayed what I'd seen of the Phage's attack in my mind. There was a repeatable rhythm to the swirl, I realized; the Phage didn't move at random. I came up out of the bond for a moment, landed heavy in my own skin, and adapted quickly. I started to reach for the controls, then stopped myself.

We were a team. We needed to work as one.

"Bea, break down their patterns. I caught a couple of repetitions in the way they form up immediately after an attack. If we can anticipate, we can really fuck them up with an immediate second burst."

She was in the bond now too, the three of us working smoothly as a team. I sensed Starcurrent, outside the bond, struggling to convince the very independent construction gang of their safety, but that was zis problem right now. We had a swarm to smash.

Typhon was on the edges of my awareness, a black, angry shadow, but very distant now. He'd gone at a tangent to separate the swarm as much as possible, and it was working. Our half was starting to slow down, while Nadim was powering up from the onrushing, nourishing sun.

It was all looking good.

That was when it all started to go very bad.

I felt the pain first, echoing through Nadim from an unexpected source: the docking bay, where Starcurrent was supposed to be keeping a lid on the situation. It was sudden, sharp, and shocking, and Nadim's effortless flight faltered, more from surprise than any real disability. The Phage responded instantly to the second of hesitation in a lightning-fast attack. They hit the shields in a rain of bodies, destroying hundreds, but that didn't matter; there were tens of thousands in the swarm. The Phage didn't care about their own injuries. They cared about the prize. In other circumstances, I would have probably felt some admiration for that, but now, I just wanted to kill them all, *fast*. Nadim twisted, rolled, evaded, and the swarm fell behind again, but not far behind. They were tireless. They were ruthless. And they would not stop coming.

"Do you have enough for a dark run?" I asked Nadim. Stealth mode might save us right now. For how long, I didn't know.

"I do," he said. I caught a hint of falsehood to that; he had enough power to start one, but he wasn't sure how long he could hold on to it. "When?"

"Bea, dual fire: particle laser and rail guns. Pick your shots. Nadim, as soon as she fires, use the confusion to go dark. Change course. Go under the sun, slingshot around, head back to Typhon."

"Got it," Bea said. "Analyzing the patterns . . . okay, locked in. Firing in three, two . . ."

One was silent, but Nadim's whole body shuddered with the force of all his guns firing, and then he was moving fast, and shifting his body chemistry at the same time. Organic tech, bizarre and wonderful.

I need you, he told me, and I immediately leapt from my skin and into the bond, wholly committed. He caught me, and we merged into one creature.

Zadim went dark.

We rolled and swam for the star that burned and sang ahead. Dipped low, spread now-invisible solar sails to catch the streaming energy of the sun, the vibrant song of a new star hissing in our cells, singing in our bones, an aching and ancient melody that rose and fell like tides: the beat of a heart, a living thing. We felt the cold scrabble of the Phage as the swarm boiled and struggled for a target. Confused now that we had vanished. A quarter of the swarm drifted, smashed and silent.

A single Phage followed, as if it might sense our trail. Uncertain.

Now, the Zara part of us whispered, and we felt the surge ripple through our body as the dark run receded, showing us to the swarm.

It chased, thinking nothing of the danger, wondering nothing of the reasons.

We screamed into the gravity of the sun, folded our sails, and the song of the light rose to a screech, discordant and beautiful and ravenous. The armor protected us from the heat momentarily. Pain woke, and we pushed the sensations aside. The gravity crushed us, but we skimmed the edges like a stone, let it draw us forward and the momentum push us back out into the dark, looking down on the swarm that followed blindly on our trail.

Their mass was smaller, composed of tiny fragile pieces, and one by one, the sun dragged the spiral apart, scattered and destroyed them. Some escaped, but they were few and weak, and spun away into the dark. Lost.

We separated, me into my small, soft body, Nadim to his, and the loneliness of it, the loss, made my eyes water as I opened them and took in a deep breath, bracing myself on the console.

Bea knew what we'd done, but she didn't comment. She was busy reporting. "We're clear for now," she said. "Heading back toward the Sliver, tracking Typhon's course."

Nadim showed me how that fight was going before I could even ask. We had problems in the docking bay too, but Starcurrent would have to cope until we put down the Phage. I'd never been more conscious of how much a Leviathan needed a deep bond for max combat effectiveness. Whatever Typhon was getting from Marko and Chao-Xing, it wasn't enough. I didn't see any of the quicksilver intuition that came when Bea, Nadim, and I were working at peak efficiency.

Maybe Typhon's wounds were slowing him down, or maybe—well, I didn't know. But if we didn't help him, he might not survive this fight. Nadim didn't have enough energy for another dark run, and we were already running low on juice. Our lasers might just draw the Phage onto us, and I didn't have a final solution for dealing with them. The rail guns could injure Typhon at this range.

I didn't know nearly enough about the Phage.

While I was chewing on our next strategy, we arrived at the Sliver.

It was a mess. With Nadim gone, some of the swarm after Typhon had drawn off to attack the Sliver, whose silver shield was still up, but I could see by the readouts that it was stressing badly. As I watched, drone ships like the ones that had chased us on the dead planet poured out of the honeycomb docking area—Bacia's holdout tech, I assumed, something they would only use in an emergency. The drones were small and light, completely automated, and they had weapons. They engaged the Phage one-on-one, blowing them effortlessly away, though it would take a while for that finite number of drones to eat their way through a swarm.

One added benefit: the movement and vibration of the drones lured more of the Phage away from the Elder.

"Now. Fire now."

Bea switched to manual controls and unleashed a massive particle burst. We took out some of the drones as well. Too damn bad; Bacia could make more.

The drones had no sense of self-preservation, and some of them even seemed programmed for kamikaze maneuvers; they headed straight for the center of the biggest part of the swarm and detonated. Effective, but expensive, and not possible for us to imitate unless we built some drone ships of our own.

Typhon was burning through the last of his fuel cells, the shimmer of his shields faltering. Dammit, he just couldn't get it through his head that going balls-out wasn't always the solution.

"Fight smarter, not harder," I muttered.

Bea nodded. "They're going to lose power, maybe even life support."

"Typhon is desperate," Nadim said, and his fear laced through me. "The massacre . . . it damaged him. He isn't capable of strategy, only attack."

PTSD, I guessed, or some Leviathan equivalent.

"He's going to get himself and everyone on board killed. Talk to him, Nadim. This battle is winnable, but he needs to fall back. We can handle cleanup."

I didn't hear the Leviathan exchange, but I sensed it. Then Nadim said, "He's afraid of being boarded again."

It had to be terrifying for Typhon to admit that, but maybe it was also progress, a sign that he'd started seeing

Nadim as an equal. "Tell him to trust us and kick clear."

With Bacia's drones, we could mop up the rest of the Phage, even with our limited resources. I was known for coming up aces when I seemed to have a nothing hand and . . .

A shuddering boom rocked us from the docking bay, and another lance of pain tore through Nadim. I swore.

"How is it those damn contractors can't settle down and be thankful they're not getting their faces eaten in vacuum?"

"I'll go," Bea said.

"Try singing to them." I was only half-kidding, and judging from her thoughtful expression, she was considering it.

I focused on the view screen, where Typhon was finally pulling away from the Phage. His retreat forced another split between the surviving swarm; some tried to chase him while Bacia's drones picked them apart, and the rest came after us.

We can do this. Almost there.

I got on the controls and aimed a sweep across the tightest cluster of Phage, and it was unnerving how impervious they were. As one died in agony, the survivors writhed onward, like an amoeba with no higher thought. These organisms scared the shit out of me.

We were down to five shots, max.

If I didn't make them count, we'd have passengers on

the hull, testing that new plating, searching for the way in. And then—

Nope. Not happening.

Still, my stomach churned with dread. The idea of these things hurting Nadim made me want to go supernova, as if my whole body was a bomb. *I have to protect him. I must.*

"Zara, calm. We're together. We have this." Nadim's reassuring tone grounded me.

He leapt, away from the Phage, graceful as ever, and that reminded me he wasn't hurt, and wasn't damaged like Typhon. The massacre had left him grieving, but he still had Bea and me, so he wasn't living in the dark like the Elder. Our teasing retreat left the Phage faltering because they couldn't catch Nadim, and the drones picked off the slow, stupid ones.

"Another shot," I said.

We blazed half the remaining Phage, and I let slip a little relief. That was when another boom came from the docking bay, and all our power dropped. *Shit.* I fiddled with the controls frantically, no luck. Soon, we'd be overrun with alien contractors, and I wouldn't last long without life support. Nadim could still move, of course, but without power, his weapons wouldn't cycle, and the Phage . . .

"No good deed goes unpunished. Starcurrent, what the hell . . . ?"

"Is fine, on it, restore soon."

Sure enough, the lights came on about a minute later,

and maybe the explosion had worked to settle our unwilling passengers, but the distraction still cost us. The Phage had nearly reached Nadim. He reacted quick; a sweep of his tail lashed most of them away, and Bacia's drones picked off a couple that made it to the plating. I felt the tiny explosions against his covered skin.

"You okay?"

"Fine. But whatever Starcurrent did drained my reserves. I am . . . tired." The simplicity of that statement spoke volumes.

He needed to stop fighting, needed to heal properly from the right type of star. If Nadim kept pushing himself, he might slip into dark sleep. I could use the alarm to shock him awake now, but even so . . . it would only be for an emergency burst, if we were in real trouble. We needed to get him nourishment quickly.

And there were still Phage to kill. The drones were almost gone, tag-teamed by groups of individual Phage and ripped apart. We'd told Typhon to step out, and that had to hold. So, what now? We had a few thousand of these damn bugs left to swat, and I legit did not know—

"Zeerakull, we arrive! Death to our enemies!" A triumphant roar came across our comm and my mouth dropped open.

"Suncross?"

"Sorry, am late to party. Docking bay discharge problems."

The lizards' ship—surprisingly elegant and needle-sharp for such a blunt-object species—appeared on-screen, and I had never been so glad to see anyone in my life. Suncross commenced firing a weapon I'd never seen before, short burst missiles that exploded at the heart of the Phage. He also had something that jetted from the front of the ship and seemed to . . . glue them together, for lack of a better word.

That cohesion made them a better target for Bacia's few remaining drones. Between those and Suncross's obvious delight in slaughtering Phage, we managed one more rail-gun shot and finished the stragglers near the Sliver.

If there were any Phage left, they damn sure were going to have a story to tell at happy hour, and that story would be *Do not fuck with us.*

I let out a breath and then contacted Starcurrent.

"Get those assholes off my ship."

And then? We were having words with Bacia. If they had weapons effective against the Phage, it could mean they knew something about them. And I wanted every scrap of data before we blew this shitty station.

Deep down, I had chills that wouldn't quit. Because Bacia had been right. The Dark Travelers did draw the Phage. These monsters were *hunting.*

Hunting Typhon and Nadim.

Tip # 465

Out there, the single greatest threat you'll face is the Phage.

Depending on the type of ship, danger levels vary. Leviathan berths are difficult to secure, and if you're lucky enough to be chosen, you'll end up fighting this plague sooner or later. Explosive deep-space drones are most efficient. Since these beasts are small and fast, many typical ship weapons are ineffective. If possible, we recommend a matter-fusion gun, which magnetizes their chitin temporarily, resulting in a larger cluster for a pleasing and glorious target-rich encounter.

Many ships have been lost to the Phage and their hunger, but their bodies break down for excellent salvage value! There is nothing quite so satisfying as profiting from victory in battle, brave explorer.

CHAPTER SEVENTEEN

Binding Wrath

BACIA WANTED TO see us the second we docked. Fine. I wanted to see their shiny ass too. I left Bea in charge and stomped down to the docking bay.

The second I opened the door, I scanned the crowd, found the boss in his heavy metal suit, and pointed at him. "You!" I made that a full roar. "Get over here *now!*"

There had been some serious battling done in here. Half the crew looked wrecked; those who'd been able to remove their suits looked bruised, some bloody, in all the assorted colors that might entail. The crew boss clanked over to me, and that expressionless faceplate stared down at me.

"Well?" I glared right back. "What the hell? We saved your asses, and you know it!"

"All we know is you kidnapped us. With no provision for ransom or overtime." I thought if he could have shrugged, he would have. "Should have given us terms. If ransoming, transmit details. If overtime pay, we have to approve."

"We were *about to be killed* and so were you!"

"If we died, station pays out to our designated kin, but only up to quitting time. You put that at risk." He pulled a handheld and did something to it. "Double-time mynt for keeping us after end of shift. Triple fita for kidnap bonus." He thrust it at me. "Sign."

"Are you kidding me?"

"Sign or we start taking off the armor plates. Self-drilling. Self-uninstalling too, in case of nonpayment."

Now I was angry. Seeing-red angry. I should've left these assholes to die. Since I'd transferred the remainder of my mynt and fita to Suncross, I couldn't afford to pay out this bonus. They were removing Nadim's upgrades over my dead body, though.

"Fine," I growled. "It was a kidnapping. Pay your ransom or I'll end you."

"You can't demand retroactive ransom after releasing prisoners!"

I got right up in his faceplate, ready to crack it open like a walnut and drag his ass out of the suit for a beating. "And you can't call our rescue a criminal act!"

"Supervisor Khem." Bacia's voice boomed out of the communicator attached to the crew boss's utility belt. Though I couldn't see his expression and doubted I could read it, even if I could, there was no mistaking the tremor as he picked up the unit.

"Yes, High One?" That was a weird way to translate the honorific, but this alien was just about performing an obeisance to his comm.

"I need to speak with Zara Cole. You will not delay her. You have been paid in full. Do you understand this?"

"Yes, High One." Then he bowed to me, or at least that was what it looked like.

I was still mad, but since I wanted to see Bacia too, there was no point in fighting with one of their minions. Marko caught up with me as I strode through the docking honeycomb toward the long, dark tunnel that would deposit us on Tier One.

"Bea told me to keep you from blowing up the Sliver, but given your current expression, that might've been ambitious. Maybe we could just take out a few tiers?"

"Keep laughing," I muttered.

He was right, though. If I went in on Bacia at a million watts, I'd lose the negotiation. At least theoretically, they owed us something for defending their outlaw space station, and I'd get more out of this deal if I didn't storm in ready to pull their face off. As I emerged onto Tier One, I took a deep breath. Another. The air smelled faintly of chemicals, of alien bodies, and the wash of that strange chemical cocktail comforted me, oddly. It wasn't the smoke and spice of the Zone, but it reminded me that I could adapt anywhere, and that flexibility made me strong.

"You've never gone for a face-to-face with Bacia," I said to Marko.

He shook his head. "Chao-Xing prepped me. Don't make eye contact. Don't let them get too deep in my head."

"Sure," I said. "Let's see how well that works out."

I launched off the platform and luxuriated in the rush of the gravity well carrying me up to the Peak. Landing smoothly, I waited for Marko, secretly amused at his reaction when we came up to the featureless white wall. For a few seconds, I considered being an ass and seeing how long it would take him to figure things out.

We didn't have time to burn, though. Typhon must have been going wild with the desire to bail on the Sliver and get out there, continue searching for Leviathan survivors. Nadim shared that worry, but he wasn't irrational with it. Yet. I tried to imagine how I'd feel, if Bea and I were the only humans alive as far as I knew; I figured I'd be desperate too, not knowing if our cousins were out there. I hurried us through the tech-checks and only savored Marko's reaction a little when our breath got us into Bacia's inner sanctum.

"Nadim?" I whispered.

"I'm here." Hearing his voice was reassuring, but it helped even more when he touched my mind lightly, not a full bond, but just letting me know I had backup.

Okay, game time.

Inside, everything was the same as before, and I made sure not to look right at Bacia. Even so, their presence crashed over me, a commingling of dismay and awe that left my stomach spinning. Marko grabbed onto me for support; that was how unprepared he was for the impact of Bacia's preternatural charisma.

Bacia leaned forward, and even though I was holding up every bit of mental shielding I could manage, I still felt the impact of their attention. Like being hit by a grenade. "You have my thanks, Zara Cole. I would have lost much, if you and your Dark Travelers had chosen not to defend."

"We didn't do it out of fealty," I said. "And we don't have to do it again, either."

They didn't like that. The room chilled, so that I could see my breath. "Do not test me, human. I could turn you into a smear on the floor, and no one could gainsay me."

Marko tried to speak, possibly to argue that claim, but he ended up choking at a fleeting glance. His pale cheeks reddened. *Up to me, then.* I had the advantage of a full and perfect bond with Nadim, strength Marko couldn't depend on from Typhon. Bacia was trying a power play, wanting to show us who was boss and that we ought to be damn well grateful for their largesse. Beside me, Marko's knees buckled, and I felt unseen hands dragging me down too. They wanted us beaten and begging.

Lightly, I dropped into the bond, getting distance from Bacia's glamour or whatever the hell it was. With Nadim as a buffer, I held on, stood straight, and gazed over their head. I couldn't manage a bored expression, and some strain showed in my voice when I spoke next. *No helping that.* "Can we get down to business? Because I'm damn tired of carrying your water, Bacia."

The pressure dropped so fast my ears popped. Marko staggered, and I hauled him upright without making a thing of it. He leaned against me, which spoke volumes on how shaky he was feeling. Bacia's power was no joke, but I knew better than to let them see they could shake me. Powerful people—on Earth or in deep space—had one thing in common. If you showed weakness, it only made them want to hurt you more.

"I'm done testing," they said then. "You will not be asked to kneel."

"Asked?" Marko kept it to a private murmur. He was trying to get his equilibrium back. Good.

Bacia didn't seem to notice. "I respect your strength, Zara Cole. And yes, we have business to transact. I want you gone from my demesne, but you tally our accounts correctly. I owe you a debt for protecting what is mine."

Unexpectedly reasonable, but welcome, after dealing with that cockamamie crew boss. "I know what I want in return. The only question is if you're willing to give it."

"Ask." Bacia made that sound like an order.

I gritted my teeth on the surge of annoyance and controlled my temper. My mother was in my head, talking about sugar and vinegar and catching flies, but I never had time for any of that mess. Deep breath.

"You owe us, like you said. And what we need most is drone tech, like we first saw on the dead planet you sent us to, tech you just used on the Phage."

Earth had drones, of course, but they weren't built to withstand the pressures of deep space, and we hadn't aimed our research at energy cells that could run weapons that were compact but powerful, possibly because Earth scientists didn't know shit about the Phage. The Leviathan still didn't trust us completely; they'd given us *safe* tech, not stuff we could use to develop greater weapons of mass destruction.

Safe wouldn't defeat the Phage. Safe wouldn't save Nadim, Typhon, and any surviving Leviathan we found later.

"This is a great deal of fita," they said. Textbook negotiating. *Oh, no, if I pay that you're taking food from my children.* "This tech is a legacy from the Great Ones."

"The *designs* might be legacy, but you're still building

them. That makes it *current* tech. Up for barter."

They sat back. I wasn't sure which part of my answer shocked them, but on reflection, it was probably the idea that I knew they weren't a god, or whatever their real name was, because damned if I'd be calling their shiny ass High One any time soon. "You dare too much, human."

Maybe, but they hadn't slapped me down yet. And they could have. "Why did you want Lifekiller, anyway?"

The name *Lifekiller* went through them like lightning. They didn't move. Just stared at me, silent. I waited them out.

Finally, they said, "I require a genetic sample of the Great One. Then he may join his ancestors in peace and glory."

Meaning, they intended to kill him. Okay. I was fine with that. Danger, I could handle. Lifekiller didn't belong in our skies.

"Sounds good," I said. "So. Drone tech?"

"In exchange for what?"

"Bacia. Come on. You already admitted you owe us."

After a moment, they held up a hand—there was something subtly wrong about their hands, but I couldn't tell what it was; it just made my mind do that stutter-stop thing as it tried frantically to fit what it saw into an understandable framework—and Jelly Butler came floating out of concealment.

"Transmit drone designs and configurations to the Leviathan ships," Bacia said. "Arrange for delivery of required materials for construction." They flicked their fingers, and Jelly Butler drifted off. "Is that acceptable, Zara Cole? You must construct these devices yourself. It will take a great deal of time, but you did not ask for manufacturing thereof."

They sounded smug. Well, they should be. I'd gotten ahead of myself, and I'd specifically asked for the tech designs. Debating with the devil was a tough business.

"How much to have the construction done here?"

Before Bacia answered me, the Sliver penthouse tier went shrill with klaxons, and the whole damn room flashed red. And I saw something in Bacia's expression then that I'd never expected.

Fear.

"Or how about you give us the drones, fully operational?" I asked them, because *this* was the moment to hit that button, hard.

"Fine," they snapped. "Yes, they will be delivered fully operational. Out. Now."

We got kicked out of the inner sanctum before I could process what was going on. Obviously, events had taken a catastrophic turn, but Bacia refused to say if it was more Phage or system failure, so I glanced at Marko, wondering if he'd noticed anything that had slipped past me. But he was looking woozy, a memento of his first face-to-face with Bacia.

For a few seconds, he crouched, like he was trying to get over motion sickness. "Your bond with Nadim shields you?" he guessed.

"Somewhat. Typhon didn't help?" My mind was elsewhere, replaying the meeting.

He stared at me. "I can't feel him at this distance, Zara."

Right. I didn't mean to rub it in.

I sighed. "Well, at least we got paid. In theory." Which reminded me . . . *shit*. I'd forgotten to specify a time frame. It'd be just like Bacia to stiff us with some far-future delivery date.

Outside their lair, the alarm wasn't as glaring, so maybe it wasn't a station-wide emergency. Could be more of a personal issue. Or hell, it wouldn't surprise me if Bacia had set the whole thing up, to keep us from getting our due. At that thought I wheeled and almost tried their security system, but Marko put a hand on my arm.

"Let's not start a fight if we can avoid one. They agreed to our terms. Now we just need to wait."

The pause made me remember Bacia's reaction too. Whatever was going down, we probably wanted to get some distance from it, because I recalled that flash of fear. With a mumbled curse, I shook him off and pretended he was talking me down. "Fine, I hear you. Bacia knows what we want. I'll give them time to deliver before I shake the tree."

"Are you sure you made the right choice? Wouldn't the data be better than the finished drones? We could learn a lot from the designs," Marko asked.

"Normally, I'd say data would be better, but we don't have a production facility, and let's face it, it's not exactly calm out there. How long would it take us to create a functioning drone army on our own? We need weapons, not hobbies."

"Then we might want to think about a contract, where Bacia agrees to supply us with a certain number of drones, renewable as we use them to fight the Phage."

"Too bad you didn't mention it when I was making the deal." I was kicking myself. I admit, I'd had it in my head that Marko was all hat and no cattle, like my grandma used to say, but he'd just shown me otherwise. I hadn't considered a long-term contract. Bacia probably didn't think we'd be alive long enough to need one, either. I wondered what my shot was at amending that deal.

Probably zero.

Marko smiled at me, not the PR expression he used so often on Earth, but a real one that crinkled the corners of his eyes. "Sorry. My head wasn't on right during the negotiations. But there's no point in hanging around here. We should get back to Nadim and Typhon."

"If Bacia doesn't send word about drone delivery soon, I'll come back to collect."

As I leapt from the platform into the slipstream, the klaxons from Bacia's sanctum burst on station speakers. Lights flashed as I plummeted, halogen brightness mingled with the twirling red that usually meant a dire emergency. Marko landed hard behind me, stumbling on his still-healing leg. Which was weird. I still had my cast on, so walking was awkward, but it didn't *hurt* anymore. Shouldn't Marko be better by now? Or maybe I was the weird one. Come to think of it, EMITU had mentioned that one of my other wounds shouldn't have healed as fast as it did. Making a mental note to get my ankle checked out, I watched the aliens scramble on Tier One. All around us, they were locking down their shops, packing up hover dollies, and pulling chains and fences up around them wherever possible.

"What the hell?" It was more of a rhetorical question, but Marko seemed to take it seriously.

"I have a bad feeling about this," he said.

"You and me both. We need to scramble."

Too damn bad the entire lower-tier population of the Sliver had the same idea. The press of bodies swept us up, pushing us toward the tunnel that led to the honeycomb of the docking area. I got shoved into one of the Jellies, and the tentacles carried a shock-charge that left me twitching. Raising a fist, I about went full gladiator on its quivering ass, but Marko stepped closer and put his body between me and the rest of the scrum.

"It won't take much for this to turn violent." He spoke into my ear. "These people are scared, they want out. We can't fight all of them."

I took a deep breath, knowing he was right. There was a time to throw down and a time to haul ass. I was smart enough to distinguish between the two. I grabbed the nearest alien; from the suit design, it looked like one of Suncross's kinfolk.

"What do the sirens mean?" I demanded.

The lizard held up two hands in a gesture I recognized as a shrug. "Been here four years, never heard them before. Can't mean anything good. Even the Phage attack was level two. This is level three."

Everyone was bailing on the assumption that they didn't want to meet what could make Bacia's personnel hit the panic button? Fair enough. They must have ships capable of carrying them away from the Sliver. Anyone who didn't have a ride off-station was screwed. Desperate aliens shoved through the throng, eagerly trying to book passage on somebody's ship, shouting outlandish offers of mynt and fita, which didn't matter a damn in the chaos. That coin only carried value *here*, not out in the black.

I smothered a twinge of sympathy. Nadim and Bea might be willing to take in strays, but Marko showed no such inclination. He forged forward, trying to clear a path for us. There was a lot of damn shoving on the way to the tunnel, and then it got downright claustrophobic with tall, lumpy-headed aliens hemming me in on all sides. Before this I wouldn't have said I feared enclosed spaces, but I couldn't see anything but mech armor, jelly tentacles, face-plates, everywhere I looked. It got hard to breathe, and we were creeping along. There was a logjam somewhere up ahead, and people piling up behind us.

Marko was trying to calm me down, but I was about to start punching people when Nadim came through on comms. "Zara, what's wrong?"

Funny how just hearing his voice felt like a shot of seda-tive. Suddenly I could breathe, could tolerate how trapped I felt. "Something's going on, not sure what. We're work-ing on evac, but everyone is trying to leave at once, so it must be bad."

"Be careful. Come back to me soon."

"On it."

We had reached the midpoint, and I could feel the deep chill of the honeycomb ahead, likely due to its proximity to vacuum, when the red lights stopped flashing and the alarms went deathly quiet. For some reason, that didn't reassure me. I had zero confidence that Bacia had quietly dealt with the problem and was now sounding the all clear.

To me, this felt more like the eye of the storm.

Extract from Just the FAQs! Your preferred e-choice
for hot gossip

Recently, we caught up with billionaire and entrepreneur **Torian Deluca** at his tower HQ in New York. Let me tell you, he was wearing a Spinelli suit, perfectly tailored, and he offered us some vintage cognac, which I virtuously declined. (Okay, I had a nip!)

He's promising us big news in the future, but for now, we found out that he's in talks with the Russian monarchy about his lovely daughter's engagement. Do we hear wedding bells? Let's hope **Princess Ivonne** doesn't forget us when she's in **Prince Alexei**'s arms.

Just the FAQs also got the scoop from Mr. Deluca's new assistant (an impressive young man with a mysterious past), **Derry McKinnon**, on what it's like working for the most powerful man in North America. Watch for that interview, coming soon!

CHAPTER EIGHTEEN

Binding Eternity

ALL AROUND, THE aliens were calming down, taking stock. Some seemed to think everything was good and were turning to make their way back toward Tier One, while others were wary like me, still shoving toward the docking annex.

Marko grabbed my wrist. "Let's get out while we can."

It wasn't like I was hesitating, but with the crowd now of mixed minds, leaving was like being a salmon determined to spawn upstream. I shoulder-checked and shoved my way toward the exit. I'd never wondered if I could parkour off somebody's back before, but it was starting to seem tempting. So many Jellies, though, I'd probably hit one and get wrapped up and stung to death. Avoiding their swirling appendages would take a fair bit of maneuvering, but—

The Sliver rocked. The tremors hit like an earthquake, or the shudder of a massive explosion. Everyone listed to the side and I slammed into a wall, Marko right on top of me. I cussed and shoved him off as my remote link with Nadim sparked to life.

"Zara, there are multiple fires on the Sliver, several breach points. I'm reading a huge energy source and—"

Bacia cut in, jamming the transmission somehow, and their voice was in my head, on my H2, on my remote link; they were everywhere, booming a request that felt more like a demand. "Zara Cole, I need you and your Dark Travelers immediately! The god-king is risen and has broken containment. You must retrieve. If you fail, the Phage will not matter. All life dies in his wake!"

Bacia sounded deeply shook, and even if they were being honest, I smelled a deal in the making. "We already retrieved your pet god," I told them. "What's in it for us?"

"*All life dies* if you do not!"

"And?"

Bacia's voice took on an edge that said I wasn't going to like coming back here next time. "If you succeed, you will have all the drones you need, forever."

Now *that* was an offer I couldn't refuse. "Deal."

Suddenly, Bacia's voice was everywhere, ringing from the walls, the floors, every surface. "Stand aside for the softskins!"

As soon as Bacia's order came through, the Jellies nearby cleared a path for Marko and me, stinging and stunning everybody blocking our way who were slow to comply. Many retreated, and more fell—just knocked out, I hoped. But either way, we finally had a route to the Hopper, paved with twitching bodies.

Didn't much bother Marko, who ran forward without my urging. He was still favoring that leg, and I had to steady him a couple of times; walking over bodies required good balance. He saved me from a tumble once. But then we passed through into the clear space of our docking bay, and there was our Hopper, ready to go.

"How exactly are we supposed to hunt down a god?" Marko asked. A damn fine question. Nadim and Typhon were both drained, and replenishing at a star wasn't an option if we went tearing off after Lifekiller. "And what do we do when we catch it?"

"We've got the recordings we used before; those seemed to work to lull him back into a trance. Starcurrent said zis people managed to take down almost all of them, so maybe they've got a handy manual on How to Kill Your Gods lying around. We make do." I flashed him a grin, more attitude than humor.

Marko grinned back. He was starting to develop a ruthless streak; I liked it on him. He and Chao-Xing made a good, balanced team, but I wished Typhon could appreciate what he had. They might not feel exactly like the pilot and starsinger he'd lost, but from what I'd observed of the Leviathan, they needed a deep emotional connection to thrive. While Typhon might've existed for a long time, he wasn't really living.

After a glance at Marko, who shook his head, I got in the cockpit. All of us had flight training, but Bea and Chao-Xing were our best. "You sure?" I asked.

"Your scores were higher than mine, trust me."

I took some time to check my calculations on the nav computer because exiting the pull of the Sliver was higher geometry, and a mistake could cost our lives. To my relief, we launched smoothly; Bacia must have locked down all the other bays, because not one ship was in our way on the exit. Once we grabbed some distance, it was clear the Sliver was in bad shape. The Peak looked trashed, and so did several levels below. There was a blowout on the opposite side from us that must have taken several docking bays. The venting, burning air made thick candles marking the damage, and all of it burned a peculiar teal blue.

We had to avoid some spinning, frozen bodies on the way out. Ejected from the Sliver before the shields kicked in for emergency venting, I'd guess. I could see about thirty. None of them were moving on their own, and as far as I could tell, none had been in space-quality protection. No rescues to be made. I silently steered around the corpses and poured on speed to get back to Nadim. As I disembarked, Marko shifted to the pilot's seat and sped away so fast I barely had time to clear the bay. We only had the one working Hopper between the two ships for right now, but our busted-ass vehicle was starting to heal up on its own. Organic tech. Useful as hell.

I felt Nadim's intense relief course through me in a thick, cool wave as he drew me closer. The bond was an embrace, sweet as anything I'd ever known, even at this light level. Just being part of him, and him part of me, gave me a wicked surge of energy, and I felt it flood into his system as well. An added boost we both needed right now. "Welcome back," he said, and the tone of his spoken voice felt just as intimate as the blend of our minds. "Are we in trouble again?"

"Are we ever not?" I asked.

I moved toward the control center—because I shared Nadim's awareness of where everyone was—so I knew Bea and Starcurrent were there. "This kind of trouble may be the good kind. Gets us what we need to fight the Phage."

"Then whatever we have to do will be worth the effort."

"That's the spirit." I kept my doubts well away from

him, and I suspected he was doing the same to protect me. Dumb, but kind. "Get Typhon on the line for me."

I ran the rest of the way, which reminded me that though I'd had workouts aplenty on the Sliver, the grav there wasn't quite as heavy as human normal, which meant my muscles needed conditioning. I'd put in a sparring session later, if I lived that long. Meanwhile the run pumped me up, though I arrived a little short of breath.

Bea threw herself into my arms, a full-body hug that I felt spark between us into Nadim's bond, and then she headed back to the boards. Starcurrent lifted several tentacles and shook them in greeting.

"Good to see both of you," I said. I felt safe here. Confident. Probably stupid, but I felt like I could take on a god with these people, easy. "Where's Suncross and his boys?"

"Not far," Nadim said. "They dropped Beatriz and Starcurrent off a while ago, and they're awaiting your orders. I think they like you, Zara."

"Everybody likes Zara," Bea said. "Or else."

"Keep that mess to yourself," I told her, and hip-checked her. She bumped back. "Typhon? Are you there?"

"Here." His voice sounded like an earthquake in vocal form. "What is it you want?"

"You chill again? Can you hold it together if we go after the Lifekiller together, or are you going to go all berserker? Because we don't need that right now. We need to be smart, and precise. Lifekiller's all volume, all the time. Can't fight that direct. Understand?"

"I've existed for a thousand of your years," Typhon rumbled at me. "I understand. I will comply."

"Chao-Xing? Yusuf?"

"Yeah, we're listening." It was Yusuf who answered, which somehow surprised me. He sounded stronger. Steadier. "We'll keep him calm. Zara? Need some fuel. Soon."

"Copy that."

Bea had her H2 in hand, scrolling the latest intel from Bacia. "Looks like Lifekiller's stolen a ship heading who knows where."

I nodded, saving a smile just for her. "Then we need to get on his tail. We'll try to map a course that takes us close to healthy sources. Good enough?"

"Not much choice," Yusuf said. "Let's do it."

With traffic locked down in and out of the Sliver, we easily tracked the lone ship racing away from us. The god-king must have been batshit after all that time in cryo, and there was no telling what he was planning. If the Abyin Dommas had decided this race had to be stopped, I didn't want to consider the consequences of failure. Bacia had read me all wrong: I would have done this for free.

Nadim leapt after the enemy vessel, and at Leviathan

speed, we should've been able to overtake a mech ship in a matter of hours. But no matter what we did, no matter how we adjusted or checked our numbers, the god-king's ship just kept putting on speed. Bea stared at the charts, then slammed her fist against her thigh.

"This . . . this isn't possible. That's not how physics works. The laws of thermodynamics . . . There's just no way that ship has the power—"

"Is burning life force, the most powerful fuel in the universe," said Starcurrent. "Will need more soon."

"Wait." I stared at the Abyin Dommas, unable to process what I was hearing. "Are you saying that the god-king can convert biological energy and feed it to a fully mechanical starship?"

"More complex than that, but . . . yes."

I didn't like the vision that came to me, of that creature with a captive crew on board, sacrificing soul after soul to make his ship go faster. Nauseating.

But Starcurrent wasn't done. "If Lifekiller powers up fully, will be very bad."

"How far ahead of us is he, Nadim?"

"We won't catch up unless he stops."

"To refuel," Starcurrent said. "He will run out of lives soon, must take on more."

Meaning that ship would find an inhabited world and start grabbing sacrifices. I felt a wild, strange wish that

I still believed in God, that I had the faith my mother did in His love, because it would have come in damn handy right now. I hated having no options; reminded me of the worst days in the Zone, when I couldn't even afford sticky rice because Derry had spent our food money on chem. No, worse than that: this felt like being a child again, tied down on a dirty table in a church where I'd lost my faith while a fake preacher had held a knife to my head.

Deep bonding might comfort me, and it was an advantage in combat, but I couldn't feed my energy to Nadim just to help him move faster. Had to save up for now because we'd for damn sure need it later. He touched my mind, lightly, and reassurance drifted through me. Nadim didn't doubt we'd be okay; we were the extra-special Honors team, who'd graduated to the Journey without completing the Tour. Or some such shit.

I sighed. "Let's stay on the ion trail. And let me know if you can figure out where this relic is headed, Bea."

She nodded. "I'm on it, collaborating with Yusuf and Marko on analyzing possible targets. Based on what Starcurrent said . . ." Her voice trailed off to a mumble, which meant she was thinking aloud.

"Talk to Suncross," I told her. "He might have valuable intel about the systems up ahead."

The Sliver receded behind us, and at this remove, it gleamed like a knife. Ahead, there were shimmering colors, golds and purples, swirls of stardust. From orientation, I'd learned that the brightest colors often carried the most dangerous radiation, just like snakes on Earth. All these celestial bodies had names, but I preferred appreciating the beauty without slapping on labels like supernova remnant, quasar, or barred spiral. Nadim kept the wall clear, so I could see the austere allure of the stars we were chasing the god-king through. Filaments and ice dust, a cluster of burning blue that stole my breath. Space might kill me, but I couldn't be sorry, even for a minute, when I appreciated how damn lovely it was.

"What's that?" Nadim would know the name.

"Neutron star. Good for Elder Leviathan. If we slow, it would help Typhon."

"Do it. How does it sound?"

In answer, Nadim drew me to him. Human equivalent, his arms around my shoulders, as my head hit his chest. Only for us, it was mind to mind, and I dropped into *we*, the most comfortable clothes I owned. In the link, we heard the low purr, soothing and deep like a bass drum. The song rolled over us, but there were discordant notes, echoing in the distance. We slid apart. I stumbled a little, drawing a look from Bea, but she was too busy to do more than cock a brow.

I shook my head. "What was that?"

"The god-king and his ship. It is a bond that should

not be," Nadim said. He sounded more bothered than I'd have thought. "Impossible to have such a bond with mechanicals!"

"I think I've found a probable target." Before Bea could elaborate, we passed from the ice and dust cloud into a bigger debris field, all flat surfaces, hard edges, everything spinning and twisting at different velocities.

I tensed. The last time this happened, we'd stumbled into a Leviathan graveyard. "What is this?" I demanded.

"Rock, mostly. Some metallic deposits."

"Organic material?" Starcurrent asked before I could.

"Zara, there are life signs." Bea looked as freaked as I felt.

My stomach dropped. "Something's still alive? In the middle of *this*? Is it the god-king?"

"No," Nadim said. "Something else. But we must cross this field to follow Lifekiller's ship."

"Safely?" No answer. I sighed. "Do it."

Nadim twisted and dove, but sometimes he couldn't avoid all the debris; it sparked and scraped on his protective plating, though, so I wasn't too worried about him getting injured. Instead, I was thinking about a world that Life-killer would find, somewhere up ahead. How he'd break it open like a snack machine back home, eating everything in sight.

I felt a weird surge through my nerve endings, an instinct that I'd learned to heed, and I said, "Nadim?

Where are those life signs exactly?"

"The debris field disrupts smaller readings, but—"

Starcurrent shouted, "Phage!"

Damn, I hated being right. These twisting, turning rocks were perfect cover for the Phage. They were all over this asteroid field, some swimming in vacuum, and others leapfrogging from rock to rock. I figured they'd be on us fast. "Ready whatever we have!" I shouted. "Nadim, can you do any kind of evasive in this?"

"Not much," he said. "It's all right, Zara. I have armor now. They will have to work much harder. We will be all right."

It sounded gentle, and sweet, and sure. It was also a lie. Nadim knew better. Both Leviathan were still tired, maybe up to 80 percent energy for Nadim, but Typhon was still healing from his last Phage attack, and probably no better than 60 percent. We'd lost the key advantage of maneuverability and speed, though if we had to blast out of here I'd do it, regardless of the damage. We didn't have the energy reserves for a fight against both the god-king *and* the Phage, not now, maybe not ever.

Hell, I wasn't even sure how we were going to contain that bastard. If I was him, I'd have developed countermeasures against the Abyin Dommas, like, yesterday, but so far, he didn't seem to be long on strategy. That was our one ace in the hole.

I tensed up for the fight, because the Phage were coming

at us fast, swarming forward in a broad, sweeping arc of bodies climbing and jumping and surging . . . "Bea! Do we have enough power for weapons?"

"No," she said. "One shot, maybe. Nothing much now." She sounded shaky, but she was standing. We all were. If this was it, then we'd make a fight of it hand to hand if we had to. I'd killed the bastards before. I could do it again.

"Wait," Starcurrent said. "Something is different."

Ze was right. I expected that swarm to break in two and go right for us and Typhon, but . . . it broke *around* us.

The Phage *ignored us.*

I felt them skittering over Nadim's armor, scrapes of chitin on plate, and I couldn't help but convulsively shiver with revulsion; it was like being covered in roaches. But they were touching down from behind him, using him for a launchpad, and moving on.

Typhon boomed on our comms then, and he sounded . . . well, like he was unraveling. "The Phage have never done this. There must be easier targets ahead, weak but living cousins. We must save them!"

"Whoa, whoa, back up. We don't know what's out there, or why they're running. Maybe it's from something, not toward it." *Toward the god-king's ship.* I sure hoped that wasn't true, but I felt a sick certainty it was.

"More speed!" Typhon ordered. "We must find what they hunt!"

He wasn't going to listen to me, and I supposed he wasn't going to listen to his crew, either. "Bea," I said. "Anything on the projected course for the Phage?"

"Nothing evident. I don't understand. Leviathan are their preferred prey. This is . . . unprecedented."

"Keep Typhon calm. Don't know what will happen if he lashes out right now. If they're ignoring us, let them think we're big chunks of rock."

"I will," Nadim promised. "Typhon understands."

I wished I did. No joke, the Phage made me shudder. I could *see* them as we wove through the asteroid field. The rocks didn't hurt us, and neither did our greatest foe. That was some inexplicable shit. Up close, the beasties were worse than alien; they were . . . empty. No individuality, no distractions. The closest comparison I could find was to an insect hive, but even that didn't describe the behavior I was witnessing; not a single Phage demonstrated individual curiosity at anything around them. I was shivering, hard, by the time we cleared the rocks.

"It's like they can't see us. Or hear us," Bea whispered. "Why? What's blinding them?"

"Something is *very* wrong." That came from Marko, connected via vid.

"No shit," I mumbled. "Try to keep Typhon on track if you can. We don't have any other Leviathan on sensors; do you?"

"Nothing," Marko confirmed.

"Nadim, can you hear your kin singing?"

"No, Zara. I wish I could."

"Me too."

Just then, a blaze started on the viewport. In space, there wasn't anything like a horizon, but the glow was such that it was like an inferno, even many light years away. Not huge yet due to sheer distance, but I could tell this star was massive. We'd come from the Sliver to a galaxy whose name I didn't even know. Bea might be able to look up the Earth designation for it, probably just letters and numbers, glimpsed on high-powered telescopes.

The planets in this system were gray and dead, pocked from a rain of comets and other celestial detritus. Around us, colors swirled in deadly glory, red and violet, laced with silver and gold. I couldn't see the god-king's ship with my naked eye, but we must have been on the right track.

Nadim said, "It's racing toward the sun."

"Does he want to die?" Bea asked.

"Does not track," Starcurrent said. "God-kings are not prone to self-ending. Murder, yes. Not suicide."

We followed but with more caution, while the god-king didn't seem to care about heat, radiation, or gravitational pull. The star just got bigger and brighter, until Nadim had to add layer upon layer of diffusing shielding, and even then, it was hard to look directly at it. Outside, it would have cooked us like lobsters in boiling pots.

"Nadim, be careful. Don't hurt yourself."

"I'm approaching my limit," he admitted. "I cannot go any closer. But the spectrum of energy is very good for both me and Typhon."

"This is where we guessed our god-king was going," Bea said then. "Not that being right does us any real good now."

I considered our next move. Bacia might still want this thing, but I was aligning with Starcurrent. It would probably be better to kill this creature, if we even could. Ideally, I'd have liked to launch the god-king's ship into the sun, but I had no idea how to get that done with our existing weapons. Attacking might just piss the Lifekiller off. Probably would; he didn't seem like the stable type anyway.

The sun's titian glow flickered, darkening at the edges like a cigarette burning down. It took a second to parse what I was seeing. And then, it just happened *so fast*, there was no stopping it. One second, the star was full and alive and seething with energy, and then it was like the lights had just . . . turned out.

I blinked, washing the afterimages from my vision.

There was no sun now. Nothing that radiated any kind of brightness at all.

It was ash and shadow.

"Nadim?" I had trouble getting the name out. "Are we

in trouble here? Is there a gravitational wave coming?"

"No," Nadim said. He sounded . . . afraid. "Nothing. Lifekiller ate *everything*. There's nothing left, not even energy. Not even a black hole. It's as if . . ."

"As if it never existed," I finished for him. "As if he erased it from existence."

There was a deep moment of silence.

"Lifekiller has power now," said Starcurrent. "We should run."

ENCRYPTED PRIVATE SERVMAIL

From: Torian Deluca [September 18, 2142 3:34 AM, EST]
To: Claudius Acorn, WHSC coordinator
Subject: RE: A small request

Dear Mr. Acorn,
  Yeah, right.
  Look, asshole, I don't care who you are, who your father is,
or where you went to school. You know what I have on you.
I'm asking for a small favor, that's all. Drag somebody down.
Derry McKinnon goes up as an Honors alternate, or I burn
your life to the ground. I don't give a shit if he's qualified.
You make it happen.
  That's it. I catch you trying to go around me again? Well,
they didn't find the last guy.

–TD

CHAPTER NINETEEN

Binding Despair

THIS THING DRANK stars.

Not just stars. *Huge* stars. Monster red giants. What was it Nadim had hinted to me? That stars were, in some sense, alive? If this god-king could prey on a sun, how could specks of dust like us ever, *ever* fight him, much less beat him?

"Zara," Nadim said. "Join."

I ached for that comfort, and I leapt into the bond, deep as I could, submerging *I* into an entirely new entity, one with one mind, soul, thought.

Zadim looked out on the devastation with Leviathan senses.

This system had never been a cradle; these ancient, battered planets had never developed life in their own right. But the sun, the *sun* had been vast and vital and beautiful, and Zadim could still hear the echoes of its last, anguished song spreading through the universe, carried on pulses of light. The death of such a thing was deeply unnatural. Stars did die, slowly or quickly; they guttered out into sparks and darkness, spinning out their plasma as they aged, and some died in fury, collapsing inward and reversing into a gravity so relentless it allowed no song, no light, to escape. A selfish death, one never quite accomplished; those black holes remained frozen at the moment of oblivion, never to achieve it. Hungry, haunted places.

But this was different.

This was murder.

The silvery form of Lifekiller's ship—a mechanical thing, lifeless—exploded without warning, shedding metal fragments in all directions. Beneath that shed skin was something else, larger and harder, a sleek, jet-black hull that was kin to the Phage's chitinous surfaces. It bristled with sharp points and edges, an aggressive, organic form that made the human part of us cringe. The Zara part glimpsed something that Nadim did not, a hint of something awful beneath. Her discomfited perceptions spread into Zadim's awareness, and something emerged beneath the darkness of the black shell . . . a writhing, twisting wrongness that was beyond Nadim's individual perceptions. Humans were attuned to predators.

Lifekiller was changing. Growing.

Soon, it would emerge, stronger than ever before.

Typhon, Zadim reached out. *It must be now.*

We cannot destroy this construct, Typhon replied, still alone, still lonely, though his Honors glowed bright within him. Zadim mourned for his empty, grieving solitude. *All our weapons, all our strength will not damage the carapace it has forged. I am too weak, and you are too young, and this creature is too vastly powerful.*

Typhon, admitting defeat. It was worth a moment of wonder. But Zadim forged on. *A physical attack will not be successful. But a different kind might be. Can you feel any living cousins? Anywhere, no matter how far?*

Zadim was too young for senses to stretch so far; there was nothing in our reach, no whisper of Leviathan song.

Typhon finally replied, *Yes. Groupings in other galaxies. A few scattered here, nearer.*

Tell them to sing, Zadim said. *All of them. Sing of rest, of peace, of sleep.*

Zadim knew this was a danger. The harmonics of such songs, the kind that crossed empty space and found reception in Leviathan flesh . . . such songs could influence them, and Nadim was still tired, even with all solar sails deployed and drinking as much watery, distant light as possible. They had not been in the presence of the red giant for long before its horrible death. He already drifted close to dark sleep, even with all that Zara could do. The Leviathan song would resonate in him too. It would be a tide pulling him into sleep, the same as it would the Lifekiller.

You are too weak, Typhon said. *I am too weak. We will sing ourselves away.*

Make a bond, Zadim told him. *You must. Now. It will hold you.*

Typhon said, *I am afraid.*

He never would have said such to Zara Cole or to any small and relatively vulnerable Honor inside him. He would never have said it to Zadim but for the fear that this, at last, could be his last battle.

Don't be afraid.

It was a faint new voice. Only a whisper. Typhon's presence echoed with the feeling of small hands touching walls, of small voices lifted together. Almost insignificant. And yet.

Don't be afraid. One voice, leading two more. The Zara piece of Zadim recognized it as belonging to Yusuf, as damaged as Typhon, as bitterly grieving. *We are strong. We will be stronger.*

Marko and Chao-Xing. She no longer held herself back; her blazing warmth shone clear. Marko was as steady as gravity, holding them together. With Yusuf, they were three planets circling an unwilling star.

Don't be afraid, Zadim echoed with kindness and understanding for the pain and loss and anguish that Typhon had felt, still felt, would feel again. *We are with you.*

Typhon let go and sank into the bond.

What came into existence was a new thing, strong and tough, with Typhon's bitter, hard-won survival and Chao-Xing's battle wisdom and Marko's cool control and Yusuf's lightning edge of beauty and pain.

We are Lightstorm. The new creature took the name with awe and exaltation. It reflected none of their names, but that didn't matter; they were one, and the one was strong.

Bea fell into Zadim, adding brilliance and joy and a persistent kindness. Starcurrent swam in too, rich with songs and stories, bitter with scars. *Can two Leviathan also merge?* The question came from the fused being Zadim had become, larger than just pilot and ship.

Try, said Lightstorm. There was an edge of pure joy in it.

A leap together and again, something new was born: a resonance of minds, a giddy storm of thoughts, feelings, sensations. *We are Men Shen.* That name came from Chao-Xing, along with an image of two gods standing guard against two doors. Warriors. Protectors. *Gods.*

From somewhere deep in the shared consciousness, Zara Cole approved. *Gods to fight a god.*

The song of distant Leviathan, boosted through Typhon,

hit like the leading edge of a storm. It swept through the shared tissues of Men Shen, built, amplified as Typhon and Nadim added more resonance. Yusuf, Zara, and Chao-Xing shaped the weapon made of the song. Starcurrent, Bea, and Marko found the target, a tiny point of weakness in the thick chitinous covering of the Lifekiller, and drove the song in like a lance of pure power.

The shell cracked, exposing the form within to vacuum. A wave of thick, viscous liquid roped out. *Amniotic fluid.* That came from Beatriz, or perhaps from Marko; their individual voices blurred now, became shifting and indistinct in the new creature. *It isn't ready to be born. Hit it again.*

Before Men Shen could shape another lance of power, the carapace shattered down the center, spinning away in two ragged halves, and a monster swam free. The humans in the bond felt a wave of sickness, wrongness, bitter nausea; Starcurrent felt fury and horror, a familiar evil waking ghosts.

Lifekiller might not be finished in his new form, but he was very large, almost the size of Typhon. He had no form, or all forms; he shifted and boiled, formed appendages and faces and snapping teeth, and with the speed of a predator, he grabbed for the enemy closest to it.

Nadim.

No, you fucking don't. That was Zara's voice, crisp and

calm. Even as it rang through them, she, Chao-Xing, and Yusuf surged forward in the bond to take the lead, warriors, while the crafters—Marko, Bea, Starcurrent—formed the weapons warriors would wield. Song was a weapon, at the right modulations, and Typhon and Nadim channeled it in ever-louder pulses. This time the warriors used it as a blunt object, hurtling in a broad fist to strike Lifekiller, and the flexing tendril that attached to Nadim ripped free from both Nadim and Lifekiller's body. The dead flesh drifted limp and desiccated away into the darkness.

Lifekiller retreated. It could run, the two halves of Men Shen realized. With just two Leviathan, it was impossible to block every route, but they began to move in parallel, circling the god-king. The song pounded the creature relentlessly, wave upon wave, and its skin began to gray. *Sleep*, the combined song of Leviathan shouted. Aboard Nadim, Starcurrent added the recordings of zis own songs, and Lifekiller faltered.

It was working.

Men Shen was so fixed on the mission that the arrival of the Phage came as a shock.

Yusuf was the first to notice and called out—a small sound that drew little attention from the battle until Chao-Xing joined it, then Marko. Men Shen turned their joined attention outward.

Covering the god-king's withdrawal, the dark swarm

boiled from the darkness. The Phage from the asteroid field arrived in numbers so great their bodies blotted out the distant stars. The Men Shen's song faltered, and Lifekiller took the chance. It fled behind the mindless, devouring shield, past the dead sun, and away into a universe that wasn't ready for the danger.

Surrounded! Men Shen formed the thought even as that deepest of bonds splintered, and broke again, and again, dropping Zara—no, *me*—onto the floor. My knees would barely hold me, so I used the console to haul myself upright. Bea was on the floor nearby, and I gave her a hand up; she looked spun out, but I didn't have the time. Starcurrent flailed, a ball of tentacles and indistinct noise. No help there.

Focus.

I was all over the instrument panel, trying for a brainstorm that would get us out of this mess and back on Lifekiller's trail. We'd come so close, and now he was out there, powered up and free to menace the whole damn universe. It was impossible not to feel responsible for the lives he was going to take, though Bacia couldn't escape the greater share of blame.

Nearby, Starcurrent braced on the wall, using all tentacles and filaments to stay up. The Phage had ignored us before; they were attacking at max, now. They swarmed Nadim's hull, biting and drilling the plating, and with them covering us like maggots on a carcass, many of our weapons were useless. Nadim rolled and flipped some free, but there were so many, *too many*. There was no way we could fight them all.

"Dark run?" I felt short of breath. Crushed with anxiety. Even as I said it, I knew the answer.

"I don't have enough energy, Zara, and even if I did, I wouldn't leave Typhon." Nadim was loyal to the core.

Snarling beneath my breath, I uplinked to Typhon. "Solutions, people. If we don't shake the Phage *now*, we die along with this star."

"Run," Yusuf said. "Got to run."

We ran, but we couldn't shake the Phage. I had the worst case of claustrophobia, knowing they were crawling all over Nadim, looking for a weak point, trying to get *in*. The shudder that wracked me nearly bent me double. Nadim was doing his best speed, and so was Typhon, but the Phage were keeping up, and for each one we managed to shake loose, another clamped down. The armor was holding. For now. I felt a new, sharp fondness for that construction boss who'd been such a pain in our asses because *damn*, quality work.

"I'm going out there. I'll shoot them one by one if I have to." I meant it. I knew I was exhausted and strung out with worry. I could feel the light, constant tremor in my hands.

I needed food and sleep and a little time for the damn stress to subside, but I wasn't going to get any of that now. I'd rather kill things.

"Zara, no!" Nadim sensed my desperation, of course. It was keeping me from thinking clearly, along with all that other mess. "You're far too tired. You can't."

Thankfully, Bea was, if not completely calm, then logically wrangling the problem. "Nadim. You and Typhon both have plating . . ."

She was onto something. I grabbed the tail end and ran with it, remembering how Nadim had said, *We do not use weapons on each other.* "Punishment!" I shouted, at the same time Bea said, "Discipline!"

I grinned at her, and she gestured that I should say it. I activated the comm to make sure the message broadcast to everyone. "Typhon, use your tail like you did over Nadim's alleged bad behavior—which, don't think I've forgotten that. Leviathan have trouble when they're alone against the Phage, but we're partners. So *help* each other!"

Nadim got it before Typhon did. He slapped the *shit* out of the Elder, like he'd just been waiting for the excuse. I couldn't control a half-crazy laugh. The plating protected Typhon from physical harm, but it smashed the Phage crawling over his armor. Like lightning, Typhon returned the blow, so hard that Nadim spun out. I tumbled sideways and latched on to Bea. Starcurrent grabbed both of us with several tentacles. Handy having our own mobile safety harness, not that ze wasn't good for other stuff. I was getting to like zim a lot, especially when ze crisply said, "Pardon my touch. Am respectful of boundaries. But better you do not die."

To an external observer, it would probably look like a Leviathan slap fight, but they weren't seriously hurting each other, and the Phage died by the hundreds with each strike. It took human ingenuity to come up with a solution this basic, because the Leviathan explored alone and *died* alone, once they encountered the Phage. They also weren't killers, not like humanity or Suncross's people. I wasn't sure how the slapping thing had evolved in them, but I guessed there were territorial battles, ceremonial things, something that had developed into elder/younger protocols.

From this point on, surviving Leviathan needed to travel in pairs, at least until the threat passed. And slap each other. Dumb and basic, but effective as hell.

"Put on some speed now and roll," I said over the comms.

The incredible burst Typhon and Nadim put in in tandem drained the last of their reserves, but it also scoured the last of the Phage from them, as far as I could tell. Even if there were stragglers as we blazed back toward the Sliver, they would be slow and stupid, easily put down. I might get my spacewalk hunting mission yet.

Not at this speed, of course. That would be suicide,

because we were going to have to hit the brakes, and momentum was a bitch. But when we got to the crim station, I could check for stowaways. Honestly, the prospect of killing the Phage up close and personal sounded damn tempting. I was sick and tired of their inexplicable bullshit.

And then Starcurrent made it sickeningly explicable.

"Is true, then," Starcurrent said.

"What is?" Bea asked.

"That god-kings command the Phage."

That snagged everyone's attention, hard. A babble of questions came from the console—Chao-Xing, Marko, and Yusuf all asking stuff at once. Bea just stared for a few seconds, her brow furrowing like it did when she was tackling a knotty puzzle. As I reviewed the chain of events, I realized it made sense. "Wait, wait, wait," I said. "That wasn't coincidence that they showed up? They didn't come tracking us, either?"

"They ignored us in the asteroid field," Nadim pointed out helpfully.

"Yes," Starcurrent said. "They were summoned. Responded to Lifekiller's call."

"*Damn*," I whispered. "And they went after us on his orders too. I did think it was too damn coincidental that they swarmed just as we had that bastard on the ropes."

"Good," said Starcurrent, and flashed tentacles. "You understand."

"How could it command them?" I asked, because I felt

like Starcurrent was still holding something back, and I didn't like it. Zis tentacles fluttered nervously and turned the colors of discomfort. Kid couldn't bluff to save zis life. "Nobody else can."

"Nobody else drinks stars, either," Bea said, but I shook my head, attention on Starcurrent. I wasn't about to let zim slide on this one.

"Legend only," ze finally admitted. "Phage were made by conquered peoples, long dead now, to serve god-kings. When god-kings died, Phage did not."

"So somebody bred an army and set it loose without a general. *Great.*"

Starcurrent's embarrassment flushed rainbows through zim. "My people thought Phage would die without god-kings to sustain. Were wrong."

I was angry now. Sharply angry. "Damn right you were! These things have been eating *Leviathan*! And you knew about that?"

All zis tentacles went up in surrender. "Is not our fault! Did not make Phage, do not know how to stop! But now is bigger problem. Now, Lifekiller can command."

Lifekiller had a fucking army. Great. Well, at least now I had a sound grasp of our predicament, even if it felt like a sucker punch. If the god-king wasn't enough to contend with, now we had the Phage as his shock troops.

In that moment, it was so hard not to just . . . quit. I

was so tired; it felt like forever since I'd had a full night's sleep or a decent meal. The little kid in me wanted to whine about how none of this shit should be my problem, and yet it was. All of it. Dispirited, I sank down into a nearby chair.

Bea put a hand lightly on my shoulder, then Starcurrent added a tentacle. That silent contact said, *We're here. You're not alone.* Some of the weight lifted, and when Nadim opened himself to me, it felt like a full embrace. I dropped into the bond long enough to give and take comfort, offering strength to both of us. Not long in actual time, but when I opened my eyes, I felt a lot better.

Chao-Xing was on-screen, looking serious. "We need your gift, Zara. Find us a weakness."

"I'll try to come up with something."

Of course, everyone asked what that was about, so I had to give the nutshell version, explaining my supposed superpower. To my surprise, they all reacted like it was . . . right, that Chao-Xing had seen something special in me, an ability I'd never realized I possessed. And it felt good, really good. To be valued like that. The Leviathan DNA in my head might mean I was a better-than-average candidate for bonding, but this skill was mine, pure Zara Cole. It meant something.

"Approaching the Sliver," Nadim said then. "Zara? What are we going to tell Bacia about losing our quarry?"

I swore. Bacia wouldn't like us returning empty handed,

but what were we supposed to do, two Leviathan against a fully fueled-up god-king and his Phage army? Come on. All factors considered, we were lucky we'd survived that encounter. Typhon or Nadim alone? Unlikely. And I grieved for all the Leviathan who'd died in the black.

It occurred to me then . . . we'd thought the Leviathan had been killed in a mass slaughter at the Gathering, but what if the Phage had picked them off one by one as they arrived? It would've left the same carnage, but made more sense, tactically speaking. If we'd come up with a solution between two cooperating Leviathan, then their Honors could have too. They could have used their bulk, formed defenses, *fought back.*

Unless each one died alone, got devoured, and the Phage saved an infested corpse to jump the next arrival, a decoy of sorts. *That's exactly what happened to Nadim.* The strategic part of my brain activated, telling me I was on target. They were viruses, infecting and controlling another creature.

Before I could work out how this insight benefited us, a sharp pain broke over me. Not excruciating, more like the sting of an insect. A glance at Bea told me she hadn't felt it. Neither had Starcurrent. But I checked my arms and legs to see if I was bleeding; that clarified whose pain I'd sensed.

At once I reached for Nadim. "You okay?" I didn't know

if I was talking or thinking.

His silence scared me, and then his sheer terror hit me like a wall of dark water. "Zara, it's inside!"

Oh shit. There was no question he meant the Phage. I'd thought I could crush any stragglers on his armor, but one of them had found a soft spot to burrow in? First, I calmed Nadim because his fear made it hard for me to function, then I ran for the armory to gear up with one thought looping:

Gotta destroy this thing before it breeds.

Transcript from **Good Day, New Detroit**, *with hosts Kephana Washington and Saladin Al-Masih, September 20, 2142*

WASHINGTON: Good morning, New Detroit! This is poised to be a historic show. Coming up, we have a first look at the latest personal hovercraft, a new release from Obari–your favorite Nigerian pop idol–and finally, an incredible, unprecedented Honors announcement.

AL-MASIH: (feigns surprise) Are you serious, Keph? I thought we were done with Honors coverage for a while.

WASHINGTON: Oh, this is incredible! Just wait for it.

AL-MASIH: Come on, not even Obari can compare to an Honors exclusive. Let's not keep our viewers in suspense! Can't you give us a little hint?

WASHINGTON: (pretending to give in) Oh, all right! Two of our Honors have already been promoted to the Journey, without completing the Tour! And one of those extraordinary young women is a local–wild-card pick Zara Cole! She's gone onward with her flight partner, Beatriz Teixeira, with their original Leviathan.

AL-MASIH: Oh my God. This has never happened, has it, Keph?

WASHINGTON: Never! We have a first look at their replacements: Kashvi Baphna from Bhilwara, India, and Derry McKinnon—another local boy! We'll be interviewing Mr. McKinnon on a live linkup, later in the show.

Interlude: Nadim

All I know is terror.

I remember, I cannot forget, can never forget, the husks of my cousins, drifting as detritus. Devoured from within.

I can never wash away the horror of the mindless hunger, a thousand plague cells in Leviathan skin, attacking with a ferocity we barely survived.

I'm pretending to be calm—for Zara, for Beatriz, and for Starcurrent too. They are so precious, my beloved partners, and my fear might hurt them. I cannot permit this monster to harm them. I want to reach for them, but the bond would comfort only me and reveal secrets they must not know.

I am powerless.

All the weapons from that one, Bacia Annont, the heavy plating, my shields. None of that can save me from this intruder with fangs like steel knives and a relentless determination to infest. I can only trust in the ones who protect me, even as I care for them.

Typhon is powering up his guns. I will not tell the others.

But he will kill us himself—a merciful death—before allowing us to fall. He has seen too much death, too many of our kind lost. Even now, I am not sure how many remain. Their songs are distant and fearful, full of misery and mourning. And the Elder will not survive using weapons on me. Despair will claim him, and his partners along with him.

It must not come to that.

CHAPTER TWENTY

Binding Prisoners

"YUSUF! ANYBODY LISTENING on Typhon?" I shouted, hoping Nadim would relay the signal. "Check for stragglers who might've gotten inside. Do it now! We can't let these things build a nest and breed!" I had no idea how long that would take, but it couldn't be much time . . . they'd overtaken Leviathan fast enough to ambush the next to arrive. "Nadim, can you pinpoint it?"

"No," he said. He sounded strained and shaken. "My senses don't work on it. I can feel movement, but . . ."

"Where? Block out the rest of us and tell me where you feel it!"

He bonded with me and showed me, and the storm of his fear and helplessness made me stagger a little. I sent what reassurance I could, and ran as fast as I could for the area he'd indicated . . . but when I got there, it was a blank wall. "Nadim!"

"It's in a place not fitted for humans," he said. Growing panic in his voice too. "I don't have the resources to make it safe, Zara . . ."

I switched gears. "Bea! Bring the skinsuits! Nadim, what's on the other side of the wall specifically?"

"Gases that are toxic to you," he said. "They would kill you, Zara."

"Can you vent them out somehow?"

"No, I need them."

Dammit. "Can you form an entry door?"

"Zara—"

"I'll wait until Bea gets here with the skinsuit," I promised.

"Zara, *you cannot go in without one.* It will kill you on contact!"

"Can you give me a door?"

He did. It cost him; I could feel the burn of energy as he reshaped his flesh and created an opening that was sealed off from me by a thin membrane. On the other side was a small chamber, and another membrane. An airlock system. I'd have to break the membrane, step in, let him seal it up, then break the one into the toxic chamber. "Can you recycle from the airlock and keep the toxins from getting into our section?" I asked him.

"Yes." A clipped, distracted answer. "Wait for the suit, Zara. Bea is almost here."

Bea arrived, running flat out, and tossed me a skinsuit. It unfurled in the air, and if I could have done some magical vid thing and jumped into it in slow motion, I would have, but I had to step in and pull it on, yanking so hard I thought I might rip it apart. It held. I rolled the hood down and adjusted to instant insect-vision, which was much sharper and better once I got used to it.

I pulled my gun and said, "Going in. Bea, back me up. You and Starcurrent need to kill the *shit* out of this thing if it makes it through."

"We will," she promised. She was pulling on her own skinsuit—prepped, I realized, to go in to get me if something went badly sideways. Starcurrent already had on zis tentacle condoms, and could manifest zis bubble helmet at a moment's notice, so we were okay.

Now I just had to kick some Phage ass.

I walked up to the thin membrane and pressed on it. A slit formed, and I squeezed through. It snapped shut behind me.

As I pushed through into the second chamber, though, there was no way to mistake it. The suit's warnings went off, lights in my vision blinking, tones sounding, and I could *smell* whatever was in here. Filtered down enough, I assumed, that it wouldn't melt me inside the suit, but it burned my nose and mouth, and made my eyes water. *Not good.* I needed all my alertness on my surroundings right now. I blinked the pain away, shoved it aside, and took stock of what I was seeing.

Bioluminescence shimmered in the walls, providing me with a dim half-light; I wanted to turn it up, but every lumen of it was costing Nadim core energy. I let it stay as it was. The chamber was a big vaulting place, with organic, arching ribbing veining the walls and jutting out like the supports of old cathedrals back home. It was filled with a thick, yellow haze. It drifted down in lazy curtains, and I couldn't see far.

I used the bond to avoid opening my mouth. *Nadim. Where?* I saw the overlay of where I stood with where he had detected the movement and moved right, around a thick column that spread out thinner filaments like branches, anchored up toward the dim ceiling. He guided me with a pulse of light along the wall.

Ahead, I saw a red pulse flash. I couldn't see what was there. The yellow mist hid it.

I readied my gun. *Can you clear the mist? Just for a second?*

Something like a breeze stirred through the room. The mist lessened, and . . . I saw it.

The Phage lay on its side, leaking fluids onto the floor. Its chitinous limbs moved slowly. It looked like a repulsive, deadly monster, but at least it was *dying*.

Not slow enough. I got braced to shoot, looking for a good target.

A voice, processed and weird through my translators, said, "No."

I froze. "Bea? Bea, did you say that?"

Bea, on comms, said, "Say what? Zara? Are you all right? What's happening?"

"Hold," I said. "Nadim. Did you hear it?"

"Yes," he said. "But I don't know what it is."

I could end this with one easy pull of the trigger. Drill a shot right through that ugly, horror-show head. All my instincts told me to do it, *now*, before it hurt Nadim or worse.

"No," it said again. "Please."

It was the *please* that made me shudder. *No* could have been a glitch, the translator accidentally interpreting random noise wrong. But not *please*.

Please had meaning. Awareness of individual danger.

Please was a plea for mercy.

Most of me wanted to kill this thing. About 90 percent, maybe 95.

I didn't shoot. Didn't put the gun away, though. "Give me a reason not to."

"Can help," the Phage said. The words came through strangely accented, but they were words. Had meaning. "Please not kill me."

I felt sick and short of breath suddenly and drew in a burning breath that made me sicker. The warning light in my suit was blinking faster. Tones sounded louder. *Shit.* I was losing suit integrity in here.

"Dying," the Phage said. "Can help you. Want to."

It was bad enough that the monsters I'd thought were as smart as hammers could talk. Now it was begging for its life.

And offering me something of value.

"How many others made it in here?" I asked. My throat felt like I'd gargled burning lighter fluid. I swallowed. Tasted a trace of blood.

"None," it said. "Please. Help."

I chose mercy.

Chao-Xing had said, *Find us a weakness.* And here it was. Where the other Phage had no regard for their own existence, this one cared enough about its own life to beg for it. I pulled it out of the toxic gas, past the organic airlock, where Bea and Starcurrent were waiting with weapons.

"Stay back," I said.

They both started to bombard me with questions, but there was no time. The Phage cell felt oddly light and fragile as I hauled it, leaving a green-gray blood trail. If I didn't act fast, this thing wouldn't survive long enough to fulfill its offer of help. Starcurrent lent me some tentacles and we got the creature to medical quickly after that.

EMITU rolled out of its docking station and leaned toward the Phage. "I'm a med unit, but this is not a patient, Honor Cole. Do you want to put it out of its misery?"

"I brought you your biggest challenge yet. Scan it. And save it."

Starcurrent and I plopped the patient in the treatment bed, though the Phage cell didn't quite fit. I backed off and gave EMITU some room; the autodoc did some stuff that looked inventively dangerous, but the intruder did stop bleeding. From where I was standing, EMITU seemed to be using chemicals instead of medicine—at least in human terms—but then again, I didn't even know if the Phage was a carbon-based life-form.

Don't care if it dies, I told myself. *Better if it does.*

"Zara, be careful." Bea was still near the doorway, weapon cocked and locked. Girl was tense. Didn't blame her. This had been a hell of a day. "I don't like this."

"Look, the thing spoke. You ever talked to the Phage before?" It was a rhetorical question, and when they didn't answer, I went on, "This thing's an anomaly. It claims it can help us, and at this point, we need to take any advantage we can get."

"But . . ." Bea swallowed her protest. "I can see that you're dead set on this. Let's set up containment."

That was a damn clever idea. I hadn't thought about what would come next, but I should have. I was tired, scraped raw, exhausted . . . and so were we all. Nadim most of all. I needed to consider his safety first.

Maybe Bea and Starcurrent were right. Maybe this was a trick. We knew jack shit about the Phage, so maybe they were evolving, and this one was trying to work a con. Like, if we accepted it as an ally, it would split into two and then four, and soon we'd be overrun and infested from the inside. I couldn't take my eyes off this thing for a minute.

"Nadim," I started. "Ask Typhon if he's ever heard of—"

The Phage in the treatment chair started shuddering as EMITU did something to it. Shit, it might die anyway. Somehow, failing to save something felt completely different from choosing to kill it. White froth bubbled from the Phage's mandible, and then EMITU said, "Well, that's not a good sign."

"That's not what we want to hear!"

"I'm working on it, Honor Cole. These things don't come with a manual."

A few moments later, the seizure and foaming had stopped. For a few long seconds, I thought it was dead . . . but the readouts showed life in it yet. EMITU said, "Huh. That shouldn't have worked." I let out a sigh. I still couldn't stand looking directly at the thing, but it was hard to call it a monster when it had enough self to beg for mercy. Seeing someone, anyone at their most desperate gave them a reality that was hard to shake.

The Phage was unconscious for a while. Bea and Starcurrent eventually left to consult with the others, leaving me on watch. The medbay was probably the best for containment, so I stayed, conscious of the needles of Nadim's discomfort. I'd tried to open a channel to talk about my decision to spare this creature, but now Nadim was quiet. Resting, and still resisting.

"It'll be okay," I said then. "If it's dangerous or it betrays us, I can always kill it."

"Do you know of the Trojan horse, Zara?" Nadim finally spoke. "It's a human story I learned a long time ago."

And yeah, I did. I froze when I processed the implications. "You think this Phage is *carrying* something? Like a virus that'll make us sick?"

I didn't know if it was good that we'd rubbed off on each other like this. Once, being cynical and suspicious had been my full-time job, but now Nadim was talking like me, and I was erring on the side of kindness. That was some fully mixed-up shit right there.

And he was right. Completely right. I had taken the Trojan horse into the city walls because it had asked nicely. The old Zara, running the streets in New Detroit—she never would have fallen for it.

My fingers flexed on my weapon. It would be so easy to kill the Phage while it was out, recovering from whatever experimental medical shit EMITU had just done. I turned to the autodoc. "Can you run some tests while it's out, see if it has a viral payload to deliver?"

"I'm not a wizard, Honor Cole. My ability to extrapolate and interpret data from a unique specimen is limited. If you bring me others to study and compare—"

"Never mind," I said. "Guess that only leaves one option."

EMITU rolled over to block my way. "I must warn you that I am medically obligated to fuck you up if you attempt harm to a being in my care."

"I wasn't going to . . ."

"I'm also not a lie detector, but I can read acceleration of respiration, heartbeat, and an intent to do harm. Cheer up. If I do have to grievously wound you, I can immediately slap a pressure bandage on the wound."

Funny as the bot could be, I didn't doubt its sincerity. I might be able to shoot the autodoc into scrap, but I couldn't otherwise get around it. Wrecking our medic in the middle of a war would be stupidly disastrous.

Chao-Xing arrived with Yusuf and Marko while I was thinking that over. Damn, the situation was dire if they'd *all* bailed on Typhon to come over here. C-X was already striding toward the unconscious Phage, weapon out, when I grabbed her arm and wheeled her around.

"Are you insane?" she demanded. EMITU started his speech again, and came to a quick stop when she pointed the gun at its mechanical face. "Shut up."

"Yes, good plan," EMITU agreed, though it didn't move out of her path, either.

"We thought Beatriz was joking when she first told us," Yusuf said. He had his hand on his weapon as well. Lots of aggression in him too. "Move your medical unit if you don't want to lose it."

"No! Dammit, I saved the Phage for a reason!" Even if I didn't know for sure that I'd made a good call. I glanced at Marko, thinking he might be a likely ally . . . but I didn't see any sympathy. Only wary doubt. "You understand why I took the risk, right?"

"My instinct is to kill it," Marko said. "But I also know that I'm full of Typhon's unbounded hate, and so are these two. I'm trying to control that, but I can't vouch for Typhon. He's . . . not handling this well. He sees no option but to kill every Phage we find."

"Then one of you should go back to console him. This is *one* creature and it's injured. I'm not killing it until I hear what deal it's offering."

Surprisingly, Chao-Xing seemed most keyed in to Typhon's rage, and she tried to shove past me, determined to blast the Phage cell to atomic dust. "Let me go!" she snarled at Yusuf when he held her back.

I put my body between her and the target, half unable to believe I was protecting the enemy. "Get her out of here. I'm taking responsibility for this. Me. Nobody else. And Typhon's not at risk unless you start something. Go home. Now!"

"Can't do that either," Yusuf said. "Chao-Xing's right. That thing has to die, for all our sakes." His gaze was hard and pitiless. "It would kill our Leviathan without mercy. We can't take the risk."

I took in a deep breath. "Chao-Xing. Are you listening to me?" She wasn't. Her gaze went right over my shoulder, fixed on the unconscious Phage. *"Warbitch!"* That snapped her right out of it, and onto me with the same furious intensity. "You said I had a gift, remember? Well, my instincts are telling me that this Phage cell is a weakness for them. It can help us. It might even win us the damn war. *So back off.*"

The shell of her rage fractured, even if it didn't break completely; somewhere inside, Chao-Xing struggled to process my words and understand what I meant, pushing back against Typhon's heavy influence. She finally nodded once, sharply. She knew what I was talking about. She'd trust me.

God help us all, she trusted me.

Nadim said, just for my ears, *Zara. Is this worth it?*

It has to be.

Yusuf never did come around, and it didn't look like he trusted my judgment, either. When he hustled Chao-Xing out of the medbay, he carried a shadow with him, but I could only deal with one crisis at a time. Marko stared at the Phage cell with a conflicted expression. "Are you sure this is wise, Zara?"

I laughed bitterly. "Hell no. I live expecting shit to go sideways. Maybe this thing will give us some fatal disease, just like Nadim fears, and if it does, gut up and take whatever measures you have to, to save Nadim and Typhon. But . . . I can't kill it, because that means giving up on hope. Right now, this is the only possible advantage we have against the Phage. I can feel that."

He nodded. "Then I'll wait with you." He looked faintly sick, though. Too pale, even for white-boy complexions. I pulled over a stool, and he gratefully sat down. "Sorry. Typhon is . . . not pleased with us just now."

"Tell him to shut up and wait," I said.

"That might work on Nadim, but . . ."

"Yeah, I know." I looked at EMITU, who was still rolling indecisively between the two of us and the bed of its patient. "Don't suppose you've got any booze."

"I have germicidal alcohol," it said. "And olives." It paused. "I am lying about the olives. Also, I suggest that removing all soft, vulnerable bodies from this area might be an excellent idea, as I believe my patient is beginning to come around."

"We'll stay," I said. "Bring on the hooch."

"I was also lying about the alcohol."

We sealed the medbay door behind us. Containment was key. If this shit soured on us, each ship would still have enough Honors. He didn't say that was a factor in his decision to stay with me, but I could read it in his somber expression. Seemed like some Honors were ready to become heroic sacrifices at the drop of a hat. I'd been in that headspace in the temple of doom, but I'd hurt Nadim a lot then too. This time, I wouldn't make that mistake. I'd do everything I could to survive.

Nadim's relief surged through me, like he could sense my state of mind. I touched the wall lightly in reassurance, got a color pop back.

And at last, the Phage stirred. Barbed limbs thrashed against restraints, then stilled, though I guessed it probably could have cut through those like a hot wire through butter. The shape of the thing still revolted me; it was something out of collective human nightmares, like we'd always known something like this existed out in the dark, and known how dangerous it would be. Could the universe itself have a collective unconscious? I'd have to ask Nadim.

"I live," the Phage said. I expected that without the

flattening effect of the translators, it might have seemed surprised. Now, I could hear the Phage's language. It was as unsettling as its appearance; thin whistles and clicks and rattles. Reminded me of dead deserts and living poison.

"You do for now," I said. "And you will if you're honest, and you're useful to us. Do you understand?"

"Yes."

"You said you could help us."

"I can."

"How?"

To my amazement, it told us.

Honored members of the committee:

I have upon several occasions registered my most strenuous objection to the unprecedented breaks of protocol this year, including the unscheduled arrival of a Leviathan Elder, the astonishing decision to hold a hasty Honors selection to replace Honors Teixeira and Cole in the program, the equally astonishing (and unjustified) decision to strip said Honors of their rank and privileges for abandonment of duties, and revert them to private citizen status in their absence. I have said, many times, that this is a hasty and unwise decision made in advance of facts, as the Elder has provided little information to us of the circumstances of their absence from the Tour.

But what causes me to tender my resignation from the program is more serious. There is evidence that the selection of one Derry McKinnon as one of the two replacement Honors has been engineered by external

forces, in a violation of everything our program holds
sacred. I have sounded warnings of this undue influence
on two prior occasions. Nevertheless, the committee
achieved a majority of votes to pass this candidate
and affirm the selection, though his history is clearly
unsuitable, as is his psychological profile.

I can no longer serve honorably in a program that has
abandoned the honor it confers on others. I can no longer
be assured that our cause is just or that our process is
pure, and that raises disturbing questions of exactly what
we do here.

It has been my privilege to serve the young people we
send to the Tour, and the Journey. I will not stain that
memory by cooperating in this appointment.

[DNA signature]

CHAPTER TWENTY-ONE

Binding Offer

"CAN HEAR SWARM," it said, which was a stunning statement, and one I immediately doubted. A glance at Marko told me the same. "No kill now?"

"Why?" I wasn't sure it would—or could, for that matter—answer the question, but I wanted to see if it understood the concept. I couldn't read body language, facial expressions—not that this thing had a face, exactly; it had a *maw*—and all I had right now was the words it spoke. Truth or lie, at least it was talking.

The Phage took its damn time replying, and I stood watching it, rocking back and forth on my heels. I was exhausted. I stank of the poisonous gas that had seeped through my suit, and my eyes felt raw. So did my throat. I'd ask EMITU to check me out, but we were all a little preoccupied. Still, I was aware of all these annoyances, and aware that they might be prejudicing me, or impairing my ability to judge things right. I thought about bonding with Nadim, but that wasn't fair, either; he had a visceral horror of these creatures, and besides, he had his own weariness to handle.

Right now, it was me and Marko and the Phage stuck in a bottle. Either we'd all come out, or none of us would.

"Woke," the Phage suddenly said. "Bathed in light of god-king. No longer just hunger."

Marko leaned forward, elbows on knees. "You mean, you became . . . aware? Because of the god-king's presence?"

"Yes."

Marko raised his eyebrows and looked at me. Did this mean *all* the Phage that had swarmed off with Lifekiller now had individual consciousness? Or did that mean this one was weird? Either could be true, provided it wasn't a super-elaborate trap that was about to blow us all to kingdom come.

"EMITU, scan the Phage for explosives," I said, because why not cover that base?

"Already done," EMITU replied. "Alas, we will all die."

I snapped to attention. Marko did too.

"Someday," EMITU finished, now that he'd gotten his desired response. "But not from blowing up. The Phage contains no dangerous materials. I also completed a virus scan but found nothing recognizable. If you die of something, it will be gloriously new."

"Great." I glared at it. "I'm going to reprogram you into a toaster."

"Then you won't be needing me anymore." EMITU tossed off that salt, then rolled into his dock and powered down.

"Jerk," I said to it, and turned back to the Phage, who might not have understood any of that. I wasn't sure how nuances translated, though Starcurrent seemed to get by okay. "Okay. So, you . . . woke up. Did any others?"

"Others of the swarm? A few. They do not follow."

"Follow what?"

"The trail of hunger."

"To the Leviathan?"

"Yes."

"But you did."

Silence. The Phage finally said, "I was hungry. I only aware of . . . of nature of prey when felt consciousness within. Kindred mind. Sorry for pain."

In its clumsy way, this thing was describing . . . empathy. Awareness that it was causing pain, and regret. "Holy shit," I said to Marko. "It understands what it's done."

"Yes," the Phage said. It almost sounded eager. "Understands. Individual. All individual." Pause, and a long one. "Few of my kind are so. Most content to be . . . one. Directed by the Mind." Somehow, I knew there was a capitalization on that noun.

"You mean, the god-king?" Marko asked.

"No. God-king newly arrived. Mind there always."

"Something else is . . . ordering these attacks, then?"

The Phage shook all over, a definite *vibration*, and I was reminded of some boring vid I'd seen once in rehab about bees, and how they communicated by complex dances and vibrations. Huh. That probably meant something to another Phage. It just looked freaky and disturbing to me. "No," it said. "Mind is Mind. All of us together in swarm."

"Collective consciousness," I said. "Like a hive. Only I think maybe the Phage aren't so specialized. They just . . . swarm, eat, move on."

"Yes," our Phage cell affirmed. "But different. Now god-king plans. Swarm obeys."

"Can you still hear it? The Mind?"

"Yes."

"What is it saying?"

The Phage shifted a little, and every time those razor-edged nightmare limbs started moving, I got a little sick and sweaty, but it didn't seem to be contemplating an attack. "Following god-king. Will do as god-king commands.

Much food to be seized. Much . . ." The Phage stopped and vibrated again. "No. Do not wish to listen. Very bad."

"Hang on a second. You said you could track the swarm. Can you actually disrupt it?"

"I must surrender to the Mind to do so. Must be released from . . . flesh prison."

I really wasn't sure if it meant the restraints, or containment, or Nadim, but whatever way, that was a hard no. "Get used to being on a leash. You're lucky you're not in a thousand pieces right about now. When you surrender to the Mind, don't you just become, I don't know, a mindless drone again?"

"Yes. No. Not sure. Possible I remain I alone within the swarm. Others may be within. Can link together. Direct the Mind."

So, an internal revolution was what he was offering. But what if these mutated Phage, the individuals, were few and far between? Seemed to me that hive behavior would be to turn on them and rip them apart, and get on with things. The death of a few drones wouldn't bother the Mind a bit.

"Too risky," I said. "You can give us valuable intel for now."

"Will keep me alive?"

"For now," I repeated.

"How long alive?"

Great, the Phage was a damn negotiator. Five hot seconds

ago, it was a mindless killing machine. "Let's say until you do something that makes us not trust you anymore."

"Define."

"Trying to eat something except what we give you to eat. Being aggressive to any of us. Damaging any of us even accidentally. Drawing more Phage to us. Do you understand these conditions?"

"Yes."

"Marko? Anything to add?"

"Us also means any and all Leviathan," Marko said. "Nadim, Typhon, any others we might encounter. In fact, any conscious being of any type, ever. No eating. No killing. No hurting unless in defense of others."

Basic stuff, all good. "Hear that? What he said too."

"I understand these things. I will not violate." The Phage hesitated a second, then went on. "And in turn . . . ?"

"We'll give you food," I said. We had stores, but I figured we could barter for something gross on the Sliver that could be used exclusively for the Phage. We might need to buy a whole lot of it, though. These things could *eat*. "You stay in containment, and don't stray from where we put you without permission. Follow the rules, you'll be safe. Break them, we'll kill you. No questions asked."

"Yes," it said. "I agree."

"Remember: we're taking a risk with you. Don't screw it up. We'll kill you."

"Can get up now?"

"Yeah, let me—" I started forward to release the restraints, *not* that I was eager to do it, but as soon as I spoke, the Phage effortlessly sliced through all of them with one easy gesture and got out of the chair. I backed away, hand on my gun. Marko stood so fast the stool overturned, and EMITU buzzed out to set it upright again with fussy care. "Okay, stop there. Stop!"

The Phage obligingly paused and stood quietly. It twitched a little. Maybe still unconsciously trying to communicate with motion and vibration. I took a breath, looked at Marko, who was also on guard, and we both nodded and took our hands off our weapons.

"So," I said to the Phage. "What the hell do we call you?"

It cocked two of its cutting arms at a weird angle and said, "I do not know. My kind do not have names. Only the Mind."

"Well, you get to pick your own now." Because if I named it, I'd probably pick something like Bug-Ugly.

"I will think," it said. "Need more data."

"EMITU, make yourself useful."

"How may I be of service, Honor Cole? May I rub your feet, or—"

"We need to figure out the best delivery mechanism for information to the entity we just, uh, acquired. And anything else you can determine about it."

EMITU spun in place, faced the Phage, and made a totally unnecessary *hmmm* sound, then spun back. "This life-form's senses operate best in limited light. It has limited hearing, although it can communicate in its way by biological movement. It has excellent visual perception. It also senses very minute organic particles. It does not need to breathe, but it does need to eat at periodic intervals to sustain its processes. I would assess that visual information delivered in specific bandwidths would be best for information exchange. It seems to learn rapidly. Is that enough, or should I break out a Ouija board and crystals?"

"Thanks," I said. "Go back to bed."

Marko looked at me oddly. "What are you thinking?"

Why did people look so worried when I had promising ideas?

I left the Phage in the media room, absorbing great gobs of Earth culture. Nothing top secret that could let it head an invasion, fluffy stuff that might familiarize it quickly with human customs. Marko agreed to stand guard. Made sense, as he *was* stuck here for a while. Yusuf and Chao-Xing had gone back to calm Typhon, and we still had only one Hopper. That meant my mission to Bacia would require facilitation.

I hated asking for anything, especially under these circumstances. Swearing quietly, I activated the comm and got in touch with the docking center. "Patch me through to Bacia. Please." I added the latter grudgingly. Never hurt to be polite.

"They are waiting for your call."

That . . . was not reassuring. Within seconds, Bacia's face was on my screen. "Did you complete your task?"

"About that . . ."

"Where is he?" Their voice rolled like thunder, and I could feel them trying to exert presence, but the technology connecting us dimmed some of Bacia's pull.

"I'm not sure. We couldn't stop him." That was a massive failure, and I strangled the urge to make excuses as I outlined the situation.

"You are useless!" Judgment boomed out, and Bacia looked like they were ready to start a war over this. "You insignificant pustule—"

"Look, I get that you're mad . . . and probably worried too. I mean, you did dig up a huge threat to the universe and somehow *lose control of it* when we delivered it to you safe and sound, with all the tools to keep it asleep. But hey, let's not argue over who owns the problem because we played a role in that too. That's why we're not running. We have to find this thing and kill it, and you still owe us some drones. We need them."

"You *dare*?" They looked like they couldn't believe I'd interrupted. "There is no payment for failure!"

Time to play our ace in the hole.

"Look, I don't know what plans you had for that relic, but one of our crew took some genetic samples while it was on board. I guess if you're not interested, I can ask around for a buyer. You're probably not the only collector of god-kings in the universe. Or the only drone manufacturer." Actually, I was bluffing, testing the waters. I had no idea if either of those statements would be true.

Bacia immediately folded their cards. *Boom.* "I will send a shuttle. Let's talk in person. Bring the samples, or we have nothing to discuss."

It surprised me that they remembered that our Hopper had gotten jacked on the dead planet. They didn't seem like the type who remembered the trivial things. Then again, they ran a complicated, criminal-heavy outpost, so maybe they were better at details than I could imagine.

"I'm on the way," I said.

Before heading to the docking bay, I took a deep breath. "Nadim, do you think handing off the god-king DNA that Starcurrent collected is a sound idea?"

"I don't know." He sounded as worried as I felt. Like me, he was being forced to handle a lot of shit in a hurry, all of it new and incredibly dangerous.

"Seems like our two options are bad or worse. Bacia probably won't try to take over the universe with it, right?" *Probably.*

Nadim was silent for a bit, and I could feel that he was weighing our situation, sorting through memories for anything helpful. Finally, he answered, "I feel there is some danger to that, but Lifekiller is the immediate threat. Even Typhon has never encountered a life force so voracious, so destructive. Alongside the Phage . . . together, they would be devastating. If there is a long-term cost for bartering with Bacia, it is a problem for later. We must fight what's in front of us first."

Hearing Nadim articulate my own thoughts shored up my resolve. "That's what I think too. If we're in this together, we'll be okay."

I wanted to say more, but words were never my best friend. So even though time was ticking down, I pressed my hand against the wall and just felt Nadim, all shades and layers. It was like being lifted and twirled, all exuberance, even if we were worried. That moment of union left me feeling lighter but also like I could face down a whole pantheon of gods and devils, as long as I had Nadim.

"Thank you, Zara." Three words, but he was saying so much more.

As far as he was concerned, I was the damn chosen one, destined to bond with him and save the universe. Hell, maybe it was even a tiny bit true.

I swaggered a little on the way to the docking bay to await my ride. "Starcurrent?"

Ze answered right away. "Problem with the Phage?"

"No, I need backup for a meet with Bacia. You down for it?"

"Am on this level, Zara. Is not down?"

I tried again. "Will you come? And bring the samples you took from Lifekiller." I threw that in like an afterthought. I hated being sly with my friends, but it seemed important right now.

"Pleased to. Going now." The translation matrix gave a little trill that made me think ze really was happy to be asked. I felt bad about that. I was dragging zim into something without proper intel, but . . . priorities.

Five minutes after we both got to the bay, Bacia's shuttle arrived. It delivered us to a private docking area, directly adjacent to the Peak—I'd thought something like that must exist, a secret landing area away from the unwashed masses. Bacia would only travel in style. An honor guard of six of Suncross's people—the Bruqvisz—marched alongside Starcurrent and me, herding us as much as escorting, I thought. There was no security check, either. Bacia clearly didn't think we had the stones to hurt them.

Bacia waited for us in what I'd come to consider their throne room and didn't waste time on pleasantries. "You have the samples?"

"Not so fast. You knew we had no chance in hell of stopping that thing when you sent us out there. I'm not thrilled with being sent on two suicide missions. We're not your pawns, Bacia."

The gigantic, shimmering being shrugged. "Thought you might destroy each other. Good for me, either way."

At least they were admitting to the bullshit, even if I didn't like it. They were also copping to the fact that they saw the Dark Travelers as a threat, which was *interesting*. Now that Nadim and Typhon were geared up for war, they ought to be worried . . . and thinking about how to stay on our good side. They'd have to save face while doing it, of course.

"I could have my tentacled friend here smash these samples you're so desperate to have all to shit. I'm petty like that." I smiled. They pushed at me, trying to drive me down, but I was developing a certain immunity. "Let me guess: when you started to take samples, Lifekiller's dead ass woke up again. And you didn't have the right stuff in place to stop him. So even though we handed him over, you didn't get what you wanted before he blew out half your station and left."

Bacia made a sound of pure rage. "Do not destroy the samples. That would be . . . unwise. They are your only bargaining chip."

Which meant that they *were* a bargaining chip, which up to that moment I hadn't been a hundred percent sure about. Nice.

Considering this was zis first encounter with Bacia, Starcurrent was faring well. Ze didn't get sucked in, and the trilling sound ze made didn't translate, but I recognized a pissed-off alien when I heard one. I had some explaining to do when we got back.

At a gesture, the six-pack of Bruqvisz stirred and closed in around us. I took a defensive position. Starcurrent flared zis tentacles, which went purple, and zis ruff stood up. "Fighting, Zara?"

"We could. Or we could hammer out the terms of our agreement. Your choice, B-ball." That was a purposefully disrespectful nickname. "Are we allies . . . or enemies? And remember, we're the only ones in the universe who've got what you want right now."

The crime lord swore, or at least, I assumed they did. Those sounds didn't come across as words I could understand, but Starcurrent's filaments turned a pasty peach. Must have been impressive.

Eventually, Bacia snarled, "Fine. We deal."

My time in the Zone came in handy as we haggled for a good half hour. In the end, I was happy with the terms—and the number of drones we'd receive on the regular, arriving in self-piloted fleets under our command. We did a DNA-breath deal, like the one I'd signed with Suncross, and then I turned to Starcurrent. "Hand over the samples."

I hoped this didn't turn ugly, but Starcurrent's filaments

floated like ze was giving in over zis better judgment. Then ze gave the case to the honor guard. To Bacia, I added, "Pleasure doing business."

"I truly loathe you, softskin." Bacia's starry eyes narrowed.

For some reason, hearing that made me happy. It felt like an admission of respect. "Likewise. We'll be expecting the first drone shipment within half a Sliver day."

"Understood. And after that?" Seemed like Bacia wanted to know our plans.

"We go hunting."

I started to leave then, but Bacia's question stopped me. "Why are you keeping silent, one wonders?"

"About what?"

"You have avoided any mention of the Phage cell you've separated from the swarm. What are you planning to do with it?"

"None of your business."

"Perhaps I could offer you a better deal. If you add the Phage sample to our original agreement, I'll double the number of drones."

Damn, that was tempting. But I couldn't be sure that pure mechanical assets would outweigh the benefit of a live wiretap on the swarm. For one thing, our Phage cell was a built-in early-warning system, if we kept it happy. "Sorry, no bargain."

"I must have it!" Bacia thundered. "Phage are rarely seen alone, and never captured alive. This splinter cell is unprecedented."

"What are you, a collector? Do you have a secret display room where you hoard weird shit?" It was a joke, but the honor guard seemed not to think so. They were eyeing me like I'd pulled my pants down in public.

"That creature is unique, the only one of its kind." Softer, Bacia added, "Like me."

Maybe if I was tenderhearted, I'd have been moved by that, but I shook my head. "Our business is concluded. We may not be back for a while, so watch your six. Lifekiller probably holds a grudge."

DIRECT-H2-APP-SCORPIONXPOISON-ENCODED

From: Torian Deluca
To: Derry McKinnon

I gave you wings. Now fly. And kill Zara Cole.

CHAPTER TWENTY-TWO

Binding Mercy

FOR A RIDICULOUSLY low price, I bought a small amount of something called flaff that Bea, on analyzing, assured me would be nutritionally adequate for our Phage—not that she'd come to terms with the fact we were making one welcome. I tried to tell the vendor I needed all he could give me. For answer, he shoved something about the size of a loaf of bread at me. It came in its own steel box. Oh no, no way was I opening another damn sealed box on the Sliver. I shoved it back. "I need a thousand times more than that!" I barked.

In response, the vendor—a short, squatty grayish

creature I hadn't seen before on the station—entered a code. He pulled out another identical box and opened it. That one was empty. He also pulled out a gigantic, terrifyingly large knife that was more like a scimitar, and then he opened the first box.

Immediately, the substance inside—a weird, moving, wetly green organism—swelled to twice its size. The proprietor swung the sword, cut it cleanly at the top of the box, jammed the excess into the *other* box, and slammed and locked both boxes. "Grows very fast," he said. "A pest. You want, no refunds, no complaints."

Something that was nutritional, dangerous, and grew at a furious pace? That sounded ideal for the Phage to chew on. "Got a flaff-killer in case it gets out of control?"

"Absolutely." It thumped down another box and flipped the lid to show me about a hundred small bottles. "One bottle kills completely. Box a sample before using if you want to preserve flaff for later."

"Neat," I said. "How much?"

I suppose it shouldn't have been a shock that the stuff to kill flaff was twice as expensive as the flaff, but it clearly was a worthwhile investment. I paid. Bacia had given us some station credit, which they damn well should have.

Drones arrived on schedule, a massive fleet of them that just barely fit, even stacked one on top of another inside the docking bay. We'd have to deploy some to land a second Hopper, but I figured that was a decent tradeoff.

So. Stacking it was, but at least, once programmed by Bea, they did that all by themselves. Smart, deadly things, with sharp lines and alien sensibilities.

We'd also negotiated for high-intensity artificial sunlight to be blasting at precisely regulated frequencies at both ships while we waited, so by the time we'd finished our station duties, Typhon and Nadim seemed a little steadier. I hated taking them back into battle like this, but chances were Lifekiller would play hard to get for a while, and we'd have a chance to orbit some suns and get both ships back up to full strength.

At least, that's what I was hoping.

"Suncross and I made a decision," Bea said. "Construction is installing weapons on both Nadim and Typhon like what the Bruqvisz carry. They seemed very effective against the Phage."

"The globulators?" I asked.

"That is not a word," Bea said.

"The things that glue things together, right? Those are cool. How much does it cost?"

Suncross's image filled the screen behind her on the bridge. He pounded his console with four fists. But lightly, as I assumed it wasn't quite as sturdy as the bar table in Pinky's. "Nothing!" he boomed. "Made bets. Won big while away. Bet on Abyin Dommas again, but only for preliminary rounds. Never bet on finals."

"Good plan," I said. "And thanks."

All four lizard palms showed toward me. "No thanks," he said. "We thank you for chance at decent combats. Boring out here. No real opponents who don't fall apart in the first pass. Phage are worthy of our time."

I wouldn't have put it quite that way, but yeah, I got the sentiment. Good enemies were hard to find. "Well, we're grateful anyway. Gives us a better shot at fighting this thing. Listen, you're not obliged to come with us again; far as I'm concerned, you more than paid your debts . . ."

"Zeerakull. Do you really believe we would pass up the chance to fight a legendary god-king? Never!" Suncross's enthusiasm was like a little kid visiting a toy store for the first time. "Our families will write of our battles one day."

"Your family will *write* of the battles . . . ?" Somehow, I was expected drinking songs.

"Yes. Of course." He blinked at me, as if he couldn't quite believe I'd asked the question.

Starcurrent said, "The Bruqvisz are renowned for their novels and histories. Bestsellers in kiosks across the system."

I just . . . okay. "Great," I said. "Well, be sure to get my name right when you do it."

"Where are we going first?" Suncross asked.

"Don't know," I said. "I'll consult our, uh, expert." I

hadn't told him about the Phage. I didn't even like the fact that Bacia knew. I wondered if their Bruqvisz guards were chatty, and word would spread all over the Sliver; wouldn't take long to reach Suncross's ears if so. But he didn't seem to be bothered, at least for now.

I took the flaff down to the hold where we'd locked up the Phage. It was a big, empty space, but as I stepped inside I noticed that the Phage had, somehow, built itself some amenities. A thin silky construction that stretched from one side of the room to the other. Another silky one that ran ceiling to floor. I didn't know what they were for, but I was pretty sure it built them out of extruded material, like a spider.

The Phage was climbing the vertical rope when I entered with one of the flaff boxes. I unlocked it but didn't open the lid. I kept my eyes on the shiny, nauseatingly jointed carapace as it twirled and spun on the rope. Was it doing something useful? Exercising? Having fun? I couldn't tell, but it suddenly released the rope and thumped to the floor, and I came instantly upright with a hand on my gun.

The Phage spread all its limbs, except the two it was using for legs, and showed me a sickly gray underbelly. "I come in peace," it said. "Zara Cole. That is your name, yes?"

"Yes," I said. "Hi. Brought you food."

It tilted its head a little downward and said, "Flaff."

"Hope that's okay. Bea said it would nourish you."

"Is . . . home food. We eat when nothing else available."

"You know how fast it grows?"

"Will manage growth and eat small," it said. "Will lock up when finished. I thank you for the meal."

The Phage was polite, and it was getting on my nerves. "Yeah, well, fine. Don't make a mess." I cleared my throat. "Where do we go to find Lifekiller?"

The Phage pointed to the box. I moved away, as far as I could go, and pressed my shoulders against Nadim's skin. Felt him with me, watching closely. He didn't speak aloud, but I clearly got the image that if he felt something was about to go wrong, he'd take action. I wasn't sure what he could do, though.

I still got the wonderful, steadying sense that he was looking out for me.

I watched as the Phage opened the box with a flick of a talon, and in a lightning-fast move, sliced the first bulge of growth off the flaff, and closed the lid. The flaff it had sliced off was still growing, but the Phage's maw began chewing it away faster than a blender, and in a matter of seconds, it was gone. Nothing left. I felt sick and light-headed watching that.

"Is good," the Phage said. "Thank you."

"Sure. Lifekiller. Directions. Now."

It was silent for a moment, then said, "Ready to provide

coordinates." It reeled off a set of numbers, impossibly long, and then climbed up its rope again to twirl. "Will not be there long. You should hurry."

"Okay," I said. I wasn't going to hurry. Our ships were in no shape yet for a pitched battle. I just wanted to confirm the Phage was giving us good intel, so we could head that direction and make sure it wasn't just spouting random bullshit for its supper. "What are you doing?" I couldn't resist asking.

"Talking," it said.

"I mean, on the rope."

It didn't answer me. Maybe it didn't know. I shrugged and started to leave.

"Zara Cole," it said. "I have thought of a name. I will be called Xyll."

Not a human name. "Okay. What does it mean?"

"In the Abyin Dommas tongue, it means 'alone.'"

I blinked. No. I was not going to feel sorry for this eating machine that had torn its way through Leviathan bodies without remorse. I was *not*.

"Xyll it is," I said. "If you're lying to us, Xyll, I'll kill you."

It kept twirling.

Bea caught up with me outside, and I had the distinct impression she'd been lingering as backup. She was even armed, which for her was far from the usual. She looked good in a gun belt, though. I noticed she'd taken to weaving her hair into a single, thick, square braid at the back of her head. The little curls that escaped around her face looked delicate and sweet. So did her relieved smile.

"Thanks for not dying," she said. "Honestly, that thing scares me. Doesn't it you?"

"Sure," I said, though I wasn't sure that was a hundred percent right anymore. I hated what it had done too. But the fear was way down now that it had demonstrated an ability to understand social interactions. "It says it wants to be called Xyll."

"I'm not calling it that."

"Why not? You're okay with Starcurrent and Suncross and ships big enough to blot out the sun having names and personalities—"

"It doesn't have a *personality*."

"Bea."

"I don't want to think of it that way."

I didn't push it. Wasn't even sure why I cared, really. Xyll was an enemy, pure and simple; whether on its own or as part of a swarm, it could do tremendous damage to all of us. We needed to be on guard. Maybe Bea was right to keep her distance.

"Did you get the coordinates?" I asked her. She nodded. "Are they valid?"

"Well, they designate a point in space," she said. "As to whether the swarm is there, and Lifekiller . . . I guess we won't know that until we get there."

She was right about that.

"I don't think it was lying, Beatriz," Nadim said helpfully. "And it seems to be behaving as it promised. Apart from building webs in its room."

Ugh, now that he'd called them *webs* I wasn't going to sleep again. "How close do we need to get to find out if he's telling the truth?"

"I expect Typhon's better at sensing the Phage," he said. "I will ask."

While there were no immediate fires to put out, I took the chance to clean up, take care of my hair and skin. I put a silk wrap around my head and went down to the kitchen to wolf down some food. I was tired as hell, but I didn't feel like napping was the right thing to do while we were Phage hunting. Still, I figured it wouldn't hurt to lie down for just a bit on the couch. I'd just close my eyes.

About an hour later, Nadim woke me up to tell me, "Typhon cannot hear the Phage yet, but we are half a day away, even at this speed. I am sorry to disturb you."

No sorrier than I was. I yawned and stretched. The hour's nap had made my muscles feel thick and achy, and my head pounded with the desire to lie down again. "It'll be a few hours then, at least."

"Definitely. I can tell that you are tired, Zara. Recent events have been difficult for everyone. Too much fear, not enough peace. If you don't recharge, you won't have the strength for what is to come. And *you* cannot drink starlight." His voice was sheer tenderness, to the point that the top of my head tingled.

Getting geared up for war hadn't changed Nadim at the heart. I didn't have the energy to argue when I wanted some downtime too.

I went back to my room, grabbed my blanket, and lay down on the floor. It had been a while since we'd bonded like this, and while I wasn't looking to go flying as Zadim, we could both use a little snuggle time. I closed my eyes; they would summon me if anything dire happened or if Xyll decided to munch on something other than its supply of flaff.

I dropped into a light bond and savored the sweet click of homecoming. In a way, this unity was more nourishing than sleep. Because I was joined with Nadim, I had hazy, secondhand impressions of starsong skimming through me like smooth jazz. Somehow, I was starting to process the sounds like music too, and I could swear that I was almost able to pick out trumpets, sax, and trombone. The high call of a lonely voice, gravelly at the bottom like Nina Simone. Deep down I knew that was my human brain's way of processing the alien and unfamiliar, but it still sounded beautiful.

But it was also muted. Distant. "It feels different," I mumbled.

"What does?"

"Energy. The plating . . . it blocks some of your ability to heal, interferes with absorption efficiency." When I realized it, I snapped fully awake. "Why didn't you tell me there were side effects?"

Nadim was silent a long time. Finally, he said, "To keep you from worrying. There are no perfect solutions, Zara. For every choice, there is a trade-off. Each road taken means another path closes."

"I'm not interested in philosophical double-talk. You yelled at me before for not looping you in, and that was fair. I apologized. Don't you owe me the same?" Okay, so maybe this wasn't on the same level as deciding to die like a big damn hero, but still.

"I am sorry." And he *did* sound it. "Believe me when I say the additional protection is worth the exchange. One day, when it's safe, perhaps I can remove the armor and feel the starlight on my skin again." There was a pulse of mourning, buried deep, that he didn't want me to feel, almost like . . . homesickness.

Back home in the Honors footage, they always talked about how serious it was to make the decision to go on the Journey. There was a reason each Leviathan returned to Earth after the Tour; if an Honor was offered a place on the Journey—which I now realized meant fighting the Phage—they were also given the chance to tie up loose ends at home. Saying good-bye to their families, closing bank accounts, ending their old human lives.

I'd been so swept up in the life-and-death dramatics of this great adventure that I hadn't really considered the implications of all that. There might only be Derry's betrayal waiting for me on Earth—and Deluca's revenge, and a father I didn't ever want to see again—but Mom and Kiz, they were on Mars. And I hadn't told them I loved them one last time or anything. I hadn't said good-bye.

"Zara?" As ever, he felt my shifting mood.

"Are we really never allowed to go back home?" I asked quietly. And then I told him what I was thinking, about my mom and sister. "I mean, it was extraordinary circumstances with Bea and me, and she left *so* many people behind who love her."

"I am sorry, Zara. But we cannot tell those on Earth about the risks we encounter here. Long ago, our Elders judged that humans were too dangerous and violent to be allowed to know of other worlds. Perhaps someday, when your people have proven themselves—"

"Hang on a hot second, what?" This time, I sat up. Tired as I was, a good shot of anger burned my weariness back. "*We're* too dangerous and violent? What do you call all these other backstabbing pirates we rubbed elbows with on the Sliver? What do you call Bacia?"

"Bacia, and those other species, were in space long before you." Nadim sounded prim now. Made me madder.

"Your species lacks the control to be allowed to—"

"Excuse *me*, but I'm right here. Are you telling me I don't have enough self-control?"

"You are different, Zara."

"I'm *not*. Bea's not either. We are *human*. And you're treating humanity like a mess somebody should clean up, or a virus you don't want the universe to catch. Well, screw that." I flopped back down. "If we want to go home, we will. If we want to tell the world about what we've been through, *we will*."

I knew what he was trying to say about us, though. Seemed like I remembered reading a book in rehab, an old one that dated back before the Leviathan came, where some so-called expert theorized that the reason we hadn't encountered intelligent life in the cosmos was that sentient beings tended to repeat a cycle of technological advancement that ended in self-annihilation.

Back then, that idea seemed stupid to me because we'd met the Leviathan long before I was born, so that notion was obviously wrong. Except maybe he was onto something, only the percentage of killers that evolved was high, but not the sum of all life. After all, while the Leviathan were explorers and the Abyin Dommas were peaceable, humanity, the Bruqvisz, and the Jellies were violent. Bacia had a sociopathic streak. I'd run into plenty of warlike races . . . more than peaceful ones. So why hold *humanity* back, specifically?

"You will destroy the Honors program if you do."

"Maybe we should." I closed my eyes. "Tell the truth. Part of the reason you don't tell humanity the truth is you need soldiers for your war. A lot of Honors have died out in the black, and our people at home have no idea. That's not right, Nadim."

It made me mad all over again that we were fighting this shitty covert war. Didn't change anything that I was good at it, or that I liked it most of the time. The Honors program was the biggest damn con of all time, set in motion by a race that was supposed to be benevolent and good. And maybe they were, mostly. But they were afraid. And they'd tricked us.

"No," he said softly. "I know it isn't right. But is destroying the progress that your world has made a better choice? If they reject the Honors program, if they reject the trade we offer, what then?"

"Then they get to make an honest choice for a change," I said. "And the Leviathan get to stop lying. What's wrong with that?"

Before he could tell me, my H2 popped with Bea's worried face. "Zara, you awake? We've arrived at the coordinates the Phage gave us, and . . . just come to Ops."

"What is it?" I scrambled up, tossing the blanket back on my bed. "Bea?"

"Just come."

From: Derry McKinnon
To: Torian Deluca

Made your offer to the Leviathan Elder. You were right. Everybody wants weapons. Gave a little demo of the advanced prototype you sent up with me and made the deal.

I am clear to go find Zara. My ship doesn't like it much, but she'll do what I want, at least as long as she knows I can hurt her. Send the rest of the chem supply. I can't break orbit unless I have enough to last this trip. You don't want me going through withdrawal, do you? That would blow all your plans.

Don't worry. I'll bring you Zara's head on a plate.

CHAPTER TWENTY-THREE

Binding Forces

"WHAT AM I looking at?" I asked.

The dead rock on-screen wasn't remarkable. Dull gray, with darker striations. Readings seemed to indicate there was a thin atmosphere and our equipment was showing the dead remnants of civilization, though the settlements were in ruins. Whoever had once lived here, there was no sign of life now. It didn't seem like an emergency.

Bea's hands trembled as she brought up another series of images. These were shockingly different—a planet bursting with colorful hues, with vivid greens and blues that reminded me of Earth. Not in the same configurations, of course, and there were slashes of deep red and shocking purple as well. A gorgeous place.

Bea said, "Typhon took these scans long-range, an hour ago."

I stared. "Can't be. He was looking at another planet?"

"No. He wasn't. An hour ago, that's how it looked."

"You're telling me that in the space of an hour, the planet went from alive and vibrant to . . . to *that*?" She didn't need to tell what could've done that. I knew. "This verifies that Xyll can track the swarm, at least." My calm words covered horror swirling like cold grease in my stomach. I had to swallow to keep it down. "Who lived here?"

Bea nodded toward the chairs not far away. Starcurrent sat slumped limply, all silent grief, like when we'd pulled zim from zis escape pod after the Leviathan slaughter.

I knelt beside zim. "Starcurrent? What can you tell me about this place?"

Zis tentacles barely fluttered, and I didn't like zis color at all, pale gray, deepening to charcoal on filament tips. Maybe I wasn't an expert on Abyin Dommas chromatology, but this singer in the deep radiated sheer sorrow. Deep shock.

"Is Darkwell, among first colonies founded in the diaspora." Starcurrent's translated voice was flat, but I could feel the waves of enormous horror coming off zim. "Home to a hundred universities. The Library of Zuran. Not the birthplace of Abyin Dommas, but a singing jewel to us." A high, thin whistle cut across the translator, like keening. "All dead. All gone now."

"I'm so sorry." It wasn't enough, nothing could be. Before now, or maybe more accurately, before seeing that red star die right in front of us, I never could've fathomed destruction on this scale. Hell, I thought humans were good at killing, but *this* . . . it had taken less than an hour to reduce a whole planet, and every living thing on it, to rock and ruin. "How many?" I asked finally, mostly because I didn't know what else to say.

"Five million? It was a small colony, mostly Abyin Dommas, a few Bruqvisz." Tentacles flared then, and I hurt for Starcurrent. And Suncross's people too. I didn't think he'd take it well.

That wasn't small. It was a goddamn massacre. I'd thought the most horrible thing I'd ever see was that Leviathan slaughter, but that had been perhaps a hundred ships, at most. "Is there anything I can do for you right now?"

I expected a sad negative, but Starcurrent wrapped a few tentacles around my arms, and now that I was used to the feeling of zis skin, it didn't bother me. But the strength of it put me on guard. That was going to leave a mark. "Sing. Sing them to their rest with me."

I almost said, *that's Bea's thing,* but this was such a small ask. It didn't matter if I sounded good; the point was, being willing to offer a little comfort. "Call the tune. I won't know the words, so I'll hum along."

"Me too," Bea said.

"I will, as well."

I couldn't remember ever hearing Nadim sing with his physical voice, the one he used with us, though I knew he called to other Leviathan, or maybe resonated was the better word. Regardless, Starcurrent started singing in a bass so low that I felt it through the soles of my feet, and it was pure loss, mourning that pierced deep even as I tried to match it several octaves higher. Bea weighed in with her soaring soprano and Nadim sang too, a lovely baritone. It should've been an atonal mess, but instead it was so moving that tears sprang to my eyes. I didn't cry easily, ever, but I could feel the awful loss of this, the waste of it.

We must've kept it up for five minutes, as we looked down on the dead colony, now just ash and dust. Nadim orbited once, long enough for us to finish paying our respects.

Chao-Xing came on the comm just as Starcurrent fell silent. "What are you doing? We can't wait here. We should keep moving! Get new coordinates from that abomination."

"Xyll," I said.

"What?" She was mad as hell over the pointless

slaughter, but now that I knew her better, I could also see the pain. C-X was blaming herself for this. So was I. If we'd done something different—

But what-if was a fool's game, a bet you couldn't win. Excoriating ourselves couldn't bring anyone back. We just had to do better, faster.

"The Phage cell asked to be called Xyll," I said.

"I don't bother learning the names of my enemies," she said coldly. "It's dead when we're done with it, even if I have to go through all of you to do it."

Yeah, it wasn't time to argue. "We're moving out; will forward the next location when we have one."

"Do it fast," she said. "I'm not losing anyone else to these bastards." She was off the screen before I could even try to make a comeback. Not that I had it in me.

On my way out of the hub, I went over to Bea, lowering my voice to a whisper. "Any survivors at *all*?"

She grabbed my hand, holding on so tight it almost hurt. We'd seen what Lifekiller did to that star, but I still couldn't wrap my head around what I was seeing. "There are no signs of life whatsoever."

"Like, down to plants and animals?"

"Down to *anything*. No biological life of any kind. The god-king devoured everything. This world is a husk, and the colonists have been reduced to ash."

"This wasn't a Phage attack?"

She shook her head. "I don't think so. They leave . . . pieces."

I shuddered. Where the Phage devoured everything, at least they were eating, turning that life into fuel. Ruthless, but that was the essence of life. It was something I could understand. The god-king, though . . . I couldn't see any sense to him. He seemed to be swelling like a tick or a mosquito, and then I had the awful thought that maybe he was gearing up for another radical metamorphosis. Like, if he could suck up enough energy, it would power a change. I suspected we did *not* want to see his leveled-up form.

Poring over the awful images wouldn't change anything, so I steeled myself. Since we'd missed the god-king by a frustratingly short time—and this world had paid the price—I couldn't let my emotions cost us another victory. Like Chao-Xing had said after our first decisive win, *we are at war.*

Since we were paused assessing damage, Marko took the chance to return to Typhon on the Hopper we were sharing. Ours would be operational soon.

Then we left Darkfell behind and found a cluster of stars that would nourish Typhon and Nadim. Soon both ships were recharging and healing, which was good. We needed every advantage for the next round.

I went back to Xyll—to learn where to find our enemy.

Xyll was, at first glance, in a cocoon, and for a second I thought, *Kill it with fire*, because I did not want to see a metamorphosis form of the Phage, either . . . but then the silk chrysalis it was in parted down the middle, and Xyll jumped out to crouch in the middle of the floor.

It was still the same. I didn't see any menacing upgrades.

"What the hell is that?" I pointed at the thick cocoon, which was a lump in the middle of the horizontal silken rope.

"Bed," the Phage said. "Have you not such?"

I wasn't here to compare decorating tips. "We missed the swarm. Where are they now?"

"You are angry," Xyll observed.

"Damn right. There's a planet down there that's an empty rock, and it used to be full of life."

"Lifekiller," Xyll said. "The god-king is enraged."

"Yeah, well, me too. Tell me where he's going."

"Cannot."

"Why?"

"Cannot feel Phage now. Dormant."

"What does that mean?"

Xyll lifted all its limbs. It looked like a threat. I kept my hand on my gun. "Dormant. Bed. Sleep. Cannot track when asleep."

Shit. I'd never thought about it, but everything living needed rest, at least everything I'd ever heard about. The

Phage had collectively fallen asleep, maybe after they'd picked a course to follow . . . but Xyll couldn't access the Mind while it rested.

Unless it was lying.

I pulled my gun. Xyll lowered its arms, which looked *less* combative, but I couldn't be sure of that. Not at all. "Why threaten?" it asked me. "Telling truth."

"I need to be sure. Do you regrow those legs?"

For answer, I got a hiss from Xyll, and something in me squirmed and shuddered. It sounded like every vile, poisonous thing on Earth, coming to get me. Man, these Phage could tap into the fear center with no effort at all. Made it extra hard to be objective about them. "Yes," it said. "Will regrow. But painful."

"You don't want me to shoot something off you."

"Is not my choice."

"Then tell me the truth," I said. "Tell me where the Phage are heading."

"Do not know," Xyll said. "Mind is dormant. Phage cannot be reached."

"But they *had* a course before the Mind went to sleep."

"Yes."

"Tell me where that leads, then." It was a risk. If the Phage changed their course somehow, or Lifekiller changed it for them, we could miss the mark altogether. Lives were on the line—not just ours, but planets full of life. Darkwell had been a living, breathing, vital place, and now not even viruses or bacteria survived.

I couldn't let that happen again. We had to catch them.

The Phage rattled off another sequence of targeting numbers, and I asked Nadim if he got it; he said yes, and I holstered my gun. Xyll didn't move. "Would have shot me?" it asked.

"If you hadn't answered me? Yes."

The Phage's armor glistened as it shifted, but I couldn't read what, if anything, that really conveyed. "You hate," it said. "Why?"

"You chewed up Leviathan," I said. "What other reason do I need?"

It didn't answer me. It hesitated a moment, then crawled back up on the rope and buried itself in its cocoon again.

Did I feel a little guilty? Hell yeah. Xyll had done nothing since arriving on board to make me doubt its intentions, but still . . . the only measure I had for its kind was hunger and violence. Scaled up to intelligence, that was an incredibly dangerous combination. I had to be careful with this thing. I had to *understand* before I could trust.

I left the containment room and leaned against the wall outside, eyes shut for a moment. "Nadim, you know what to do."

"Yes, Zara," he said. "It's a gamble, isn't it?"

"Only one we have," I said. But that wasn't what I was

thinking about. "At best speed, do you think we can over-take them?"

Nadim was silent for a moment, and then he said, quietly, "I do not believe we can. We will try. But Lifekiller has given the Phage a much greater advantage. If we knew their destination, we could attempt an intercept course."

"What's on that route?"

"Many things. Too many planets to protect." He sounded deeply shaken. I understood that.

But I was overcome by something else too. What I'd just said to Xyll. What Nadim had said to me. I sank down the wall and put my head in my hands, fighting not to cry from the overwhelming surge of knowledge that came over me like a cold wave.

"Zara? What is it?" When I didn't answer, Nadim attempted a bond, a light one. I fended it off. "Please tell me."

"We're the Phage," I said. My voice shook. "You're treating us like *we're the Phage*. Humanity. You're trying to rehabilitate us. That's what the Honors program is. That's why you've given us all the tech to make our lives easier. You're hoping that we'll lose our violent edges and become . . . civilized enough for the rest of the galaxy."

"Humans are *not* like the Phage," he said. "You are young. You come from one of the cruelest, most angry planets that exist. You have been forced to fight it, and lower life-forms, for tens of thousands of your years. But when there was nothing left to fight, humans turned on each other. When you had conquered your environment, you poisoned it. When you were no longer threatened by your companion animals of Earth, you exterminated them. You are not like the Phage." He paused for a long, painful moment. "I am sorry to say this, Zara, but in some way, humans are more dangerous, because humans do not do this from hunger."

My heart collapsed inside me, and the tears slid free, not for me, not for my own pain, but for the cold fact that humanity had the darkest of edges in us, something that even the Phage lacked. A vicious streak that we used on each other, when nothing else was available. I knew that. We all knew it, deep down, for all our art and culture, beauty and kindness. Deep inside, there was a disturbing, limitless darkness. It was there in every culture, in every age.

"That's why the Leviathan wanted us," I said. "Not for our intelligence. Not for our curiosity. Not for anything *good*. Leviathan wanted us for our darkness. Because that's what you need to fight the Phage."

"That's not entirely true. If it was, why would the Elders have first asked for scholars, scientists, and musicians, instead of criminals, killers, and soldiers?"

"I don't know," I said. I felt miserable now, sick, strangely betrayed even though nothing had really changed. "You tell me."

"The Elders wanted to find the best in you and teach you that you could all reach those heights." He sounded so incredibly gentle now. "They wanted the best, and Zara, they chose *you*."

"Because I'm a criminal."

"Because you are strong, yes. But I think because they saw something else in you, just as they did in Beatriz, in Marko, in Chao-Xing. You are all strong, you all have vital instincts we need. But you are balanced by such goodness. Such love."

That made sense, but the words weren't enough. I reached out to him because Nadim could lie to me in words, but never like this. I was anguished and angry and sad and broken, and he flooded into me like warm sunlight, filling up the cracks in my heart. I couldn't convey the horror I felt at that possibility, but he felt it. And he let me know that it was all right, somehow. That we were what we were, and there was nothing to regret.

I love you as you are, Zara, he said. *There is darkness in you, yes. But there is a light like a million stars, and this, we have learned from humans too: that both may exist together. That both may be useful and good. Your strength comes from struggle and pain and survival. You must wear that with pride. Because I am proud of you. And yes, the Elders chose humanity partly for this reason. But I choose you for you. Always.*

I threw myself into the bond completely, and spun into starlight and song, and the harmony of it was beyond any measure of peace. Zadim loved, and was loved, and I was aware that Zara's physical body had collapsed to the hallway floor, eyes open and black, but it didn't matter.

I was home.

Let's go.

Zadim leapt forward, released, whole, and Typhon fused together. *Lightstorm.* The small, flitting needles of Suncross and his crew gliding with us, stitching a straight course as the Leviathan swam in great leaps, sails spread to catch song and light. Beatriz joined the bond first, and then Starcurrent, with all zis gray anguish. All together.

We are one. We are Starocean. Before, we hadn't articulated a name. Now it was time.

This is the strength we need, Zadim thought. And Lightstorm pulsed an agreement. *But we need more.*

We felt rather than heard Suncross's transmission that blasted on a wide band through the stars, giving course instructions.

We were calling an army.

The resonant deep song of Leviathan belled through stars, through darkness, seeking cousins, and Zadim felt the strong reverberance of replies. Distant, but responding.

From a thousand planets, we felt the call, heard the response.

Yes.

We were going to war, and gods should tremble.

FROM THE FIRSTWORLD TEMPLE OF BIIYAN,
FRAGMENTARY TRANSLATION
Provided by Honor Sunfire Victory, with permission
from the Bruqvisz Planetary Database

Spike of sharp fear
As god-kings return
To bend light and murder stars
And end all that oppose
We fear
We fight
We die
We win
Sing the dawn of new days
Sing the dusk of old
Sing it never to come again

CHAPTER TWENTY-FOUR

Binding Gods

WE FLEW.

Through starsong and incandescent colors that hissed like silk around us, food and heat and life. The armor was heavy, and it altered our maneuverability. We had sacrificed some grace and dexterity for durability and self-defense. It was acceptable. In our present form, we were unstoppable.

It lies to us, Lightstorm said. *The monster. They are not on this course. It remains loyal to them. Kill it.*

No, part of Starocean said. *Not yet.*

The Leviathan aspects wanted Xyll dead, but one within

the fusion refused . . . and then two. Zara, and Starcurrent. *It is of use*, Starcurrent's part said, still bitter as ashes. *It may die later.*

Our course is wrong, Lightstorm said again.

Wait, Starocean said. *Watch. Listen.*

At some remove, a gulf of time later, we heard the scratching wrongness of the Phage, their awful disharmony, and the noise drew nearer. Some portion of us heard the alarming cacophony, but others were talking, and Starocean grew less. Smaller. Starcurrent was gone. Beatriz. We wanted to fight, but smaller words scraped away insistently at our attention, like the hand on someone's cheek, barely felt, but there.

Dropping from the bond, I opened my eyes and sat up to find Bea shaking me. "Come back! We need you here!"

I felt a little dizzy, and if *I* did, maybe Nadim did too. He could *not* plummet into dark sleep now, so Bea was probably right. A deep bond should be a strategy, not what we did because I was emotionally wrecked, when we were both exhausted. I stood up and groaned; all my muscles had seized up.

I struggled to focus. "Right, okay. What's wrong?"

"Xyll got out. I don't know where it is!" She swallowed hard. "Can't pick it up on sensors."

Shit.

Was this the moment that Nadim's Trojan horse

prediction came true, and Xyll started destroying our Leviathan from within? At this juncture, we couldn't spare the time to hunt down an internal saboteur, especially if Xyll burrowed into some part of Nadim that we couldn't easily reach. I had the most experience in navigating his biosystems, but we were also chasing down a damn god-king, and the Phage lurking somewhere ahead of us were as big a problem, if not bigger. But what if Xyll hurt Nadim somehow, infected him? Laid eggs or reproduced via parthenogenesis? I didn't have a clue how Phage biology worked, only that it did, and *fast*.

I still had a gun on my hip from gearing up to face the Phage earlier, and the weapon was in my hands before I knew it.

"Hello." The metallic clatter of its voice came from . . . overhead.

My first thought was, blindly, *Giant roach-spider, kill it fast*, and I aimed my gun. It scuttled backward, still clinging to the ceiling, which was wrong on *so many levels*.

"Get down from there!"

Xyll dropped, landing easily on the floor. "Have an importance, could not wait. Looking for you."

My trigger finger was taut, ready to blast this thing into bits, but so far, I had no evidence it had done anything other than leave its quarters. "Nadim? You good?"

"I detect no internal damage, Zara." I noticed the strain

in him, though. He wanted Xyll contained. Preferably, gone.

"Hear that?" I said to Xyll. "Nadim just saved your life. You have thirty seconds to tell me what's so crucial that you broke the rules."

"Empty ones, the eaters, are coming."

"The Phage hive mind?" Last I knew, they were following the god-king's commands, but maybe— "Have they been ordered to hunt us down?"

"True," said Xyll. "Soon, now. Must defend. Will help if possible."

Making a quick decision, I put away my weapon. "I'm trusting you. Now that we're on alert, go back to your room, unless you can't hear the swarm in there?" That was a test. There were no blockers in place, no reason that should be true. If Xyll lied and claimed it needed to be elsewhere, then maybe I couldn't trust its intel.

"Going," Xyll answered. "Will keep promise to aid. Permit comms access? Had none before. Had to leave to tell importance."

Starcurrent joined me in the corridor to escort the Phage back to its quarters. Once we saw Xyll inside, ze said, "It does not lie."

"How can you tell?"

"Hearing truth, this is not a thing that humans do?" Ze seemed surprised.

"Not really. Some people are better at gauging deception than others. There's a whole subset of psychology devoted to it."

"Then, is difficult to explain."

Taking the declaration at face value, I said, "You think Xyll is really an ally?"

"Harder to distinguish personal motive from simple true false. But . . . Xyll wishes to live, true. Hard to thrive as an individual in the swarm. Could be eaten."

Again, that tracked for me. For someone who had to be grieving deeply, first for zis Leviathan, and then for the whole colony of Darkwell, ze was coping admirably right now, though zis tentacles remained a muted gray. Or maybe it only seemed that way because I *didn't* fully understand zis people.

"Noted." I hesitated for a second. "You all right, my friend?"

Starcurrent seemed startled, or at least, that was what the ripple of tendrils told me. "No," ze said. "Loosed a god-king, Zara. Caused death of an ancient star, death of Darkwell. Am not all right at all. Are you?"

I stared at zim for a long few seconds, because it was a damn good question, but that was, I realized, how humans rolled. We put things in boxes until we had the space to deal with them. I'd be guilty as hell later, but right now, I only cared about survival. About Nadim. About stopping the god-king from doing worse.

"I'm all right because I have to be," I told him. "Am I telling the truth?"

That got a stir of tentacles from him. "Yes. Truth."

"Then let's leave it there."

As I headed back toward Ops, Nadim said, with an admirable economy of words, "Phage sighted."

Chills rippled through me, because this time, the fight would be different. Instead of mindless hunger, these creatures were attacking on Lifekiller's orders. Finally, the devourers had strategy behind their destruction, an army with a general, not just a rampaging mob.

And they wanted us dead.

Even if they couldn't manage it, the delay of a drawn-out battle might cost thousands of lives elsewhere. We couldn't let another outpost fall like Darkwell had.

"Nadim, does Typhon know they're coming?"

"He's aware."

"Good, then we're on the same page. We can't lose too much time here. This strike could be meant to slow us down, keep us away from the god-king."

"Zara . . ." Nadim's voice was tentative. "Lifekiller is stronger now. We could lose this battle. You know that."

"I don't," I said crisply. "And you never go into a battle afraid of losing. We fight, Nadim. Together. Always."

"Always," he said. But there was a slight, troubling note

in his voice. I didn't know what he was thinking. I didn't have time to find out.

Before, our fight had been about saving the Leviathan—and we still needed to—but the threat was even bigger now. The god-king wouldn't stop at destroying our ships.

Shivering, I remembered Nadim's translation from Lifekiller's icy sepulchre: *Here rests the fallen god-king, life-eater, song-swallower. Tread not upon him; never speak his name. Let him return to dust and may the silence never be broken. Death comes for any who forsake the way.*

We couldn't even claim we hadn't been warned.

"Get ready for a hell of a fight," I told Bea.

She took one side of the console while I settled on the other, sending orders to the drones in the docking bay. On-screen, I saw Suncross's ship come alongside, much smaller than Typhon or Nadim, but strapped for Armageddon, then the Bruqvisz's face appeared on-screen, all teeth and excited neck frills. I took that to mean he was eager for battle.

"Obliteration!" Suncross yelled. His crew echoed the war cry.

I couldn't raise an answering call. Too much was riding on our results here.

"Try to clear us a path through this," I said. "We'll supplement with the drones."

"Understood, Zeerakull. Today the stars will sing and our enemies burn!"

Suncross vanished from the screen, and his ships went weapons hot, putting on a sunburst of speed that boosted his vessel out in front, a small but mighty vanguard for our two behemoths. It was impossible not to feel awed by the momentous events unfolding. On Earth, they had no idea of the stakes behind the public pageantry of the Honors. It was all just smiles and uniforms to them.

This was life and death.

If we fall here, Mom and Kiz will never know the truth. For a few seconds, the sorrow of that washed over me, and then I put the sadness aside. No matter what happened, I wasn't sorry. Not for anything. If I had to do it all over again, I'd still come to Nadim. Maybe it would sound strange to anyone else, but he completed me, and I'd come to care so much for everyone; Bea, Starcurrent, Chao-Xing, Yusuf, and Marko had become my family.

Wild, when I considered what a loner I used to be, how I fought permanent attachments. No wonder I always felt trapped on Earth. I needed a whole universe to call my own. For once, I didn't feel like that was too much to ask. For me to be here? This was meant to be, and I was honor bound to give everything to this cause.

Lightly, I touched minds with my Nadim, and from there reached out to my Beatriz, and my Starcurrent. They were *all* my family, and I'd give this everything I had. Immediately warmth filled me, along with conviction and strength.

"We can win," Nadim said.

"We have to," I answered.

And launched the first barrage of drones at the swarm.

Suncross's ship used their globulators to clump the Phage together. Nadim and Typhon followed with their own weapons, blasting with abandon. I stood at the console, watching the battle rage silently beyond. We were close to a binary sun system, one that radiated cool blue with a hot, orange core, and the light slid over the shifting, twisting movements of the Phage as the swarm turned, broke, reformed, attacked. Through Nadim, I felt the impact of the bodies hitting his armor and latching on, but to negligible effect.

Bea reached over and said, "I made an improvement." She hit a control in front of me and held it, and through Nadim, again, I felt a mild buzz, like a pleasant little shock.

Not so pleasant for the Phage. She'd connected the forcefield generators to the plating. The Phage weren't prepared for the current, and they drifted into space, twitching.

"You made a bug zapper!" I high-fived her.

We spun back to our jobs, watching for anything out of the ordinary, targeting and firing on the swarm with rail guns and energy weapons.

"Nadim, did that hurt?" Bea asked.

"No," he said. "It felt good. Like . . . sunlight."

"Great. Then I'll keep zapping. Tell me when we've got enough in the kill box."

I smiled at Bea, despite the severity of our situation. "Look at you, working the army-talk."

Typhon dove straight into the swarm, ramming, twisting, slapping, and crushing hundreds at a time. But he was getting too far ahead. I tapped the comm. "Chao-Xing, rein it in! Stay in the formation!"

"Trying," she said tersely. "He's a little wild right now."

The big, scarred Leviathan let out a deep, resonant pulse that punched through me like a fist, and I staggered. So did Bea. Even Nadim felt it.

It blew apart about a thousand Phage in one go, shattered them into broken shells and drifting fluid, and I grabbed the console, shaken. "What the hell was *that*?"

"I don't know," Nadim said. "I've never seen him do it before."

It was Yusuf who replied, "Nadim can run in stealth mode. Typhon has sonic disintegration." Yusuf sounded steady, very much part of Typhon's crew.

"Well, that would have been pretty damn useful in literally every other fight we've been in!"

"He couldn't do it before," Yusuf said. "He wasn't strong enough. He's only just reached enough reserve power to use it . . . but it's limited."

"Still an advantage. Let's push. We have to get clear."

For answer, Typhon lunged forward, an athletic leap of grace and power, the force of the pulse radiating from him in a scintillant glow. It pummeled the Phage, destroying the first waves, sending the next spinning out of control. There were a hundred thousand of the creatures, but every booming attack from him drove them back and apart. Suncross's ships went after stragglers, spearing them with light beams that cut them in two and sent the opposite halves spinning.

"Beware!" That was Xyll, on comms, and the stannic screech of its voice made me wince and clench my teeth.

We were so focused on driving through the swarm that we'd missed a dark whip snaking out from around the blue sun. More Phage. Reinforcements, flanking us.

"Typhon!" I sent coordinates. "Take them out. We'll deal with this."

Typhon's resonant cry was incredibly effective against the Phage, and I understood why; Lifekiller had the same vulnerability to resonance, music, song. It was a power that threaded through the entire universe, and one I never would have guessed. But now I understood why the Leviathan had pilots and singers. It was nurturing.

It was also a weapon.

"Bea," I said. "Get ready for Lifekiller. We're going to need songs. Abyin Dommas songs, human harmonies, Leviathan calls, anything and everything. Get it prepped."

"On it, I'll loop in Marko," she said. "You okay here?"

"Yes. Go."

She moved another console and began to set up a symphony that would slow down, and hopefully damage, a god-king. No pressure. I watched her for a second, but she was confident, moving with urgency and authority.

Quite a change from a girl who'd been terrified to let people hear her sing when she came aboard. Who'd been prostrate at the sight of open space.

I felt a wave of love for her. For all of them.

Starcurrent arrived, swarming in on a blur of tentacles, and joined Beatriz. Ze leaned back and waved a few tendrils in my direction. "Do you require assistance, Zara?"

"Nope. I got this."

I concentrated on destroying the Phage ahead of us, while Typhon devastated the swarm behind us . . . but then I felt a sudden burst of worry. Not mine. Nadim's. "He's exhausted," Nadim said. "He will lose the ability to sing that frequency soon. He must pull back."

Dammit, too soon. Both ships were drinking light from the binary suns, but the armor cut down absorption by 30 percent. Typhon was blowing through his reserves too fast.

I hit comms. "Yusuf?"

"I know," he said. "I'm on it. Stubborn son of a bitch argues, but he's not stupid."

"Save it for Lifekiller," I said. Then I turned to Xyll. "Can you access the hive mind?"

"Can try," Xyll said quickly.

"If possible, confuse the swarm around Typhon. Try sending it in another direction."

"Phantom ship," Xyll said. "Yes."

I zapped the last few thousand Phage from the original swarm as they abandoned any kind of strategy and latched on to Nadim's armor, hoping to drill inside. Tough as the plating was, I was afraid they might just make it, given enough time. A couple of hits from the zapper, and they drifted away, prey for Suncross's ships to slice apart.

"Xyll," I said. No answer. "Xyll!"

"Swarm is moving away," Xyll said. It sounded faint. "Difficult. Apology."

I didn't have time for that. "Where's Lifekiller?"

For answer, Xyll reeled off another string of numbers. Nadim grabbed and displayed them, and I didn't know what I was looking at. A planet, obviously. A large one. The scan showed a lush world with what looked like green seas, a few atolls of land masses, white ice at the poles. Delightful place. Not unlike Earth, though the atmosphere looked cloudier. Gases that would probably be toxic to us without suits or filters.

"Nadim?" I asked. "What planet is this?"

Nadim might have answered, but it was drowned out by

the burst of discordant noise from Starcurrent, who was suddenly *there*, staring at the planet. I'd never seen zim quite so distressed, every tentacle unfurled and shaking. Not gray in the tips this time.

A vivid, violent black. Zis barbs were out.

"Home," ze said. "That is my homeworld. Greenheld."

For a second I didn't know what to do, what to say. I was a kid from the New Detroit streets. What did I know about saving an entire homeworld, an entire damn *people*? I finally got my voice back, and said, "How many—"

"Billions," Nadim said. "There are billions of Abyin Dommas here. It is the heart of their civilization. Zara, I think the god-king means to exterminate them!"

"Because we sang them silent," Starcurrent said. It was almost a keen. "Is revenge."

"How far away is Lifekiller? Xyll?"

"Minutes," the answer came.

I didn't have time for horror or fear. I boxed it up, steadied my feet, and said, "Starcurrent, warn your people. If they have defenses, get 'em up. Nadim—"

"Yes," he said. "Hold on."

He leapt forward with such strength that it sent Phage corpses spinning like asteroids, heading for the sun, and I'd never felt such urgency or speed in him before. He was tapping into dangerous reserves, but I let him. We both had to delve deep now. I told Yusuf what we were doing, and Typhon abandoned the Phage and followed, passing us in the next tremendous push. Stars blurred. Gauzy clouds of stellar dust brushed by us.

We ran with all the incredible power that Leviathan could bring.

We'd just touched the outer edges of the system when Xyll announced, tonelessly, "Lifekiller has arrived."

On the screen, I saw a shimmering golden shield encase the planet. Through my link with Nadim, I heard the incredible singing of the people abiding below in those oceans, Starcurrent's kin, a united and beautiful chorus that grew stronger by the second.

They were singing their defense. And their song created a shield that might save them, at least for long enough.

I saw the vast, unfinished form of Lifekiller drift closer to the planet, and heard the strain, the fear woven into their desperate song.

Without hesitation, I leapt for Nadim and gave everything to the bond, pulling Starcurrent and Bea with me. Starocean flowered open, bold and bright and brave, and then we called to our others, a deep fusion that twined us together in an incandescent explosion to bring Men Shen into existence again, and we were mighty beyond reckoning. A single creature, with a single purpose.

There were glimmers of fear, but we shone purple and red, valor and rage that this demon would try to extinguish so many lights, so many songs. Men Shen boomed a warning, all defiant resonance:

WE STAND

WE DEFEND

NO SURRENDER

Here as one, amid these swirling stars, we would save Greenheld or fall forever.

ACKNOWLEDGMENTS

First, we tip our hats to our faithful readers. Thank you for sticking with us and allowing us to create a story this bizarre, big, bold, and beautiful.

RACHEL:

Thanks to my co-writer, Ann Aguirre, who helps me steer our OTP so beautifully. All the love to my wonderful husband, Cat Conrad, who has been there for me for over twenty-five years and continues to stand by me for better or worse. The last year has been a challenge, so he should know how much I appreciate him. Extra thanks to Lucienne Diver, for always believing in me and being the best agent in the world. Thanks also to Justina Ireland and Sarah Weiss-Simpson. This book wouldn't exist without their invaluable contributions. Finally, I send much affection to book lovers everywhere. Thank you for loving and living in the worlds we build.

ANN:

I'm starting with Rachel Caine again. I still can't believe we've written two books together! It never feels like work; it's all joy, all the time. Next, I thank my wonderful husband, Andres, who always asks, "Is there anything I can do?" Somehow the question always makes me feel better, even when the answer is no. Thanks to Claudia Gabel, who never seems to think our ideas are too weird for deep space, and great appreciation to my agent, Lucienne Diver, who is the answer to a question I didn't know I was asking. Special thanks to Justina Ireland for her critical insights and to Peter Stenson, who named the Sliver. (I promised to give him credit!) Thanks to my son, who always listens to my plot problems and sometimes he solves them. I also need to thank the people who supported me while I was working on this book, including but not limited to: Bree Bridges, Karen Alderman, Fedora Chen, Kate Elliott, Charlotte Stein, and Suleikha Snyder. Finally, much love to the readers who are all in for sexy space whales. We're writing your book of love.

Want to be an Honor? Enroll at www.thehonorsbooks.com.